D0149516

FATAL
ENQUIRY

Center Point
Large Print

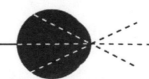

**This Large Print Book carries the
Seal of Approval of N.A.V.H.**

FATAL ENQUIRY

WILL THOMAS

CENTER POINT LARGE PRINT
THORNDIKE, MAINE

Library of Congress Cataloging-in-Publication Data

Thomas, Will, 1958–
   Fatal enquiry / Will Thomas. — Center Point Large Print edition.
      pages ; cm
   Summary: "In Victorian London, private enquiry agent Cyrus Barker
and his assistant, Thomas Llewellyn match wits with Sebastian
Nightwine, whom the British government has granted immunity for his
past crimes, believing they need his help"—Provided by publisher.
   ISBN 978-1-62899-215-1 (library binding : alk. paper)
   1. Barker, Cyrus (Fictitious character)—Fiction.
      2. Private investigators—England—London—Fiction.
      3. Great Britain—History—Victoria, 1837–1901—Fiction.
      4. London (England)—Fiction. 5. Large type books. I. Title.
PS3620.H644F38 2014b
813′.6—dc23
                                                            2014019450

_____Acknowledgments

One of the pleasures of writing is having the opportunity to work with so many talented and capable people. In my case, I would like to thank my agent, Maria Carvainis, for her longtime support, along with Martha Guzman and Elizabeth Copps at the agency, who take care of so many details on my behalf. I would also like to thank my editor, Keith Kahla, for his fresh perspective on Barker and Llewelyn, as well as the wonderful team who worked on this book, including Cassandra Galante, Paul Hochman, Courtney Sanks, Hector DeJean, and Hannah Braaten.

Many thanks to my family for their encouragement and support, especially to my wife, Julie, who cares about the characters in my books as passionately as I do.

_____Chapter One

It is a truth universally acknowledged, at least among private enquiry agents, that the most momentous of cases, the real corkers, begin on the blandest, most ordinary of days. I'm not sure why that is. One would think that criminals, on a beautiful morning like the one that occurred in early April 1886, would want to stretch themselves upon the grass of Hampstead Heath like the rest of the populace, and plot their next bit of deviltry some other day. It is a dreary little island from which Britannia governs its empire, and one must take every opportunity to enjoy a rare perfect Saturday, or so I told my employer, Cyrus Barker. Not that he ever listens to the advice of his assistant.

"Have you noticed there's not a bit of green in this entire court?" I asked, stepping away from the bow window of our chambers. "Not a blade of grass or a sprig of ivy, not so much as a weed. Nothing living except the three of us and that poor blighted shrub on the table there behind your desk."

"It is a penjing tree," my employer rumbled from the recesses of his green leather chair.

"It's a bush you take delight in tormenting. It might thrive if you let it alone."

The Guv opened his mouth to give me a dissertation on the history and practice of Chinese pruning techniques from the Han dynasty to present, but closed it again with a sigh. Apparently, I wasn't worth the effort.

"I might take Juno for a gallop in Battersea Park this afternoon," I continued. "It seems a shame to waste the entire day indoors."

"I was under the impression that the Welsh are a hardworking race," my employer mused. "Apparently, I was misinformed."

"It's hot in here," I said, ignoring his remarks upon the Welsh character, which is above reproach.

"As I recall, last week you were complaining that it was too cold."

"It was too cold last week. April's like that; variable," I replied. "Do you know what this morning would be perfect for? Book shopping. All the shops in Charing Cross will have their front doors open and their fresh discards in bins on the pavement. But if we go this afternoon when it is likely to rain, all the good books will be gone, because rainy days are when other people go to bookshops."

"Thank you for the suggestion," Barker said.

"Who would notice if we lock up a few hours early?"

"The potential client who needs our help and trusts that when we say we are open on Saturdays until noon, we are men of our word, but then, I suppose that is out of fashion nowadays."

I stopped myself from rolling my eyes. Cyrus Barker is convinced with all his Puritan soul that everything has gone to seed and nothing stands between us and the Lord's Return save a few final ticks of the clock. I would not mind so much if I were not always presented as the example of Man's Spiritual Decline.

"Well, lad, we cannot have you standing about all morning with nothing to do. Go to that news kiosk on Northumberland and buy the morning newspapers."

"You've already read *The Times*. Which ones shall I get?"

"*The Star*, the *Gazette*, *The Standard*, *The Chronicle*, *The Globe*, and anything else that strikes your fancy."

"*The Illustrated Police News*!" our clerk Jenkins called in from the outer room.

"And of course, *The Illustrated Police News*."

"Right," I said, actually glad for something to do. "Back in a few ticks."

I nipped out the door into Craig's Court and rounded the corner into Whitehall Street, almost colliding with a young woman who had stopped to study her Baedeker guide. She lifted the metal tip of her parasol from the pavement in order to ward off my unexpected advances and I was forced to hop over it. When I looked up, I realized I was standing nearly face-to-face with a beautiful girl.

She wore a traveling suit of heather tweed, with a choker of black velvet, which set off loosely gathered hair, so pale as to look like spun silver. Her face was equally fair, but her brows and lashes were dark. I realized it must have been some sort of artifice: kohl, perhaps, or some other weapon of the female arts. It gave her eyes, almost gold, a foxlike look to them which was most attractive.

"Oh, I do beg your pardon," she said, before I could speak.

"You needn't beg for what is easily given, and anyway, the fault is clearly mine. May I help you?"

She held out the map in her hands. "I'm afraid I am quite lost."

"If it's any help, this is London," I said.

She smiled in spite of herself. "I'd worked that out for myself, thank you."

"What are you looking for?"

"Trafalgar Square."

"It is due north, in that direction," I said, pointing. "It's but a few streets away."

"And Westminster Palace?"

"The palace is south. Look for the big clock tower. You can't miss it. Are you here on holiday?"

"How can you tell?"

"The Baedeker, of course. Do you require a cab?"

"Not if, as you say, I'm within walking distance. Thank you for your help."

"There's a price," I said, turning back to her. "I must have your name."

She looked at me under long black lashes, assessing me carefully. Whatever I said must have passed muster. "Sofia. My name is Sofia Ilyanova."

"I'm Thomas Llewelyn," I said, bowing. "It is a pleasure to meet you."

"And you, sir," she said, smiling. She had a very nice smile.

"Enjoy your walk."

One rule, when speaking to attractive women, is to leave them wanting. Rather than fumble for something further to say, I pinched the brim of my hat and went on my way, sincerely hoping my existence did not evaporate immediately from her memory.

I clattered off to the nearby kiosk and seized one of everything, making certain that I had not neglected to get Jenkins's *Police News*. Passing back through Trafalgar Square, I looked around, hoping for a second look at the girl, just to convince myself she was as attractive as I thought she was, but she had disappeared like a morning mist.

Back in our chambers, I put the hallowed pages of the *News* on Jenkins's desk and deposited the rest in front of Cyrus Barker. I seized the *Pall Mall Gazette* for myself, if only to tweak the conservative nose of my employer, and retreated to my chair. He lifted the first newspaper off the stack and settled back to read. Things were improving, I told myself. While other workers in London were struggling with heavy machinery or tabulating long columns of figures, I was being paid simply to read the newspaper. If I could continue this until noon, I would consider it a successful day.

The outer door opened then, and all of us looked up to see the bewhiskered visage of Inspector Terence Poole of Scotland Yard. He came in like a shunter in a rail yard going along its allotted route, until he came to a stop in front of Barker's large mahogany desk.

"May I consult?" he asked, falling into the visitor's chair in front of my employer. He looked tired and the edges of his pendulous side whiskers were frayed from where he had been tugging them. I knew something above the usual petty thievery or domestic squabble must have occurred.

Barker's thick, black mustache bowed in distaste. "You know I do not consult. After your men have trod all over everything and carted away the clues, you wish me to go somewhere and perform a magic trick? I'll take an unsullied crime scene, and if it's not too much trouble, a paying client."

"Ah, but you see, there is no crime scene. In fact, there is no crime . . . yet. All we have so far is a potential victim asking for protection."

Barker waved his hand dismissively. "I don't do bodyguard work, but I have a good man I could suggest if you require one."

"No need. I myself have been given the duty. I understand Commissioner Warren asked for me especially. I only wish I could say I care for the assignment."

"I doubt the new commissioner loses much sleep at night worrying whether or not his inspectors like the assignments he gives them."

"True," Poole conceded. "At any rate, a steamer will be arriving tomorrow from Calcutta with a passenger who has been afforded diplomatic status."

"You are drawing this out on purpose. You must really want me to ask. Very well. Who is this man, Terry, and from whom are you protecting him?"

"I am to protect this man from a certain Mr. Cyrus Barker of Craig's Court, Whitehall."

The Guv's brows furrowed. "You've been hired to protect someone from me?"

"You have been known to take a man apart like a watch."

Barker considered this. "Not unless he deserved

it. Who is this fellow who claims I'm an imminent threat to his safety?"

"You're the enquiry agent. You work it out."

"I can't possibly—oh, no. Surely you don't mean *him*."

"Who?" I spoke up.

"Please tell me Her Majesty's government would never grant him diplomatic status."

"Who?" I repeated.

"They have, Cyrus. I'm sorry."

"Damn and blast!" Barker growled.

"Who is it?" I demanded. "Will someone please tell me?"

"Sebastian Nightwine!" they barked simultaneously.

"Oh," I said faintly, sitting back in my chair.

We had crossed paths with the Honorable Sebastian Nightwine a little over two years before, during my very first case. He met us in a jungle of a conservatory, accompanied by a live jaguar. At the time I had guessed him to be a large-game hunter, but apparently he was a criminal, whose father had been a noted explorer and philosopher. I got the impression from Barker that the two had a long and problematic history together.

"How long have you known of this?" my employer asked.

"All of about an hour. It is a state secret."

Barker unhurriedly struck a vesta against the

striker on his desk and lit his pipe before settling back in his chair again. I admit I was surprised by his reaction, or lack of it. I had met Sebastian Nightwine only once, but I thought it might have provoked some kind of response.

"Did the commissioner send you here to warn me to stay away, or did you come on your own?"

"He sent me, actually," Poole said.

"I was not aware he knew of my existence."

"He has since Nightwine insisted he needed protection from you."

"The man is not even in town and is blackening my name already."

"Warren wants you to know that if you go to the docks and attempt to interfere with his arrival in any way, he shall have me effect your immediate arrest."

"You'll put the darbies on my wrists yourself, then?" His fifteen-stone frame, his square jaw overshadowed by that proscenium arch of a mustache, and the black-lensed spectacles covering an old scar on his right brow and cheek made him a man to reckon with.

"If I am ordered to, I must, yes." Poole looked for a minute at the Guv. "So, you won't come, then?"

Barker raised a finger. "I have not decided yet. I must consider what action to take."

"Don't be mule-headed. You don't want to do anything that will harm your reputation."

"You admit, then, that he is damaging my reputation. What has he said about me, precisely?"

"Merely that he fears moving about the city freely with you in it."

"He has reason to fear me." Barker leaned back in his chair and tented his fingers.

"I'll trod on him like the vermin he is."

Poole leaned forward with his hands on Barker's desk. "You're not going to listen to reason, are you? As an official of Scotland Yard, I'm warning you to stay away from the docks."

"Which docks in particular would that be? I'd hate to be working on a case tomorrow and accidentally pass by the one dock I was supposed to avoid, only I didn't know it."

"Just stay away from all the docks," Poole answered, running a finger over his mustache.

"I would not want to inconvenience Captain Nightwine when he arrives."

"That's Colonel Nightwine. He has been promoted."

"Really? When last I saw him he was slinking out of town with a knot in his tail. How is it that he is returning two years later with diplomatic status?"

Poole shrugged. "I only know what the commissioner told me."

"Do you still have the files you collected?" Barker asked.

"They are hidden where I can get to them if I need them."

"Good. You understand him, then. He's got powerful friends and a long memory."

"I don't believe I was chosen to protect him out of pure chance. I'm having my nose rubbed in it." Poole stood. "I should be getting back. You've been officially warned off."

Without a good-bye, the inspector quitted our chambers. There was silence in Barker's office, save for the occasional drawing on his pipe.

"He forbade you to go, but I suppose you'll go all the same?" I asked.

"Of course."

"And what was that about files?"

"I gave Poole a copy of everything I'd gathered for years on Sebastian Nightwine. I was naïve enough to believe it would at least make the CID aware of the scope of his activities.

"Then Terry made some of the information known to Henderson and it even reached the point where the former commissioner considered doing something about it, but the aristocracy closed ranks against him. After that, Henderson dropped the investigation. Poole told me later he went to 'A' Division every morning for six months believing he was going to be sacked. In the end, however, it was Henderson who was dismissed."

"Black Monday," I said.

"Aye."

Two months before, on February 8, two rival unions had organized demonstrations in Trafalgar Square. The meetings occurred without incident, but afterward, the crowd, five thousand strong, had no way to work off the emotion engendered by the impassioned speeches. The mob smashed windows in Pall Mall and St. James's, waking aged peers from their club chairs. A similar meeting in Hyde Park that evening resulted in looting in Oxford Street.

Two days later, during one of London's "particulars," word got out of another approaching mob and the citizens panicked. However such false rumors spread, Scotland Yard was blamed for instigating the warning and probably for the fog, as well. Realizing that he was about to become the scapegoat in the whole affair, Henderson promptly resigned. Feeling, perhaps, that radical unionism required a firmer hand, the selection committee replaced him with a commissioner who had a background in the military.

"I thought the commissioner was sacked over the riot."

"He was, but they were already inclined against him for daring to make charges against Nightwine. That's why I'm a private enquiry agent and not a CID man. I prefer to be beholden to as few men as possible."

"Did they ever offer you a position?"

"No, they didn't."

I thought about that. If I were in charge of hiring constables, would I choose a man who wore black spectacles and knew a hundred ways to kill people?

"Their loss, then," I replied.

Barker flashed me a rare grin. "I was of the same opinion."

Chapter Two

Cyrus Barker may not be an aristocrat, or the son of a famous explorer and philosopher, but his money has allowed him to grow accustomed to being waited on. It was one of my duties whenever I attended the sparring matches he held irregularly with Brother Andrew McClain to tie on his boxing gloves. He didn't thank me; he was off in that little self-contained world of his behind his quartz spectacles, fighting whatever demons dwelled there. His arm was out, and I was tying up his glove, but the Guv seemed unaware of my existence.

"Brother Andrew," I murmured to his opponent, before stepping between the ropes and down to the floor. We were in the reverend's mission in

Mile End Road, where he kept a boxing ring according to professional standards in the basement.

"Tommy Boy," he said back to me at once, patting me on the shoulder.

"Do you need help with your gloves?" I asked, standing on the verge outside and holding onto the ropes.

"I learned how to tie on my own gloves before you were born. What's got your master's blood up?"

"He didn't tell you? Nightwine's coming to town."

I hopped down to the floor and tugged once on the string attached to the clapper of a bell, causing it to clang. I had not so much as turned around when the two men met and began trading blows. Looking over my shoulder, I saw that Barker had crossed the canvas and engaged the missionary to Darkest England in his own corner.

There was a smile on Andrew's lips even after a punch to his jaw rocked his head back. Not so Barker, who looked grim and determined. Having attended dozens of these sessions in this manner, I could state it was not his custom to charge his partner. Normally, he waited to be advanced upon and counter-punched. As McClain had said, his blood was up.

The two men's bodies were a study in contrasts. McClain was of average height, but bandy-legged, with a stout belly and muscular arms. Barker was taller, his muscles more defined, but his Adonis-like form was marred with tattoos, scars, and burns from a rough life spent in battle. Many of the marks were from secret societies to which he had belonged at one time or another. Barker had the longer reach, but McClain the extra weight. If anyone thought his stomach made of fat, they were mistaken. It was harder than a medicine ball. He was one of the few men in England whom my employer could consider an equal in the ring.

McClain's only weakness was the gloves he wore. He had been heavyweight bare-knuckle champion of England, before the Marquess of Queensberry rules changed everything in an effort to make the sport less brutal and more civilized. To him the gloves would always be an impediment. In McClain's eyes, it was man's nature to tinker with everything until it becomes finally and irretrievably broken, boxing included. After the rules changed, McClain had taken to drink, until a chance encounter with an evangelized prostitute had changed his life. He now used his not inconsiderable skills at oration and head thumping to good effect in the East End, where some would say it was needed most.

The two of them were not boxing per se, although I've seen them box according to both the old rules and the new. What they practiced most of the time was a sport I'd dubbed "Dirty Fighting." It was all one had learned in the mean streets of London against everything the other had acquired in the ports of Asia. The only restriction was the gloves themselves, which limited the use of throws and joint locks, and only an occasional kick or two. I have been in the ring with both of them. With McClain, I felt like a mosquito on the hide of a rhinoceros, while kicking Barker was akin to wrapping one's shin around an ancient oak. When they went at each other, I considered moving to another room. It was like watching antediluvian carnivores fight over a wounded prey. It was a wonder no one was permanently maimed in these friendly matches of theirs.

"Enough!" Handy Andy cried, pushing Barker back after being cornered in the ring. "I ain't the one you're angry with. It's Nightwine."

"You'll do in a pinch, old man," the Guv replied.

" 'Old,' he says," the missionary called to me. "He's no young pullet, himself."

It was a dialogue they'd honed for several years, verbal sparring, each of them searching for signs of weakness which in all probability did not exist. Barker thumped a fist into Brother Andrew's ribs.

"What was that?" Andrew rasped, dancing away. "Is there a bottle fly buzzing about? Has it begun to rain?"

"Raining blows, perhaps," Barker growled,

pursuing him about the ring. He came too close and Brother Andrew shot out a left that caught him on the bridge of the nose.

"He's got you careless, Cyrus," Andy said. "When you're careless, you'll make mistakes."

Barker grunted, whether in agreement or dissent, and then launched a flurry of blows, most of which Andy repelled with his thick muscular forearms. When it was done, both had reddened chests. McClain slid the braces off his shoulders, so that they dangled at his knees as if to say "I've been playing with you, but now I'm getting serious." My employer's only reaction was a look of grim satisfaction.

He charged in and launched a left, which Andrew blocked, but it was a feint to cover a right hook which caught the side of the missionary's head, causing him to stagger a few steps. Such a blow would have left me unconscious for half an hour, but he shook it off and looked exultant.

"Now that was a blow. Good one!"

It took me back to when Andrew himself had taught me how to block.

"Boxing is a thinking man's game, Tommy," he had instructed. "It's not all brawn and flailing away and hoping to get lucky. You must outthink your opponent to take him down, and you must be willing to step within his striking distance and expect to trade blows."

When they quit five minutes later, Barker was bleeding freely from the nose and McClain's left brow was starting to swell. Their arms and chests looked like sides of beef.

"Take out the rest of your frustrations on the heavy bag, Cyrus," his opponent ordered, stepping out between the ropes. "We're done here. I've got lunch to prepare."

"You want to take a tour of the ring with me?" Barker asked as he wiped his face with a towel.

"I'm fine," I assured him.

"Nightwine always does this to him," McClain said in my ear.

"I know."

The Guv climbed down out of the ring and began slamming away at the weighted canvas bag at the side of the room. As I watched him pound the bag, I was particularly glad I hadn't accepted his offer.

A few minutes later, McClain returned from upstairs, where he had seen to the preparation of lunch for his flock, most of whom were indigent. Barker was rubbing his hair with a towel, still lost in thought.

"Cyrus! Can I talk to you in my office for a moment?" Andy turned to me. "Have a seat, lad. We'll be out in a minute."

The two disappeared down the corridor while I sat and looked around the room. The chamber must have been built at least a hundred and fifty years before. The stone ceiling was crumbling in places and in need of a mason's attention. It was like Andy's ministry in a way, built for hard work and not for show.

The heavy bag still swayed back and forth, showing dents in the canvas from Barker's final blows. *What was going on in his head?* I wondered. I had never before seen any news drive him to see Brother Andrew. Come to think of it, I believe he'd been agitated the first time he'd taken me to see Sebastian Nightwine, during the week I'd been hired.

I tried to picture the man as I'd seen him last. He was tall, well built, and deeply tanned. The two might have been carved from the same timber, only Nightwine's had been sanded and polished to a sheen, while Barker was still rough-hewn. Nightwine had thick blond hair and a trim mustache, with amber-colored eyes that reminded me of a tiger.

I peeled off my jacket and waistcoat and had a try at the heavy bag myself. It's never a good idea to try anything right after Barker has done it. One is certain to feel inferior. In my defense, I'm almost a foot shorter, and the sand at the bottom of the bag is harder packed and heavier than in the middle where he struck it. I almost turned my wrist on the first blow. Afterward, I punched a little higher.

The meeting lasted longer than the minute

promised by Brother Andrew. I had grown bored with the bag and donned my jacket again before they finally returned. Normally they did not discuss a topic so sensitive that it required closeting themselves in McClain's chambers. My employer patted my shoulder as he walked by.

"Practicing on the heavy bag is a good use of your time, lad," he said.

I was no longer breathing heavily from the bag, which had come to a standstill behind me. How did he know that I had been practicing? It took me a moment to notice the small dents where my fists had been. Cyrus Barker has trained himself to observe everything in a room, either in connection with a murder or as a potential weapon to be used. He would not enter a room that had no sure exit, and he preferred to keep his back to the wall to avoid being attacked from behind. Would I ever learn the skills needed to be the kind of private enquiry agent he was, or was I fooling myself?

"Good-bye, Thomas," Brother Andrew said. "Come by sometime when this one isn't leading you about by the nose."

"Yes, sir, I will," I promised.

Barker and I walked to Commercial Road and eventually found a hansom cab heading west. The Guv didn't say a word. In the distance, I heard the Bow Bells peal the twelfth hour. Technically, the rest of the day and the Sabbath were my own.

All I had to do was get him to acknowledge the fact.

"Sir, it is noon." It doesn't pay to be subtle with Cyrus Barker.

"Is it?" he asked vaguely, as if half of his brain were engaged upon something else.

"Yes, sir, unless you've got something else you need me to do."

"Could you do one thing for me? Go to the Public Records Office and copy down the passenger list for a ship called the SS *Rangoon*."

"Would this be a ship arriving from Calcutta tomorrow?" I asked.

"It might."

"How did you get the name, since Inspector Poole refused to give it to you?"

"Oh, come now, Thomas. You know all incoming vessels are listed in *The Times*."

"What are you planning to do with the information?"

"I intend to board the *Rangoon*, of course. What odd ideas you get into your head sometimes."

"But he warned you off, and I have a police record, as you recall."

"Legally, I am free to enter the vessel so long as I do not molest Nightwine in any way or keep Poole and his men from performing their duties. My defense will be iron-clad if I can find someone aboard ship with whom I am acquainted and will vouch for my attendance there."

"Hence the passenger list."

"Ah, light breaketh."

I sighed. One does that a lot when working for Barker.

"I don't believe Inspector Poole will split hairs the way you do. He'd be more inclined to tear a clump out of my scalp."

"We'll play the cards as they come, I suppose," he said.

"I thought Baptists didn't play cards."

"Touché," he replied. "I'll see you back at our chambers within the hour, then."

"Yes, sir."

There is nothing more scalding than doing work beyond the time one is being paid, but then I am salaried, so technically all my time was his. It is a mercy that he allows me to sleep at night, but then I could recall on both hands times when I was awakened over some matter involving a case.

The sooner I shinned out to the Public Records Office, the sooner I'd get my freedom under way, so I let Barker take the cab back to Whitehall and took one of my own. The PRO is not the most entertaining place to spend a Saturday afternoon, but the queue moved swiftly and the information was readily accessible. There were close to eighty names on the list, and of course, Sebastian Nightwine was one of them. If I needed any proof that he was really coming, there it was in black-and-white.

Once I was back in the office, I set my notebook in front of Barker. He picked it up and began reading it carefully, name by name, rather than scanning it as I had supposed. What was he looking for? I wondered. Accomplices or past adversaries? He was at the bottom of the second page when he stopped and pointed a thick finger at a name there.

"Sir Alan Garrick," he said. "He'll do, I think. I did some work for him a few years ago involving a stolen racehorse. He's also a Mason. He should get me close enough to Nightwine."

"Close enough to do what, precisely?"

"To inform him that we are aware he is in town. That shall be enough for now."

_____Chapter Three

A nd so my time had come. Having ascertained that Barker had no real plans beyond working in his garden and ruminating about Nightwine, I was free to do all the things I had planned to do. I went book shopping in Charing Cross, where I found a complete set of the works of George Meredith for one pound ten, and then took a prolonged stroll through Trafalgar Square in the vain hope that beautiful strangers might be in need of directions. Alas, the fox-eyed vision was nowhere to be found, and so I took Juno out for her gallop in Battersea Park, which we both enjoyed very much.

Saturday evenings, I often ended up at the Barbados Coffee House off Cornhill Street, in St. Michael's Alley, where the bean was first imported to London and Englishmen first tasted the West India Company's viable alternative to tea. There I was one of a coterie of assorted wags and geniuses who called themselves the Wanderers of Kilburn, although, come to think of it, no one recalls why. The leader of our group was my closest friend, Israel Zangwill. Generally, we spend the evening holding court, drinking Voltairean amounts of coffee, arguing about whatever happened to be in the newspaper, and assuring each other that eventually our abilities would be noted by those in authority and the reins of government (or literature, or philosophy, et cetera) would eventually be placed in our capable hands.

"What is Mr. Barker up to these days?" Israel asked. He is always interested in the doings of my employer, though we have an agreement that he, a reporter for *The Jewish Chronicle*, will not publish anything I tell him without asking me first.

"He's been out of sorts all day. An old adversary of his is coming to town. Have I ever mentioned Sebastian Nightwine?"

"No, but I've heard the name. You're sure he's returning? It isn't just a rumor?"

"I've seen it in print with my own eyes. Why?"

"As I recall, he left London owing a lot of money to the Jewish moneylenders. Does Mr. Barker intend to confront the fellow?"

"He's been warned off by Scotland Yard, but that's never stopped him before."

"Why should Scotland Yard protect a *gonif* like Nightwine? This I would very much like to know."

"You and me both," I responded. Since knowing Israel, my English has been permanently riddled with Jewish phrases.

"Should I tell them?"

"Hold off, if you would, until I speak to Barker."

Zangwill shrugged his bony shoulders. "They have waited this long. Another day or two shouldn't matter. I would like to tell them myself, if possible. It never hurts to have bankers looking favorably upon you."

A few hours later, I went home and climbed the stairs to my employer's aerie at the top of the house. He was in his silk Asian dressing gown, reading a biography of Bunyan. Beside his chair was a small table containing an earthenware teapot with a bamboo handle and some small matching cups. Only in Barker could such disparate subjects as Chinese pottery and the author of *The Pilgrim's Progress*, the solidly English Baptist John Bunyan, find their nexus.

"Was your time profitable?" he asked, laying the book in his lap.

"It was. I have some news. Possibly even a suggestion."

He indicated the chair on the other side of the teapot. "Enlighten me."

I told him about the moneylenders to whom Nightwine was indebted. It proved a good move on my part. I so rarely earn one of his smiles that I basked in this one for the rest of the evening. However, I left his rooms not knowing whether he would take the suggestion or not.

The next day began as most Sabbaths do in the Barker household, with attendance at the Baptist tabernacle just down the street. Charles Haddon Spurgeon was in good form, his voice clanging like a bell as he expounded from the podium. Afterward, we returned to Barker's residence for our Sunday joint. It was beef that week, my personal favorite, rather than Barker's, which is mutton. Mashed potatoes swimming in butter, carrots, peas, and Brussels sprouts, rolls, salty gravy made from the drippings, and cherry tarts, washed down with tea or strong coffee, and all for just two men. It is a wonder we were not as round as billiard balls.

After such a meal it is only natural to attempt to read a good book and fall asleep over it. Our butler, Mac, woke me in plenty of time to dress in my Sunday best for the arrival of our good friend, whom I'd never met, Sir Alan Garrick. In the hall, Cyrus Barker impressed me by passing over his customary bowler for the top hat on the hall stand. It wasn't silk, but made of good, proper beaver skin. Mac took it from his hand and applied a brush to it vigorously, swirling the crown to an immaculate circle before setting it upon our master's head at precisely the proper angle. I don't know whether there are schools for butlers, or if men are simply born to the trade. Nature or nurture, our old friend Sir Francis Galton would say. Barker took an ebony stick with a silver tip from the stand, while I chose a humbler one made of maple and brass, thinking to myself that I might feel the need to clout a head that afternoon. Then out we proceeded to keep our appointment with Colonel Sebastian Nightwine.

Despite the fact that steam engines built by no less than James Watt himself kept the water of St. Katharine Docks artificially higher than the nearby tidal river, the twin basins of the docks were not deep enough to accommodate the largest steam vessels. In an age which equates size with innovation, the arrival of the major steamships brought attention from the press. The wealthy traveler always looked for the latest in ostentation and scale, while schoolboys argued crossing records and knots per hour. Under such conditions the St. Katharine Docks rarely got attention in the newspapers, and may even have been considered a liability as far as international commerce was concerned. Hence, these docks were the perfect ones in which to bring someone like Colonel Sebastian Nightwine into London, under cover of darkness, so to speak, though in fact it was afternoon on a conspicuously sunny day, a rare enough thing in London. Nature herself seemed to be welcoming Nightwine with open arms.

The SS *Rangoon* steamed in, its funnels belching, and as it came to a slow stop I could not help scanning the crowd below and visually picking out those individuals with distinctly Semitic features. At the Guv's request, I had sent a message to Israel that he might warn a certain number of creditors of the pending arrival of someone they'd wanted very much to speak to for some time. I also noted Inspector Terence Poole, with a squad of constables in tow. Unfortunately, he had noticed us first and was headed in our direction with thunder in his eyes.

"What shall I do with you?" he demanded. "Do you mind telling me that? I should arrest you right now."

"For what?" Barker countered, not in the least agitated. "I have come to welcome an old friend who is on this ship."

34

"You say one word to Sebastian Nightwine and I'll throw you in irons!"

"I'm not referring to the colonel. I've come to welcome Sir Alan Garrick. He and I have had business dealings in the past."

Poole wagged a finger in his face. He was one of five people I knew brave enough to get away with it. I was not one of those people.

"You're up to something."

"Of course I'm up to something. I'm a private enquiry agent. We live by our wits. However, you quite clearly stated what I can and cannot do, and since you were kind enough to do so, I intend to abide by that statement. That much and no more."

"You will not attempt to attack him?"

"I will not."

"You will not speak to him?"

"No."

Poole tapped his mustache in thought. "You will not bar him from leaving the ship or dock?"

"Never."

"And the lad here?"

"He will be a shining example of restraint. Won't you, Thomas?"

Poole looked at me dubiously.

"A shining example," I assured him.

"You'd clown at your own funeral," he said.

"Not mine. Yours, perhaps."

He took a step toward me but I moved behind Barker where it was safe.

"There he is," my employer said, raising his stick. The two of us made our way to the foot of the gangplank where passengers were starting to disembark. I'd had no description of Garrick, but Barker seemed intent upon a man of about five and fifty years with iron-gray hair and nearly white side whiskers.

"Sir Alan, welcome to London again," Barker boomed, and let me assure you, he can boom when he wants to. It arrested our quarry in his tracks midway down the gangplank.

"Er . . . Mr. Barker?" he asked, dredging the name from his memory.

"I hope the journey from Calcutta was uneventful."

Either pressured from the people behind, anxious to set foot on terra firma again, or curious as to why he was being addressed, Garrick resumed his descent and soon the two grasped hands. As they did so, Poole came up beside us and frowned at me. I looked up in time to see a head of very thick, very blond hair among the crowd still on deck. Only one man I knew had hair like that, an almost strawlike yellow that is quite easy to spot even at a distance.

Looking down, I noticed that Barker was pumping Sir Alan's hand in an unusual way. His index and middle fingers were almost hooked over the top of his hand, while the ring and little finger curled around the bottom. *Freemasons*, I told myself. Barker was giving him a secret Masonic greeting.

Poole stepped around Barker and stood almost between the two men, who immediately put down their hands.

"Sir Alan Garrick, I take it?"

"Yes," the peer answered.

"I am Inspector Poole of Scotland Yard. Are you acquainted with this person?"

"Of course. He is Cyrus Barker, an associate of mine."

"Did you two gentlemen plan to meet here today?"

Garrick and Barker looked each other in the eye, or rather, Garrick looked at his reflection in Barker's spectacles.

"We did not, but I'm glad he came to welcome me. We have business to discuss."

Poole cursed under his breath, but not specifically at us. The blond head was about halfway down the plank, near the spot where Sir Alan had stopped when first addressed by Barker.

"Would you gentlemen please step over behind the swagged chain there? You are impeding the progress of others."

Obediently, we moved to stand behind a chain which separated passengers from those coming to greet them. Turning back, I saw Poole and his constables begin to cluster around Nightwine, hindering him from coming forward, right after

Poole had warned us about doing that very thing. I had not gotten a good look at him yet. Everyone seemed to be working in concert to keep me from viewing his face.

At some point, Nightwine's shoes must have touched the actual dock itself and his long journey was ended. There was a sudden movement among the crowd and I heard one of the constables say, "Oy! You there!" A man brushed past me in a long coat and homburg hat, raising an umbrella as if leading a charge. From the sidelines we watched as half a dozen or more middle-aged men tried to break through the cordon of officers, while Poole cried warnings for everyone to step back. Finally Barker and Garrick stepped apart and I got a good look at Sebastian Nightwine. No sooner had I laid eyes on him than someone grasped the lapel of his suit and began shouting. His face flushed darkly as he remonstrated with the determined group of moneylenders that Israel Zangwill had let loose on him, before catching sight of Barker and me at the foot of the gangway. At just the proper moment, my employer raised his beaver-skin top hat in greeting and then turned away.

"Come along then, lad," he said, settling the hat back on his head and turning to Garrick beside him. "I have a cab waiting, Sir Alan. May we take you anywhere?"

_____Chapter Four

After we dropped Sir Alan in Fleet Street, Cyrus Barker reached into the pocket of his waistcoat and consulted his battered pocket watch.

"I'm sure you must have plans for the rest of the afternoon."

"I do," I admitted. "But I'll share a cab with you back to Whitehall."

The Guv grunted his assent, but something in his statement suggested to me that he was trying to rid himself of my company. He had needed my presence for Nightwine's arrival, and now suddenly my services were no longer required. Meaning is as much in how we say a thing as in what we say. Even his grunt held a tone of disappointment.

We shared a hansom cab back to our offices and once inside my employer seated himself as if intending to stay there for some time. It was the Sabbath Day. I don't wish to imply that he never worked on Sunday, since our profession is an elastic one which takes no heed of days and times. However, Barker does not work then unless he has a particular reason to do so.

Nightwine's arrival in town certainly warranted a bending of this rule, but there was no reason for him to return to the office afterward; no reason of which I could conceive, anyway. I thought his behavior highly suspicious.

He looked pointedly at the clock on the mantelpiece and I regarded it as well. It was seven minutes to three. The Guv had an appointment. He was expecting a visitor and he didn't want me there.

"I thought you were in a hurry to be away," he said.

"As you often tell me, I must cultivate patience."

The Guv pursed his lips and rose from his chair. He looked out the bow window into Whitehall Street while a minute ticked by.

"Would you prefer I go?" I asked. "I mean, if you've got something on . . ."

"Not a thing," he assured me. Going to the smoking cabinet in his bookcases, he removed a pipe carved like the head of a lion and began thumbing tobacco into it. "Stay all afternoon if you wish."

I stretched, a prolonged, catlike movement, which would have been censured by Barker as unprofessional during the week, but was perfectly allowable on a Sunday, the day of rest, when one wasn't supposed to be working. All the same, it got under Cyrus Barker's thick hide, which was what it was intended to do. Another minute ticked by.

While Barker smoked, I looked through the various cubbyholes in my rolltop desk.

"Are you looking for something?"

"Am I bothering you, sir?"

"Not in the least."

"Just looking for a fresh pencil. Here's one."

"Good."

It was four minutes to three. Barker's head was encircled by smoke like a diaphanous halo. I decided I'd strained his patience long enough.

"Best be on my way, then. Tell Mac I shan't be home for dinner. Cheerio!"

"Enjoy your day, lad," he replied, visibly relaxing.

I stepped out into Craig's Court and turned the corner into Whitehall Street. As it happened, I was standing in the exact spot where a day earlier I had encountered the girl named Sofia. Traffic in the street was a third of what it would be on Monday and foot traffic was minimal. It was not difficult to deduce that the man walking toward me was intended for number 7. One of the reasons Barker hired me, or so he has told me, is my ability to be unnoticeable. Just then I leaned against the wall with my hands in my pockets and one foot against the brick, my head down. The passing fellow paid me no heed at all. When he was gone, I took out my pad and pencil and began to scribble in Pitman shorthand. It's how I think best. If it isn't recorded, it didn't happen.

Five feet ten, medium build, late fifties. Well dressed, morning coat (hasn't changed since church?), graying hair, clean shaven, walking stick, homburg hat, no overcoat. Purposeful stride. Appearance of wealth. Does not look lost.

The man turned into Craig's Court. I wasn't about to put my head around the corner and have Barker see me, but I had to wonder, who was this fellow and what business did he have with Barker on a Sunday?

Casual acquaintances have joked with me about enjoying mysteries, as if when an enquiry agent's assistant has time off he prefers to spend it reading Wilkie Collins. The truth is: I despise mysteries. They really get under my fingernails. I already have enough elements of my life that have no answers; I don't require any more, thank you. True, I derive some satisfaction when we capture a criminal and prove without doubt that he has stepped outside of the law and deprived someone of their property and often their lives. That does not mean I would go looking for imaginary cases in my free time. Do barristers while away their evenings poring over legal briefs or do engineers read boiler manuals by candlelight, a cup of tea at their elbow? I rather think not.

I was walking away with the intent to avoid my

employer on the off chance that he himself might step out of the office to see what mischief I was getting into, when up ahead I saw a familiar sight. It was a white lace parasol just disappearing ahead of me into Northumberland Street. On any given day, of course, London teems with white parasols, and the chances of finding a particular girl under any one of them are far less than finding a pea under one of three walnut shells manipulated by a confidence trickster. However, I was twenty-two and sound of limb, and would have crossed London for the opportunity to flirt with a pretty girl. And so I gave chase, as any sane young man would.

By the time I reached the corner and turned into Northumberland Street my quarry was well down the road. She was remarkably fleet of foot. Was it Sofia? The odds were almost astronomically against it. I was not so vain as to think she would hang about the area hoping for another chance to speak to me; almost vain enough, perhaps, but not quite. From where I trotted a hundred yards behind, the woman under the parasol could or could not be her. She was about the girl's height, and was wearing a different dress, but then she would be wearing something different. This dress was almost fawn colored, and when she lifted her heels, her boots were white leather. The parasol was like a thousand others. Behind, I willed her to turn around and give me the slightest glimpse of her face, but then I'd never gotten a woman to do anything even by speaking. How did I expect it by willing it? She passed a small courtyard in front of the Northumberland Arms, and about twenty seconds later, I did so, as well.

"Mr. Lancelyn, is it not?"

I skidded to a halt and nearly fell on the cobblestones. My heart began beating faster, I could feel it in my breast. At one of the tables Sebastian Nightwine was just rising.

Ahead of me, the girl turned the corner and disappeared.

"It is Llewelyn, as I'm sure you are aware."

"Lancelyn, Llewelyn, no matter. I've never been good with names. Perhaps we should all be Welsh and call ourselves Jones."

"An excellent suggestion," I replied. "You should pass it on to your friends in the government."

"That was an interesting reception at the docks. Mr. Barker's idea, I take it."

"No, actually I'm the one with the Jewish friends these days."

"Ah. You're not as callow as you were two years ago. Come have a seat. I'll buy you a drink, or a cup of tea, if you prefer."

"Nothing for me, thank you. It might be poisoned."

Nightwine sighed. "I believe I can get through an entire conversation without killing someone,

44

although you do try my patience. I suppose, like your employer, you feel you cannot break bread with the Bad, Bad Man."

"Something like that."

"Just sit down, then. We need to talk."

With a good deal of reluctance, I sat. Normally I prefer bars or glass between myself and a viper. On the other hand, there was a kind of exhilaration at being this close to a man Barker considered his nemesis.

"Well? You want to talk? Let's talk."

"I'm making a fresh start," he said. "I'm tired of my old ways and trying to rehabilitate myself. I've got several friends willing to overlook my past and to help me put my best foot forward. I could convince a lot of people to give me a second chance, but not your employer. Never him. There's been too much water over that bridge."

"Why the change of heart?"

"I'm not getting any younger, and I don't intend to lead a hand-to-mouth existence for the rest of my life. I've got plans."

"Plans involving diplomatic status."

"As usual, I see Cyrus is well informed. Yes, plans that would go a good deal more smoothly if he were not trailing me about trying to stop them. He gets excitable, you see. Once he gets an idea in his head, there's no letting up on his part."

"You mean ideas such as you're a professional criminal?"

Nightwine was not angered by my words, but he waved a finger in my face.

"Now, now, Mr. Llewelyn. Be careful. You're awfully close to slander and I have an excellent solicitor. All you have is hearsay and much of it based upon the word of a man who is permanently prejudiced against me."

"And why shouldn't he be?" I demanded.

"I know you highly regard your employer, but the truth is he has carried the insane notion in his head for twenty years that I killed his brother."

My jaw must have dropped. Certainly I had no rejoinder at hand for that remark. Barker had not even intimated in the two years I had known him that he had a brother.

"I can see he hasn't told you," Nightwine went on. "He's always been tight-lipped. I suppose he hasn't mentioned we were in the army together, either, or that we were the closest of friends. Oh, dear, he has been holding out on you, hasn't he? He really doesn't trust anyone, your boss."

"You're lying," I told him, but even as I said it, I realized I was on shaky ground.

After all, I'd just caught the Guv hiding something from me. What kind of a working relationship can one have with a man who carries so many secrets?

"Am I? Ask him how we met, then. The one thing I can say in Cyrus's favor is that he never lies."

At this point a waiter interrupted us. Nightwine drank only water and I nothing so far, and they needed the table for paying customers. I ordered coffee. If Nightwine poisoned it, perhaps I wouldn't have to go back and confront my employer.

"No bread?" Nightwine asked, raising an eyebrow.

"Not at present, thank you. Do you have a message you want me to give him when I return, or is the fact that I've been waylaid here these few minutes talking with you enough of a threat?"

"Bravo. You really are coming along. I must admit I wasn't impressed at our first meeting."

"I'd known Mr. Barker all of about forty-eight hours then. The message?"

"Tell him we should meet. Let bygones be bygones, shake hands, and settle our differences and all that. He can name the place. I'm staying at the Army Navy Club. You see? I'm all aboveboard. Unlike him, I have no secrets."

"I'm not the one you have to convince."

The coffee arrived. I pulled it away from his reach and drained it in one pull, though it scalded my tongue. Bravado, I believe the Italians call it. I threw some coins onto the table.

"I must get back," I said, standing.

"He's got you working on the Sabbath? You know, you really need to put your foot down or he'll take all your time."

"When I want advice, I'll ask my father."

"Fair enough, then. I'll be waiting for his decision. What's it to be, do you think? Olive branches or arrows?"

"I'd say, keep the quiver handy."

I walked away then, leaving him alone at the table, proceeding calmly and sedately until I reached Whitehall, where I made a mad dash to Craig's Court and threw open the door. Barker's chamber was full of pipe smoke but no visitor.

"Nightwine," I cried, out of breath, pointing behind me. He came around the desk and we both ran to the Northumberland Arms. Of course, the table was empty. Without a word, Barker turned and surveyed the streets in every direction, searching for his adversary but not finding him.

"Tell me everything," he ordered.

You first, I said to myself.

Chapter Five _____

I recounted every word Nightwine had said; every nuance and inflection, as we made our way back to our chambers. My employer walked with his hands clasped behind his back and his head sunken on his breast. I was determined to get it all out before he spoke.

"Obviously, he was trying to drive a wedge between us."

"And has he succeeded?" he asked. That's Barker for you. No need for a hundred words when four will do.

I raised my hands. "I understand how you work. If you wish to remain silent about your private life, that is your own affair. I suppose if I believe a piece of information you hold is required, I shall ask for it."

We entered the office, the door of which had been thrown open in our haste to leave, and took our chairs again.

"Do you think my past with Nightwine is such a piece of information?" he asked.

"You would be better placed to answer that question than I would, sir."

"You do realize," he said, "that sometimes information can just as easily get you killed as save your life."

"I understand that, yes."

He exhaled half a barrel full of air and then sat back in his green chair. I sat up. He was finally going to tell me something of his past.

"I suppose the first thing you should know is that I did have an elder brother. Caleb was two years older than I, and while my parents were missionaries in Foochow, dressing in Chinese clothing to make the Western religion more palatable for the natives, Caleb was sent to a proper English boarding school in Shanghai.

"You must understand there is a major tragedy in China every couple of years: a flood, an invasion, an earthquake. In this case, it happened to be cholera. It swept through Foochow and my parents set up a makeshift hospital to care for the sick and dying. Before I knew it, both my parents had contracted the disease, leaving me, at twelve years old, to fend for myself in a strange country.

"I was small and quick and could steal from market stalls and vegetable gardens, but by the time I was sixteen, I was nearly six feet tall. I had to work to eat and there was precious little chance of work while the country was at war. I dug ditches, worked on boats, harvested in the rice paddies, and carried palanquins, but mostly I starved. By my calculation, I had been starving for four years.

"I hardly even remember the time when my parents were alive, except for a party my mother had thrown the night before Caleb had gone off to school. She had contrived to serve roast mutton and had assembled a cake from local ingredients. I thought of that cake for years. It was an inconceivable time. People were dying by the millions. A foreign boy on his own in China would have found an early grave, and so I became one of them, simply to survive.

"China had become a nation of refugees. The

Taiping Rebellion was blowing north, consuming as it came, and soon overtook Foochow. It was rumored that Shanghai was the only safe place to go, but the boats were full and the prices exorbitant. I realized my only chance of survival was to find my brother, and in desperation, I set out to find him. Over the course of six months, I walked four hundred miles barefoot. Shanghai was in chaos when I arrived, choked with panicked refugees, both Chinese and European. At least I knew where I was going, to the St. Francis Xavier College northeast of the Bund, the European quarter of the city. When I arrived, the English guards had no use for a ragged scarecrow and refused me entry, but I was determined to find my brother, my only living relative for almost six thousand miles. Caleb would know what to do, I told myself. I climbed a fence one night in the midst of a rainstorm, timing my entrance with the metronomic pace of the guards' beat, and made my way to the college, but when I arrived, I found it boarded up and abandoned. I have to admit I broke down, convinced my brother was on a ship halfway to Perth and the comfort of distant relatives who no doubt believed me buried with our parents.

"I was fast approaching the point where I could not go on without food. There was but one way to get a full belly in Shanghai at that time, by joining the multinational army gathering to

51

defend the city. I made my way to an encampment outside of Shanghai called Kuang-fu-lin. Less desperate recruiters might have questioned my age, but I was tall and already sported a smudge on my upper lip which would eventually become a mustache. The ironically named Ever Victorious Army needed bodies, and if I had marched from wherever I'd come from, I might be tough enough to last five minutes in battle, which was the best one could hope for.

"The recruiter, a British sergeant broiled red by the sun, expected me to make my mark. I took the pen and signed my name in Chinese: *Shi Shi Ji*. Then I thanked him in English. He was surprised by the fact that I could speak English, and told me to report to a certain tent after I was fed.

"The young man whose tent I was sent to arrived on that very same January day. His uniform had been made for him at Huntsman's in London, and his boots were hand-tooled. One wouldn't know by his looks and professional appearance that he had just been turned out of Sandhurst Military Academy for numerous offenses, and sent to China to temper his high spirits. With the phrase 'Right Honorable' in front of one's name, one could write one's own ticket. That wasn't to say that everything was rosy. He told me later he knew no one in this half of the world, and everyone on the other half had told him what a disappointment he had turned out to be. While the American brigadier in command of the general army was trying to figure out where to put a young Englishman in boots so new they squeaked, he sat in his tent and looked about at the crates of supplies and the Enfield rifle still waiting to be fired, wondering what would become of him. He felt a few card games and some spirited larks had not merited being banished to a country where one found heads lined up along the ground like cabbages, but it was far too late to argue now. He knew he must learn to adapt and change, as his father, a close friend of Darwin and an explorer and scientific author in his own right, would have said. He supposed, he told me later, that if his father had not put the family name on the map, it wouldn't have been necessary to send his son so very far away.

" 'What in hell do you want?' he snapped when I lifted the flap and stepped in.

"I explained to him I was told to come there. He ordered me to give his horse a good rubbing down. And that was the beginning of a long and complicated relationship."

"Obviously the officer in question was Sebastian Nightwine."

"Correct. No doubt to the surprise of Frederick Townsend Ward, the American brigadier in charge of the defense of Shanghai, the young popinjay the English government had foisted upon him proved to be a capable leader. He was fearless in battle, could quote strategies from Marcus Aurelius and Caesar, and seemed to know automatically how to attack a fortified camp. He was soon well liked by the men, not least because he always returned from a raid with spoils, and he understood how to acquire or build whatever was needed with the skill of an engineer. Granted, he was something of a freebooter, but then Ward himself had attended West Point in the same era that would produce George Custer and was something of a glory hunter himself, if one listened to the local gossip. The important thing was that Captain Nightwine could perform the task at hand, whatever it might be, which is an important ability when fighting on foreign soil.

"He began sending me into various villages to bring back intelligence, such as the fact that most villagers were more afraid of the southern rebels than loyal to the Ching government. My hair was so dark, and my features so swarthy that with the front of my head shaved, a long queue, and my round Asian spectacles, I easily passed as a native among the Chinese. Of course, by that time I had spoken Cantonese for so long, I considered it my first language. A large percentage of our soldiers would bolt or switch sides if given the opportunity, mostly due to the fact that they had few weapons and were expected to scavenge battle-fields for them. The rebellion was led by a man named Hong Xiuquan, a failed scholar, who, having read some Christian tracts, came to believe himself the younger brother of Jesus Christ, mandated to free his country from the oppression of the hated Manchu government. His mental capacity was questioned but not his success. He'd already taken southern China.

"Without proper funds, Ward could not be expected to create an efficient modern army. All he had were his so-called Devil Soldiers, wildcatting Americans who were willing to jump into the dragon's mouth, and a few thousand untrained Chinese soldiers who had been farmers just months before. Men like Nightwine and me were the best that he could hope for under the circumstances.

"One day, a year after I'd enlisted, my brother arrived in camp. When the school had shut down, he had been recruited by his headmaster as an interpreter and taken to Peking. He enjoyed the work, and being involved in various palace intrigues, but eventually he and his master had fallen into disfavor at court and their usefulness to Her Majesty's government had come to an end. He came to Kuang-fu-lin, much in the same way I had.

"I was thrilled to see him. He hadn't changed much, save that he'd somehow turned into an adult since last we met, with a mustache, a cigarette, and a civilian suit.

"He had believed me dead, after combing Foochow looking for me and learning that our parents were dead. Now he saw me masquerading as a Chinaman. I couldn't exactly stand up and declare myself a Scot after all that time. Only Nightwine knew, for I had told him soon after we met. Caleb asked if Ward still needed interpreters, and I took him to the officers' tent. Nightwine was very interested in him and both were on their best behavior. They discussed the political aspects of the war, Chinese history, the imperial government, and the right of people to govern themselves, but they were giving each other what they wanted to hear. Even before it was over, I knew their mutual cordiality was false. Caleb and I were not fifteen feet from the tent when he warned me of Nightwine's unsavory reputation.

" 'Do you fight at his side?' he asked.

"I told him the truth. After I had collected enough intelligence in one quarter, he sent me to another before he attacked so I would not be implicated as a spy.

"He'd heard in Peking that Nightwine was a butcher, who rode his horse through the lines, running citizens through as if he were playing at pig-sticking. Women, children, old people, he hacked them to pieces. He rode into houses and looted and raped and made certain there was no one alive afterward to implicate him. He was a monster.

"I was young and naïve and didn't believe that a friend of mine could be so ruthless. I argued that he was only obeying orders.

" 'Perhaps he is,' Caleb said. 'On the other hand, a subordinate is not going to tell Ward that Nightwine enjoys hacking limbs from peasants or beheading captured rebels. I suspect your so-called friend does not possess a conscience. He's using you, lad. You're risking life and limb in the rebel camps, knowing the punishment for spying is beheading, while he sits in his tent all afternoon drinking and shining his boots, or tending to his charger.'

"I had to admit, I attended to his boots and his horse.

"Of course, I didn't want to believe it. Sebastian was my best friend, possibly my only one. His ruthlessness, however, was something I suspected. He had a way of deflecting any of what he considered the weaker virtues. Privately, he called the Chinese no better than cattle, but then he felt much the same about the English. He didn't care a fig about people unless he knew them well, and even then he could go cold suddenly, as if his compassion were shut off with a gas cock. Perhaps I knew it all along, but was too ashamed to admit it. I was out in the enemy camps away from our own soldiers who might have warned me. To them, I was a Chinese orderly, there to wash clothes and cook meals.

Perhaps, I reasoned, he had isolated me so I wouldn't hear how he was putting my intelligence to use.

"When I returned to his tent after walking Caleb back, Nightwine seemed genial enough, and asked if he would be willing to interpret for him. They were raiding the hills near the Old Armory.

"I offered to go with him, but he refused, telling me, 'You're too valuable for that. One stray arrow and where would the Ever Victorious Army be?'

"I should have seen it, Thomas. I should have recognized it from Second Samuel. David wanted to rid himself of Uriah the Hittite, and so he led him into battle and then ordered his men to withdraw."

"Oh, no," I murmured.

"Even though I was forewarned, I didn't think Nightwine capable of such base treachery then. I went off blindly northward toward my next assignment, where my commanding officer sent me. When I found the rebel camp two days later, they were in the midst of a major celebration. Word had arrived that Ward had been killed. It was said that the Devil Soldiers were withdrawing. There was confidence among the rebel forces that the Ever Victorious Army would finally lose. I was in the wrong place. I turned about and began the long march back to Shanghai.

"The rumor proved to be true. The Americans

were withdrawing in disorder and Nightwine was nominally in charge, while England decided on a more permanent and high-ranking successor. The war over China would go on. I searched for Caleb and learned from some of the Chinese soldiers that he had fallen in battle, pierced by no less than three arrows. He hadn't so much as a pocketknife to defend himself. After all my searching and my bloody walk from Foochow, I had spoken with him for less than half a day and wasted most of that precious time arguing about Nightwine's character in a vain attempt to make them like each other. I have no doubt that it was deliberate murder. Sebastian Nightwine killed my only brother, and I will never forgive him."

_____Chapter Six

The following day, and the start of our working week, Cyrus Barker actually refused a prospective client. A manufacturer in Leatherhead by the name of Ferguson was convinced one of his employees was stealing designs and plans and selling them to his competitors. He had no wish to make accusations without proof and risk losing some of his better employees. As he explained his predicament, the Guv pulled a slip of paper from his desk and wrote a name and address upon it. The man's explanation trailed off as the paper was set in front of him.

"What's this?" he asked suspiciously.

"It is the name of a rival of mine who is better suited to this case. He is young and ambitious and you will find him competent."

"You're turning me down?"

"This sort of work requires someone working within your company for days or weeks. Even if I could afford the time, I'm too recognizable and would be quickly spotted.

"Sending my assistant would leave me with little to do and unable to take on a second case."

"But I want your agency to handle the situation. You have the best reputation."

"I would not recommend someone unless I thought him professionally capable of handling the work."

"This is no way to do business," Ferguson said, rising from the visitor's chair.

"If you don't like my recommendation, I suggest you consult one of the other agencies in this court. Good day, sir."

After the fellow left, looking angry and befuddled, I put away my notebook and sat back in my chair.

"You want to leave your time free in case Nightwine chooses to retaliate over the incident at the dock," I challenged.

"If he made an open attempt upon my life or these offices, you would not be able to leave the role you were forced to play in Leatherhead."

"I suppose you're right," I conceded. "I would remind you, however, it does not reflect well on us when we refuse custom."

"Duly noted."

"Perhaps it is Nightwine's strategy to cause you to turn away clients until eventually your reputation suffers."

"I believe—" Barker began, but I never learned what he believed because Inspector Poole slipped into our offices again.

"I thought you were guarding Nightwine," the Guv said, frowning at him.

"I am," he told us. "We work in shifts. I've just been next door, checking in at 'A' Division.

"Have you heard the news?"

"He's been busy turning away clients," I said. "What has happened?"

"Five people are dead this morning and three more in hospital, including two constables. A residence has been placed under quarantine, and just happens to belong to Seamus O'Muircheartaigh. Someone has done for him. He's barely hanging on to his life, and is not expected to recover."

The Guv looked at me and gave a low whistle of surprise. "Someone is very brash to make a play at the Irishman," he said, "if not suicidal.

The man is a human cobra. What have you discovered so far?"

The inspector dug into a coat pocket for his notebook and began flipping pages, while I pulled out my own from the rolltop desk, ready to take shorthand.

"This morning, a young woman delivered a package at number 47 Old Jewry, the City, shortly after eight o'clock. That's about all O'Muircheartaigh was able to tell us before he collapsed. There was parcel wrapping in the outer office and a sword and scabbard on the Persian rug in front of his desk."

"Was the sword in the scabbard?" my employer asked.

"No, they were lying side by side. When our constables arrived, everyone in the office was dead or dying, without so much as a scratch on them. PCs Roche and Halston were summoned by a secretary, a Miss Callahan, now deceased. Whatever it is, a microbe or what-have-you, it got them, as well. They're in St. Bart's Hospital, choking out their lungs at the moment."

"Do you have a description of the girl who delivered the package?"

"Heavily veiled, dark dress, average height. Could have been any woman in London, or even a small man in disguise."

"Interesting," Barker murmured in his low

voice, so piercing I could feel the wood desk under my hand vibrate as I wrote.

"What kind of sword was it?" Barker went on. "Foil? Saber?"

"No, it was in your line," Poole said. "Wide blade, not very long. Possibly Asian. The handle is copper and represents a flower of some sort."

"Offhand, I'd say it was ricin that killed your constables, Terry, a substance produced in the manufacture of castor oil. It is fatal if inhaled. It was probably in the toe of the sheath. The drawing of the sword to view the blade released the substance into the air."

"How do we clean it up?" Poole asked.

"Very carefully, and with a wet neckerchief covering your face. The residue will have settled on everything, and this substance doesn't become inert. O'Muircheartaigh should be quarantined, as well. One good cough and the ricin in his lungs becomes airborne again. It's nasty stuff."

"This all sounds vaguely foreign," Poole stated. "I've never heard of ricin before, and of course, O'Muircheartaigh is an Irish criminal. Then there's the sword. Do you suppose it could be a rival Irish faction, working out of France, perhaps?"

Poole, an Englishman to the core, is always suspicious of anything or anyone outside his own culture. The French are not to be trusted, the Germans covet our navy, and the Russians want to wrest India from our grasp. As a Scot and a Welshman, the Guv and I have wondered about his opinions closer to home, but he is a good friend, and has saved our hides on more than one occasion.

"I'd have called O'Muircheartaigh the most dangerous man in London," Barker stated, "but whoever made the attempt on his life this morning would more closely earn that title."

The thought occurred to me that whoever the messenger was, he had done me a favor. The Irishman had sworn he'd kill me one day. In our second case, I had been responsible for causing an explosion which killed a woman who had been his paramour. That she was going to use the bomb she carried to harm a member of the royal family he found irrelevant.

My employer looked at Poole. "You've given me very little information to work with."

"It's all we have at the moment," Poole said, standing. "I've got to get back. The Yard is hopping today. We'll talk later."

When he was gone, I turned to my employer.

"Do you think there's a connection between Nightwine's arrival and this attack upon O'Muircheartaigh?"

"I am convinced of it. Nightwine sold his criminal interests to the Irishman before he left for Asia. Seamus would be furious to hear he was coming back."

"Not even if Nightwine declared himself reformed?"

"If you believe that, lad, you are more naïve than I think you are."

"So, someone working for Nightwine attacked O'Muircheartaigh, attempting to bring him down first?"

"I would, were I in his situation," Barker said. "Wouldn't you?"

"I suppose I would."

Standing, he filled his pipe and crossed to the window, where he looked out onto the courtyard. "Mark my words, Thomas. O'Muirchartaigh already knew of Nightwine's arrival and was planning a move of his own when events overtook him."

"Should we go into the City then?" I asked.

"Even if we tried to enter his offices, we would be stopped by the police, and I do not believe Seamus would be able to speak if we went to St. Bart's. We should stay here until we have more information."

I was about to venture a remark, no doubt something decisive and necessary to the investigation, when I was interrupted by the bell of the telephone set on the Guv's desk.

I got up from my chair and lifted the receiver to my ear.

"Barker Agency," I said.

There was a short crackle on the other end, and then the operator spoke in a monotone voice.

65

"Good morning. I have an incoming call for Mr. Waterstone," he said.

"I'm sorry. You must have reached this number by mistake. There's no one here by that name."

"Thank you," the operator said, and rung off promptly.

"Who was it?" Barker asked.

"Wrong number," I stated. "He wanted someone named Waterstone."

There was a sharp tink as Barker's pipe hit the floor and the amber stem broke.

Before I knew it, his hands dug into my lapels and jerked me around the desk, as he dragged me toward the narrow hallway behind our chambers.

Barker stopped at a door on the right and opened it. It was a lumber room with a ladder affixed to the wall at the far end, leading to the basement. He pointed and I climbed down quickly, with him close behind.

Reaching the empty basement, he led me across to a door in the wall and plunged inside. It was a tunnel, narrow and unlit. I hadn't gone ten feet before my shoulders came in contact with something cold and reptilian. I gasped, my mind conjuring snakes.

"Telephone cables," my employer called out ahead of me. "We're under the exchange."

We scuttled along, bent double, for at least fifty yards, until we saw a faint light ahead. My employer clambered up a set of stone steps and I heard the metallic squeal of a bolt being drawn before we burst out through a trapdoor onto the embankment overlooking the Thames.

"Take the footbridge," the Guv shouted, pointing overhead. "The sooner we are out of Whitehall, the better."

There is a time to ask questions and a time to be silent and this was definitely the latter. We climbed the bridge and loped across it, fast enough to cover ground but slow enough not to attract attention. We passed the spot where two years earlier I had been blown into the Thames by an explosion. I had promised myself I'd never come this way again, but apparently, this was a day for breaking promises.

"We've got company," Barker called back, as three constables trotted toward us from the far end of the bridge. I thought perhaps we could appeal to them for help, but instead, the Guv charged them. Though he dispatched the first easily, the second was thick enough to believe he could tackle Cyrus Barker. He threw his arms around him, locking his hands behind Barker's back, his helmet hard against my employer's rib cage. The Guv hesitated, choosing the right spot, possibly even the precise vertebra, and then brought his elbow down sharply. This would have been enough for most men, but the constable was tough. He doggedly held on. Barker had to drive a knee up hard into his diaphragm, lifting him off the ground, before the man finally let go and slid down onto the bridge. As I came around, the third officer was about to take a swing at my employer's head with a heavy truncheon, so I caught his hand and swung it down, cracking the ash across his kneecap. He gave a sharp cry and fell, holding the injured limb. Tugging his whistle from his pocket, he tried to bring it to his lips, but I thumped him on the helmet with his own stick. He stopped moving and I turned to my employer, aware we'd just assaulted three civil servants.

"Secure them," he said to me, a trifle winded, and tossed me the Hiatt master key he always kept in his waistcoat pocket.

"Don't forget their whistles," I said, as I dragged a constable to the side of the bridge and cuffed him to a bracket there.

"Good thinking. Now, find us a cab."

We hailed a passing hansom at the far end of the bridge and climbed aboard. Barker sat back and immediately sank into himself in that way he has. I let him think a minute or two before speaking.

"Where are we going?" I demanded.

"The Bank of England. We need money."

"I take it the name 'Mr. Waterstone' is some kind of warning. Who sent it?"

"Terence Poole."

"What are you talking about? I know he's a

friend, but he's threatened to arrest us a dozen times. He's had me in lockup at least twice."

"Never for something that could impede our liberty altogether."

"What do you mean?" I asked, feeling a cold tingle between my shoulder blades. "What sort of something?"

In answer, he merely shrugged those thick shoulders of his.

"So, right now, our offices are being stormed by Scotland Yard?" I speculated. "Poor Jenkins. They'll probably haul him in for questioning. At least he can claim ignorance."

"Terry wouldn't warn me over anything short of murder. We must assume a warrant has been issued for my arrest."

"I still don't understand, sir. Why not stay and prove you didn't do whatever it is you've been accused of?"

"If there was a way to prove my innocence immediately, Poole wouldn't have called," Barker said, his brows so knitted they had descended behind the twin moons of his black-lensed spectacles. "Whatever it is, it must be damning."

Chapter Seven _____

I'd never been inside the Old Lady of Threadneedle Street before, though I'd passed down the street itself on several occasions. Barker holds accounts in various banks across London, but generally uses a branch of Cox and Company within Craig's Court. I better understood why he had an account at the Bank of England when I read a plaque inside that said the establishment was founded in 1694 by a Scotsman, William Paterson. My employer prefers old established companies with which to do business, and sends his money north of Hadrian's Wall whenever possible.

I wasn't prepared for the vaulting marble ceilings or the cavernous echo of footsteps and voices therein. One could be excused for mistaking the bank for part of a cathedral or royal palace. In the hush of those grand walls, I was painfully aware that I had just chained three police constables to a bridge. I stood beside my employer, trying to look professional and businesslike, but inside, my nerves were ajangle.

Cyrus Barker wrote a cheque while I surveyed the room. We crossed to a long counter manned by tellers, hard-faced men with most of the color drained out of them, who looked as if they had not smiled once in their entire lives. The Guv set the paper down in front of one of them, a man so desiccated he would not have been out of place among the mummies in the British Museum. He scrutinized the slip of paper distastefully, but then I expected that. Barker's handwriting is nearly illegible.

"I'll be right back, sir," the teller said. "I must get this amount approved." He turned and passed into the room behind.

The Guv's hand opened on the counter, as if to tap on it, and then closed again, willing patience. I cleared my throat and looked about. Everything appeared normal. People walked about sedately, discussing loans and rates. Men filled out forms, and conferred in corners. Money was accruing, and an empire was being financed.

The Guv grunted something in a low voice that I could not understand.

"I beg your pardon?" I asked, a knot suddenly forming in my stomach.

"I said, run!"

I turned and dashed toward the door just as two burly men came around the far end of the desk and gave chase. As we ran, Barker pulled a handful of sharpened coins from his pocket, which he uses to stop anything short of a bull elephant. There was a clang as he banked them off the hard marble floor behind us. One man took a coin in the shoulder. The other one received a deep cut in the cheek. The last I heard before breaking out into Threadneedle Street again was the sound of one of them falling with a groan.

From there it was only a short distance to London Bridge and the relative safety of Lambeth on the other side. Barker and I first attempted a straight line to the bridge via Gracechurch Street, but at one point, he diverted me into Lombard. It was none too soon, as a squad of constables trotted by, heading north toward the bank. The Guv pulled me into a shop that sold general sundries, looking about momentarily at domestic items that had no meaning in our lives: hairpins, bolts of fabric, and combs. After a minute or two, he pulled me out again, and we skirted a tailor's shop. The third business along the row was a coffeehouse, and as he opened the door, I was momentarily treated to the aroma of freshly brewing beans. However, it was all I was treated to, as we crossed the main room and passed through the kitchen, whose help stared at us without even so much as a protest. We exited into a sooty alley which led into King William's Street before finally coming to ground in an evil-smelling barber shop.

"We need our hair cut," Barker stated.

"Not my hair!" I protested.

"Especially your hair, lad. It distinguishes you."

The shop was worlds apart from Truefitt's of Old Bond Street, our customary barbers. It looked like it hadn't been cleaned since the Worshipful Company of Barbers was first organized in 1308. The shaving mugs were cracked, the floor filthy, and the barbers little better than inebriants, with but a single set of proper teeth between the three of them. It came as no surprise that the shop was empty. We settled uneasily into two ancient chairs and unwashed sheets were tucked around our throats.

"What'll it be, then?" the barber leered, brandishing his scissors.

I sighed. "Cut it short."

"Righto."

As the first lock tumbled down the sheet, I felt like a sheep being shorn. It reminded me exactly of my first haircut in Oxford Prison prior to my employment with Barker. It never occurred to me that such a humiliation could happen twice in one lifetime.

I was so concerned with the state of my own head that I hadn't noticed the Guv's.

When I finally looked his way, his face was being patted with a towel. Gone was the heavy black mustache that reached to his chin. His face looked naked without it, his upper lip pale against his swarthy chin. My hair was short, the familiar curls gone, but the barber had reduced his to mere stubble.

It was demeaning to pay these fellows for the butchery they had done to us, but I did so, clapping my bowler on my head, where it promptly slid down over my ears. Stepping out into the sunshine I had so admired that morning, I turned back and bowled the hat back inside, where it kicked up layers of dust and hair on the dirty floor.

"This gets better and better. We should have had them pull a few teeth, as well. No one would recognize us then."

"Step in there a moment, Thomas," the Guv said, pointing to a villainous-looking alley, black with soot.

I obeyed, wondering what further indignity I was about to endure. Immediately, the April sunshine disappeared and the temperature dropped sharply. Barker reached into the pocket of his coat and took out an eye patch.

"Where did you get that?" I asked.

"From the millinery shop we were in earlier."

"I don't recall paying for it."

"You didn't. I stole it," he said.

"You *stole* it?" I asked. Barker's integrity is so exaggerated that he would walk a mile to pay back tuppence. "Why didn't you simply pay for it?"

"Scotland Yard will trace the cabman who

brought us to the City. They will track down the barber and find out how we've changed our hair. I needed something else to alter my appearance that they couldn't possibly know about."

Looking away from me, he removed his spectacles and put them in his pocket before tying the patch over his right eye, the one bisected by the scar. Then he turned back to face me.

I had never seen Barker's eyes before. Either from a habitual squint or heredity, his left eye was little more than a horizontal slit in his face. The iris looked black as coal.

"Well?" he asked.

"Excellent," I replied. "No one would recognize you."

My employer stepped out into the street again and regarded his reflection critically in the window of a pawnshop, running a hand over his stubbled head. Whatever he saw didn't fully satisfy him, because he pushed me back into the alleyway again.

"We still look too much like ourselves. I'm afraid we must lose our collars and ties."

"But this is my favorite tie, sir!"

"It can't be helped, Thomas."

"Blast!" I cried, and ripped off the collar. Somewhere, perhaps even now, some down-and-outer is wearing my best tie.

"Satisfactory," he growled. "Now, we must get

out of the City, but we do not dare use a cab. I'm afraid we will be walking the rest of the day."

"Where should we go? Ho's restaurant? Reverend McClain's?"

The Guv shook his head. "Terry knows them both. He also has Fu Ying's address in Three Colt Lane." Bok Fu Ying was Barker's ward, who also cared for his prized Pekingese, Harm. She lived in Limehouse in the middle of the Chinese district, a few streets from the tearoom of Ho, my employer's closest friend.

"Would Poole give that information to his superiors?"

"Of course. He would have to. You know he is CID through and through. He was walking a beat when you were in short pants."

"Then why did he warn us, if he bleeds Metropolitan blue?"

"Because we are friends. He felt it his duty to warn me, but he would not go so far as to obstruct an investigation."

"Then where can we go?" I asked. "We certainly can't check into a respectable hotel anymore, dressed like this."

"I know a place, but it will mean several miles' walk. Be glad that it isn't pouring rain."

"Not yet, anyway," I remarked.

"There's that Welsh pessimism."

"I don't believe you know anything at all about Wales, actually."

We put our heads down and walked. When we finally reached the bridge, there were half a dozen policemen there, attempting to set up a cordon to capture a certain pair of desperate enquiry agents, but it was proving a challenge due to the high volume of traffic that fills the bridge at all hours. Barker strode ahead and engaged a perfect stranger in conversation, a slatternly looking man who already appeared drunk before noon. I fell back, searching the crowd for a traveling companion of my own, but found none. Instead, I followed along closely behind a family, trying to look like a wayward brother, until we had crossed the bridge. It worked well enough. I was scrutinized, but passed over unmolested.

In Southwark Street, the Guv parted from his companion and made his way to an ironmonger's shop. I stepped back from the group and followed him in.

"Hunting that Barker fellow?" the proprietor asked Barker immediately. "You'll need a good lantern."

"What Barker fellow?" the Guv asked.

"There's this bloke named Barker who killed a lord. He sapped three peelers and is at large in the City. Someone's put up a reward for whoever brings him in. Two hundred and fifty quid. I've sold six lamps so far. Only got two left."

"Two hundred fifty quid is a lot of money,"

Barker said. "A fellow could retire on that."

"You'll 'ave to catch him first. He's a slippery one from what I hear. Some kind of detective. And you'll 'ave to fight off a few hundred other people out looking for him, too."

"What's he look like?"

"Big fella. Dresses like a toff. Mustache and dark-lensed spectacles."

"That don't sound too hard to find. Where was he last seen?"

"Right here in Lambeth, headed north by cab. It's been a boon to business, I don't mind saying, though I wisht I was out looking myself. I could find something to do with that reward money."

"Why don't we make that two lanterns, then?" Barker asked. "Who's giving this money away? Scotland Yard?"

"Not bloody likely they'll want our help, is it? No, it's private, like."

"Could it just be a rumor, then?" I asked. "Is it in the newspapers?"

"Not yet," the man admitted. "But it's all over London. Common knowledge by now."

"Is he traveling alone?" I asked.

"Far as I know. Reward's only for Push hisself."

"Push?" Barker asked.

"It's 'is moniker. Rhyming slang. Push-Comes-to-Shove. Guv."

"So you know him, then."

"Oh, everyone knows Barker. Don't expect 'im

to just walk up and let you clap irons on him, though. He's stubborn as two mules and kicks harder."

"Ta for the warning."

A few minutes later we were walking down Southwark, swinging our unlit lanterns.

"First the police are after us and now there is a reward," I said, shaking my head. "Your bank accounts are frozen and half of London is out hunting for us. Nightwine's behind this, too."

"Aye. It's no coincidence that the Irishman and I have both been brought low on the same morning."

"Why don't we catch up with Vic and find out what he's heard?"

Barker has watchers all over London who provide him with goods and information, most of whom answer to the phrase "Barker sent me." My least favorite among them was a street Arab and constant irritant that went by the name Soho Vic. As I understood it, he was a miniature Fagan, running a warren full of underage messengers in Whitechapel.

"That's the last thing I want to do," Barker countered. "Two hundred and fifty pounds might not be much to us under normal circumstances, but it's a fortune for Vic. I don't want to put him in the way of so much temptation, especially with the number of mouths he has to feed. Besides, people know he delivers messages for us and will be following him, hoping he'll lead them to us."

"So, we're alone, then. Cut off from all effectual aid. Nightwine certainly knows what he's about. What o'clock is it?"

"Nearly four," he said, consulting his old repeater. I'd left my pocket watch back on my desk in Craig's Court, the special one given to Barker by the Prince of Wales.

"If we were to have a pint at the right kind of public house, we might learn more about this reward."

"Thomas, that is a canny suggestion, the first one you've made today. I know just the place."

Ten minutes later we were sitting in a dark tavern with pint glasses in front of us. I was glad it was dark so I couldn't see how dirty the table was, or what was crawling about underfoot. I was also relieved I hadn't ordered any food, even though we'd missed lunch. I'd hoped for a better class of public house, but understood that matters such as a rumored reward would be more likely to be discussed openly in a tavern like this one in George Street, which was called the Regency Buck.

"They say the Irishman will live," someone said at a nearby table.

"Take more than a bit of poison to bring him down. Seamus is a tough old bird. So's Push, for that matter."

"I'd have paid cash money," another man said, "to see the Guv take apart three blues and chain them like a necklace 'crost Charing Cross footbridge."

"Where'd ye s'pose the Moor's got to?"

"Bound to be somewheres. Can't have one wiffout t'other."

"Is it true there's a big reward, then?"

Barker had hoped to slip the question in unobserved, but in a place like this, one has to establish one's bona fides before being allowed to participate in such rarefied conversations. However, it was a juicy question, one that everyone wanted to discuss anyway, and so they let it slip by, which I'm sure was what the Guv had intended.

"What reward might that be, mister?" the publican asked, coolly.

"Two hundred and fifty quid for Barker's head on a pole, that's what reward. Personally, I don't believe it. Somebody's pulling our leg."

"That's where you're wrong then, mister. The Elephant and Castle gang have been spreading the message, and swore the bloke that started it spread out the entire amount in front of them in ten-pound notes, to show he had 'em."

"What did he look like, this chap with the notes?"

"They didn't say and I didn't ask. Who wants to know?"

"Name's Shadwell," Barker said. "Me and my boy are up from Surrey. We don't wanna waste our time. How many are out lookin'?"

"Go back where you come from, then," one of the crowd advised. "There's hoondreds of us. Some 'ud hunt down Cyrus Barker for nothin', just to knock him off his bleedin' perch. Put my cousin in Holloway two months ago, he did."

"Isn't the Met looking for him, as well?" Barker asked.

"That's why we're here," one man said. "The manhunt starts in about harf an hour on the embankment in front of Scotland Yard. We're gettin' our last drinks in before we sign up."

"What do you say, boy?" Barker asked. "Shall we hunt this detective fellow or go home?"

"Whatever you say, Da," I replied, trying not to look intelligent, which my contemporaries will tell you is not difficult.

"Wouldn't hurt to look about for an hour or two, would it? Might bump into this Barker bloke by accident, like."

"Who's this Moor fellow, then?" I asked.

"Barker's assistant," the publican explained.

"Wha', is he a blackamoor?"

"Nah, though he's dark enough. Stands for: More-the-Merrier, Barker's terrier!"

Everyone enjoyed a laugh over that. The problem with nicknames, I've always thought, is that one never gets to invent one's own.

"Shall we go?" Barker asked.

I put down my sour beer, and dropped a few coins upon the ringed and dirty table. "Gladly."

_____Chapter Eight

Instead of retreating to the anonymity and relative safety of the east or south once we were in the street, Barker herded me back along the Thames toward the embankment again.

"Surely you don't intend for us to go back to the bridge?" I asked, alarmed.

"Thomas, I didn't shave my mustache and put on this eye patch merely to cower in a corner somewhere. We're heading along the river for a few miles, and the easiest way to reach it is by the embankment."

"But it'll be swarming with constables."

"Constables who will be looking for a pair of desperate fugitives, not men offering to help in the search. The trick is to be bold as brass. Now, stop dawdling."

A quarter hour later we were standing where we had begun our journey that morning, at the Charing Cross Railway and Footbridge. What a change a few hours had wrought. Though it had stood near empty hours before, the far shore now teemed with people milling about like ants on a mound. I wondered how the rumor of the reward had already reached into every corner of London. Had not one person come forward to defend the reputation of Cyrus Barker?

"Shall we cross?" he asked, though it was obvious he had every intention of doing so.

"In for a penny," I quoted.

"Exactly."

When we reached the bridge it had been barricaded completely, and a queue had formed. Constables questioned anyone attempting to cross.

"Your name, sir?" a bored constable asked as we came forward.

"Shadwell," the Guv replied. "Robert Shadwell. Bruiser Bob, they call me. This here's me son, Alf."

"Shadwell," the constable wrote on a clipboard. "And your purpose for being here?"

"Come to hunt for this Barker bloke like everyone else. Heard there might be a reward."

He made a notation on the form and nodded.

"Very well, gentlemen, you may pass."

As we neared our offices and Scotland Yard, I could hear a man below addressing the crowd in a loud, clear voice.

"Again, we have not established the rumor of a reward for the capture of Cyrus Barker. Scotland

Yard disavows any knowledge of such an offer and, frankly, we doubt its veracity. A definite source has not been located. Also, the Yard will brook no interference in this investigation. We will arrest anyone whom we believe to be hindering this manhunt for personal gain!"

"Who's the fellow speaking?" Barker asked a constable at the checkpoint on the other side.

"That's Inspector Abberline. He's in charge of the hunt."

"Any leads? Where was he last seen?"

"You'll have to ask him that," he said, pointing his thumb at his superior on the bank.

"Don't think I won't," my employer said. "Come along, boy. Pick up your feet."

We descended the steps and found a mixed crowd of would-be man-hunters and newspaper reporters, pestering the officer with questions. Abberline was about thirty, of less than medium height, with good features, a small mustache, and black hair beginning to recede. He looked bright as a new penny and very capable of running such a large-scale operation. The questions with which they peppered him he answered back with aplomb and logic.

"What about the rumor that after mowing down your constables like skittles, he turned back and is hiding somewhere in his rooms?" a reporter asked.

"Absolutely unfounded. We thought of that

possibility and have tossed every room in the immediate area from cellar to attic."

"How are the injured constables?"

"All three of them were admitted to Charing Cross Hospital. As I understand, two have been released, while the third will remain with a broken knee."

"Is it true that his assistant is with him?"

"Yes, it is. Initially, he was not charged, but now we have reason to believe he is also a fugitive of the law. Mr. Thomas Llewelyn is considered dangerous and was the one responsible for breaking PC Raife's knee. He was imprisoned three years ago, I understand, for attacking a nobleman with the intent of robbery."

So much for British justice, I thought bitterly. Though I had paid my debt to society, my past would be brought up repeatedly throughout my life. There are events in our lives that define us. Mine was lifting a single coin from a stack on the mantelpiece of an upperclassman at Oxford at the precise moment he walked in. The coin meant life or death for my young wife, lying ill in a garret on the other side of town. As it turned out, 'twas death for her, and eight months in Oxford Prison for me on a charge of theft. When I claim Life is a cruel taskmaster, believe me that I know whereof I speak.

"How long will the bridges be cordoned off?" one of the reporters asked.

"Until noon tomorrow, at Commissioner Warren's discretion."

"What makes you sure Barker done it?" the Guv called out. "Were there witnesses?"

"No," Abberline answered. "But he left behind one of his calling cards. I cannot comment further."

Barker turned away and walked to the river's edge, raising his lantern to light it. I backed away from the crowd casually and followed. The sun was starting to set and the Thames looked as black and thin as india ink. Barker scratched under his chin, which I knew to be a sign he was thinking fiercely while the crowds behind us continued to pelt Abberline with increasingly inane questions. My employer turned and headed south along the embankment.

So, I thought, *the victim had one of Barker's business cards on his person.* That did not sound so damning. They were readily available in a pewter stand in our outer office for anyone to take, and he handed them out whenever he had the opportunity, believing that advertisement resulted in clients. It took me a minute or two to realize that it wasn't those cards to which he referred. The victim must have been found with one of Barker's sharpened pence buried in a hand or leg. I couldn't think of a single thing that would point more strongly in Barker's direction than one of his sharpened coins, a novelty that to my knowledge the Guv alone employed, and which he'd just used that very day in Threadneedle Street, thereby damaging his case further.

"Let's separate, lad," my employer ordered, as he helped me light my lantern. "Stay just in view of my light."

"Do you have a destination in mind, sir?"

"I do."

"Might I hope there is food there, and that it isn't far?" I asked, dwelling on the fact that we hadn't had lunch or dinner.

"Aye," he said, turning around and marching along the embankment. "You're entitled to hope as much as you like."

With that less than encouraging news, I followed behind. At first, I was forced to push my way through the crowd, lantern held high, but as we headed south most of them dispersed over Westminster Bridge or into Whitehall. In ten minutes' walk we were the only two men that I could see following the Thames, but I still hung back, because if I understood him at all, he needed to think.

Perhaps there will come a time someday when there will be a paved path along the Thames in London, a promenade that will go on for miles, but for now it was rough going. I was constantly stepping up and down, barking my toes on something or backtracking and going round. A couple of times I lost sight of the lantern for several minutes. Free though I was, I did not enjoy my solitary walk along the river. Normally at that time, I'd have already eaten a wonderful supper prepared by Etienne Dummolard, our cook, enjoyed a hot soak in the bathhouse, and would currently be reading or going out with my friend Israel Zangwill to a concert or coffeehouse. Now my life was in ruins. Why bother wasting time and effort climbing out of the muck if you're fated to be tossed back in again?

At one point, I was stopped by a constable who asked me if I'd seen anything unusual or anyone hiding along the waterfront. I told him that with all the activity along the river that evening, it didn't seem possible for anyone to escape being found. I was even so bold as to ask if the rumor of a reward was true. He responded that he doubted it, and in any case, it wouldn't be going into the pocket of his tunic, anyway. I lit a cigarette for him, wondering what the commissioner or Inspector Abberline would say to this officer casually chatting up one of the suspects they were presently hunting all over London.

Not long after, I nearly stumbled over Barker. He was sitting on the edge of a dock with his feet dangling over the water, and his candle had guttered and gone out. By then the moon had risen and we were bathed in a cool blue light. I put down my lantern and shook out my arm, for it had been a chore to carry it all that distance. I was tired and hungry and despondent about our predicament.

"Why have we stopped?" I demanded, though it felt good to rest for a moment and stretch my aching limbs.

In response, Barker looked over his shoulder. I turned my head and barely discerned a pair of heavy boots in the moonlight, the man inside them obscured by the shadow of an outbuilding.

"Who's there?" I asked, half to Barker and half to whoever had stopped him.

A man I had never seen before stepped forward into the moonlight. He was massive, over eighteen stone, and taller than Barker, with the misshapen nose of a boxer, and ears that were mere lumps on the side of his head. He had very large black side whiskers and looked capable of thrashing even Cyrus Barker.

"James Briggs," my employer said.

"Not 'Bully Boy' Briggs?" I asked. The latter had been one of the Guv's associates. Barker had occasionally recommended Briggs as a bodyguard to clients.

"Sorry, Barker." The huge man spoke at last, taking off an enormous bowler hat that still managed to look too small for his large head. "I've fallen on hard times. I know we been friends for years, but I could really use that reward."

Barker reached for a piling and pulled himself up. "It was very shrewd of you to work out where I was going, James."

"You always was a water man, Cyrus. It's the sea captain in you. It weren't that hard to figure out where you might go."

"Perhaps not," Barker conceded, "but I don't intend to make things easy for you."

The man's face creased into a grin. "Wouldn't have it any other way. Haven't had me a proper scrap in two years or more."

"But you're hardly unarmed. I assume the priest is with you?"

"Aye, his holiness is by my side as always." Briggs shook his arm and something slid out of his sleeve, a lethal-looking metal club with a bulbous knob at one end and a leather thong at the other. Though a priest is used to club salmon in fishing, Briggs had converted his to become a clubber of men. He went into a crouch and moved toward the Guv.

"Toss me a weapon, lad," Barker ordered. "Look behind you."

I reached for the first thing that came to hand, a boat hook about six feet long, sticking out of a beached dinghy, and tossed it to my employer.

"That don't seem quite fair, Cyrus. It's too long," Briggs complained.

"You never used to be so particular, Jimmy. There's an oar behind you. It's your choice."

Briggs hefted the oar as if testing it, and then without warning, swung it at my employer's head. The Guv ducked backward out of reach, avoiding it so narrowly I would swear it rustled his newly shorn head. Then as its arc cleared him, he stepped forward again and smacked the wooden end of the pole hard into Briggs's rib cage. The man let out a woofing sound and bent double. Barker wrapped the boat hook around his neck and pulled him forward so quickly that he was forced to trot to keep his balance. With a sharp crack, Briggs's forehead came in contact with a piling. He fell back like a stone, spread-eagle on the dock. The entire fight, if one could even call it that, had lasted less than five seconds.

I hurried over to see if he was alive. He was bleeding and unconscious, but he would live. As I debated whether to tend his wounds, the Guv seized him by the wrists and began to drag him across the dock.

"What are you doing?" I exclaimed.

Barker didn't answer, struggling with the heavy load. When he reached the edge, he unceremoniously kicked his friend over into the water with a splash.

"But he'll drown!" I cried, wondering if my employer had gone temporarily mad. I couldn't imagine a situation where Barker would kill in order to protect himself, even in these dire circumstances. Instead of replying, he jumped in after him.

"We're taking him with us!" Barker called, when he surfaced.

"Why?" I demanded.

"He knows where we're going, and I can't carry him far. Are you coming?"

Before I could protest, he flipped Briggs over onto his back and began swimming, one meaty arm around the man's throat. It was April, and though the weather was agreeable enough, it would be a few months until the Thames was warm enough for a proper swim.

"But—" I said, and then gave it up.

Barker and his heavy load were already being swept along with the current. I ran down the bank and took my first tentative step into the icy water, which sloshed over the tops of my boots. There was no time for complaint.

I dived in, every part of my body protesting, and began swimming after him as fast as I could.

"H-how far?" I called a few minutes later, my teeth beginning to chatter.

"Not far," he called. "Half a league or so."

My brain tried to recall exactly how far a league was. Was it half a mile? Two miles? I hadn't the slightest idea.

Ahead of me in the darkness, I heard a thrashing sound and then a dull thump.

"What happened?" I asked.

"He tried to wake up."

"The cheek," I murmured, though I was too tired to say it aloud. The frigid water was quickly draining me of all energy.

When I caught up with Barker, he looked as exhausted as I felt, but he stroked along in the Thames doggedly, keeping Briggs's head above water. The exertion in the cold river was almost more than I could take, and I wasn't dragging a huge man behind me. After what seemed an interminable time, Barker motioned me toward the bank as a police steam launch came around a bend into sight. We hid in the shadow of a barge, treading water weakly, and watched the launch pass slowly by. Being caught would have been a bad end to the day after all we'd been through, but on the other hand, I realized, the police would have dry blankets, a hot boiler, and maybe even mugs of cocoa. The Thames River Police do know how to make an excellent cup of cocoa. For a moment, I thought it might almost be worth getting caught. Instead, I bit my tongue as we waited for the launch to pass.

"I don't think I can go much farther, sir," I confessed, when it was finally gone. "I'm knackered. I'm sorry."

"Don't be. We're here." Barker seized a ladder attached to the side of the barge while I took possession of the limp Briggs. When he'd climbcd aboard, he disappeared for a minute and came back with a rope to haul the man's outsized body out of the water. After ten minutes of struggle, the three of us lay supine on the deck, gasping for air.

Finally, I sat up and looked about. We were on a decrepit old barge with a homemade structure of castoff wood atop it, festooned with wind chimes that clamored lackadaisically in the river breeze. I hadn't been so naïve as to expect a hotel for the night, but I had at least hoped for a proper room.

A door opened behind us and a boy emerged, guarding a candle with the palm of one hand. He was Chinese, with a queue down his back, a small pillbox hat, and no shoes. He took in the sight of the three of us lying on his barge with the kind of stoic calm I've seen his people exhibit in the face of disaster. Coming forward, he engaged Barker in low conversation in what I assumed was Cantonese.

I wanted to ask where we were, but couldn't muster the strength, or perhaps I simply saw the futility of asking. Barker looked in no mood to answer questions, and I doubted the boy spoke English. Luckily for me, Bully Boy Briggs had awakened and favored a more direct approach.

"Where the hell am I?" he suddenly bellowed into the night.

I couldn't have put it better myself.

Chapter Nine_____

Within minutes, the boy pressed small cups of strong, black tea into our hands, and I began to suspect that, all things being considered, I just might live. Briggs had fallen into a sullen silence, probably irked at how easily he had been overcome by my employer. In spite of what he'd called out, he appeared incurious of his surroundings, or of his sodden clothing, but then, he was likely nursing a concussion.

The boy soon returned with bowls of rice flavored with egg but with neither spoons nor chopsticks to eat them with. Barker dug his fingers into the bowl and shoved a handful into his mouth. Briggs sniffed the bowl suspiciously, decided the contents wouldn't kill him, and began to do likewise. I followed suit. When we were done, Barker patted his pockets, then remembered his pipe lying on the floor in our offices with its stem broken. He frowned and sniffed, mentally tightening his belt.

"Lad," he said. "Leave James and me to talk. There are berths down below. Get some sleep. You'll need it."

I wanted to hear what plan the Guv had

concocted, but at the same time, I was cold and exhausted. I nodded and said good night, then went through the door of the makeshift structure and down a narrow set of steps. The boy met me there and led me through an ill-lit corridor to the stern of the ship. There, divesting myself of every stitch of clothing I had, I climbed into the unfamiliar bed, and was asleep almost instantly.

Hours later, I woke to the sound of the river slapping against the barnacle-laden timbers near my head. The cabin was smoky with the acrid scent of whale oil, and I felt nauseous from the fumes. Pushing myself out of the berth, I looked about for my clothes, but they were gone. Wrapping the blanket around me like a toga, I staggered to the door and threw it open. When I was certain I wasn't going to be ill, I shuffled down the corridor. Ahead of me I heard a tinkling sound, almost like sleigh bells. In the main cabin, I was treated to a sight which almost made me forget my nausea entirely.

Cyrus Barker was stripped to the waist and there were stout steel rings suspended from his forearms, seven or eight on each one. They were an inch thick and a little wider than the circumference of his arms. He was performing one of his Chinese forms, like a ballet, but an earthbound one, under the accumulated weight of the rings. So deep was the strain, in fact, that the Guv's body dripped with sweat and the short hair spiked upon his head. Barker had taught me several rudimentary forms but I had not seen one like this before. I waited until he was done before daring to speak.

"Where is Briggs?"

"I let him go," he said, as he let the rings slide down his arm onto the floor with a musical clatter.

"You trust him to keep our whereabouts secret?"

"I trust him to do that which is in his own self-interest. I paid him off with a few damp bills from your trouser pockets. It should buy us some time, at least."

"I hope you didn't give him too many. Goodness knows how long we must live off them."

"It's only money, lad, and easily gotten," he said, putting on a shirt.

"The words of a rich man," I countered. "I've never found it so."

"Yesterday morning you awoke in a comfortably appointed bed in an elegant house, where you dressed in the latest fashion and were fed by London's finest chef. I would say you're not doing too poorly for yourself."

I couldn't argue with that, but I put out my hand and reclaimed the wallet, which I found had been emptied of twenty-five much-needed pounds. Scotsmen are like that, I've found, penny-wise and pound foolish, but it was his money, and he could do with it as he pleased.

"What are we going to do today, sir?" I asked. "Shall we lie low?"

"We have an appointment later, but first we are expecting breakfast."

"More rice and egg, I suppose?"

"The egg is considered a treat," the Guv explained. "Normally they just have rice. They are giving us the best they have."

"There's nothing like a bit of rice and egg to break one's fast," I said, trying to sound enthusiastic.

"It's nourishing, at least. That is why half a continent lives upon it."

"To be sure," I agreed. "Sir, could you tell me what has become of my clothes? I don't relish going about in a bedsheet all day."

"They've been washed and mended and are drying on deck. They should be ready after breakfast."

The tea arrived first, piping hot, but practically tasteless. Were I to mention it, no doubt I'd be told the flavor was subtle and I needed to refine my tastes. I prefer coffee to tea, and that as black as the devil's heart, but I drank the tea and ate the rice anyway. The boy offered me chopsticks, but I still hadn't mastered them yet, unlike Barker, who could pick up a single grain between the tips.

"This barge belongs to the Lo family, our

gardeners," Barker explained. "The boy's name is Yuk."

Soon after, Yuk came down with my clothes. They were still slightly damp, but it was better than spending the day dressed like a Roman senator in a grammar-school version of *Julius Caesar*. After changing, I returned from our cabin.

"What's on for today, then?" I asked.

"We're going out, but it's early yet."

"In that case, do we have time to finish the story you began yesterday? Your brother didn't return from battle. What happened next?"

Barker's brows went flat across the top of his spectacles like a storm head gathering.

He was not inclined to open the vault of his remembrances so soon after his last revelation. Under normal circumstances, I'd back away and leave him to himself, but not this time. This time I had the justification of my convictions. This time I was right. He had told but half a story, and I wanted and deserved the rest of it. What had happened after his brother was so cruelly slain in the field? Did he confront Nightwine, and if so, what happened next? There are times when you can just tell that a momentous story is about to be told, and I refused to be cheated out of his because of a man's natural or perhaps unnatural reticence.

He cleared his throat a couple of times, perhaps hoping I'd take pity on him, but I was stern as granite. He rubbed a hand over his fringe of hair and began to speak.

"I did not learn of my brother's death right away. Townsend Ward had been killed at the siege of Chang-Sheng-Chun and the army was in disarray. Some joined the captain's force and others began to pack up to go to America with the Devil Soldiers. Colonel Charles Gordon was coming; the Americans were out, for the most part, at least, and the British were coming in. The rebels took advantage of this time of command confusion and launched an attack upon an unnamed hillside town south of Shanghai, and during that offensive, my brother had been killed. No one but Nightwine knew of our connection, of course, and who would associate a Chinese spy among the rebels with General Ward's Scottish-born interpreter? It was three days after the siege before I heard he was missing in action.

"The first thing I did was to buy some bottles of plum wine and get blind drunk. Then I strapped a dagger to my wrist and went to Nightwine's tent, determined to avenge Caleb's death. It was a stupid mistake, but I was young. He waited in bed until I had the knife raised to strike, then pulled his pistol and sang out. The tent was immediately full of guards, and I was thrown in the stockade. Being in charge at the time, Nightwine could keep me there indefinitely without trial, or as he put it, I could stay there and rot.

"In a Chinese jail, one has no expectation of ever coming out again. It is akin to being sealed in one's own tomb."

"Like the Count of Monte Cristo," I blurted out.

Barker frowned.

"Sorry, sir. I meant like the French prisons during the revolution. One goes in and is pretty well forgotten."

"I suppose. I have not studied the subject. In any case, I was held in a small, circular stone cell that had once been the town armory. It was hot as blazes in there, and there was but one window and that too high for me to reach. The walls were several feet thick. Any thought of escape was futile.

"I had a lot of time to think. I'd been a complete fool, walking into Sebastian's trap. He had planned and acted, while I had merely reacted. I was never going to avenge my brother's death without an organized and well-thought-out plan. To that end, I became friendly enough with the guards that they kept me apprised of what was going on in camp. A week later, General Gordon arrived and officially took over duties as head of the Ever Victorious Army. A smart man, I told myself, could turn this to his advantage."

"How?" I asked.

"The room was a natural echo chamber. You see, the Chinese like to hear their prisoners' groans and cries for mercy. So, I began to sing."

"Sing what?"

"It didn't matter what. Scraps of songs, whatever came to my head. You see, the cell window faced east, in the direction of the general's tent. And as you have remarked in chapel, Thomas, my voice carries. A few days later, I had an epiphany. I recalled all the wonderful old hymns I had learned at my mother's knee. You see, there was supposed to be a quiet Chinese spy in there. How would Nightwine explain when Gordon heard someone bellowing good Presbyterian hymns in broad Scots?

"I sang for hours. I sang for days. The guards rushed in and beat me into unconsciousness, and when I woke up again, I sang again. I understand I could be heard by the enemy a mile away."

I could picture it all too easily, having sat beside him in church these past few years. Cyrus Barker makes up in volume and vigor what he lacks in pitch. At the Metropolitan Tabernacle in Newington Causeway, I have heard him drag entire rows out of tune. It was very believable that he could drive an army camp mad with his singing. Three verses into "Amazing Grace" sung off-key in basso profundo and I sometimes wanted to strangle him myself.

"Eventually I was taken before Charles Gordon and asked to explain myself, and for the first time in years, I did. I revealed that I was a Scotsman who had gone native working as a spy among the

Chinese rebels for the Ever Victorious Army and Captain Nightwine in particular. That is, until my brother was killed under suspicious circumstances. After careful consideration, Gordon gave me one more week in the stockade, to be augmented if I should begin to sing again, and a transfer to another captain when I was free. Should I attempt to endanger the life of the captain, the general might conveniently forget my true lineage and have me beheaded. Gordon was fair but he could be hard when he had to be. I didn't agree to it, but then I had been given no choice. The camp needed uninterrupted sleep.

"A week later I was released, handed an old and ill-conditioned Sharps rifle, and ordered to report to a Captain Macanaya, leader of a platoon of Manila-born mercenaries. Macanaya had the look of a pirate. He had me drilled in shooting and gave me a cramming course in Filipino. A few days later, I saw action again.

"The rebel forces in Chansu were much larger than the attacking Ever Victorious Army, but armed with only traditional weapons. I survived the first volley of arrows with a wound in my shoulder, and was unscathed by the ancient cannons that made more noise than damage. However, after the first few shots with the Sharps, I found myself without adequate time to reload my weapon. I used the butt end on thick Chinese skulls, and stabbed when I could with my bayonet, but they kept coming and coming. I felt that all of southern China was waiting to challenge me with halberds, spears, broadswords, and cudgels. My tunic was reduced to shreds and there were cuts all across my torso, mostly surface abrasions that would heal quickly and leave few scars.

"My arms ached from defending myself and I wondered how long I could go on, when a relief column swept in from their flank. I was about to cheer with my comrades when I saw the horse that belonged to Sebastian Nightwine. He came thundering past and there was a momentary look of recognition in his eyes, before I felt a sword slide past my cheek, nipping my ear. There was a sharp tug and the next I knew my hair fell about my eyes as my former commanding officer rode away with my queue in his hands.

"You must understand, Thomas, that when a Chinaman renounced the Ching government, he showed that renunciation by cutting off his queue, which the Manchus had imposed upon the Chinese Han people as a symbol of obedience. Loose hair was the symbol of the Tai-Ping, and with one swift stroke of his saber, he had labeled me a rebel. Soldiers who had run with me into battle now found a rebel in their midst.

"Nightwine came galloping back and raised his sword before him. There was murder in his eyes, and no one to protest that he was killing a soldier from his own side. My empty rifle seemed inadequate for defense under the circumstances. I debated for a moment whether to take up a spear and bring down the horse, or find a broadsword and merely take on the rider. At the last second, I found the broadsword, raising it to defend myself. There was a sharp clang as we met, and I was knocked ten feet by the locomotion of my attacker, but I was not injured. Better still, I had slowed my enemy's progress. The captain rode into a phalanx of rebels, who were stabbing at him and trying to swarm up the side of the horse. He cut himself free, hacking and slashing in all directions. He and his men had had enough. He signaled and someone gave the bugle cry for retreat. The Ever Victorious Army began to back away or in many cases turned and ran. The few mounted cavalry, many on bleeding mounts, thundered past, thrusting their own Chinese soldiers out of the way.

"I lay on the ground for some time, my head bleeding, surrounded by the bodies of anonymous Chinamen. No one gave a cheer when the army retreated from the field. They turned silently and began walking in the other direction.

"I slept for a while, until I felt hands in my pockets. Someone was trying to rob me. I waved him away and pushed myself to my feet. There was no one who cared whether or not I returned to camp. As far as Nightwine was concerned, I was dead. I turned and headed south, realizing that if I was going to get another meal, it would be with the rebels."

"So," I said, knowing I could get in trouble for what I was about to say, "you were a deserter."

"That's a very fine point, I'll admit," Barker said, raising a finger. "My brother and I did join the Imperial Army, but I never actually took the queen's shilling. Aye, I suppose I am a deserter. If the Ching government should decide they want me back, they can come here and take me."

"Didn't you tell me once that you were anti-Ching? 'Destroy the Ching and restore the Ming' and all that?"

"I see you have been paying attention. Yes, I eventually became critical of the Manchus, who had taken over China two hundred years earlier. I had hoped to help my adopted country win its freedom, though the rebel forces of the Taiping Rebellion were not the proper way to go about it."

"So what became of Nightwine after that?"

"After Hong Xiuquan's death in 1864, the rebellion fell apart. So, too, in a way, did the Ever Victorious Army. It was disbanded. Nightwine stayed in Shanghai for a while, but if there is one thing I know about him it is that he bores easily. He tried Macao, Hong Kong, Formosa, even Tokyo. He gambled or spent what money he had acquired in the war. He lived off rich widows and befriended and borrowed from other Englishmen, playing upon his name. Essentially, he was the same blackguard and rascal then that he is today."

Here Barker clamped his jaw shut. Sometimes it seems as if he has a daily limit to his conversation and one cannot get another word out of him. I thanked him and went to my cabin, knowing he would call me when he needed me. It did not take long.

An hour later, Barker came into my cabin.

"Are you ready, Thomas? We've got an appointment to keep."

I'd gone back to my berth to digest the story he'd spun. When he entered, he had tied a scarf around his neck which, with the eye patch and stubble, gave him a piratical cast.

"Where are we going?" I asked.

"Westminster Abbey."

"That's awfully close to Scotland Yard."

"It can't be helped. Years ago, Terry and I worked out that if he ever had to warn me with the name 'Waterstone,' we were to meet the following noon at the Abbey, if at all possible. I hope he can answer the questions I have."

"That's good," I said, crawling out of the berth and donning my jacket. "I've got a few of my own."

_____Chapter Ten

Westminster Abbey is so steeped in history, and so many people visit its vaulted halls to see the famous figures entombed or memorialized therein, that it is easy to forget it is still a functioning church. Services are maintained morning and evening, and there are weddings and christenings daily. Though it is owned by the government and therefore subject to the Church of England, the Abbey itself is ecumenical, perhaps not enough to please a staunch Baptist such as Cyrus Barker, but by Anglican standards, surely.

Every time I enter these hallowed halls and tread upon the lords entombed underfoot, I castigate myself for not visiting more often. It is but half a mile from our chambers and straight as the arrow flies. Many people wish to see this famous shrine all their lives and never shall and here it is at my very door.

I was conscious as we entered of the dust motes suspended in the air by sunlight streaming through leaded windows, and the general feeling of age. True, I have stood in older buildings, but none that had quite this combination of agedness and hallowed ground. Barker is not so sentimental. He may revere a writer such as Bunyan or a leader like Cromwell and never feel the need to see where the man's dust is laid. Once the spirit has departed, there is nothing left to interest him. It is but clay. He prefers to meet them in the works they left behind.

We came in through the north transept which, according to a Westminster Abbey guidebook, is known as Solomon's Porch. My first impression, I regret to say, was that the wood paneling and window frames looked worm-eaten and in need of restoration. The deeper we went into the interior, however, the grander was the entire aspect: an ornate altar backed with an immense choir screen; arched ceilings so high and beautiful it made one giddy to stand and look up at them; gold leaf overhead and tributes to prime ministers at our feet.

The Westminster Abbey church, also known as the Church of St. Peter, was built in a cruciform shape with the head of the cross facing east and its foot facing west. To our left lay the ornate tomb of Edward the Confessor, and ahead was the famous Poet's Corner, which I was particularly interested in seeing. Barker was merely looking for Inspector Poole, with whom we had the appointment, and the task was not an easy one. For a structure first built in 1096, it is immense. Looking for one individual is not an easy task, but then I wasn't much help to my employer.

Putting a classics scholar in front of a tribute to poets is a dangerous thing.

The Georgian wag Addison once claimed in *The Spectator* that the Abbey had "poets who had no monuments and monuments which had no poets." I thought that a bit harsh. They had, for example, the crypts of Chaucer and Spencer. But for the most part, the Poet's Corner is a collection of plaques and busts and the remains of the actual poets lie elsewhere. For all that, it is an impressive display and a proper acknowledgment of what this country has produced in the way of lyrical writing. I was impressed by the newest bust of Barker's countryman Robert Burns, which had been funded—a pasteboard sign informed us—by shilling subscription from both highborn and low. The Scots were not going to allow their poet laureate to be forgotten.

"Lad," Barker murmured from a dozen feet away. I joined him behind the altar, where an old chair sat by itself, looking precisely like what it was, an ancient throne. I didn't understand what I beheld until I saw the heavy piece of granite on a shelf underneath. It was the coronation chair, with the fabled Stone of Scone, which according to legend, Jacob of the Old Testament used as a pillow.

"Now is your chance," I whispered. "You'd be a national hero if we could just spirit that rock north to Scotland."

There was a cough nearby and I turned, wondering if we'd been discovered. As far as I was concerned, they could add stealing national treasures to our ever-mounting list of crimes. But it was only Inspector Poole sitting in a pew and peering from behind a woman in a large hat. We did not hurry, but casually strolled down the aisle to the row behind him, taking seats on either side of his broad back. Just then the organ, which had been playing quietly the entire time we'd been inside, gave vent to strong soaring chords.

The mass was about to begin.

"It's about time," Poole muttered to us.

"I've found that men from the Yard are often in want of some sound hours in church," my employer said.

"I'll choose my own services, thank you."

At this point we were shushed by an old matron who looked at us with ill-concealed disfavor. I was wont to frown back at her, but this was Westminster Abbey after all. The three of us looked suitably ecumenical as we stood and began to sing Martin Luther's "A Mighty Fortress Is Our God," suitably Protestant for anyone save perhaps the Pentecostals.

"You're in a good deal of trouble," Poole muttered after we all sat down again. "What were you doing visiting Lord Clayton late on Sunday night?"

"I cannot say," Barker replied with an air of finality.

"I like that," the inspector said, glancing my way. "I go far out on a limb on his behalf, endangering my professional reputation, but he cannot say."

"I made a promise."

"Well, unmake it!" he snapped. "I'm not the village gossip. I need the information for professional reasons."

"It doesn't matter," Barker said stonily. "I gave my word, which is inviolate."

Realizing he'd get nothing from my employer, he turned to me. "Where did he go Sunday?" Poole demanded.

"You know I can't tell you that."

"Don't have the foggiest notion, do you?"

"I'm afraid not, as the old rope said. He never tells me when he goes out. I wasn't even aware he'd left."

He turned back to my employer. "Did you meet Clayton's son? What's his name? Gerald?"

"Briefly," Barker admitted.

"Well, you seem to have made an impression on him," he muttered out of the corner of his mouth. "He claims you tried to blackmail his father."

"Preposterous," the Guv barked. "Over what?"

"He was coy about that, but I believe he said you claimed to have compromising letters from a young lady."

"He obviously doesn't realize the kind of enquiry agent Barker is," I said. "He's confused him with a common detective."

"Yes, I'd worked that out for myself, thank you," Poole said acidly. "About what time did you have this meeting, Cyrus?"

"Early evening, before eight o'clock. I was back in my chambers around nine-fifteen, as Mac will attest."

"Sorry, but loyal retainers do not count as proper witnesses. Lord Clayton was found around ten-thirty. He'd been dead over an hour."

"Where was he found?"

"Beside a folly at the far edge of his property. It must be very secluded that time of night."

"Interesting," the Guv said.

"Glad to be so bloody entertaining."

"No, interesting that he should have had a private rendezvous so far from the house, when an hour earlier he'd invited a vile blackmailer like myself in the front door and up to his private study. It's difficult having to come back and kill someone. If I were better organized, I'd have done it on my first visit."

"He didn't do it," I said to Inspector Poole. "But I'm sure you worked that out for yourself, too."

"That's enough out of you," he snapped.

We stood and sang another hymn and waited for a reading from Ecclesiastes before sitting down again.

"A young woman," the Guv said. "The only reason to see someone on a clandestine rendez-vous outside of the house would be to meet an unescorted female."

"You mean like the one who dropped off the present at O'Muircheartaigh's door yesterday morning?" Poole asked. "You think everything is related?"

"Isn't it usually?"

Poole turned to Barker. "You claim then that you were set up?"

"The Irishman is near death, and I'm on the lam. We have been got neatly out of the way."

"Can you tell me, Cyrus, what you've done to incense Commissioner Warren against you?"

Barker shook his head slightly. "Not in the least. I've never even met the man."

"Well, you've succeeded in jumping up his nose. He's baying for your blood. Apparently he hates all private enquiry agents and you in particular. If he had his way he would revoke all private licenses and you'd be having your neck stretched for you in Wormwood Scrubs. He seems to think you a deserter from the army, which puts you one step beyond Satan in his eyes."

"Shhh!" The old woman leaned toward him again.

"Beg pardon, ma'am," Poole said.

Barker's tone went icy. "Has Nightwine been speaking to Commissioner Warren?"

115

Poole looked uncomfortable. "They dined together yesterday at the Army Navy Club. Oh, Christ help us!"

"What is it?" I asked.

"It's Abberline, coming this way. Hook it!"

We didn't need a second invitation, but scissored out of the pew, down the aisle, and behind the choir loft.

"Hurry!" I heard Inspector Abberline cry, though I'm sure the constables were having difficulty running in the Abbey in the middle of a service. I thought it likely the good Lord would forgive us under those particular circumstances, and therefore ran as fast as my legs would carry me.

Ecclesiastes will tell you that there is a time for everything under the sun. Despite the fact that we were in one of the most sacrosanct spots in the whole of England, it was time to put shoe leather to paving slabs and get out of there. To do so, we would be forced to raise a clangor and disturb that fine peace, for there is a terrible echo in the Abbey and it is impossible to run silently. As I glanced back at Barker, I caught something out of the corner of my eye. Poole was not following us. In fact, he was moving toward Abberline, blocking his progress. I wanted to yell back at him, to call him a bloody fool for throwing away a good career, but Barker's hands came down on my back and propelled me forward and I was forced to save my breath or tumble full length across the tombs. Abberline had not come alone, but had brought along half a dozen constables and any number of officers dressed as ordinary citizens.

The CID had recently created a "plain clothes" squad, as skilled in makeup and costume as any actor. I realize I am Welsh, and as such am not entitled to an opinion, but I cannot help but think it decidedly un-English. Costumed spies are all well and good on the Continent, but we don't go for that sort of thing in London Town.

It was after one of them had seized my coattail and I was giving him a good, straight kick to the pit of his stomach that it occurred to me that I could do anything I liked to the fellow. In theory, how was I to know this was an officer in disguise? He hadn't identified himself as such. He wasn't like the constable on the bridge whose knee I had clouted. The fellow reluctantly let go of my boot and lay in the aisle, holding his stomach. Before the next assailant, a bobby in a regulation helmet and waxed cape had caught me up, I hared away and was soon running toward a large staircase. Truth to say, I had no knowledge of the entrances and exits there, and for once my employer was no wiser than I. Of a sudden, Barker jammed a shoulder into me, knocking me like a billiard ball toward a set of anonymous doors. It took a moment to get myself in stride again, and as I reached them, I shot a glance over my shoulder and saw blue-black oilskins and helmeted figures pouring in from the south entrance. Had we gone that way, we'd have been captured for certain.

I hit the doors hard, conscious of the fact that they had hung there for centuries, and wincing when they banged against the wall. I was in a deserted corridor, heading toward the west entrance with Barker right behind me and the constables just behind him. The Guv stopped abruptly, bringing down the first row of men behind him, then turned in the immediate confusion of officers tumbling over one another like a football scrum and caught me up again.

With the west door almost within reach, Barker thrust me through a doorway into a short hall and out through the far side, crossing a square of lawn. It had begun raining and there was horse traffic just a few yards away on the other side of an iron fence. Barker sprinted past me and I ran as fast as my legs could go. Before we were fully prepared, we had shot into traffic, shying horses and slowing carriages on both sides. It was a wonder we weren't both crushed under the wheels of a passing vehicle, but before I knew it both of us stood on the other side of the street safe and sound.

I muttered a curse, considering it miraculous to be alive.

"Lad," Barker warned.

As if escaping from Westminster Abbey were something he did on a regular basis, he raised his hand and hailed an approaching cab. We clattered aboard and I looked at him curiously. The Guv was barely breathing hard.

"Where to, gentlemen?" the bored-sounding cabman asked through the trapdoor over our heads.

"Soho," Barker replied.

"Why Soho?" I asked when the cab began to move.

"Because it is not Westminster at the moment."

We bowled off toward the west. Somewhere behind I heard a chorus of police whistles. When we were safely away I dared sit back in my seat and asked the question that was uppermost in my mind.

"What do you suppose will happen to Poole?"

I knew the atmosphere at Scotland Yard. While it had the appearance of male camaraderie, in reality, it was every man for himself. Inspectors chaff each other and engage in bluff banter, but in fact, it was a fierce competition; each man responsible for creating a list of informants and bullying subordinates into helping him. One only helped a superior in order to ride his coattails to a better position, and an inspector who disgraced himself was immediately attacked from all sides: from his superiors, anxious to distance themselves from any scandal, and from subordinates, eager for his position.

The Guv leaned back against the seat cushion, his one visible eye closed, considering the question. "I don't know what will happen, but without a doubt, Terry is finding himself in a good bit of trouble on our account."

Chapter Eleven_____

Eventually, our cab slowed in Glasshouse Street, but rolled by the entrance to the Café Royal, which I had assumed would be our destination. The café is the unofficial headquarters of Mr. Pollock Forbes, who is himself unofficial, being the head of a Masonic organization wielding great power within the government, and a history stretching back to the Crusades. Barker and I were coming to beg favors. Across the street in Shaftesbury Avenue, I could see the building where Cyrus Barker had recently leased a room to begin his Antagonistics classes again. He had been planning the defensive fighting classes for several weeks, yet another disruption in our lives. The cab came to a halt at the Guv's command, in front of a white, nondescript door, and we alighted. Barker proceeded to pick the lock while I covered him and stared down anyone nearby who looked too inquisitive. For a secret society, the door opened too readily to his hand, I think. Barker tapped me on the shoulder and we slipped through.

Inside was a large, airy chamber of white marble, dominated by a staircase of the same material that appeared completely unsupported. There were no handrails and nothing underneath to support the structure visibly. I supposed it was some kind of engineering marvel. Overhead, the ceiling was carved in gilt arcane symbols, some recognizable to me, others not. With a start, I realized Barker had broken into the establishment's Masonic temple. It ruffled my plain Methodist feathers just to be there.

"Find Pollock," Barker ordered, and I pushed through the door into an outer hall which skirted the dining room, trying not to draw attention to myself from the waiters bustling by in their long aprons. Entering the room, I passed among the elegant diners enjoying one of the most popular restaurants in London, until I finally spotted Forbes at a table near the front entrance, sipping a cup of mocha while scrutinizing the move of his opponent at dominoes. The young Scotsman had no official office anywhere, but conducted important matters over this frivolous game in plain sight of everyone. He caught my eye and waved, and I nodded in the direction of the temple before making my way through the tables again. Reluctantly, I stepped back into the cool marble chamber which, for all its elegance and symbolism, resembled the interior of a mausoleum. For a moment, I fancied what it would be like to be interred inside.

"He's coming," I told my employer. "He's finishing a game. It shouldn't take long."

"I don't have time for games," Barker grumbled.

"I could go back, knock over the table, and drag him in here, if you prefer," I replied.

"That won't be necessary. Forgive my ill humor. I've got a lot on my mind at the moment."

There was a squeak of the outer door and a feel of pressure changing in the hermetically sealed room as Pollock Forbes entered. He has a reputation as a genial young man, but for once, he showed his edge.

"Cyrus, this is most irregular," he complained. "You know Mr. Llewelyn is not a member. You're breaking protocol."

"I'm sorry, Pollock, special circumstances warrant. I didn't want the lad in the street revealing my presence to all and sundry."

"That's quite a costume you're wearing today. I suppose I should be glad you didn't come through the dining room. I hear you're in a spot of trouble."

"I am," Barker admitted. "The banks have frozen my assets, and my home and offices are no longer safe. Sebastian Nightwine is in town, which cannot be a coincidence. Oh, and Scotland Yard is hunting me. I understand there is a price on my head. Did you know Scotland Yard suspects me in the murder of Lord Clayton?"

"I understand there was an eyewitness who claims he saw the two of you argue two nights ago. It was Clayton's son, Gerald."

"He's lying. Clayton and I spoke amicably and parted the best of friends."

"A knife was found on Lord Clayton's body, along with one of your sharpened coins."

"Anyone can leave behind a knife. It proves nothing."

"I'm sorry, Cyrus, but it was not an anonymous weapon. It was a dagger about nine inches long and had your name and crest imprinted on the blade, a rampant lion."

The Guv suddenly launched himself off the marble bench and began pacing about the room. Forbes and I looked at each other, startled. Coming up to a wall, he smote it with the palm of his hand, producing another echo in the chamber.

"It is my own fault," he growled. "When Nightwine was in London two years ago, I pressed a knife blade into his front door as a warning. Evidently, he took it with him as a souvenir."

"That wasn't very wise," Forbes said. "Is that the only knife you've ever given away?"

"I'm not in the habit of giving them as gifts, if that is what you mean. It was a warning, and now he has used it against me. I should have known better than to let my emotions get the best of me."

"What can I do for you?" Pollock Forbes asked, always practical. "How are you fixed?"

"We'll make do," my employer said. I was certain he hadn't the slightest idea how little money was in his wallet, which was just under five pounds. What he meant was that whatever situation in which we found ourselves, we would make do.

"Do you need a place to stay? I've got a few rooms outside of London where I can tuck you away."

"No, thank you. I don't wish to put you in the position where you can be blamed for helping me."

The remark or the feelings behind it set Forbes coughing. He was slowly losing a battle with tuberculosis. He sat down on a bench, choking into a handkerchief, and when the spasm was over, stuffed the silk into his breast pocket until he needed it again. Since I had known him he had stopped wearing white shirts, which collected the fine spray of bloody droplets. The one he wore now was a dark gray.

"What do you need, then?" he asked weakly.

"Information. Inspector Poole told me Nightwine's been given diplomatic status. I want to know why and how, and by whom. What is he here for beyond causing me trouble? He arrived from Calcutta two days ago aboard the SS *Rangoon*."

"Have you any idea where he was before that?"

"He tends to travel about a good deal, but his favorite location is along the border between Nepal and Tibet. His father explored the area years ago."

"His father was Sir Elias Nightwine, the explorer?"

"Aye," Barker said. "Sir Elias tutored him himself and took him along on his expeditions. You'll recall he was an extreme social Darwinist and raised his son on the principle of survival of the fittest. Some might say he raised a monster with no interest or compassion for anyone except himself."

"Expeditions," Pollock repeated. He never committed anything to paper, but stored everything in that well-ordered brain of his.

"You recall something?" Barker asked.

"I've got a fellow in the Foreign Office. There was a meeting there yesterday, very sub rosa. He was not allowed to attend but took a pencil to a notepad, scribbling to see what had been written on the sheet before it. Someone had written 'Shambhala Expedition.' That's in Tibet, isn't it?"

"It is, as I recall. It's some sort of mythical city."

"Does it have any significance in relation to Nightwine?"

"It might. Tibet has always held a strange fascination for Sebastian. Foreigners are forbidden to set so much as a foot in the country, which makes him want to go there all the more. I think his sudden arrival and this meeting is too much of a coincidence. If you would, concentrate your efforts in learning about this so-called expedition."

"I was going to, anyway. It sounds intriguing."

"Knowing Nightwine, there is intrigue and to spare."

Forbes frowned. "You called him Sebastian a minute ago. Do you know each other?"

Barker's mouth went grim. "Too well, if anything."

"I'll ask around for you, then," Forbes said. "While you're here, may I at least feed the two of you? There's no telling when your next meal will be. We keep a table by the kitchen for bailiffs. Some of our regulars are, alas, insolvent, generally writers and painters. I assure you the food is no different at that table than at any other here."

I was certain Barker would refuse. He always had in the past. We had come here at least once a month in the two years I'd worked for him, and

126

yet never had I tasted anything but the coffee mocha. To my surprise Barker accepted, perhaps only to spite me.

At the bailiff's table one is given no choice as to the menu, but the food is plentiful and it is free, as long as one has a purpose in being there. We began with turtle soup, then turbot, beef cutlets in brown sauce with roasted potatoes, haricots verts, apples in brandy, and a salad. It was a welcome change after several meals of hard, dry rice.

"You're eating very sparingly, sir," I noted. "Are you feeling well?"

"Never better. I have allowed this town and its rich food to add some poundage to my frame. I think it best under my current circumstances to subtract them. It would be best," the Guv went on, "if you did not mention our having dined here to Etienne. He and Mr. Nicholson, who owns this establishment, are the bitterest of enemies."

I lifted a forkful of roasted apples braised in brandy and thought of Barker's cook and his hot temper which could be kindled by the slightest spark.

"Why am I not surprised?"

Once we were outside again and walking through Soho, I turned to my employer. "May I ask you something?"

"You may," he said cautiously. "I cannot promise I shall answer."

"How does Forbes come by his information?

Do people just tell him things, or is there some way with the full weight of his office he can force confidences from his brothers? I don't understand how it works."

"How could you, not being a member?" he answered. "The first thing you should understand is that police work does not pay well and offers few benefits. By joining the Freemasonry, constables receive insurance and supplemental pay if they are injured. It is more than a fraternal organization. The majority of the Metropolitan Police are members, as are Her Majesty's Army."

"I didn't know that."

"Their members also include MPs, the Home Office, the clergy, and the judiciary. Often the only connection between these offices is the bond of Masonry. If one needs information and cannot not go directly to the source, one could go to Pollock and barter information, or as you would put it, go begging. We certainly had our hat in our hands today."

"Is that why you did not ask for money?"

"Aye. He was already giving us information and food. I did not wish to be indebted to him any more than I must. If he were to ask us certain questions in exchange, I would prefer we have the freedom to say no, if we choose."

_____Chapter Twelve

W e were walking through Leicester Square a few minutes later when Barker suddenly pointed to an alleyway so narrow it would be unnoticeable a dozen paces away. I dipped in and Barker followed, flattening himself against the wall. I did the same, realizing we were being followed. I had not noticed him turn around and look once since we left the café, so he must have used every window we passed to scan the crowd behind us. The arrival of plate glass in London had no doubt been a boon to enquiry agencies.

We waited nearly half a minute and I was beginning to think that for once Cyrus Barker was wrong, when suddenly he gave a mighty heave and a man shot past and struck the wall in front of us like a salmon pulled from a Speyside stream. He was about five and twenty and wore a gray serge suit and a silk topper over long curling hair the color of honey, which reached nearly to his shoulders. I can honestly say that if I had any professional instincts to jangle, they jangled then. I recognized a professional criminal when I saw one and stepped forward, pinning him to the wall with my forearm.

"Careful," he said. "You'll rend the fabric."

"I'll rend more than that. How long have you been following us?"

He shrugged. "Ten minutes or so. I've been sent to fetch you."

"By whom?" I pressed, still pushing him against the brick.

"The Irishman."

Barker put a hand on my shoulder and I let the dandy stand at ease. He immediately began to pick imagined specks of dust from his jacket and rearranged his clothes to his satisfaction.

"He's still alive?" Barker rumbled.

"It would take more than a mere plague to kill him."

"I don't think we should place ourselves in criminal hands at this particular time, sir," I told my employer.

"Mr. O'Muircheartaigh said you'd say something like that," the young man stated. "He told me to say he wishes to extend the olive branch. He understands that your professional relationship has been breached, but the present situation warrants a meeting."

"I don't trust him," I argued.

"Probably best," the young man agreed.

"I'm not talking to you!" I said, pushing him against the wall again. "What's your name, anyway?"

"Psmith, with a *P*. The *P* is silent."

"Then why bring it up?" I asked.

"I didn't want you to think I'd made it up."

"I do think you made it up," I answered. I didn't much like this mannequin and his suave manner.

"I don't believe you," Barker said. "Or rather, I don't believe him."

"He said you'd say that as well. He wanted me to assure you that the olive branch only extends until our mutual obstacle has been eliminated. Then the gloves come off once more."

" 'The enemy of my enemy is my friend,' " Barker quoted.

"Something like that."

"That sounds more like Seamus."

The dandy's face creased into a smile. "The Irishman is no politician. He would rather be feared than admired. Are you coming? I've got a vehicle waiting just down the road."

"What made you think I would go to the Café Royal?"

"I didn't, but the boss did. You took your time getting here, too. I've waited close to a day. Thought I'd go out of my mind with boredom waiting for you to turn up."

I looked at Barker, who had crossed his arms and was staring at the man. He came to a decision quickly.

"Very well. We will hear what Seamus has to say."

The young man led us to a new-looking

landau on the other side of the square. It was gleaming black with red wheels and an interior of cream leather. It emphasized in my mind that while we were practically living on the street, O'Muircheartaigh was a success, at least as far as his finances were concerned. We climbed in and Psmith stretched out across from us, his arms strewn across the back of the seat, as if the vehicle belonged to him.

"And how is your master?" Barker asked politely. He was exercising some of that patience he was always telling me to cultivate.

"I call no man master, Mr. Barker. Mr. O'Muircheartaigh is recovering, or so his doctors inform me. You'll find him gravely changed, however. It is possible he will remain an invalid the rest of his life, but then it was his brain that has gotten him this far."

We pulled into Commercial Road, headed for the City. The day was warm and the sun beat down unmercifully upon us.

"You're not what I expected, you know," Psmith said, after a few minutes. "I mean, being the best detective in London and all. I heard you had a good tailor."

"This is not a time to be spotted in my sartorial best, Mr. Psmith." There was a moment of silence before Barker spoke again. "Is Seamus still in hospital?"

"No, at his request he's been moved to rooms

around the corner from the Old Jewry. He keeps his own doctors and nurses on the premises."

"I suppose you have been given orders to kill them if he dies," the Guv said.

Psmith chuckled. "You know him rather well."

"Better than I would wish. You are a shootist, then. Why are shootists always interested in clothing?"

In response, Psmith opened his jacket. He had two small pistols jammed into the waistband of his trousers, with the butts facing forward.

"It's clean work," the young man said. "As long as you don't stand too close."

"Twenty-two-caliber Remingtons, I see. You must be very accurate."

"It's a gift. I hear you're not bad with a pistol yourself. Is it your weapon of choice?"

"No, it is merely a necessary evil," my employer said.

"What's your weapon?" Psmith asked, turning to me.

"Him," I said.

The young man grinned like a jackal. He smiled too easily for my comfort. "Good answer."

The cab deposited us at the corner of Old Jewry and Cresham. Psmith unlocked the door of an affluent-looking red brick residence. Inside, two very large gentlemen were seated in the front room and exchanged glances with Psmith as we walked by. We walked down a nondescript corridor until we saw a nurse in her caped uniform and followed her into a sickroom. There were two other nurses there, flanking a bed with a still body resting on an oversized pillow, a counterpane pulled up to his chin.

"All of you, leave us!" O'Muircheartaigh cried peevishly from the bed. "I wish to consult with Messrs. Barker and Llewelyn privately."

We waited until everyone left the room, and then my employer and I moved closer to O'Muircheartaigh.

I could not believe the change the man had undergone since last I saw him. O'Muircheartaigh's eyes were sunken in their sockets and he had lost much of his hair, what remained lying lank and colorless against his scalp. The ricin, or whatever it had been, had broken capillaries across his face, leaving it etched in purplish tracks. His skin was jaundiced, the color of cheese rind; even his eyes were an unhealthy yellow. He lay shrunken in his pillows, clutching a small tank in clawlike hands with a valve and a rubber hose from which he breathed periodically.

"Come sit close by the bed," he said. "There are chairs here. Do not be alarmed at my appearance. The doctors assure me that I shall live, which is well for them. Come, look me over and get it done with. We have much to discuss. You will forgive the tank. It contains pure oxygen. I am reduced to sucking from a bottle like a helpless,

134

mewling babe. I am alive, however, which is more than I can say for my comrades, or for Sebastian Nightwine when I get hold of him."

"You know, then," I murmured.

"Oh, yes, Mr. Llewelyn. It has been a while since I bought out his enterprises and he sailed off to points east. I knew he would eventually run out of cash. He always does. I give him credit for stealing into town unnoticed, without his usual fanfare."

"I had hoped we had seen the last of him," my employer said.

"Cyrus," O'Muircheartaigh said from his pillow. "We've had our differences in the past, and I know how you feel about me personally, but I want you to consider taking me as a client."

"Under no circumstances."

"No, please! Hear me out!"

Barker had waved a dismissive hand in his direction.

"Hear me out," he continued, weakly. "You must be short of funds with your accounts frozen. I've got all you could possibly require. I could fund an army if you need it to bring down Nightwine. I want you to set aside your high-minded principles for once and take me on."

"Seamus," Barker said gravely, "you know I'm going after Nightwine for my own reasons. I don't want your money and I'd never take a client who would exact such revenge upon the people I bring in. They deserve punishment, but only after justice has been meted out."

"Perhaps I was wrong about you, and it is better on my side of the fence, where an eye still requires an eye in return."

"I'm going after your man, Seamus," Barker said mildly, not the least put out by the Irishman's rhetoric. "But I don't want your money. You are coming out ahead. You have nothing to complain about."

"You are as unbending as a bar of pig iron."

"Thank you. But if you really want to help, there is one favor you can do for me, Seamus. Stay out of my way. Don't attempt to go after Nightwine with men like Psmith. They'll confuse the issue and hinder my enquiry. Lie back, for once, and let your money accrue."

"And if I don't?" O'Muircheartaigh asked, breathing heavily.

"Let us just say things would get lively for quite a while. And I do not believe either of us would be the last man standing."

The Irishman took several breaths from his cylinder, and tried to compose himself. The room seemed monastically quiet all of a sudden.

"Very well," he finally answered. "I'll keep my money if it's not good enough for you. Starve if you like. But I expect reports. I must know what's going on."

"When there is something to know, you will know it."

My employer made no move to rise and neither did I.

"What is it?" his old enemy demanded. "You're shaking your head."

"I was just thinking what a tough old bird you are, Seamus. How did you survive when all of your younger colleagues did not?"

"We had opened the office at seven-thirty, as usual. I generally wait for the first post before walking to the Exchange Building to see how my stocks are trading. My secretary, Miss Jonah, entered with a package about two feet long. I opened it after noting there was no address of any kind. Inside was a leather case containing a short sword. I'm not a connoisseur of weapons, but I could tell it was expensive and probably old. I lifted it out of its case gingerly, because it seemed fragile rather than because I thought it might be dangerous. When I pulled the sword from the scabbard, Miss Jonah and my bodyguard, Mr. Bing, were standing on the other side of the desk. When I drew the sword in an outward gesture, they both suddenly clutched their throats and Bing began choking. In a few seconds, they both fell to the floor.

"Realizing it was an attempt on my life, I threw down the sword and backed into my office and opened a window, actually sitting on the ledge. I called for aid upstairs where some of my associates were sleeping late, having done some work for me the night before. Two of them used the back stair but one came down through the lobby, and passing through the contaminated room, brought the contagion with him into my office. By the time he reached my desk, he was gasping, his eyes starting from his head. Soon his companions joined him, fighting for breath. Then it felt as if all the air had been sucked from the room. I recall ripping open my collar and trying to get another window open for circulation, but my fingers were like sausages at the ends of my hands. I fell out of the window into the street. That's the last I recall, until I awoke in St. Bart's Hospital hours later, as you see me."

"You had a very close call. Was it ricin, then?"

"Mixed with something else, I think. Some sort of vegetable alkaloid Nightwine picked up in the Orient, I shouldn't wonder."

I wondered how both of them would be familiar with substances such as ricinus and vegetable alkaloids and the like. The things one had to know to work in the Underworld.

"You have something to contribute, Mr. Llewelyn?" O'Muircheartaigh asked, studying me closely.

"Nothing, sir. It is a most remarkable story."

"Yours are the last ears that shall ever hear

that story from my lips," he rasped. "Good day, gentlemen."

Before we were even out of the room, the staff came in and crowded about him, to his irritation. On our way out the door, we encountered Psmith in the reception room, seated with the two guards. He said not a word, but aimed a finger at me and squeezed off a shot.

Not if I see you first, I thought.

Chapter Thirteen

To be perfectly honest, I was getting tired. We had narrowly avoided being arrested in Westminster Abbey, broken into a Masonic temple in order to talk to Pollock Forbes, and had an interview with a very much alive Seamus O'Muircheartaigh. Perhaps it was the Irishman who exhausted me most. He had a way of draining the energy from a room, as if he fed upon it. Had going to see the Irishman been worth the danger? I couldn't say.

It was my wish that we could go back to the barge, and quit risking capture for the rest of the day. I would put up with the tasteless tea and the repetitive menu. I would even make do without a book and go to bed early. Unfortunately,

Cyrus Barker didn't see things my way. Though the sun was obscured by clouds, it was still up in the sky somewhere and his pocket watch told him it was just three o'clock. There was plenty of daylight left.

"While we're this close to the East End, I should like to see to the safety of Fu Ying," my employer said, referring to the Chinese girl who was his ward. "Nightwine would never hesitate to use one's relations against him."

"But, sir," I said. "Anyone who knows you well will be watching her rooms in Three Colt Lane, hoping you'll appear. Inspector Abberline is sure to have plainclothesmen in the area waiting to arrest you. If you try to see her, you'll be jugged like a hare."

"Then we'll bypass Limehouse and try Mile End Road. I want Andrew to keep an eye on her, even if it means bringing her to the mission. I trust his abilities over anyone's in London."

"Do you really think no one's considered Handy Andy, sir?" I argued. "I mean, everyone knows you have been supporting his ministry for years, not to mention the fact that he is your sparring partner."

"Aye, but his mission is a warren and I know all the exits. Also, McClain's followers may help divert any pursuers."

"It's still a risk."

"Nothing is a sure thing, but I'll have one of

the most able fighters in London to protect me."

"I've fought Brother Andrew in the ring, sir," I admitted. "He's very good."

"I was talking about you, lad."

"Oh," I said, surprised. Barker rarely pays a compliment.

We took the tram at Aldgate Station, taking care to separate. It is a wearing thing when you're looking at everyone as if they would suddenly recognize you and call for the police. I sat several rows behind the Guv, trying not to look at his stubbled head. The more one tries not to look at something the harder it is. I focused my attention instead on the street, but it was a depressing sight. Everyone looked dirty, ill, and poor, from the women selling paper flowers to the tradesmen desperately hawking their wares. The streets were grimier here, too. There were no crossing sweepers where there was no money to be made. The job generally fell to young girls and boys in the better parts of London, but here, no one bothered. The hooves of our tram horses were muffled by the layers of debris and refuse on the ground. I couldn't help but marvel at the difference twenty minutes' travel makes in London.

When we arrived, I saw immediately that something was wrong in Mile End Road. There were people milling about the street to no purpose, as if something had occurred, but I couldn't tell what it was. Barker alighted from the tram and I followed at a short distance, crossing the street to the far side. The Guv had a cautious eye on a policeman talking to a man I recognized as one of McClain's volunteers. We passed an alleyway when a voice spoke almost in my ear.

"Go down the road and cut back this way in the next."

I glanced over my shoulder. The voice belonged to a man in a trilby hat with the collar of his macintosh pulled up, obscuring his face. I recognized the voice, but couldn't place it.

"Who was that?" I asked, after I had caught up with my employer.

"I don't know," Barker admitted. "But we are about to find out."

He steered us into another alleyway, which we traversed until we reached Bridge Street and doubled back. I noticed there were fewer people there, and also no sense of excitement or tension. We came to the far end of the alley and found the man standing there awaiting us. His hand, which had been clutching his collar over the lower half of his face, fell away and I recognized him instantly.

Robert Forrester was chief warder of Her Majesty's Yeoman Guards, responsible for the Tower of London, Her Majesty's Crown Jewels, and the so-called Tower Hamlets: Whitechapel, the City of London, Poplar, Bethnal Green, and several other neighborhoods in the East End. It was a grave responsibility, but one that appeared to rest on competent shoulders. Forrester was a sturdily built man in his sixties with a beard like a king from a playing card. It went perfectly with his dress blue uniform or his more formal red and gold tunic for ceremonial occasions, but less so with a trilby and a macintosh. I suppose there's a reason why military men avoid mufti whenever possible.

"Cyrus," he said, looking my employer square in the eye. "You must prepare yourself. I have some news."

"What has happened?"

"It's Andrew McClain. He had a heart attack this morning and didn't make it. I'm very sorry to bear such terrible news. I know what he meant to you. If it is any consolation, he died in the ring, as he would have liked."

Barker put his hand on the wall behind him and bent over as if he'd been gut punched. He didn't speak for at least a minute. I was reeling myself. It didn't seem possible. We had seen him just two days before and he had been fit and vigorous and full of life. He could have run rings around me, and had on numerous occasions. I knew what Barker was thinking, or at least I thought I did. A man with a heart as big as Andy McClain's should have outlasted us all.

"Was he boxing at the time?" the Guv finally

asked. I noticed he was having some difficulty speaking.

"No," Forrester answered. "The local beat constable told me Andy had been showing a potential patron around the mission."

"Will there be a postmortem?"

"It is standard procedure, though his death appeared to be due to natural causes. He was in his mid-fifties after all, and had subjected his body to heavy abuse for years." The warder put his hand on Barker's shoulder. "Sometimes the heart just gives out, Cyrus."

"I shall need to see the postmortem all the same. Some men simply have weak hearts, but Andy was different. He watched his diet carefully and exercised every day. I would have thought he would live to be an octogenarian. Who was this patron? Did you get a name?"

Forrester shook his head. "No name."

"He canna be dead!" Barker burst out. "He had plans. There were things he needed to accomplish."

When Cyrus Barker became upset, I had noticed in the past, his Lowland Scots began to spill out.

"I'm sorry, Cyrus," Forrester repeated. "I know what he meant to you. This must be quite a blow."

My employer's hand still rested on the wall, as if for support. For once, the fight seemed to have gone out of him. "More than you could possibly realize. Thank you for telling me, Robert. It means a great deal that you were the one who did."

"I didn't want you to hear it on the street," Forrester replied.

"I need to walk and think. Excuse me."

Cyrus Barker turned and left the alleyway. Forrester and I nodded to each other and I turned to follow my employer. The Guv was clearly agitated, and if I didn't hurry along, I would lose him in the teeming streets of the East End. When I caught up to him, there was a bleak look on his face.

"It is my own fault," he lamented, lurching through the street as if he weren't even aware of where he was going.

"What are you talking about? How can it be your fault? Brother Andrew had a heart attack."

"If you believe that, lad, you have under-estimated Nightwine entirely."

The remark stung a little, I must admit, but I had never seen Cyrus Barker looking so bereft, so completely and utterly overwhelmed. I felt as if I could have pushed him over with the slightest effort.

"It is just a coincidence," I argued. "He is dead, and we shall both miss him terribly. The timing is dreadful, I know, but what else could it be?"

"It could be anything. Nightwine could have poisoned his tea, for all I know. Anyone who can kill people with powdered caster bean shells would know how to simulate a heart attack. An overdose of digitalis, perhaps? We won't know until the postmortem."

I had trouble believing that Brother Andrew's death was anything other than a sudden tragedy. For one thing, Nightwine was being followed about by Poole and his lot. For another, I doubted McClain would have allowed Nightwine into his mission. It didn't make sense. I began to think that perhaps the Guv was developing an obsession. We had taken one hit after another, and my rock-solid employer was crumbling right before my eyes.

Chapter Fourteen_____

It's odd how people come into our lives and we learn to rely upon them to such an extent that when they are gone we mourn them more than our natural relations. Aunts, uncles, even sisters and brothers I did not have as strong a bond with as I did with Andrew McClain. He had taught me, advised me, cheered me when I was down. I could rely upon him. He was that brick without which the entire structure comes tumbling down. If I felt that way, then Cyrus Barker must have felt it doubly so. As far as I could tell, no one deserved to be considered Barker's mentor as much as Handy Andy McClain. If anything existed that could derail my employer from a case, it was this. For once, I saw the mighty oak tremble.

"I'm sure there will be a large funeral for Brother Andrew, considering what he's done for this city," I said.

"Aye," he answered, but with little conviction.

We had found a tea shop in which to sit and mourn. It would have felt irreverent to the Reverend's memory to mourn him over a pint when he had helped so many drunkards during his ministry. The East End would never be the same without him.

"What shall become of the mission?"

"I don't know," Barker admitted. "It was undergoing a transition. I suppose it is harmless to tell you now. Andy was leaving the Church of England. That is why I spoke to Lord Clayton. He was going to provide the money for a new building. Andy had asked me to act as an intermediary. It would not be an easy break, but he had prayed long and hard over it and was convinced it was the right thing to do, even if it meant leaving the old church building behind. He would have taken the boxing ring with him, of course."

"Of course," I murmured.

"We've tempted fate long enough," Barker

said, setting down his cup. "We should get back to the barge."

It was a drawn-out process getting back to the spot where our day had begun. From start to finish it was more than an hour before we neared the dock where the Lo family's barge was berthed. When we got there, it was already far too late.

"Abberline," Barker growled as we viewed the scene from behind a nearby warehouse. The vessel was in danger of capsizing from the number of constables gathered on the deck, and moored right beside it was the police launch, whose sleek hull and brass fittings only made the barge look more weather-beaten and decrepit.

"We won't be sleeping here tonight," the Guv said, turning away, as if dismissing it from his mind.

"What about the Los?" I asked. "They're sure to be arrested."

"I must get word to Cusp," he answered, referring to his solicitor, Bram Cusp, who was expensive but generally worth the money.

"But where do we go now?" I asked. "We're nearly out of money."

"I've got a place in mind, though I must admit I haven't been there in a few years. And it shall mean another long walk. We cannot trust cabs, even were we to find one here in Chelsea Basin. Cabmen have long memories."

"It's just unfair," I said. "We've done nothing wrong and yet half of London is barking at our heels."

"No one ever claimed life is fair, lad. It's a cold and callous world."

We tramped across the city for the second time that day. "Plodded" might be a better word. Johnson said a man who is tired of London is tired of life. Just then I was heartily sick of both. I wanted cool sheets and a soft pillow and I wasn't too particular where. Barker propelled us forward, moving from shadow to shadow whenever possible to avoid notice. At one point, half dead on my feet, I imagined I heard the steady regulation boots of every police constable in the district measuring out his beat. Perhaps, I thought, we could escape to the country for a while until everything settled down. Philippa Ashleigh, Barker's companion, owned an estate in Sussex that was but an hour's ride by train. We could sit in relative ease while Scotland Yard chased its tail up here in the city.

However, I knew that the Guv would never endanger her life and had some other destination in mind. As we walked, I mulled over where Barker could be leading me. If his first choice had been a dilapidated barge, what could possibly be his lesser choice?

We crossed to the Surrey shore at Westminster, within half a mile of our home. I wondered how the old pile was faring at the moment. Was Mac awake and worrying about us? Was Barker's Pekingese, Harm, pining by the front door, wanting his master home? Probably not, if they were sensible. I wanted to prowl into the kitchen and see what Etienne had left in the larder as I had done on countless other occasions in the middle of the night.

Barker headed north into Lambeth, which is not my favorite part of the city. It has all the squalor of the East End without its poor reputation. It's dull, drab, and down-at-heel. Centuries before, in Shakespeare's day, all the theaters in London were there, including the Globe. The bawdy houses and the more riotous public houses were there, as well. Since then, Lambeth has embraced an aura of shabby respectability, but the same activities went on behind more discreet doors, I was sure.

We trudged silently down Lower Marsh Street. I'm not the wittiest conversationalist when I am this tired and footsore, and the Guv was silent, as usual. I was hungry and thirsty, and a fugitive from what passes for justice here. I was lamenting my fortune, when my employer suddenly plunged into a common lodging building. With-out stopping or asking for directions, he led me to a stairwell and began to ascend as quietly as possible. The old Georgian stairs were so tall and narrow a chap could easily break his neck on them. The halls were painted a dun yellow, and in some places wallpapered in a peeling print many years out of date. The carpet on the stairway was threadbare and musty. Here the Guv didn't seem certain where he was going. He reached the top floor and looked about with his fingertips on his lower lip, lost in thought.

"This is it," he finally said, coming to a padlocked door. He removed a key from his pocket and tried to unlock it. The lock was stiff and in need of oil, but it finally yielded to his pressure, opening with a squeal of protest. The room in front of us wasn't a room at all, but a staircase leading to an attic. I followed, curious to see what we would find at the top of the stair.

It was a room much like the one he occupied in our home in Newington, only smaller.

There were two dormer windows facing the street, a sloped ceiling, and old, mismatched furnishings, including a bedstead, a desk, and an upholstered chair with a small table.

Everything was covered in a thick layer of dust. There was a straw hat on the desk; not a boater, but a flat-brimmed one with a light tan band and a raised peak down the center of it like the keel of a boat. A suit of clothes hung from a hook that was equally tropical. I stepped closer to the desk and found it was spread with dusty maps of London and yellowed newspapers dated August 1879. There was a book written in Chinese there, and when I picked it up a square of polished wood lay under it in the dust. The entire room was like stepping into the past: Barker's past, to be more precise, when he first arrived in London. I found a pack of Swan vestas in the drawer and lit a small penny candle.

"This flat belongs to you," I said.

"Aye. I let it when I first came to England and was looking for a residence and chambers. I kept the lease, in case I should ever need it again."

Cyrus Barker is not in the least sentimental. He didn't spare a glance at the mementos, but went down on his knees and pulled an empty drawer completely out of its slides. Reaching into the recess, he retrieved an old pistol and some cartridges. He opened the revolver at the top and spun the cylinder. Like the lock on the door, it could do with a drop of oil.

"This should do us for now. As I recall, there is a grocer around the corner. We can get food there in the morning, but only one of us should go. It isn't prudent for us to travel in pairs at the moment."

"I'll go," I said. "I see there is a gas hob and a kettle. I could buy some tea and tinned food. If I had a broom and rags, I could even start cleaning up this place."

He shook his head. "Not worth the effort. Our time would be better spent sleeping."

"There's only one bed," I pointed out. "We'll have to sleep in shifts."

"I wasn't accustomed to beds when I let this room. There is a hammock stowed underneath the bed."

While he unrolled the hammock, I slowly pulled off the sheet which covered the entire bed, taking the layer of dust with it. The bedding was sound, if a trifle musty. I helped the Guv suspend the hammock from two hooks in the ceiling I hadn't noticed when we arrived. We had reached the point beyond which words were needed. Quickly, we doffed jackets, braces, shoes and socks and crawled into our beds. I blew out the candle, and we were asleep by the time the wick was cool.

In the morning, the Guv showed little inclination to leave his hammock, but he'd switched back to his black spectacles and looked more like his former self. I purchased tea and bread at a nearby shop and then brewed tea on the hob and began to sort out the place.

In spite of his advice, I gave the room a thorough cleaning. I was hoping to uncarth more of his past, right under his nose. The room, empty as it looked, was a potential treasure trove. The most likely spot to find something of interest was the desk, but I wanted to get to that last. I picked up the suit from the hook and looked at the label. It was from a tailor in Hong Kong.

"This will never fit you again," I remarked.

Barker grunted abstractly from the hammock. Digging into the pockets of the suit, I found three sharpened Chinese coins. They each had a square hole in the center, and were roughly the size of the British coppers he used now. I pocketed them and picked up the hat from the bedstead. It was from Canton, according to the label. These must have been the clothes he had worn on his journey from the Far East.

As casually as possible, I went to the desk and began straightening. *The Times* for August 1879 had yellowed with age, and the information seemed out of the dim dark past. Disraeli was prime minister and an MP was complaining because the soldiers in Africa had been reduced to rags. I could not make head or tail of the Chinese book, but at the very end of it I found the treasure I was hoping for. It was a studio portrait, octavo-sized, of four men: Barker, Ho, our cook, Etienne Dummolard, and Paul Beauchamp, who maintained Barker's boat, the *Osprey*, down in Sussex. This had been the crew of the *Osprey*, and though none would explain how, each had become rich enough in the China Seas to set up businesses of their own here in England. They all looked uncomfortable in their suits, glowering at the camera in front of a painted trompe l'oeil garden backcloth, and save for Beauchamp, all had put on weight since then. Barker was wearing the suit and the tropical hat was in his lap. I couldn't help smiling because I deduced why the photograph had been taken. It must have been Mrs. Ashleigh, Barker's lady friend, who had insisted upon it.

"What are you smiling at?" the Guv demanded.

I was caught. I really should learn to control my emotions, the way Barker does. Ruefully, I surrendered the photograph to him. He looked at it, grunted again, and tucked it into his pocket.

"The *kong*," he said.

"Kong?"

"It means 'four.' A quartet. I don't recall who first called us that."

"Friends forever," I said. "Even unto death."

"Something like that. But even that can change. Nothing stays the same forever, you know. Once, we—"

The Guv hesitated.

"Once you what?"

"Nothing," he said with a dismissive wave of his hand. "It's not important anymore."

He was intractable. Brother Andrew's death had taken all the wind from his sails. I'd never seen him so defeated. The worst part of it was that his mood was infectious.

The desk drawer which I hoped would provide me with answers to my questions proved to be empty, so instead, I set to work cleaning off surfaces and airing out the room. I opened all the

155

windows and shook out the sheet, happy for something to do. Outside, the larks, sparrows, and robins were singing their collective chorus. The sky was overcast, as gray as a strip of lead, but the clouds were content to keep the rain to themselves. I shook out the rug and swept the floor like I did when I was a child, too young to go down into the mines. I'd helped my mother with the younger children while my father and elder brothers dug coal with pickaxes until they were black as Zulu warriors. My grandfather came and walked me to school. He and my mother were convinced I would become something someday. All their hopes rested on me, and now, here I was, living in an anonymous chamber in the worst part of Lambeth, being pursued like the criminal I was.

Chapter Fifteen _____

Cyrus Barker spent the entire day brooding in his hammock. I'm not sure if brooding is a distinctly Scottish trait, but it certainly was one of his. He lay there as if encased in a giant chrysalis, not moving for hours, not even speaking save to ask for strong tea every now and again. Apart from the tea, he refused all nourishment. I found

I could not even draw him into a conversation on the merits and memories of our late friend. His responses were little more than grunts. It made for a very long day.

He wasn't speaking but I hoped he was thinking, trying to work out an answer for our increasingly dire predicament. We were running out of money. I began to look around to see what items in the flat could be pawned: the tropical suit, obviously, and perhaps the desk. All I needed was the word, but he never gave it. He merely swayed in that hammock of his and brooded.

Hungry as I was, I tried to get the Guv to share the provisions I had purchased. As night fell, I had no choice but to eat them myself. He had seriously begun to worry me.

The next morning found him up and out of his hammock. The worst of his grief appeared to have passed, though it would take more than one day to get over the loss of so good and necessary a man as the Reverend Andrew McClain. At least my employer was on two feet again. Perhaps now the case could move forward.

"Thomas, do you recall what I once said was the difference between a private enquiry agent and a detective?"

"A detective is not above breaking the law to achieve his own ends. Stealing into people's houses, for example."

"We may be forced to break that rule today."

"Oh," I said, not bothering to hide the disappointment in my voice.

"There is no other way. I must talk to Gerald Clayton. Desperate times require desperate measures."

"But isn't Clayton's estate likely to be well guarded? After all, a pair of dangerous criminals is at large."

"I did not say it was going to be easy. We certainly won't be going in the front door."

"I'll be surprised if we will be going in through the ground floor," I said.

"Good man! Now you're thinking like a detective. We shall see if we can scale the brick and climb into an upper window."

"I far preferred it when we were private enquiry agents and had at least a certain level of dignity."

"Desperate times," he repeated.

The Clayton family, I understand, has a large estate in Derby, into which their London property could be dropped like a stone in a well. For London, however, the property would be considered substantial. I hazarded a guess that the Claytons had performed a service for the Tudors or William of Orange, and had been doing well ever since. Certainly they had ingratiated themselves with someone to afford the large stone structure with its elaborate gardens and statuary, set back from the world and guarded with spear-topped iron railings and at least one constable, idly tapping on the iron tracery with his truncheon as he passed by.

"I don't like the look of those bars," I said. "No footing for almost six feet."

"Let us reconnoiter, and see if we can find a more secluded spot to climb. This is far too public in the light of day."

We circled the fence-enclosed property and found that it extended all the way around, save for a gate in front and back. The back gate was lower than the fence and was neatly hidden from view by a brace of old elms on either side, set within, which could aid us as we left the property. If there was any proper way in, I reasoned, this must be it.

"I suppose we—"

"Get back!" the Guv shouted.

I jumped off the lower rung of the gate just as something struck it from the other side with great force, something large and black and hideous, that sprayed me in drool from its gaping maw.

"Bullmastiff," Barker said, leading me down a quiet side street, as the creature began baying at us.

"My word! It's the size of a calf. Have you ever seen such an ugly creature?"

I looked down at my suit. The monster had doused my lower limbs in strands of phlegm, making me yearn for a change of clothes, but I was not in a situation where such a thing was possible. We hurried away along a quiet street of shops.

"How much money have we got left, Thomas?"

"No more than a few shillings, sorry to say."

"Give me one."

Reluctantly, I handed it over, knowing I'd seen the last of it. Though a Scot, Barker has the generous nature of a rich man. He has me, as his almoner, tip cab men liberally and never expects change back from whatever he gives. It had been some time since he had been in such reduced circumstances, I was sure. He stopped at the door of a butcher shop and turned to me.

"Go across the street to that chemist's and get a small bottle of Thompson's Licorice Elixir," he ordered.

He was standing at the corner with a packet from the butcher in his hands when I returned.

"I assume the meat and the Thompson's are for that roving gargoyle back at Clayton's," I said, turning the bottle over and reading aloud the label pasted on the back. " 'A universal panacea for the relief of pain, irritation, diarrhea, coughs, colds, cramps, catarrh, excessive secretions, and vague aches. Efficacious in the treatment of meningitis and yellow fever. Analgesic, soporific, and antitussive.' It sounds like the cure for everything."

"It's almost pure laudanum. Half the East End doses their children with it regularly," my employer said. "It is cheaper than alcohol and the licorice syrup cuts the bitter taste of the tincture of opium."

"What is catarrh, exactly?"

"It is an inflammation of the mucous membranes of the nose, but laudanum will not treat it successfully."

If I have given the impression that Barker is a know-all, let me disabuse you of the notion. As an autodidact, he either knows a good deal about a subject or nothing at all. He is well versed in medicine, which I believe is due to his working and training under a certain Dr. Wong of Canton, China. Knowing him as I do, the Guv is probably more interested in using his anatomical knowledge to bring down a fellow rather than to cure his head cold. Barker opened his package and decanted the dark green liquid over the raw meat. Kneading it repeatedly before we walked back to Clayton's estate, he made the mutton absorb a good portion of the liquid, then rewrapped it carefully and flung the package over the fence.

"Why did you rewrap it?" I asked.

"I want him to work for his reward. It will ensure that he will eat all of it and possibly even lick the wrapper. Shall we get some tea while we wait? Tell me we still have enough for a cup of tea."

"Just barely, I'm afraid. It won't kill the dog, will it?"

"No, it will merely put him into a sound sleep for most of the day."

We found a tea shop, where I regretfully parted with our last few pence. The buns newly pulled from the oven smelled especially good and the cakes on the counter made my eyes water.

"Stone-broke?" Barker asked, regarding me.

"Not so much as a farthing," I said. "Unless you count the Chinese coins in my pocket."

"I used the last of my pennies at the Bank of England, I'm afraid. It's maddening. I've got money secreted away in half a dozen places in London and I cannot get to any of them. Still, I've been in worse situations in my life than this, or at least as bad."

I drained the teapot, adding extra sugar to my cup for the energy it would bring.

"How will we make it through the day without money, sir?"

"God will provide. Mark my words. By midnight tonight, you'll go to bed with a full belly. Fair enough?"

"If you say so."

"Doubting Thomas. Your mother named you well. Let us see about a dog, shall we?"

When we returned to the Clayton estate, the bullmastiff lay prone in the corner of the lawn, its limbs sprawled and its tongue lolling from its mouth. It was not completely unconscious, but when we climbed over the gate and crossed the lawn, it gave no protest beyond a cough and a shake of its head. We walked around him, a black spot upon the green, and made our way across the lawn. Before we reached the house, we passed an ancient-looking edifice that was something in between a mausoleum and a temple. Its roof had crumbled and it was overgrown with ivy, and yet I recognized it for what it was, a folly, recently built to give the property an aesthetically pleasing air of age and sanctity. I was starving and this family was throwing its money away on buildings with no purpose. *Folly indeed,* I thought.

"That is where Lord Clayton's body was found. Rather a private spot, don't you think?" the Guv asked.

"I do. It is the perfect spot for a rendezvous of some sort. If it is a woman, she might have had a confederate nearby to kill Clayton."

"That is certainly one interpretation."

The door at the side of the house, for all its wrought-iron hardware, proved to be unlocked. Barker eased it open and stepped inside, but I hesitated on the threshold. This was it, I told myself, the day we set aside our hard-won reputations. Beyond this, we could lay no claim to dignity, either for ourselves or our work. We had truly become part of the Underworld. I stepped inside and stood beside my employer.

"What . . ." I whispered, but he put up his hand for silence. He had gone motionless in that way he has, as if turned to stone. He listened and felt the atmosphere, the temperature, possibly even the barometric pressure of the house, soaking it in through his pores.

"There is no one on this floor, unless they are seated, but someone is above our heads. In a house this size, one can expect a butler, a valet, a housekeeper, cook, upstairs and downstairs maid, perhaps a footman or two. We'll have to walk a gauntlet to get to Clayton."

"What is our purpose, exactly, in speaking to him?" I asked in a low voice. "You'll never convince him to change his mind."

"We'll see about that. If someone is squeezing him from one side, let us squeeze from the other. It shouldn't take much, I should think. When I met him, he did not strike me as a fellow with much personal resolve."

There was a sticky moment when a maid bustled past and we hid in an alcove, but eventually, we made our way upstairs to the first floor. I thought perhaps Barker knew where he was going, but we were forced to open and close doors until we finally found Gerald Clayton sitting before a fire in a faded leather armchair, sipping from a large snifter of brandy though it was not yet noon. Clayton's eyes were closed and it was difficult to tell how much he had swallowed already. Barker eased himself into the chair across from him and I stood behind, resting a forearm on the top of the chair.

"Good morning, Mr. Clayton," Barker stated in a low voice. "What have you to say for yourself?"

It was worth the price of admission to watch the man jump and spill his drink, even if it meant ruining a decent Persian rug. My first thought upon encountering Gerald Clayton was that he must have been a great disappointment to his father. He was a vision of dissipated youth, with waxy skin and protuberant eyes, his hair lank and oily-looking. There were two stacks of papers in front of him he had been working his way through. No doubt it had to do with his father's death and recent inheritance.

"Who are you?" he demanded. "What are you doing here?"

"It is I, Cyrus Barker. I've come to find out why you're ruining my name across London, Mr. Clayton. I've worked many years establishing a reputation which you have now sullied. I have come for my pound of flesh."

Clayton filled his lungs to cry for help but before he could expel a sound the Guv was over the table and had clamped a large hand about his throat.

"Now, Clayton, be reasonable," Barker said soothingly. "If you alert your servants or attempt to summon the constable in the lane, I shall be forced to get very unpleasant."

Clayton's eyes darted from Barker to me and I did my best to appear formidable. I gave him my most devilish look, and reached a hand into my inside breast pocket. What might I have in there? A clasp knife? A knuckle-duster? Actually, it was a pocket volume of Browning's poetry, but he wasn't to know that.

Barker pulled his hand away and patted Clayton's chest. "That's better. There is no reason for violence, I'm sure. Mr. Clayton, are you being blackmailed?"

"Yes," he admitted, putting his hands to his throat where Barker's thick fingers had just been. "Is it that obvious?"

"You do not strike me as a naturally vindictive person, and I did not give you cause during our brief exchange the other night to seek vengeance against me. There must be another factor. This person blackmailing you, is it a man or a woman?"

"It is a man, sir."

"Let me give you a name, then. Have you ever heard of Sebastian Nightwine?"

Clayton's brow shot up. "The very man! You seem to know everything. Is he a known black-mailer?"

"He is not, but the man is responsible for my present situation. What better way to damage my reputation than to murder the last man I spoke with, and coerce his son to say we had a public argument. What does he have on you, sir? Letters, perhaps?"

"I wish they were only letters."

"Photographs, then? The modern age has proven a boon to blackmailers."

"I was an ass," Clayton blurted out.

"I suppose it happened at university. I've heard young men frequently make fools of themselves there."

"You have no idea. I would give anything to take back what happened. Nothing really happened at all, but it looks bad."

"No doubt," Barker said, though he understood what Clayton meant no more than I.

"I was in an amateur theatrical group at Oxford," Clayton began. "We were doing *Antigone*. After the final performance we hired a photographer to take a photograph of all the players. By the time we got round to it and the photographer was prepared, we were all rather drunk, I'm afraid. The chiton tunics we wore were already short and rather askew, and we wore heavy makeup. The result was that we looked like a bacchanal of the lowest sort. Why couldn't we have done something like *Henry IV*, I ask you?"

Cyrus Barker frowned. He was not the kind to go in for amateur theatrics or to understand the kind of high-spirited antics that occur from time to time at a prestigious university such as Oxford or Cambridge.

"I'm not certain I follow you," he admitted.

In response, Clayton pulled open a drawer of the desk beside him and pitched a photograph across the table as if it were a playing card. It landed faceup in front of us. The photograph was one of those studio cards with a heavy backing, in sepia tones. It featured a group of four young men seated in front of a painted backdrop representing a classical scene. The young men wore laurel wreaths and had their hair in tight curls, and wore so much rouge they could have been mistaken for women. There were but two chairs, and two of the young men were seated in the other's laps. The costumes they wore were so short as to leave little to the imagination. I could see how it could lead one to the belief that something illicit and possibly even illegal might be going on.

"Did your father see this photograph?"

"No, thank the Lord."

"Are there more?" I asked.

"Oh, yes. Apparently the photographer was not scrupulous and knew a good thing when he saw it. I'm sure he took several. We were so drunk I didn't remember a single thing afterward."

"So there was no impropriety," Barker remarked. "Merely the impression of impropriety."

"We were merely drunk and disorderly, sir."

"Are you still acquainted with the other gentlemen in this photograph?"

"No. I'm not even certain I recall their names."

"How did Mr. Nightwine approach you?"

"He came to the house after my father died, telling me to go to the police with accusations against you. I assume he purchased the lot from whoever took the pictures."

"What did he say he would do with the other photographs? I assume they were as debauched-looking as this one?"

"Worse, if such a thing is possible. Nightwine said he would show them to all my father's old cronies, men with whom I would have dealings in the future. Mr. Barker, do you think there is any way to stop them from being circulated?"

"Frankly, sir, I do not. Nightwine got hold of them because he was looking for something like this and they were on the market. There's no telling how many copies were put out by your unscrupulous photographer. They may have been produced for sale. Luckily, it requires a good deal of effort to recognize you. I have a few suggestions."

"Name them, please!" Clayton said, leaning forward. I had not noticed until now that he was perspiring freely.

"The first is to marry quickly. Almost anyone will do. Make a proper husband of yourself and have children as soon as possible. Avoid amateur theatrics, drinking in public, and anything involving Greek literature. Above all, deny completely that the fellow in the photograph is you, should the subject arise. There is nothing I can see here to connect you to Oxford. You were heavily made up. Your father's associates will have merely the word of the photographer against yours. Have you anyone you can marry?"

"I have a maiden cousin without a penny—"

"Propose to her immediately! Elope with her. Settle money upon her. By God's grace you may learn to love her."

"But I hardly know the girl!"

"See her anyway. Don't tell her you've loved her from afar. Tell her the truth. She deserves that and might take pity on you."

"Mr. Barker," he said dryly, "it strikes me that you would say anything to get me to recant my testimony."

In return, Barker gave one of his cold smiles. "You are in worse trouble than I am. I have given you advice and it is not underhanded. May I take it that this cousin of yours is rather plain?"

"She's not famous for her looks, but she's a nice girl, if I recall."

"Do as you think best. You have made a hash of your life so far, boy. She may be your only salvation."

Clayton put down his drink. "Sir, I think you are correct. I don't know why I haven't thought of it before. But what should I do if one of my father's associates has already seen the photographs?"

"Your only course is complete denial. You'll not emerge unscathed. You could lose friends and associates, but if you marry and show evidence of a clean character, you'll find new ones."

There was a fire in the grate, and with a gesture Clayton tossed the photograph in. It began to blacken and curl.

"I'll do it. I shall write to Elizabeth this evening and go to Bristol tomorrow to speak to her. I'll throw myself on her mercy."

Barker, whom I must admit had looked as if he were ready to punish the young heir for turning our lives upside down, now sat back in his chair and regarded him steadily.

"If I handle Nightwine, will you agree to recant your testimony?"

Clayton took a large mouthful of brandy and swallowed it. He mopped his face afterward with a pocket handkerchief.

"I understand how untenable my position is. I will not emerge unscathed regardless of the outcome. I have tossed away every privilege my father gave me while he was alive, but I would like to think I have retained at least a vestige of honor. Very well. If you can make Nightwine go away, I shall do as you say. I wish you luck."

Barker reached out his hand and grasped

Clayton's. He looked my way and inclined his head toward the door. Without a word we exited the room.

In the hall we encountered a sputtering butler, but my employer paid no more attention to him than a standing hall clock. We descended the stairs, passed between two open-jawed house-maids below, and exited as we came. We didn't have to lay down our honor after all.

Outside the dog raised his head and stared at us listlessly. Barker put out an arm and stopped me beside one of the trees. We watched as the constable passed by, still swinging his truncheon. When he was gone we took advantage of the lower branches to climb over the fence, dropping onto the verge of lawn on the other side. Dusting grass from the knees of our trousers, we were away into the anonymous reaches of darkest Bayswater.

"Sir, I was rather shocked by the advice you gave Gerald Clayton. Deny everything? You usually expect people to tell the truth."

"You'll recall I told him to reveal all to his wife. As far as his creditors and associates go, in this sort of situation the punishment far exceeds the crime. A rumor sticks to one like glue. Better to deny, for no amount of explaining or assuring will convince anyone. In fact, I myself am not convinced."

"You think he—"

"Oh, the photographs may be more than he is willing to admit. It doesn't matter what he's done in the past, however. The question is: what shall Clayton do in the future?"

Something else was troubling me and I turned to my employer.

"We saw Sebastian Nightwine debark that ship with our own eyes. How could he have possibly had time to get something on Gerald Clayton? It doesn't seem possible."

"I was thinking that very thing myself, and that is not the only problem in this case. No one would attack O'Muircheartaigh's house without scrupulously keeping a vigil for days to learn their routines and habits. There's only one explanation."

"What?" I asked.

"Nightwine has an accomplice. And, if O'Muircheartaigh's secretary was correct, and there's no reason to think otherwise, it is a woman."

_____Chapter Sixteen

No one really calls it the Army Navy Club anymore, not if one considers oneself a Londoner. It is known simply as the Rag. In the last century someone had referred to a meal there as a "rag and famine affair," and the name became part of London culture, though I understand the food has since improved. The Rag was a big stone block at number 36 Pall Mall, decorated with rococo carvings and tall elegant windows. The club was built, I understand, so that wealthy military men could come into London from their estates and find something in town more in line with their home comforts than the average coaching inn. I had never been in such an establishment before. It was as I expected, however: sea and land battles fought for space on the walls with mounted animal heads and commemorative plaques, while every table was strewn with curios and medals under glass.

The eye patch Barker sported actually worked in our favor for once. It gave him the look of an ex-military man, a former soldier or sailor, which, come to think of it, he actually was on both counts. We might have been stopped and questioned at another club, but there, looking and acting as if one fit in was enough to secure entrance.

Once inside, we made a sweep of the place, looking surreptitiously around the public rooms in search of Nightwine. I was conscious of the fact that we were two wanted men searching for a man guarded by a Scotland Yard dectective. I thought it likely Nightwine would be out somewhere or up in his room. Luck was on our side for once, and we found him seated at a table in a library, with several maps spread out across a table. His back was to us, but it was guarded by a burly detective with a sour expression and a copy of *The Sporting Times* in his hands.

Barker took a piece of club stationery and pencil from a hall table and I wrote a note on it according to instructions. It read: *Inspector Abberline requests that you telephone "A" Division immediately.* That done, I folded the note in half, put it on a salver, and slipped into the room, presenting it to the detective. As noiselessly as possible, I slipped out again.

Ten seconds later the detective pushed out the door with an irritated look on his face. As soon as he was gone, we entered the room and bolted the door behind us. Nightwine turned in his seat and regarded us quizzically, though not with any degree of alarm. Far from it, in fact. He had a revolver trained on us.

"Cyrus!" he cried, flashing those bleached-bone teeth of his. "How good to see you again. Was that you who sent my detective after a telephone call?"

"I thought it high time you and I had a conversation."

"And you brought along Mr. Llewelyn. You see, I remembered your name this time. I like the eye patch, by the way, Cyrus. It suits an old pirate like you."

"How is Shambhala these days?" the Guv asked.

"Ask me that in a few months." Nightwine took a cigarette from his case and lit it. It was black with a gold tip. "I wish I knew. I've paid a king's ransom for a map of its whereabouts, but I would still be executed if I crossed Tibet's frontiers. The only way to go in is with force."

"Gurkhas?"

"Were you told that or did you guess?"

"Neither. I deduced it. Only a Gurkha tribesman is hearty enough to fight in that temperature and those altitudes. You would arm them properly, I suppose."

"Her Majesty's government will provide us with the latest repeating Enfield rifles. I understand the palace guards at Lhasa carry only Chinese-made flintlocks. If it all goes according to plan it should be a massacre."

"What will you do with the young Dalai Lama?"

"Hold him for ransom, of course. We'll see how much gold and precious stones the country is hoarding."

"Would you kill him?" I asked.

"If it suits my plans," he said, as if we were discussing something as innocuous as betting on a horse. "Five Dalai Lamas have died in the past several years, mostly by poisoning. Dalai Lamas rarely reach maturity these days. They'll simply send monks out to locate another one among the native population, like pigs hunting truffles."

"We discussed this plan years ago, didn't we, before India became part of the Empire?" Barker asked. "If Tibet falls, Nepal would be sandwiched between British colonies and could be easily taken. The other countries in the region would fall like dominoes. It is a sound plan, I must admit. It's dangerous, certainly, but then you always did enjoy a little risk in your endeavors."

Nightwine flicked the ash from his cigarette into a glass tray. "It's nice to know there is someone who understands me as well as you."

"I understand you perfectly. Of course, you are not going to succeed. I intend to stop you."

Nightwine considered this. "You're welcome to try, but I warn you, it shan't be as easy as your little trick at the dock. For one thing, you've acquired a lot of human baggage about you." So saying, he trained the pistol on me. "You know, you really need to do something about this assistant of yours. He's far too pretty. He just doesn't lend that level of gravitas a private enquiry agency requires. You should leave him with me sometime. I'll plane off some of his more delicate features."

"Thank you, Sebastian, but I believe we shall keep Mr. Llewelyn as he is," Barker murmured.

"Suit yourself," he said, curling his lip in a sneer.

"This scheme of yours is vast and complicated," the Guv continued. "The odds against your success are astronomical. You are far more likely to take an arrow to the chest or fall down a crevasse in the attempt."

"Spare me the false concern for my welfare, Cyrus. Don't you ever grow tired of trying to spoil people's plans? Are you too unimaginative to think up any of your own?"

"As I recall," Barker countered, "I did make plans. I came to London and opened a respectable agency. I bought a house and an office, I hired an assistant. I put away schemes. This plan of yours, brilliant as it is, is merely a pipe dream."

"That's where you're wrong. It is my pension. I've proven to Her Majesty's government that I'm an officer in whom it can give its trust."

"I rather think you will disappoint them, Sebastian. It's always been part of your character to deal from the bottom of the deck. As I recall, when you told me the first version of this master plan of yours years ago, you intended to sell Tibet to the highest bidder."

"Do you doubt my patriotism?" he asked mockingly. "Britain, my home country, will be given first choice. Surely you don't intend for me to be more generous than that."

"And if China or Russia offers more?" I asked.

"Then Britain will simply have to make a higher offer. It is the way of the marketplace.

178

There is nothing wrong with trying to get the most for one's assets."

"It's not going to work," Cyrus Barker said.

"That's right. You're going to stop me. In case you haven't noticed, you are incapable of stopping so much as a nosebleed. Your accounts are blocked, this morning I doubled the price on your head, and there is no man willing to call you friend."

"I have more friends than you think, Sebastian."

"Then you should warn them to avoid you during the present crisis. This is not a safe time to have Cyrus Barker for a friend."

"I'll be sure to pass on the warning."

"I hope you enjoy being chased out of churches and off barges, not knowing where your next meal is coming from. That packet of money you made in China has not insulated you from the hard times in life. It has been a fine recompense for the public humiliation you afforded me at St. Katharine Docks by the moneylenders."

"If I had not humiliated you, would you have still laid this false trail and put a price on my head?" Barker asked.

"You left your dagger behind before. It seemed a shame not to use it. Let me ask you this in return. If I had not put Scotland Yard on your tail, would you have allowed me to transact business with the Foreign Office free from interference?"

"Not a chance."

There was a sudden knock at the door. I hazarded a guess that it was the detective who had realized he'd been duped.

"There you are, then. It appears this meeting is at an end."

Barker stood and I followed his lead, wondering if we were just going to stroll out the door like club members.

Nightwine put out his cigarette. "I'm not sorry I had him killed, you know."

Cautiously, I turned to my employer. He suddenly had the admission of guilt he had waited for. I studied his face in that moment, wondering what his reaction would be. Barker was coiled, ready to snap.

"My brother, or Andrew McClain?"

"Finally hit a nerve, have I?" Nightwine said.

The knocking increased in volume until it was pounding. If I knew Scotland Yard bureaucracy, the detective would have to get permission before breaking down the door.

It was a fine door, white, with various panels. It seemed a shame to damage it.

"I believe that is our cue to leave, lad," Barker said.

He crossed to a window and lifted the sash. It had begun raining and wind and rain came spattering in, lifting Nightwine's maps momentarily, so he was forced to hold them down. By the time I reached the window Barker had already jumped out. I saw him land on the street below. Looking down at the ten-foot drop, I wondered if I would break my leg.

The door burst open behind me and I jumped. Barker steadied me as I landed on the hard and uneven cobblestones. My feet hurt like the devil, but I didn't injure myself permanently. While the detective yelled overhead, the two of us sprinted down Pall Mall Street. When we finally stopped, we raised our collars and thrust our hands into our pockets, headed toward Waterloo Bridge and the relative safety of the Surrey side.

"I thought you were going to explode in there."

"I very nearly did."

"That man wants your guts for garters," I remarked, as we trotted along in the rain. "What did we accomplish by going there? We came within a hairsbreadth of being arrested."

Barker stopped and shook his head like a dog, sending droplets everywhere. "I went because I wanted to prove to him that I was not afraid of him and he was still vulnerable.

"We both know that this is the time and place we shall end our twenty-five-year feud."

"Is there any chance of getting some food today? My stomach's wrapped around my backbone."

"You worry too much about the condition of your stomach."

"I'm sorry," I said. "It's been my loyal friend these many years."

"When we get back, perhaps you can sell my old suit for enough to fill your belly tonight."

"What about you? You've got to keep up your strength, you know."

We marched in a steady downpour, the rain drizzling down the backs of our necks. I'm not a hardship sort of fellow. If I had known I would become a private enquiry agent, instead of the poet or university don I'd set my cap to, I would have better prepared myself.

"What provoked this sudden return to the West on Nightwine's part?"

"I would say he received a positive response to his query regarding an expedition to Lhasa. I do not believe it is the idea that was so new. Rather, it is the maps he had gathered. No European has successfully cartographed the Himalayas before. It is a blank on the map."

"And now that he is here, he is taking advantage of the situation to settle your dispute once and for all."

"Aye," Barker called out over the rain. "He would not be able to enjoy his retirement knowing I would come after him."

"Would you?" I asked. "Go after him, I mean? As far as Tibet or China?"

"Of course!" he cried, as the downpour became a deluge. "I'm no more able to leave this matter unfinished than he is!"

A little over an hour later, I sat on the edge of

the bed, clad once more in a blanket. My clothes hung over the fender of the fireplace drying out. Tea was brewing on the hob, and we had cheese and biscuits on the desk after a successful barter with the pawnbroker. The Guv lay cocooned again, sodden as he was, and I could almost see vapor rising from the hammock.

"I'd give half my estate right now for a pipe and a tin of Astley's Cavendish," he remarked.

"Are we finally running out of people to see and places to investigate, sir? I think I'm getting a blister."

"You'll get worse than that before this case is done," he replied.

Not *You poor lad.* Not *Take the rest of the day off,* though, as a matter of fact, we did, if only because the rain continued to pour down on London and we had no money for a cab.

"Perhaps in a day or so you would enjoy a visit to the Reading Room at the British Museum. I would like you to investigate Shambhala for me."

"That sounds intriguing."

"I think I should send you along to see Anderson, as well."

"Robert Anderson? The spymaster general? Why would he want to see me?"

"A week ago you probably wouldn't have been permitted, but your present notoriety might work in our favor."

"It might get me arrested instead."

"Then you can rest comfortably in a cell while your blister heals."

" 'O frabjous day,' " I quoted.

"I beg pardon?"

"Nothing, sir."

I got up and hobbled to the fireplace. My suit was taking a remarkably long time to dry and the chamber had begun to smell like wet sheep. The kettle began to whistle.

"Tea's ready," I said. "You are going to eat something today, aren't you?"

There was no comment from the hammock.

Chapter Seventeen _____

The next morning the storm had rolled off toward the Continent, leaving everything bedewed and smelling of loam. I had done the best I could with a suit which had been drenched several times, a thrice-used collar, and a tie that had traveled from Canton while I was still in public school. I was going to see Robert Anderson, but not without misgivings.

"Why should we expect him to reveal anything to us, sir?" I argued. "He didn't ask for me to come and probably feels I have nothing to offer him."

"Then you must disabuse him of that opinion. What I have told you to say I would be interested in hearing, were I in his position."

"But suppose he gives me nothing in return?"

"Really, Thomas, you must work these things out for yourself. Balk! Stay seated in his chair, an impediment to the day's activities, until he either has you thrown out or finally opens his mouth."

"What if he doesn't know anything? I mean, his concern is the Irish threat. He has nothing to do with matters in Tibet."

"Since when have you been an authority on the duties of the spymaster general? Do you suppose he is not concerned about a matter which could potentially enlarge the British Empire a hundred-fold?"

"Yes, sir. I mean, no, sir. I see your point."

"We should have sold the tea kettle and bought a new collar," he went on, eyeing me critically.

"I would have liked a shoeshine, as well," I said. "It can't be helped."

"Good luck, lad," Barker said, patting my shoulder.

"I thought you didn't believe in luck," I answered.

I crossed at Westminster Bridge, aware that I was not far from where this case had first begun. I could look over and see an engine steaming across the Charing Cross Bridge. I assumed Jenkins had opened the offices as always in

Craig's Court. What day was it? It was so easy to lose track when one is on the run. By my calculations, it was Friday, April 9. Officially, we had been wanted men for five days. Generally, the Guv likes to finish a case within two weeks' time, though I seriously doubted he would make his self-determined deadline this time.

Entering the combined chambers of the Home and Foreign Office, I went up to the sentinel who guarded the building from anyone attempting to enter without proper authority. Pulling a piece of paper from my pocket, I borrowed a pen and wrote the words *RE: Shambhala expedition. T. Llewelyn* on it. I handed it to the guard, a stocky, ginger-haired fellow with a florid face.

"Give this to Robert Anderson," I said.

The man frowned at me and I understood why. One doesn't simply demand to see the spymaster general of all the British Empire without an appointment. Also, I was rather certain he recognized my name, for I had seen this particular Cerberus before. After some hesitation he pointed a pudgy finger at a bench, and stepping to a door, he conferred with a colleague before handing over my paper. Then he returned to his desk. Nothing happened for the next twenty minutes. The wheels of British government grind exceedingly slow, but finally, a civil servant, possibly the one he had spoken to, came and fetched me. As I passed I looked into the piercing blue eyes of the guard and he eyed me shrewdly. I was surprised at my own gall, but it was too late to turn back now.

Anderson was seated in his office, looking slightly harried and a bit grayer than when I had seen him last, when we had investigated a faction of Irish bombers. His office was Spartan and not particularly large, decorated with a Union Jack on a pole and a cross on the wall made of olive wood. I supposed the two represented what he stood for, God and Country.

"I'm not in the habit of speaking to wanted men, Mr. Llewelyn," he warned, writing as he spoke. "You should not be here. What do you want?"

"I won't take up much of your time. I was wondering if you could tell me the name of the gentleman leading this expedition to Tibet."

His pen paused briefly, stabbed itself into his inkwell and went on writing.

"I couldn't possibly answer that question. The names of our agents are confidential for obvious reasons. Besides, I have no idea what you will do with the information."

I would not be deterred so easily. "Very well. Do you think if I inferred that said agent was Sebastian Nightwine, I would be far off the mark? You needn't say anything. Just tap your nose with your pen."

"You have a gift for facetiousness, Mr.

Llewelyn, which is liable to get you into trouble."

"I must take that as a 'no,' then. Fine. The consequences be on your head." I rose as if to go.

"Sit down," he commanded. "To what consequences do you refer?"

"I scarce can say, and certainly would not hazard a guess. I'm sure you know that he is very dangerous. If you can explain to me why Her Majesty's government is plotting the takeover of Tibet with a man who has a file at Scotland Yard two inches thick, I'll be on my way."

"You are starting to sound like your employer."

"I've been cramming. I wanted to get it right."

"I shall tell you what I'd tell him, then. It's none of his concern what the government does. Him, least of all, under present circumstances."

"Now, see," I said. "That's what I told him. It would be far more advantageous to go to see W. T. Stead, and lay all our evidence before him."

"That scandalmonger?" he demanded. I knew I'd succeeded in getting his attention because his pen stopped.

"The *Pall Mall Gazette* is a reputable newspaper, even if they are a trifle socialist. They even print photographs!"

"If you reveal any information regarding this expedition, you may provoke an international incident."

"I believe you've got that backward, sir. If I

reveal the information I would stop the inter-national incident you are provoking."

He got up from his chair and shut the door. On the one hand it showed he was giving me his full attention, but on the other, I was trapped.

"I am not involved with the Shambhala expedition," he insisted.

"That hardly matters," I pointed out. "When Mr. Gladstone's government goes down clawing and scratching into the mud over this, saying you were not involved will hardly absolve you."

"They might consider the offer too good to refuse. Even Barker could not stop the momentum."

"The Guv says the prime minister has wanted to add new colonies ever since his opponent, Mr. Disraeli, made us an empire. The problem is there's a worm at the core of the apple."

Anderson leaned back in his chair and crossed his arms. "I presume you're referring to Sebastian Nightwine."

"Yes. In case you haven't heard, he and Mr. Barker have been acquainted for twenty-five years, ever since Nightwine killed his brother."

"Mr. Nightwine has spoken extensively about your employer. It is how I've become connected to the matter. I am considered the local authority upon Cyrus Barker. But, as you see, I still have work to do. I presume you have something to ask or tell me. I hope it is the latter."

"It is. Mr. Barker wishes me to inform you that

in his presence, Nightwine told him many years ago about this plan, only with one significant change: Nightwine intended to seize control of Lhasa and have himself declared king. He had no intention of handing it over to the British government."

Anderson shook his head. "Your powder is wet, I'm afraid. It doesn't matter what he said many years ago."

"Fair enough," I responded. "How about yesterday at 4:25 p.m. when in my presence he said he'd sell Tibet to the highest bidder? He was gracious enough to allow Britain to make the first offer, but ultimately you would need to have the winning bid."

Anderson closed his eyes and his shoulders slumped a little. "How can I verify this is true?"

"The Guv said you'd ask that. The three of us were the only ones in the room at the time. He said to give you his word."

"That's good enough for me, but not, I fear, for my associates. The negotiations are at an end. The deal is complete. Mr. Nightwine is to turn over his maps to us on Monday."

"In exchange for money, I assume," I said. "You'll never see it again. What's to keep him from pocketing it and betting at the fan-tan parlors in Shanghai?"

"This is the British government we're talking about."

"With thousands of pounds in his hand he could buy whatever he wants in Asia. He could take over Tibet as he said, or he could buy his own island and fortify it with cannons. I don't think he cares much about the British government one way or the other. He's doing it for the money. He told me to my face he was taking his retirement."

"There was talk about giving him an earldom."

"I'm sure, but the Russians would offer to make him a count, and the Chinese would make a mandarin of him."

Anderson began to scratch his beard, as if it had begun to itch. "Do not speak with Mr. Stead, for now at least. I need to talk to several people. It is probably too late to stop this, and some men on the committee will be deucedly hard to convince."

"I will tell Mr. Barker when I see him. Thank you for seeing me without an appointment."

I was actually in the corridor before he called me back in again.

"Yes, sir?" I asked, having no idea what he was about to say. He was frowning, but not in a way that looked as though he were angry with me, though he did not look me in the eye.

"Look, I just wanted to say if Cyrus should ever retire or you feel the desire to move on, come and see me."

I stared at him, nonplussed. "Are you offering me employment?"

"Perhaps, if we can reach an agreement," he said, leaning back in his chair.

"I'd never leave Barker's employ, sir," I told him. "The man's done too much for me."

"I'm not asking you to. Situations change, however, and if you should ever find yourself at loose ends someday, remember us. You've had experience with the Irish and know a primer from a fuse cap. We're always looking for capable young men."

That's because the Irish keep killing them, I wanted to say, but didn't. "I'll consider your offer, sir," I answered diplomatically.

"Do that." He took up his pen and began to write once more. After a moment, he looked up at me dismissively. "Good day, Mr. Llewelyn."

I came out of Anderson's office and down the stairs, my head preoccupied with the offer he had just made and wondering why it had made me angry. Why should anyone assume that Cyrus Barker's career was over? As long as he drew breath, to cross him off as a has-been, or worse, a never-was, well, it was an insult. Barker's career was a great social experiment. He was trying to legitimize a profession that still had one foot in the shadows.

Were my employer there, he would have pointed out that I had taken my eye off the quarry. I was so busy preparing a mental defense of my employer that I hadn't bothered to notice the subtle changes which had occurred in the lobby during my absence. Barker would never have allowed it to happen. I was nearly out the door when I felt cold steel on my wrist, and turning around, found myself staring into the intent eyes of Inspector Frederick Abberline. I found I much preferred them at a distance.

_____Chapter Eighteen

When they put you in a temporary cell in "A" Division, they cook you until you are done. That is, they give you hours to think over your misdeeds in the hope that you'll confess and possibly turn on your accomplices. It requires no effort on their part and there is no law against it, as long as it takes no more than a day. Often the delay is legitimate. Inspectors fight for space in the few interrogation rooms as barristers do in the courts. It isn't personal, but it certainly can feel that way when it is you who are locked in a cell with nothing to do but contemplate the walls and ceiling. Then one feels particularly set aside for punishment.

In the scheme of things, breaking one constable's kneecap and cuffing him to a rail is not a capital offense. We were wrestling for the truncheon and it could just as easily have been my kneecap that was broken, or so my solicitor would maintain. They could not connect me to the greater charge leveled against Cyrus Barker of murdering Lord Clayton. However, I was worried for both of us. I wondered if Gerald Clayton had followed Barker's advice and proposed marriage to his cousin. If not, could one witness be enough to convict Barker in court when the time came? I rather feared it might. I hate it when you know something is only meant to scare you, but it succeeds anyway. I may be a criminal, but I will never be a hardened one, I'm sure. Criminals such as the infamous Charley Peace could have done my few hours standing on his head.

The Guv warned there would be days like this. In fact, all things being equal, I am surprised I wasn't more upset about my predicament. Were I a stockbroker or a clerk in the Admiralty, being arrested might have been the greatest tragedy of my life. As for me, it was, well, just another day at the office.

Eventually, I was taken to the interrogation room. Abberline was there ahead of me and was perusing my file.

"This makes for interesting reading," he said. "What makes a man go from Oxford University to Oxford Prison in one fell swoop?"

"Try a sixteen-year-old wife dying of consumption and malnutrition. I don't suppose that's in the report, is it? Widower at eighteen?"

He was not impressed. An inspector hears everything in his position, most of it barefaced lies. If I were expecting him to break down in tears over my loss, I'd be disappointed.

"Where is Cyrus Barker?" he asked.

"I forget. It was right on the tip of my tongue and now I've lost it."

"That was a neat little joint lock you got me in. I'd heard your employer was clever that way."

"You would have known that move and the counter to it if he'd been allowed to continue the classes he taught for free in the CID building."

Abberline nodded absently and then went on reading the file. "It says here you are arrogant."

"Arrogant? What would I have to be arrogant about? Eight months of a university education? I have practically no possessions and am employed in a situation I am too ashamed to tell my parents about."

"Perhaps you would make them proud again if you delivered Mr. Barker into our hands."

"It is not Barker who is the criminal here, Inspector. It is Sebastian Nightwine. Everyone seems to have forgotten that. The world has gone topsy-turvy when a total blackguard is given a police escort and a good man driven from his offices."

"But your employer did disturb the peace. I was there, as you recall."

"Where? At Westminster Abbey? You weren't exactly kneeling in reverent prayer yourself. In fact, as I recall you broke up the service with your squad of blues. You didn't have to invade the sanctity of such a place."

"You know it is only a matter of time until we catch Cyrus Barker. We caught you and we found your little garret in Lambeth."

"I'm interested in learning how you knew I was at the Foreign Office," I confessed.

"We had an anonymous tip from a good citizen."

"Did he tell you about the garret, as well?"

"He did."

"Anonymous. Was it a telephone call, by chance?"

"It was, if that makes a difference. What's so funny?" Abberline suddenly asked.

"Oh, nothing. You'd have to know Barker. He's tricked us both, I'm afraid. You see, we ran out of funds a couple of days ago. He sent me to the Foreign Office and then made a telephone call to your offices with the anonymous tip."

"Why would he do that?"

"To see to my welfare. Either you'll charge and release me, after which I'll be a free man, or you'll keep me here, where I'll be clothed and fed. I work for him, you see, and he always sees to the needs of his subordinates over his own."

"What about his own? He's got no money and, if what you say is true, no roof over his head. Why would a man do that to himself?"

"Because he is tough and resourceful. If he needs anything, he'll know how to get it. He won't show his head until he's quite good and ready to do so. Until then, you don't stand a chance of finding him."

"It appears to me that Inspector Poole has allowed your employer too much latitude in many cases. He had no business revealing official CID information to an outsider. That is what got him suspended."

"To be sure," I agreed. "The fact that Barker generally solved most of these cases and allowed you chaps to take the credit for what you couldn't come up with yourselves is really immaterial."

"Your employer is a man of limited education, no background, and no experience as a police officer. He has a reputation for fighting rather than thinking his way out of a situation. His advertisements in *The Times* suggest a crass commercialism, and his leaching information from the department proves him to be opportunistic at best."

I sat up in my chair, wondering how much trouble I would get into if I punched another officer.

"You could not be more wrong about him,

Inspector. Cyrus Barker is a close friend of the Reverend Charles Haddon Spurgeon, who will vouch for his character. He speaks six languages that I know of, and though he is self-taught, knows a great deal on a variety of subjects. He is the best fighter in all Europe; I would stake a fortune on it. Nevertheless, he uses his physical skills as a last resort. He places advertisements in newspapers as a way to help people who are in need and occasionally receives no recompense for his services. He is wealthy enough to purchase this entire group of buildings and turn Great Scotland Yard into a garden he can overlook from his office window, but instead he gives to dozens of charities. He is highly respected by the inspectors in this building who are *not* Johnny-come-latelies, because he is generally willing to share information due to the fact that he gives a damn what happens in this city that he has chosen out of anywhere on the globe as his home. He is kindhearted enough to give felons like me a second chance, and if you make one more slandering remark against him, I'll teach you a half-dozen methods he's taught me for scientifically rendering a man unconscious."

Abberline was not to be swayed so easily. He was a tough egg to crack. "That was quite a speech," he commented.

"No, Inspector. It was a promise. Barker's big enough to fend for himself, but when lesser men

198

criticize him, it makes my blood boil. If you weren't so pigheaded, you could learn a lot from him."

"Terence Poole did, and look what happened to him. He'll be lucky if he's not sacked by the end of the month."

"Fine if he is," I insisted. "He can work with us. We'll get him a new desk and double his pay."

I was bluffing, of course. Poole would prefer to be reinstated with the police, I was sure, but Abberline was not to know that.

The inspector made no comment beyond briefly raising his eyebrows. There was a lull in conversation, while he regarded me steadily. I felt as if I were a safe and he was trying to break into me with a brace-and-bit. He turned to my file again.

"Let's discuss the incident in Westminster Abbey," he said after he made a notation. "You assaulted another officer."

"When?" I asked, all innocence. I can do innocence very well.

"After the service. You began to run and he attempted to detain you. You kicked him in the stomach."

"Oh, that wasn't an officer. That was a member of the public."

"I tell you, he was not a member of the public. He was Lieutenant John Wilkins, a member of our plainclothes division."

"He didn't identify himself as such. I can't be

arrested for assaulting a plainclothes officer."

"Of course you can!"

"Sorry, old bean," I said, shaking my head sadly. "I have an uncommon good solicitor, Bram Cusp, who will tell you I can't be arrested for assaulting an officer who isn't in uniform, unless he is bellowing at the top of his lungs that he's an officer of the law, which I assure you he wasn't."

The inspector rose to his feet. He was a very serious person and unaccustomed to the level of nonsense I was shoveling his way. He left the room and did not return. Score one, I thought, for the visiting team.

I was allowed to send a message to Cusp's office and then took a nap. A few hours later, I stepped into Great Scotland Yard Street a free man, free as far as a man can be with plainclothes detectives at his heels, and a charge pending. I was to appear early the next week at the Old Bailey for assault upon two police officers, but still, I felt blithe and bonnie as I walked round the corner and entered the offices of number 7 Craig's Court.

"Hello, Jenkins!" I cried as I entered. "I've just been sprung!"

"Well, I never!" he cried, jumping up from his desk. "Where's the Guv?"

"Heaven knows. Last I saw him, he was sending me off to get arrested. That's all I know."

I went over to my desk, sat down in my old,

familiar chair, and put up my feet on the corner, the way Barker often did. Late afternoon sunlight shimmered in through the windows.

"God's in his heaven, all's right with the world," I pronounced. "Until the next bloody crisis."

Chapter Nineteen

I was in one of the back rooms tying a four-in-hand and feeling relieved to wear clean clothes again, when I heard the office door open. It could have been anyone: someone trying to claim the reward, a potential client who was innocent of Barker's current situation, another Scotland Yard officer coming to harass me; in short, no one I had any interest in seeing. Jenkins appeared in the doorway, shifting his weight the way he does when he has no idea how to announce someone.

"Who is it?" I asked.

"A female, Mr. L," he said, leaning in conspiratorially. "And quite a looker she is, too, if I am any judge."

"What now?" I muttered to myself, but as I walked to the door, I had a premonition that it was Sofia Ilyanova. I was right. She stood almost with her back to me, looking through the glass into the street as she waited. She held her chin at an aristocratic angle, though I suspected there was something more down-to-earth about her than that. Her pale hair was swept up and secured in place with a small hat and a delicate pearl pin. In between two petite, gloved hands, she held a parasol, the tip resting delicately on the floor. Her dress, an exquisite color of Prussian blue, had a high collar with the merest hint of lace and had obviously been made by a dressmaker of some repute, probably in Paris. Everything about her was exotic and beautiful. It took a moment for me to speak, and when I did, I said the first thing that popped into my head.

"I never expected to see you again."

She turned slowly toward me, those gold-flecked eyes studying me seriously. "You shouldn't make assumptions about me, Thomas Llewelyn. As it turns out, I need something from you."

I gestured toward the visitor's chair and held it while she sat. Walking around the desk, I took Barker's seat and regarded her intently.

"You remembered my name, Miss Ilyanova," I noted, with some surprise.

"As you did mine."

"It wasn't difficult. I have never known anyone with a name like yours before."

"My mother's family is from St. Petersburg. My father is English."

202

"Ah." I smiled.

I watched Sofia lift a hand to brush a lock of hair that rested against her neck. I admit I had some trouble concentrating. She folded her hands in her lap and toyed with the small pocketbook she carried that matched her dress.

"What may the Barker Agency do for you?" I asked.

"It's a sensitive matter, I'm afraid."

I nodded. "That is precisely the sort of case we handle. Are you here in an official capacity?"

"I'm not entirely certain. It's hard to know where to begin."

My heart sank for a moment. Perhaps she was here to investigate the whereabouts of a past lover, or had become involved in an unsavory scandal. She seemed too genteel a lady to be a part of some unpleasant affair, but I knew it was possible. Obviously she would be sought after by men, and likely on two continents. I looked at her striking face, aware of the concern etched on her features, and suddenly wanted to thrash whoever had caused her this kind of distress.

"It's my family. My father, actually."

"Your father?" I repeated. "Perhaps you should start at the beginning."

There were things I was supposed to be doing at that moment: putting the office affairs in order after they had been neglected for days, checking the incoming correspondence, and following

Barker's instructions to research Shambhala. I wasn't supposed to be taking on new clients or wasting the agency's time talking with beautiful strangers. However, there was something about the urgency with which she had made her plea that made me feel even Barker would have listened to her, had he been there. I was conscious of the fact that with my employer gone, I was representing the agency. I furrowed my brow, concentrating, as she composed herself to speak.

"I was raised by my mother until I was sixteen years old," she said quietly. "She was abandoned by my father before they could wed, and in shame, she was sent by my grandparents to the provinces on the Siberian border where I was born. In spite of the conditions, it was a good childhood, actually. She and I were quite close. The only tension we ever had between us occurred when I asked about my father."

She paused, looking at me carefully. "You must understand that when you've never met your father, you think about him all of the time. You convince yourself he's sure to be the greatest man you've ever known, and will ride in on a white horse someday and take you away from everything. And, of course, when he finally comes, he will be as desperate to know you as you were to know him."

I shook my head almost imperceptibly. "This is going to end badly," I murmured.

"Of course it is. How could it not with such high expectations?"

"Pray continue," I urged.

"When he came, at last, nothing turned out as it was meant to. He swept into my mother's life again, much as he had the first time, delighting her with promises of what their lives would be like. They would have money, friends, position; all of the things she had been robbed of before. I was so happy to finally meet him. He was handsome and debonair, just as I imagined. I convinced myself there must have been a good reason for him to have stayed away all of those years. But instead of our being rescued, it all went horribly wrong."

"What happened?" I asked.

She paused, adjusting one of her gloves. "He killed her, of course."

"Killed her!" I exclaimed. "What do you mean?"

"Oh, he didn't do it with his bare hands, nothing as blatant as that. He's more subtle. I was a trifle to him that he momentarily wanted: the seed of his bloodline. He hired a solicitor, planning to strip my custody from her. He made her life a living hell, denying her at the last moment everything he had promised before. My mother was never strong. She took her own life with prussic acid, but I know it was truly he who killed her."

"What happened then?"

"I assumed I would go to live with my grand-parents, or if they would not take pity on me, they might settle me with a family in our village. Before that could happen, my father petitioned for custody and won, thanks to a substantial bribe to the court. He plucked me out of Russia and we have lived a nomadic existence ever since."

"Is he in London now?"

"He is, and I'm little more than a common servant to him. My grandfather sends him a quarterly allowance which is supposed to be for my welfare, though I rarely see a penny of it."

I was trying to find a delicate way to point out that she did not look as though she were in need, but she replied before I could form the words.

"It's the dress, isn't it?" she asked, looking down. "I suppose I look like the kind of spoiled child who would say anything to get what she wants, but as a colonel's daughter, I am expected to dress the part. I mean nothing to him at all."

"Colonel's daughter?" I asked, a dim light beginning to dawn. I just wasn't certain what it was, yet.

"Yes. He's a colonel in Her Majesty's Army. Perhaps you've heard his name: Sebastian Nightwine."

I sank back in Barker's chair, trying not to show my shock. I realized at once that it was undeniably true. All one had to do was look at her golden amber eyes to know she was her father's daughter.

"Nightwine, of all people," I finally managed to say.

"I see you are acquainted with his name, at least. Suffice it to say he was not the father I had always dreamed of having."

"But you were in London first," I said, remembering I had seen her the morning before we had gone to St. Katharine Docks.

"He sent me ahead to prepare for his arrival. What could I do, Mr. Llewelyn? I am wholly and completely dependent upon him. I haven't the resources to return to Russia on my own."

"Why didn't you leave him?" I implored. "What made you stay?"

"I was only sixteen then. He monitored my correspondence with my grandparents and I have no friends. What could a young girl possibly do that could gain her freedom from her own father? In the eyes of the law, I had no choice. We have now traveled together for years, every year worse than the one before. If I knew how to escape him, I would do it now without hesitation."

"Is that why I found you in front of our offices that day?"

She nodded. "I was trying to pluck up the courage to go inside and talk to Mr. Barker."

"Why didn't you do it then?"

"I had to be sure that I could trust him or that he would protect me. My father would consider this a betrayal worthy of death."

"I hate to disappoint you, but my employer is a wanted man. I was myself until just this very morning."

"I know, Mr. Llewelyn. That was my father's doing. I believe he has cast doubt upon Mr. Barker's character in order to destroy him. I have stayed here overlong already. I must get back before he suspects something."

"Stay," I urged. "Stay and I will get you to a safe place. You'll never have to see him again." I tried to imagine where I would take her, but my brain was suddenly foggy. I couldn't take her to the house in Newington; I didn't know what I would find when I got there. The barge where we had found brief refuge was not suitable for a young woman of her position, and the flat had been discovered.

"I mustn't stay now," she said calmly. "Whatever I do must be done with great care. Don't worry, Mr. Llewelyn. My immediate situation is not dire. I have simply determined that my position is no longer tenable and I will do anything in my power to change it."

"Then how may I help?" I asked, frustrated indeed. "I am at your disposal."

"You've helped already," she said. "You've listened. I will come back when I can, and perhaps together with Mr. Barker, we'll find a way out of this. In the meantime, I will look for evidence of a crime that could have my father arrested."

"You must not place yourself at any greater risk."

She stood, and extended a hand. "You've been most kind, and I appreciate it. I believe you genuinely care what happens to me."

I stood and took her gloved hand for a brief moment before letting it go. "I do. I'm here if you need me."

"I'll remember that," she said, and then she slipped out the door.

In a rush, I suddenly thought of all of the things I should have asked her. How did she know about Barker? Why had she come here, knowing he was on the run, with a price on his head? What could she realistically expect from us, anyway? I was still contemplating the feel of her delicate gloved hand in mine when Jenkins came strolling in a minute later.

"Was I right?" he demanded. "A looker, wasn't she?"

"I commend your taste in women, Jeremy."

"What was that about, Mr. L?" he asked.

I looked at him and shook my head. "I only wish I knew."

Chapter Twenty _____

B ehind Barker's green leather chair there is a
small table with a wooden panel hanging
above it, adorned by his family crest: a rampant
lion surrounded by fleurs-de-lys. It looks very
old, and may in fact be, but it hides a very modern
safe. I opened that safe then, and replenished
the money which we had spent since this case
began. I seriously hoped that wherever the Guv
was at that moment, he too would have a good
meal to eat and a bed for the night.

"I'm going to the British Museum," I said to
our clerk. "Lock up if I'm not back by five-
thirty."

Jenkins's mind was still back on Sofia Ilyanova.
I had broken the news of her unfortunate parent-
hood.

"I don't believe it, Mr. L. A girl that pretty can't
be related to a devil like him."

"A girl cannot help her parentage," I replied.

"Speaking of females, I forgot to tell you that
Mrs. Ashleigh is in town, and she's none too
pleased. You're to go to Brown's Hotel as soon as
you can to see her." Our clerk was lank limbed,
lank haired, loose jawed, and unsteady on his

feet. He'd had a merely passing acquaintance with his straight razor recently and his clothing looked as if he'd slept in them.

"Did she have any message for Barker when he returns?"

"No, sir. Only you."

I called the Brown to say I was coming and caught a hansom cab to Albemarle Street. The hansom is a modern marvel, the gondola of London, gliding noiselessly upon rubber wheels. It felt an incredible luxury after walking everywhere for the last week. I stretched out on the scat, without the Guv to occupy two thirds of the vehicle, thinking it was hard to believe that I had started the day by being arrested. I read somewhere that testing and licensing of London cabmen was very stringent. They had to know every street and how to get there in the shortest possible time, as well as which roads were being repaired. I relaxed and let my current cabman whisk me to my appointment with Mrs. Ashleigh, while I took a few moments to puzzle over Sofia Ilyanova.

I wasn't contemplating matrimony, of course, but I had to admit she had a face to look at over the breakfast table every morning. Ivory skin, moonlit hair, and golden eyes lined in black velvet. She'd be worth sweeping the front steps for, or whatever it is that husbands did for their wives these days. But I stopped myself right there, because she was the daughter of Sebastian

Nightwine, the most treacherous man in London.

I alighted at Browns' and even paying the cabman was a delight after having scrimped money for several days. In my clean suit I easily passed inspection by the desk clerk, and after notifying him to ring Mrs. Ashleigh's room, I buried myself behind the latest edition of *The Times*. While Barker and I had been occupied, apparently the world continued revolving. There had been a fire in Hammersmith and a rise in the price of corn on the exchange. However, there was no notice that a desperate enquiry agent had just been loosed on unsuspecting London.

"Thomas!" Philippa Ashleigh asked at my elbow. "Have you eaten?"

"Not since last night, ma'am."

"I think we can dispense with the formalities now. We've known each other over a year."

I shook my head. "I'm sorry, ma'am, I don't believe the Guv would approve. You know he is old-fashioned."

"Old-fashioned," she repeated, placing the emphasis on the first word rather than the second. Fashioned—forged—if you prefer, in the old ways, with the old tools. I thought it captured his essence very well.

"Where is he, Thomas?"

"I don't know. He sent me off to the Foreign Office, and then called in an anonymous tip to have me arrested."

"You must be exhausted and starved. Let's go in and have tea."

She led me into the dining room and we were seated. In just a few minutes the waiter had brought us sandwiches of cold tongue, pâté, and cucumber with watercress. He returned with cheese, pickles, and deviled eggs, with a pot of tea. As soon as food was present, my stomach had a kind of spasm from going on so little for so long, and I had to stop myself from cramming all the food in front of me into my mouth at once. Mrs. Ashleigh picked at her food and drank lots of tea and did not make me feel bad for acting gluttonous. The desserts came next: puddings and sweets, and treacle tarts. At some point I stopped myself and gave a relieved sigh.

"Thank you, ma'am."

"Certainly. Now, please tell me, coherently and in full sentences, what you and Cyrus have been doing since you ran out of your offices last week."

It was a challenge, but I rose to it. After I had given her a full summary of our exploits, I couldn't remember a word I'd actually said, but I knew I had acquitted myself well enough.

"So he is out there somewhere without a penny to his name."

"I'm afraid so."

"He sent a message to warn me that Sebastian Nightwine is in London, but actually, I knew that already. He came calling yesterday afternoon."

"Nightwine came here?"

"No, he came down to Sussex. I knew exactly what he was doing. He was showing Cyrus he could get to me if he wanted to."

"He didn't threaten or harm you in any way?"

"We talked for about an hour, that's all. I have always been able to see through his intrigues. The man hasn't changed a hair."

"You mean you know him?"

"Oh, years now. He proposed marriage to me once, but I think it was merely to get at Cyrus. You cannot fathom how deeply the two of them despise each other."

I shook my head in disbelief. It did make sense, however; they had all known each other in China.

"May I ask how Sebastian Nightwine came to propose to you or would that be impertinent of me?"

"I suppose I should tell you about Colin, my late husband," she began. "He was an engineer, mostly concerned with bridges and dams. It's the kind of occupation that will make a fortune in the East. We'd been married five years when he was hired by the government to work in southern China. We bought a house in Canton in the foreign settlement on Shameen Island. It was like a little bit of England; the husbands would go off in the mornings and we wives would pay visits or plan parties or try to stay cool in the unmerciful heat. We were not encouraged to explore the city or encounter the native population, but there was one fellow whom Colin brought home now and again, a Chinese boat captain who carried freight for him on occasion."

"Shi Shi Ji," I said, using Barker's Chinese name. "But I still can't believe you couldn't tell he was European."

"His forehead was shaved up to the crown, a queue hung down his back, and the bottom of his mustache was long and braided. With his dark spectacles, I defy you to have recognized him as a Scotsman, either. He came once a month or so for almost a year, though we rarely spoke. I did not know how well he could speak or understand English, and we really didn't speak until Colin died."

"May I ask how your husband was killed?"

"A rock gave way above an area he was surveying. It was dangerous work. That was why they had called on his expertise."

"I'm sorry," I murmured.

She looked momentarily brittle and tight, but it passed quickly. Underneath that gentle elegance there was a rod of iron.

"That was a long time ago. Cyrus came to the funeral and stood at the outer edge of the party, dressed in a white tunic as is the Chinese custom. Then he started to come by the estate to do little things, or to make improvements. He was monosyllabic and gruff but I came to rely on him. He took over our garden and grounds but he would never step in the house, not for nearly a year."

"Why did you stay in China after your husband died?"

"I did not relish returning home and becoming an object of concern to my family and friends. I did not want their pity. Also, I wanted to see that Colin's work was completed. If I could see that the improvements he had designed actually made a difference to the people there, then he had not died in vain."

"Of course."

"Eventually I began to attend social functions again. I was at a gymkhana with some neighbors when I was introduced to Sebastian. I knew right off he was the kind of man who would use a widow as his own personal bank account until she had not twopence to rub together. However, he was attentive. You cannot possibly understand what it is like to live in social seclusion for a year. It felt good to be noticed by a handsome man and for once to be the object of interest in my community."

"What was Nightwine doing then?" I asked.

"Not much of anything, I believe. He had been stationed in Hong Kong, but had gotten in trouble enough there to move to the mainland. He called one day to see me, and apparently, Cyrus saw him leave."

I sat forward quickly. "What did the Guv do?"

"He burst in the door and started barking at me in voluble Cantonese. My grasp is not good and I only caught every tenth word, but enough to know I didn't like what he said. Who was he to come into my house and make insinuations about my friends? What was he to me but a glorified gardener, after all? I argued back. And you won't guess what he said."

"What?" I demanded. "What did he say?"

"He said, 'Haud yer wiest, woman!' "

We both suddenly smiled. I could imagine this huge, agitated Chinaman telling her to hold her tongue in broad Scots, as if I were there myself.

"Well, of course, he had to come clean about being a Scotsman and then to admit that his interests extended beyond my garden. At the moment, he was in a spot, because he had come to Canton to study Chinese boxing, which is not taught to foreigners, but by the same token, I could not exactly be seen in polite society on the arm of a Chinaman, now could I? Our growing relationship had to remain a secret. Then there was Sebastian, whom once attracted is more difficult to get rid of than blight."

"I see a fight coming on," I commented.

She frowned. "Are you going to tell the story or shall I, Thomas?"

"You tell it in your own way, Mrs. Ashleigh,

but please don't drag it out. It's killing me. I do not think I can stand the suspense."

"One Saturday afternoon Sebastian came calling with flowers and chocolate and, as I suspected, a ring. I don't believe he really wanted to marry me, but there was no other way for him to legally get to my money without it. Once my name was on a document he could systematically drain everything Colin had left me. Sebastian wouldn't be denied his attempt at man's most grand gesture. He went down on one knee in front of me.

" 'Get your foul knee up off that clean floor,' a voice bellowed in the hall. Cyrus stood there in the sleeveless tunic he wore when he worked in the garden.

"Sebastian did not seem that surprised to meet his old adversary in my parlor. That's when I realized that as much as it was about the money I had, it was more about doing Cyrus out of what he wanted.

"The next I knew the two of them were destroying my house in an attempt to defeat each other. They knocked over tables and upset chairs. I tried yelling over the din but it made little difference. Paintings were knocked from walls, pots overturned, and bric-a-brac shattered. An old suit of armor that Colin had purchased in his university days fell to pieces on the marble floor with an appalling din. I stepped outside and asked a neighbor to send for the police.

"The fight ended when they ran out of things to break, and both of them were bloody and disreputable. By that time several sparrows escaped from a broken cage were flying about the room and the only piece of furniture that was not damaged was the grand piano, though they had given it a valiant effort. I gave them both the thorough tongue-lashing they deserved.

"The next I knew, the police entered the room, or rather, the English army officers who guarded our island. They seemed to disapprove of everyone, even me, as if I had engaged them to start a fracas, and began to question us individually. Then a Chinese magistrate in a tasseled hat entered and pointed to Cyrus. He questioned nobody at all but barked an order and a squad of Chinese soldiers entered and took him away. Not to be outdone, the British soldiers promptly took Sebastian in for questioning."

"My word," I exclaimed. "So, what happened then?"

"Sebastian came two days later, showing a scratch on the cheek and a split lip. He had been to his tailor and barber, who had done their best for him. We had a long chat and I told him I was not the fool he evidently thought me to be. I sent him off with a flea in his ear. He was a rascal and a charming one, but a woman who marries a rascal deserves the misery that she gets."

"And Mr. Barker?" I prompted.

"He disappeared for several days. I hired a solicitor and even spoke with a few officials but one cannot circumvent the imperial court system. One morning I received a message and called a palanquin to the magistrate's house in the middle of Canton. Cyrus was seated in the dust, chained to a *cangue*."

"What is a *cangue*?"

"It is a heavy wooden structure built like a door that is locked about a prisoner's neck. He cannot feed himself or sleep or even drink while he is locked in it. Cyrus had been beaten, as well. One eye was enormously swelled and bleeding."

"Didn't they realize he was a British citizen?" I asked.

"Apparently there had been no precedent for a Westerner to break the law while dressed as a Chinaman. The magistrate declared that he was in fact a peasant who just happened to look rather foreign. It allowed them to save face and execute justice swiftly."

"But how could the magistrate rule without a trial with witnesses and barristers?"

"You have to understand Chinese law. Cyrus, declared Chinese, was guilty of breaching the peace. Order was restored and the guilty punished. The English were responsible for punishing foreign prisoners and the Chinese their own. That was the end of it."

"How long was he in the *cangue*?"

"Three days. By the third day, he had passed out completely. It was summer and very hot. He was finally released into my care. I had him carried back to Shameen in a litter. He was bedridden for two weeks, but you know, he has told me he never regretted it. He stopped Sebastian from proposing to me. And I got what I wanted, as well."

"What was that?" I asked.

"We cut off his pigtail and made a Scotsman of him again. It was like a rebirth."

"Did Nightwine finally leave Canton when he realized he couldn't marry you?"

"He took an assignment in Peking and began intriguing there. Sebastian can thrive just about anywhere. He always sinks to the lowest spot and puts down roots. In this case he learned how to bribe the imperial eunuchs within the Forbidden City to get what he wanted."

"Which was?"

"Which was Cyrus's head upon a platter."

"Literally?" I demanded.

"Literally enough. Six months later we received an announcement from Peking ordering Shi Shi Ji to the palace. You recall, he had been declared Chinese, and was therefore under the jurisdiction of the Ching government."

"The Dowager Empress! But that's who gave him Harm. How did that come about?" I demanded. I had been trying to get the story from Barker for two years.

"I'm afraid I cannot tell you," she said. "It is his story to tell. And frankly, it is no story for a woman."

I thought about what she said and retreated from the questions I wanted to ask. Instead, I brought the matter back to the present situation.

"This feud between Mr. Barker and Nightwine isn't all about his brother, then."

"No, it isn't. Every time they meet something happens between them to add tension to the spring, so to speak. It's going to break sooner or later."

"Not sooner or later, ma'am. This time. Mr. Barker said it himself. McClain's death: it's like his brother died all over again. I don't need a gift for prophecy to see that disaster is in the air."

She set her cup down delicately. "You're supposed to reassure me that everything is all right, Thomas, not to rattle my nerves even further."

"I'm sorry," I said.

"Do your best to be there," she said, her eyes boring into mine. "I don't believe you can stop either one of them, but at least be there. At his elbow, if you can. He'll need a friend beside him."

_____Chapter Twenty-one

I t had been a long and eventful day and it was time to go home. Somehow, being away for a while had cemented the house in Newington as home in my mind. I missed its denizens and wanted more than anything to be there, and now, finally, I stood at number 3 Lion Street, Barker's private address, where I had lived for the past two years.

Holding my breath, I turned the doorknob and stepped inside. The hall looked the same. There was the hat stand with its array of sticks waiting to be used, and the standing clock by the stairs. The house smelled of beeswax and lemon oil and the must of old books. Everything was prepared for the return of its owner. My advent was inconsequential. Hard by the entrance, Jacob Maccabee's door opened and he emerged with his sawn-down shotgun pointed in my direction. The first time I'd met him our butler had pointed this same shotgun at me in defense of the house.

"Oh, it's you," he said, lowering the gun. "Thank Hashem."

The man looked shattered. His eyes were hollow and dark and he looked thinner than when I'd seen him last.

"It's good to see you, Jacob," I replied. Then I realized I had called him by his first name. I'd always called him Mac before. It was what Barker called him. When I was sore at him, which was most of the time, I called him Mr. Maccabee. I suppose I had actually been concerned for his welfare.

"Where's the Guv?" he asked.

"He's gone underground. I know he's worked out some plan, but he's keeping it to himself. I was arrested and released, pending my trial for assaulting an officer of the law." I noticed his hands were shaking. "You look as though you've had a hard time of it."

"That dratted Nightwine broke in here with members of the Elephant and Castle gang. They burst in through the back door when I was on my knees polishing the linoleum. There was a half dozen of them at least. They locked me in my room, and kicked me about when they got bored. They stayed for several days, eating everything in the pantry and drinking all the beer. Worst of all, they used a jimmy and broke open the safe. I don't know what they got away with, but they were exultant. I'm sorry I couldn't stop them."

"No one expected you to stop them," I told him. "You're not a bodyguard and things can be replaced. You know the Guv is not sentimental."

"Still, I should have done something."

"Where's Harm?" I asked, suddenly thinking of Barker's dog.

"He's outside guarding the house."

I strode down the hall and opened the back door. Harm came waddling over the bridge, looking neglected, but basically sound. I bent down to wait for him and he brushed up against my hand, a trifle warily.

"Hello, boy," I said, scratching him behind the ears. "Looks like we all survived the ordeal."

The Pekingese sniffed at my laces and wagged his tail absently. He was Barker's dog, but he tolerated me, at least enough to spend half the night on the foot of my bed most of the time. Having finished the inspection of my trouser legs, he went to the front door. He scratched against it and then resting his front paws on the door, looked back over his shoulder at me with his chocolate face and a half-hopeful, half-miserable expression as if to say, "Will you produce him now?"

"I'm sorry, boy," I said. "He's not coming home just yet."

The dog lowered himself again, heaved a snorting sigh, and then made three circles before settling himself in a ball in front of the door.

"He hasn't been eating," Mac said. "He's skin and bone beneath that coat of his."

"No less than you," I pointed out. "You're looking decidedly gaunt, the pair of you."

"Sometimes I forget to eat when it's just me in the house," he admitted.

"You should go home for a day or two, let your mother stuff you with latkes and knishes, and for heaven's sake, get some rest. You've got bags under your eyes as large as gladstones. As for you . . ."

I crossed over and passed my hand along Harm's dark back, which I noticed had lost its sheen.

"Dr. Llewelyn prescribes a pâté of chicken livers, your favorite treat."

The dog looked at me with those bulbous eyes and his ears pricked up. I've often wondered how much of what we said he understood.

"It's, uh, good to have you home, sir," Mac said. He and I had had our differences in the past, but there are times when we must all pull together.

"There's only one 'sir' who lives in this house, Jacob, and he's not here right now."

"This was a rough one," Mac continued behind me. "Having them in the house—"

He was about to go over the edge, I realized, and he would hate himself for it later. I had to say something quickly.

"Mac," I interrupted casually, my back to him. "Press some coffee for me, would you? I haven't had a decent cup since I left."

"You'll have to drink it black, I'm afraid. The cream has curdled."

"No matter," I said. "I prefer it when I am working."

He teetered for a second and I had no idea what to do if he broke down. After a moment he composed himself again.

"Very good. Where would you like me to serve it?"

"Oh, I'll be poking about. And none of that weak, watery stuff, mind. We'll need it stout, the way Etienne makes it."

"Of course."

He went into the kitchen while I crossed to the library. A few of the books had been pulled off the shelves, but otherwise, it had remained untouched. I was gratified to know the one room I considered a sanctuary in this house had not been spoiled by Nightwine's gang. Then I went into the kitchen. It was evident that they had spent most of their time there. Etienne's copper pots were strewn about, food baked in them, much of it burned on. The sink was full of glasses and crockery and the room was in general disarray. It was not like Mac at all to leave a room in such a condition. Normally, he is a dynamo. Occasionally, I have come downstairs in the middle of the night and found him working. It had been a day or two since Night-wine's men had left, yet he had not so much as washed the dishes. What had he been doing all this time—staring into space? Our cook would go on the rampage if we did not try to clean it up.

"What's become of Etienne?" I asked.

"I assume he came to the door, found it bolted, and went off in a huff. You know how temperamental he is."

"Well, I see we have some work to do here," I told him. "Let me continue looking around."

The bed in my room and the other guest rooms on the upper floor had been occupied, and the contents in the lumber room pulled out and examined very closely. Afterward, I mounted the stairs to Barker's aerie afraid of what I would find. I was relieved that Nightwine's men had confined themselves to the lower rooms. Perhaps they had assumed this was an attic.

The parlor beside the front hall contained the safe, a twin of the one in Barker's office, save that it was covered by a painting of Isonomy and his jockey. The painting had been taken off the wall and the safe had several holes drilled in the front plate. It was empty inside, of course. At least they hadn't used dynamite. I don't know how much they got away with, since it was the Guv's private safe.

"We should get the Persian carpets cleaned," Mac said cautiously, setting a cup of coffee in front of me after I had come back into the kitchen. "I know a place that does that, though they don't advertise. Then we need to see about the gardeners."

"Look," I said. "You've been shut up in this place for too long. How would you like to stretch your legs a bit and act as a messenger boy, in a hansom cab, of course?"

"It would be nice to get out," he admitted.

"Of course. Get a bialy or some gelato. Have your hair cut. Take the night off if you wish. Go see your mother and father in Newgate. Do you know where the gardeners' barge is? We'll need them back here in the morning."

"Of course I know where the barge is!" he insisted, still a trifle touchy.

"Good, then," I went on, as if he'd said nothing. "When you return, we'll get this place in shape, so when the Guv comes back everything will be back to normal. I'll help."

"All right," he said.

"I'll watch the house for a while. Frankly, I could use some time alone."

"But you haven't eaten dinner," he protested. "And I must heat the boiler in the bathhouse."

"Believe it or not, Mac," I told him, "I was able to feed myself before I met you and I might even heat a boiler without blowing up the garden."

"I changed the sheets. Someone slept in your bed and moved your books around."

"I hope he left a better-educated man than when he arrived, but I doubt it. Anyway, hop it. Get something to eat."

"There are so many things to do, now that they've gone."

"None of which need to be done tonight," I told him.

He nodded and went into his butler pantry, returning a minute later with his homburg hat and a long coat. "If you're sure, then."

"I'm sure. See you tomorrow."

After he was gone, I took off my jacket and rolled up my sleeves. In spite of what I told him, there was work to be done. In the back of the larder I found some tinned foie gras. Harm was in the kitchen watching me work, so I took down two saucers and some digestive biscuits, and between us, we finished the tin. Afterward, he rolled on his back and slept on the flagstones, waking up from time to time to inspect my progress.

When I was done I thought I deserved a cool bath in the bathhouse. On my way through the garden I stopped and listened to the sounds of night in Barker's potted Eden. Water gurgled, crickets chirped, and somewhere I heard a bullfrog adding a bass note to the melody. It was my first moment of peace since that dreaded telephone call a week earlier.

A half hour later, I returned to the house and went up to my room. Throwing on my nightshirt I climbed between the sheets of my bed. My own bed. It felt so good to be home. It occurred to me that there was a price for my freedom, and the Guv had paid it. He slept rough so I could be in my own bed. He went without, so that I could eat. He lived with a price on his head so I could go free. I was a grown man and shouldn't let someone else pay my debts. It was time to start earning my keep.

I awoke to the sound of Mac moving about in my room the next morning. I pulled the pillow over my eyes just before he threw the curtains open and bathed the chamber in light from the east-facing window. Everything was getting back to normal if he and I had already begun torturing one another.

I put down the pillow slowly and looked at Barker's factotum. Mac had seen a barber yesterday and had purchased a new yarmulke with silver stitching. He wore a new collar and cuffs as well, and though he was still rail thin, he didn't look as ill as he had when I first walked in the door.

"Is Etienne here?" I asked, hoping against hope.

"I'm afraid not," Mac said. "I'll bring up some hot water so you may shave."

"You really needn't bother."

"I'll bring up," he repeated slowly, "some water so you may shave."

"Thank you, Mac."

"Not at all, sir."

I was twenty-two and still entranced with the

process of shaving. The beaver brush and silver mug, the straight razor, and the leather strop all had their allure. The hot towel, the ewer full of steaming water, and the cake of soap whipped to a froth. There is something challenging about starting the day by putting a lethally sharp blade to one's throat.

Downstairs, I started a fire in the stove and made coffee. Most of the food was gone, but there were still eggs. I made an omelette for myself, and though it was rudimentary and not approaching the sublimity of one of Etienne's creations, it still took the edge off my hunger, which was all that concerned me.

I looked forward to going to the British Museum, which, in my opinion, did not even qualify as work. If I had been off that day I'd probably have gone there, anyway. The Reading Room might qualify as my favorite spot in London. It represents to me the height of beauty, comfort, and scholarship all brought together under one beautifully domed roof. Why would anyone want to leave it?

_____Chapter Twenty-two

S hambhala was one of those names I'd heard or read of somewhere in my studies, and one a classics scholar is supposed to know, but to tell the truth, whether the place was actual or literary, I had not the slightest idea. There wasn't a book on the subject in my employer's library. As rough-and-tumble as he was, Cyrus Barker respected the knowledge that could be obtained in books, and his collection, while not especially deep on any one subject, was large enough to attract a bibliophile like myself. So far I had skipped across it like a flat stone on a placid lake. I hadn't realized, up to that moment, how much I had come to rely upon it for information and research, if not for entertainment. Much of it was in foreign tongues and modern novels were scarce, but I was giving myself a second education through the study of Barker's haphazard book-shelf.

Before settling myself in the Reading Room, I often liked to poke about the mummies from Egypt and the Asian relics, basking in the antiquity and the wisdom of ages past, but that day, I simply made my way to the desk which I consider my own, P-16, and fell into the chair. I breathed in the must of books and listened to the echoing murmur of scholarship. The Bodleian may beat it for research, but not for the sheer joy of sitting surrounded by books for which you never have to pay a farthing. I love its perfect gold-leafed dome and its curving recessed bookcases and the blue-green-leather-clad rows of desks radiating out like the spokes of a wheel. Its staff is deferential and knowledgeable and often better dressed than the patrons who can occasionally be rather scruffy and eccentric looking, present company excluded.

"Excuse me," I said to a passing librarian. "Could you help me find something?"

"Certainly, sir," the man replied with formality. "For what, pray, are we looking today?"

"I'm searching for something called Shambhala," I told him.

"Aren't we all? If you'll excuse me, sir, I shall return in a couple of minutes."

I listened to the echoed coughs and conversations, the whisper of pencil on paper and the scrapings of chairs. It never failed to soothe my fraught nerves. It's as if the books absorbed all of the tension.

"Follow me, sir," the librarian murmured at my elbow. I got up and went after him. He moved so silently that I could not help but look down at his shoes. On his feet, he wore a pair of patent-leather opera slippers with thick felt soles attached to the bottom. Perhaps, I told myself, the staff is in its way as eccentric as the patrons. He led me to a large table not far from the front entrance, stacked high with books and notepads. A space had been cleared in front of a brace of chairs save for two small and aged volumes in imminent danger of falling into dust. The librarian donned a pair of white gloves, sat in one of the chairs, and opened the first book carefully as I seated myself beside him. He was fiftyish with gray hair and hooded eyes behind a pair of pince-nez spectacles. He was tall, of medium build, and wholly unremarkable in appearance, a bookish man, even by the standards of the people who inhabited this vast chamber.

"There isn't a great deal written about Shambhala, I'm afraid, at least very little that has been translated from the original Tibetan. Shambhala is a mythical city or country, either in Tibet or the Gobi Desert, or possibly along the ethereal plane."

"Did you just say 'ethereal plane'?" I asked.

"Yes, sir, I'm afraid I did. There is some question whether Shambhala exists on Earth at all. If it does, it is a fabulous city of gold and jewels and a highly enlightened people, a utopia, if you will, and if it does not, it is a place which exists outside of our universe, not unlike heaven, which one can enter at will only after many years of study in Tibetan Buddhism. Does that help you?"

"I have no idea. I was merely told by my employer to research Shambhala."

"Would your employer be the mysterious Mr. Barker for whom everyone is searching?"

"How did you know?"

He gave a wan smile. "I'm afraid the library staff are a group of old women when it comes to gossip. They know most of their customers by name. You, for example, are Mr. Llewelyn, who was recommended to the museum by Lord Glendeening. You like to read poetry."

"I do," I confessed. "But I notice you didn't include yourself in the group."

"Oh, I am not a librarian, Mr. Llewelyn, much as it would please me to be one. I am merely a humble scholar."

"Good heavens," I said, standing quickly. "I do apologize. I thought you were a member of the staff."

"Oh, don't apologize," he said, raising a hand and smiling. "I take it as a high compliment when someone confuses me with the staff here."

"So, you're just a patron, like me?"

"Not precisely. One could say for all intents and purposes that I live here. I'm the first in the door each morning and the last one out of the door at night. In fact, they are kind enough to let me in early most of the time. They don't like their first patron hovering outside."

It turned out that I had disturbed another of the eccentrics that, chameleonlike, had attached himself to the edifice.

"Don't you have an occupation?"

"None save the accumulation of knowledge. I have an ample private income and have nothing or no one in particular to spend it on. And I like to help people like you when I can, in an amateur capacity, of course."

"What is your field of study?"

"Any and everything. I've dipped into most of the books in this library. I do have an interest in esoterica, such as the possibly noncorporeal existence of a land known as Shambhala."

"I thought you seemed well versed in the subject."

"The information that exists is only found in these two old volumes. The first is from *The Relaceo*, by Father Estavio Cacella, a Jesuit missionary in Tibet. The second is from *The Journal of the Royal Asiatic Society* by a Hungarian Orientalist, Alexander Csoma de Koros. Both speak of a fabulous city of the north. De Koros calls it the Buddhist Jerusalem. This city may be found in China or in the north of Tibet."

"So, which is it? Is Shambhala of this world, or the next, in your opinion?"

"In my opinion?" he asked, touching his chest and leaving brown, velvety dust on his waistcoat. "Who cares about what I think?"

"I do. That is, it seems to me to be an educated opinion."

"You honor me. Either that or you are in a hurry. I really dislike giving opinions. What if I am wrong?"

"I don't intend to travel to Tibet this afternoon based upon it, if that's what you mean. Just tell me what you think and why."

He nodded. "That I can do, I suppose. Let us reason together, as Isaiah said. Shambhala cannot be a country of any size, or it would have been found by now. I know Tibet is forbidden to Western visitors and much of it is unexplored or at least uncharted, but something akin to what I've described to you could hardly pass unnoticed. Likewise, a city would require thousands of people living there, and surely travelers will have passed through and left records beyond these few paltry examples before us. The explorer Burton stole into forbidden Mecca, for example, merely to write about it."

"That leaves the so-called ethereal plane," I said.

"That, too, is problematic, at best. A place where people can project their minds or souls, it's beyond our Western understanding. I'm not certain I can fully believe it. As one gets older, one's mind is less vigorous at leaps of faith, as one's body is less vigorous at leaping over puddles."

"So, what are we left with if you eliminate both?" I asked.

"We are left with something lesser. Personally, I like lesser. It's pragmatic, especially given the chance for exaggeration by travelers. What if Shambhala is a monastery high in the Himalayas or perched in the Kunluns, or even in the middle of the Gobi Desert? Monasteries often keep valuables, being considered the safest and most well-fortified buildings. They are also places of deep meditation and some would say of miraculous occurrences. Tibet is littered with such forgotten monasteries, hidden away in high, inaccessible mountain ranges."

"Perhaps," I agreed. "But it doesn't sound nearly as exciting."

"True," he answered, "but it is more exciting than another possibility, that the kingdom of Shambhala was sacked and abandoned centuries ago, and that's why we've heard no more about it, lost to history like the Ten Tribes of Israel."

"I see what you mean. Still, it would be exciting to find."

"I'd prefer to travel to Shambhala in my mind, thank you, though if I went anywhere in the world it would be to Tibet. There is so much there I want to study. But I'm not the sort to go traipsing over far mountain ranges looking for something that may not be there."

"I agree, but it isn't me who wish to go, nor even my employer."

"Who intends to go, then?"

"A certain scoundrel I know."

"Tell me about him."

I hesitated before speaking again. After all, I did not know this man from Adam. While he waited patiently, I deliberated for a full minute before deciding to offer an expurgated version of the tale.

"There is a man in London trying to gather funds for an expedition to Tibet, possibly to Shambhala."

"Aha," he said. "Hold on just a moment."

He stood and made his way soundlessly to the center of the room to the staff desk and returned a few minutes later with an index card in his hand. "A gentleman without a membership has been here recently. He sat over there, as I recall. He requested these two books, as well as asked to study our collection of maps."

"What kind of maps?" I asked.

"Tibet and the Himalayas. Do you believe he is looking to make a fortune by finding Shambhala?"

"He may be. And if he can achieve fame or infamy along the way, I'm sure he thinks so much the better."

"Some of the monasteries in that part of the world are wealthy beyond description, having altarpieces of pure gold, studded with jewels. What army exists to defend Lhasa is small, disorganized, and poorly armed. China is attempting to usurp power but there is also a nationalist movement afoot in Tibet. The country is run by a regent, because the last several Dalai Lamas have been murdered. If Tibet is what he's after, it is a very vulnerable place at the moment."

"What else could he be after?"

"There are some powers on the earth that require a great purity and noble motives, you know, such as Galahad and the Holy Grail. Shambhala is not like that. It can be used for great good, but it can also be usurped for evil purposes, as well. We encounter people in our lives who are mean-spirited or petty, or selfish, but one may go one's entire life without finding someone who has attained pure evil."

"You sound like something of a mystic."

"I don't know that I'd go that far. I read and think a great deal. Sometimes I get an insight or two. I shall certainly be meditating over this situation."

"Sir," I said. "I'm a simple Methodist boy and Barker is as Baptist as Cromwell. I don't know anything about mysticism and Buddhists. Please don't think I mean you any disrespect, because I don't, but you needn't go meditating on my account."

"Of course not," he said, giving me a slight

smile. "You simply came upon me in your path while looking for answers to Shambhala."

"Accidentally," I added.

"If there are such things as accidents. Did you get answers? To your satisfaction, I mean?"

"Answers? I certainly got answers. Whether they are to my satisfaction is a different matter. Do you really think this man will try to get to Shambhala? Would anyone really go to so much trouble for a place that probably doesn't exist?"

"It doesn't matter what I think, Mr. Llewelyn. Your employer mentioned the name and it certainly wasn't random."

"True."

"His opinions are generally sound."

"How would you know that?" I asked. "He doesn't come here."

"Mr. Barker is of interest to a number of people, even without a price on his head. I like to keep track of him, in a loose sort of way, I mean."

"He would be gratified to hear it, I suppose," I told him.

My companion peeled off his gloves, the tips brown and powdery, and dropped them in an ash can.

"I'm sorry," I said to him. "I did not get your name."

"I did not give it. It is Liam Grant."

"Mr. Grant, from time to time our work in the private enquiry trade requires deep study on various subjects. I wonder if you would be interested in helping us. We would pay you, of course."

"Oh, keep your filthy lucre, sir. As I said, I'm an amateur. I'd do it for the research alone. I must admit, it sounds exciting, working for an enquiry agent."

"Yes, I suppose it would. I felt the same when I first took the position. But allow me to take you to lunch sometime."

"The Alpha Inn across the street grills a fine chop. I should know, I've dined and supped there every day since I moved to London. I'm not particular about food."

"Do you live close by?"

"I purchased a flat in Montague Street from a friend. It's small but snug and meets my humble needs. I lead a modest and prescribed life, Mr. Llewelyn. Truth be told, I have not gone farther than Regent's Park since I arrived eight years ago this Whitsuntide. That's the way I prefer it. My body stays put, but my mind travels on diverse planes."

"I shall leave you to your travels then, Mr. Grant. I wish you a bon voyage."

"One day I shall give you a proper tour of this place," he said, gesturing toward his circular universe. "You'll be amazed at what can be found here."

"I look forward to it. Good day, sir."

Outside I stopped, adjusted my bowler against the bright sun, and hailed a cab. I had gone in merely for some information. It wasn't until later that I realized I had chosen the first "watcher" of my career.

Chapter Twenty-three_____

I had just left the British Museum, passing the Alpha Inn where Grant took his meals every day, and I was ruminating about walking sticks. James Smith and Sons was just around the corner, the purveyor of the best walking sticks in England, if not the world. Whenever I was in this part of town I liked to visit. I stepped in the door and spent a few minutes contemplating umbrellas, life preservers, and dagger canes. I picked up a thin wand with a silver head, plain but effective, and was looking at it when someone I recognized strolled in the door with a jangle of the bell above him. It was Terence Poole.

"Are you following me?" I asked.

"You know, I think I might just be. Buying a stick?"

"There's no pulling the wool over your eyes, is there?"

He took it from me and tested it, slapping

the ball of the head into his palm before handing it back with a nod of approval. "Where is your employer?"

"Why does everyone keep asking me that? How have you been?"

"Let's see . . . Since we last met, I had a cozy chat with Commissioner Warren. He gave me some time off to—what's the phrase? Consider my future? Consider whether I like eating, more like. I preferred the old days when Henderson just turned red and bawled at me."

"Why were you following me?"

"I wasn't. I just happened to see you in the British Museum talking with that bookish fellow. Didn't want to interrupt. I've been catching you up very slowly. What was that all about?"

"Research."

"I understand that shark you call a solicitor had you sprung."

"I'm a free man, after an unjust but brief imprisonment, yes."

"Your employer may soon be free, also. Have you heard about Gerald Clayton?"

"No. Has he retracted his testimony?"

"Might as well have. He topped himself yesterday."

"Are you serious?" I exclaimed. "How?"

"Blew his brains out. He left no note behind. Now there's no witness against your guv'nor, though if I know Warren he'll still attempt to prosecute. He doesn't understand the concept of retreat."

"Poor fellow," I said.

"Who? Warren?"

"Clayton, of course."

"Ah, you're barmy. He tried to put both of you in jail. For whatever reasons he killed himself, he's done you and Barker both a favor."

I tried to fathom why he had done it. Barker had given him a logical way to lessen the impact of a scandal. Why hadn't he taken it? Unless, of course, the photograph had truly depicted what it showed, and he could not bear the shame.

"Are you going to the funeral today?" Poole asked.

"Clayton's? That's awfully quick."

"Not Clayton, you yob. Brother McClain. You're a free man now and can attend."

"I didn't know it was today. I've been concentrating on the case. Are you going?"

"Thought I would, yes. Since your governor can't appear there himself, I'd like to take his place. Besides, I'm old enough to have seen Andy in his heyday. They don't make his kind anymore. He knew more about the 'sweet science of bruising' than anyone alive today." He raised an eyebrow in my direction. "Are you going to buy that stick or not?"

"No. I don't feel like buying sticks today. I'll

have to change for the funeral. What time is the service and where will it be held?"

"Christ Church, two p.m."

"I shall meet you there."

After I hailed a hansom, I sat back in the cab and told myself I would never be like Terence Poole. I didn't want to reach the point where I accepted the death of another human being with such blasé detachment. I had spoken to Gerald Clayton only a few days earlier, and now he was a corpse in a mortuary somewhere. He was younger than I, and now all the good things in life—marriage, raising children, struggling to make a name for himself—that was all over for him now.

What had gone wrong? Had he proposed to his cousin and been turned down? He had suggested to us that she was ready enough. Perhaps he had balked at proposing to her. Certainly, in that case, there must have been several eligible women in London willing to marry him for his fortune. He was young and good-looking enough when his prospects were added to his name. Perhaps he grew despondent over his problems, his mood depressed by tumblers of whiskey until, finally, at the point of despair, he had loaded one of his father's pistols and pulled the trigger.

I arrived at Brother Andrew's funeral just in time for the service. My assumption was that few people would take much interest in an ex-boxer and street preacher, but there I would have been utterly mistaken. The service was held in Christ Church, Spitalfields, and was attended by the Lord Mayor as well as several local MPs. Members of the boxing fraternity going back generations were there alongside the poor whom Andrew had helped by the score. Cyrus Barker was sure to be somewhere in the crowd, but knowing that I was being scrutinized, I did not look for him. Besides, wherever he was, he deserved his private grief for a man who had been like a brother to him.

Andrew McClain had yet another mourner: me. I didn't know him as well as I would have liked, but I had come to rely on him. He taught Barker, and Barker taught me, and there was continuity there. Now that continuity was broken and the world was just a little colder. No more would we come to the Mile End Mission for a meal and a sermon. No more would I hear Handy Andy's rough, cheery voice calling me Tommy Boy. I was going to miss him.

To my surprise, Charles Haddon Spurgeon gave the eulogy. I would have thought that since Brother Andrew had not officially broken with the Church of England, an Anglican clergyman would have officiated. Nothing so grand as the Archbishop of Canterbury, mind, but someone with whom he had worked, who knew what he did for the downtrodden of the East End. Andrew scraped the bottom of society's barrel with a heavy ladle. He looked after the lowest tier of London citizens, drunks and former drunks, drug addicts, the maimed and crippled, and the so-called unfortunates. He always had a meal and a blanket and a kind word. He'd listen to your problems and you knew he'd beseech the Lord that night on your behalf.

Where would these people go now? I wondered. *To whom would they turn? Would the soiled doves slip away into the night, convinced the one man on earth who cared for them was gone? With Andrew in heaven, who was left down here to tell of a loving God who cares for even the lowest one?*

Spurgeon was an ugly man. I've heard a wag say he proves Darwin's theories all by himself, with his low brows and long arms, but those of us who know him would not want him any other way. He is Adonis on the inside, and anyway, an attractive, well-dressed minister would have been entirely inappropriate here. He and Brother Andrew were cut from the same bolt, rough, rude men with loud voices and the power of John the Baptist to evangelize.

Coming out of the church afterward, I found the sun too bright, the sky clear and blue as a robin's egg, the city's sparrows chirping by the thousands. The traffic in the street was heavy, dray carts and dog carts and carriages, carrying materials for new buildings, new businesses, new houses. Life was already getting on and so must I. I could not help but think, however, that it was all a bit shabbier and sadder without Andrew in it.

"Come on," Poole said suddenly at my elbow. "I'll let you buy me an ale at the Prospect of Whitby. It's the one good thing about being suspended, drinking in the middle of the day."

We walked the half mile to the old riverside public house where we soon had two ales set in front of us.

"Did you know him well?" I asked Poole as I took a drink of the ale.

"As a boy, I recall my father placing many a wager on the outcome of his fights. That was back when the Fancy was something to be admired. This earth will never see a boxer like him again. He was strong, tenacious, and quick on his feet."

"Do you recall when he suddenly gave it up to be a missionary?"

"Recall it?" he asked. "We thought the world had come to an end. He was in his thirties still, young enough to have some years left in him. You've got your facts confused, however. He quit in protest against the rules of the Marquess of Queensberry. It was later that he found religion."

"How did it come about?"

"I heard at 'H' Division where I was stationed

as a constable that he'd been arrested a few times for drinking and disorderly conduct. My father was upset to hear it, but it didn't surprise us. What do you do after you've conquered a sport all by yourself? Normally, the only way to go is down."

"Was your father an officer, too?"

"Still is. He's been behind the desk at 'C' Division these past twenty years. Anyway, the next we hear, he's been arrested in a gin palace again, only get this, he wasn't drinking. The man had gone temperance. He was protesting the way gin turned good fathers and wage earners into useless sots, forcing wives and mothers to take over all the responsibilities in the home. He vowed to open a mission where it was most needed: not in Africa, or Asia, but right here in London. My father said the man had taken one too many punches to the head. He isn't often wrong, but he was about McClain. Even a Catholic has to admit he's done fine work in Poplar, restored families, redeemed fallen women, and weaned men from the bottle. As an officer, I'll tell you one thing: his stretch of Mile End Road is as crime-free an area as you'll find in the entire East End."

"What will happen to his ministry now that he's gone?"

"Plowed under, I should imagine. His type of ministry, it's all because of the fire of the leader

251

himself. When that's extinguished, Mile End goes back to being just another street. It's up to the executor to say what will become of the mission itself."

"Who's that?" I asked.

"Your guv'nor. The responsibility for McClain's ministry will ultimately fall on his shoulders. Didn't you know?"

"I had no idea, but I suppose it makes sense."

We each took a pull from our glasses.

"What have you been doing?" I asked.

"You mean since very nearly getting sacked? I've been investigating a little on my own."

"Have you learned anything?"

"I know one thing for sure. Mr. Nightwine cannot be held responsible for Lord Clayton's death. My men were with him the entire night, and he never left the Army Navy Club. I've interviewed everyone in Clayton's neighborhood and nobody saw anything unusual that night."

I thought about that for a moment. "Barker's house was broken into by some members of the Elephant and Castle gang."

"Oh, the Elephant Boys, was it? They're a well-organized bunch. Let's not forget the Elephant Girls, as well. Some of the best thieves in London. Are you saying the Elephant Boys might have killed Clayton and made it look like Barker did it?"

"It's possible, isn't it?"

"Anything's possible, I suppose."

"Did you hear anything about this mysterious patron who was supposed to meet McClain the day he died?"

"Nothing confirmed. The people who worked at the mission said Brother Andrew seemed very secretive about whom he was meeting."

"Barker said Andrew was leaving the Church of England."

"That would have been a reason for being secretive, I suppose."

"Hmm," I said. "About how many murders occur in London annually, would you say?"

"There are about eight a year by Scotland Yard's reckoning. Why?"

"There are an awful lot of deaths occurring here. There's the eight at O'Muircheartaigh's, Clayton, McClain, and Clayton's son, Gerald. That's eleven since Nightwine arrived."

"Hold on there," Poole said. "McClain died of natural causes and Gerald Clayton was a suicide."

"You don't think it unusual to have so many deaths in so short a time?"

"I think you should concentrate on what you know to be murder, which is the attack on the Irishman and Clayton's death."

"Neither of which you can lay at Nightwine's door, since he wasn't here, or was being watched by your men."

"Which leaves the Elephant and Castle gang."

"Perhaps Scotland Yard could bring them in for questioning."

"That's what I suggested last week, before I was given the boot, only there's a catch. They've disappeared. Not a one has been seen at the E and C public house since Nightwine arrived."

"I wonder where they've got to."

"No other gang has any information concerning their whereabouts. However, they also haven't tried to annex their territory, which means they know they'll be back."

"I think your efforts would be best placed in trying to track down the Elephant Boys. And the best place to look would be with the Elephant Girls."

Poole finished his drink and wiped his mouth with a serviette. "If my wife, Minnie, finds out about this, I'll be in all sorts of trouble."

Chapter Twenty-four _____

I came out of the Prospect of Whitby feeling that at least now I understood the extent of Nightwine's plan. Walking down Ropemaker's Street, I tried to decide what to do next. Limehouse is a drab district and did nothing to improve my mood. Every building is covered in peeling paint and decay and the streets littered with horse droppings. There are chandleries, shops that cater to the Asian population, with goods from China, Japan, Malay, India, and other exotic places. None of those shops bother to put up a sign, whether in their native language or English, so in Limehouse, one simply walks into a likely looking place and discovers whether it is a shop, a restaurant, or a private dwelling.

One finds places like this in Limehouse from time to time and then can never find them again. I can't tell whether they are for Asian patrons to make them feel at home, or for foreigners like myself, interested in the exoticism they represent. I suppose it doesn't matter as long as someone buys the goods and the owner can go back to his native land a wealthy man, which is the aim of every Chinaman in this country, and mine as well, come to think of it.

These old shops sold lacquered parasols with kanji painted upon them, small scenes of pagodas carved in cork, paper wallets, carved ivory and jade, chopsticks, landscapes painted on silk, and porcelain figurines. Delicate-necked teapots, silk jackets one would be afraid to wear for ripping them, and paintings that make one long for places one will never visit. Asian shops are always stacked to the ceiling and crowding the aisles in the hope that one will break or trod on something and have to purchase it.

One of those I came upon had a few items in a dirty window, or rather, many windows, since no one north of the river could afford plate glass. Something there caught my eye and I walked in, nodding at a dour-looking Chinaman behind the counter. I went straight to the window display and found a box containing over a dozen pair of black spectacles similar to the ones my employer always wore. An idea began to form, and I lifted the box and took it to the counter.

"How much for all?" I asked.

The owner held up two fingers.

"Two pounds?" I demanded. "As much as that? A pound, surely."

"Two poun'."

"One pound fifty, then. The highest I can go."

"Two poun'."

"Two poun', two poun'! Blast you! Let me see how much I've got."

I reached into my pocket, extracted my last pound note and several coins, knowing I had more money tucked away in my back pocket. I counted them on the counter with excruciating slowness.

"Let's see. That's one pound, two shillings, and ten pence. Roughly one sixty-five."

"Two poun'."

"This is getting us nowhere. I'm just going to take all this lovely money from your counter, and carry it down the street to one of your competitors, and see if he feels like turning a profit today. Good day, Mr. Two Poun'.''

I was almost out the door when he made a sound like a rusty hinge.

"Excuse me?" I asked, putting my head back in the shop.

"Hokay," he said, as if it pained him to say it.

I quickly returned before he changed his mind. I learned that trick not from Barker but from my sainted mother. Pennies squeaked before they left her fingers.

I had taken possession of the box when the proprietor looked over my shoulder and apparently didn't care for the customer who had just come in behind me. He shook his head and waved at him with a cloth that lay on the counter. I turned to find out whom a Limehouse shopkeeper would find so disagreeable. As it turned out, he and I were of the same opinion. It was Soho Vic, Barker's messenger boy.

Vic wore a battered and rusty bowler hat, an oversized shirt and waistcoat, an evening coat with tails that had seen better decades, excessively tight trousers, and hobnailed boots. He had a fat cigar clenched between his teeth and he frowned over it, ignoring the shop owner and concentrating on me.

" 'Ello, Fathead."

"Wotcher, Ugly," I responded. One must know how to speak to these fellows.

"Wot's the idea of leaving me out in the cold?" he demanded. "Hain't I given good service? Hain't I been takin' proper care o' the agency?"

"I don't believe you've given Push any reason to complain, but he told me he wanted you out of it. Said you have too many mouths to feed."

"Does he think me too young? I know what o'clock it is," he said angrily. "I've always been quick off the blocks."

"No one said you weren't. He knew how tempting that reward money is, and he didn't want you to have to choose between him and your lads."

"I'd never peach on the Guv," Vic insisted. "Never!"

"Oh, come now, this is me you're talking to. Can you really look me in the eye and tell me you didn't at least come up with several ways to spend the reward money?"

"Never," he insisted, but he grinned around the cigar.

"Yes, well, we cannot all be the specimen of Moral Probity you are."

"The wot?"

"Never mind." I turned to Mr. Two Poun' who was still trying to remove the boy from the shop. "He's with me."

The shopkeeper went back to his stool and sat on it, watching our every move in the event we stole something.

"Did 'e really say that?" Vic asked.

"He did. I imagine he doesn't want the current circumstances to end a good working relationship."

He nodded in thought. I believe he accepted what I was telling him as the unvarnished truth.

"So what you doin' here, then? Pickin' out silk curtains for your boyfriend?"

"Satin for your coffin, more like. You and I, we've got business to discuss."

He pretended to open a door behind him. "Step into my office, then."

"How'd you like to confound Scotland Yard's new sleuth hound, Abberline?" I asked, handing him the box.

He opened it, and the second he did, a big gap-toothed grin broke out on his dirty face, not a pretty sight under normal circumstances. He reached in and pulled out a pair of black-lensed spectacles, not as fancy as Barker's, but similar enough from a distance of ten feet. He tried on a pair, looking at himself in the reflection of the window.

"Look at me!" he crowed. "I'm Cyrus Bloody Barker. 'Come quickly there, lad.' "

"There are over a dozen pair in here," I said, ignoring his imitation, which I had to admit was spot on. "Do you think you can find a similar number of large, burly men in London to wear these around town? They don't have to parade

259

or anything, just simply go about their business."

"I like 'em," he said. "Where'd you find them?"

"Bought them right here."

"Did you ask if they 'ad any more?"

"No," I admitted, "I hadn't thought of that."

"Gentlemen amateurs. No 'ead for business. Oy!" This latter was directed toward the Chinaman at the end of the counter. "You got any more o' these specs?"

Two Poun' shook his head glumly.

"Can you get us more?" I asked. "We'll buy every pair you find."

"Mebbe," he answered with a shrug.

"I'll have my boys strip the East End of every pair of black specs they've got," Vic said. "We'll start one o' them fads. You're nothin' if you ain't a-wearin' dark lenses this year."

"That's the spirit. What's your price? You know Barker will be good for it when this is over and done with."

"Just this. You claim it was me what thought of it."

"Fair enough. I accept."

Soho Vic took the cigar from his mouth and spat into his hand. The liquid was yellowish and viscous, and my gorge rose, but I followed suit, thankful that I had a pocket handkerchief to wipe my hand upon afterward. We shook solemnly as partners.

"Time's money, Bonehead, an' I'm a-wastin' it

standin' here talkin' to you. See you round. If the East End ain't crawlin' wiff Cyrus Barkers by tomorrow, it won't be my fault."

He turned and hurried away with the box under his arm, the tails of his evening jacket fluttering behind him, leaving me to feel as though I had just made a pact with the devil.

As I watched Vic leave the shop, the thought occurred to me that there might be something of interest to the case in Sebastian Nightwine's former lodgings in Chelsea. It was the only place connected to Nightwine that was large enough for the Elephant Gang to hide. The chances were likely he had given up his lease long ago, but it would be worth the effort to at least cross it from the list. I had gone to the British Museum and was left without anything to do until Barker reappeared I decided to improvise, and thereby possibly have something additional to offer when I saw him next. I hailed a cab and asked the driver to take me to Cheyne Row. There I paid him and sauntered casually past Nightwine's old address.

There was no TO LET sign in any of the windows, all of which were covered in heavy drapes. I could not see any light coming from within. I passed by and turned at the end of the street, coming back to the door. Leaning casually against it, I listened for any sound coming from inside. Possibly those were voices I heard, but they could just as easily have been the normal sounds in a settling house. I couldn't decide. Walking to the end of the street a second time I turned to my left and continued on, eventually finding an alley leading to the back of the row of semi-detached villas.

Some houses look very different from the back. Luckily, it was not difficult to spot the white stone of Nightwine's former residence. I made my way to the back gate and lifted the latch. The garden behind the house looked innocent enough. There was a good-sized larch tree, a couple of outbuildings, and a lawn in need of cutting. An empty wine bottle lay in the grass. Was it left here by an inhabitant of the house, or had someone thrown it from the alleyway? Again, there was no way to be certain. The windows in the back appeared to be covered in some kind of dark paper. One pane was not covered and I looked in where I supposed the kitchen to be. There were signs that it was lived in, crates on the floor and dishes in the sink, like the ones left at our house by the Elephant and Castle gang. I was just thinking to check whether the back door was locked when it opened suddenly and half a dozen rough-looking men swarmed out. I went into a defensive posture, but one of them, presumably the leader, pulled a pistol from the waistband of his trousers and pointed it at me. Some might say the modern pistol has rendered the old blood sports obsolete.

"Oo've we got here, then?" the man with the gun asked. He was tall and thin but intelligent looking, in a cunning way. "Looks like an intruder. What's your name?"

"Mr. Intruder," I said. Sometimes I'm too cocky for my own good.

The fellow kicked at my knee with one of his hobnailed boots, which I avoided, but not the blow to my head with the butt of his pistol.

"Take 'im downstairs to the cellar and tie him up."

I half recall being dragged through a corridor and down a flight of steps. There was blood in my eyes and trickling down my collar, but I hoped it looked worse than it actually was. The two men who carried me, a stocky fellow in a sailor's jumper and another with the sleeves of his shirt cut off, thrust me in a chair and methodically tied me to it.

That was as far as it went. They didn't hurt me, and they didn't speak to me, nor did they see to any of my comforts. I was left alone to contemplate what a complete idiot I was. I had marched right here and turned myself over to them.

A very long time later the cellar door opened and Sebastian Nightwine came down.

"Mr. Llewelyn, how nice to see you again," he said, allowing one of his lieutenants to remove his duck-fabric jacket. He slipped out his cuff links and rolled up his sleeves.

"You don't look so well," he said, examining my wound. I shook off his attentions with a toss of my head. "Your spirit is still strong, however, which is the main thing."

I watched as he took a length of rope, tied a knot in one end, and held it in the palm of his hand. It was a tough sailor's hemp and it made a rasping noise as he wrapped it around his knuckles. I watched his underlings wrap his other hand.

"Where is your master, then?" he asked.

"I don't know and I wouldn't tell you if I did."

"Wrong answer," he stated, and as the assembly watched with rapt attention he broke my nose. It was a straight punch just under the eyes, shattering the cartilage. Immediately, a torrent of blood gushed from my nostrils, staining my shirt and waistcoat. A cheer went up from the men surrounding me.

"No idea at all?" Nightwine asked. "I find that hard to believe. Surely you, as his assistant, are privy to all his bolt-holes. You must know somewhere he could be hiding."

Before I could answer, he punched me on the chin, a hook that nearly broke my jaw, hurting as much the mandibles attached to my skull as the chin itself. This was going to be far worse than I had thought, even with a vivid and classically trained imagination.

The third punch brought a welt to my right

cheek, and the fourth opened a cut over my left eyebrow. I lost count after that. The appearance of questioning me was moot; after the second punch I was no longer able to converse, anyway, so there wouldn't have been a way for me to answer him even if I'd wanted to. Nightwine switched to my torso, jabbing his fist into my stomach and ribs time and again. Finally, he drove a punch from his knees straight into my solar plexus. My heart gave a lurch and I passed out.

I awoke later staring into a pool of blood at my feet. I was alone. There was no telling how long I had been unconscious. Both of my eyes were nearly swollen shut, and everything was on fire, my face a solid mask of agony. The gas jets were off and there was very little light coming in from the window behind me. It must be evening already.

I thought it unlikely Nightwine would check on me again until the next day. No one would come to feed me, and they must be certain I was unconscious for the night. The last thing they expected, then, was that I would try to escape.

Slowly, methodically, I began testing the knots, doing my best to work my way out of them. There must be no strong tugging, which would only tighten the ropes further. The roughness chafed and cut my flesh, and I was near to passing out from the pain, but I persisted. I could do this. It was my only chance. The blood when it came greased the rope further. After about forty-five minutes my left hand was free and five minutes later I was out of the chair and hobbling up the stair.

I opened the door at the top, and found the hall deserted. Slipping across to the back door, I let myself out. Sprinting as quickly as I could to the back gate, I had to stop for a full minute in plain sight for my vision to clear. Then I went through the gate and got lost in a network of back alleys. At some point, walking became impossible, and I began to crawl.

It was impossible to raise my head anymore and I was forced to count the paving stones in front of me. Somewhere around number thirty-nine a woman screamed. That was enough, I told myself, and collapsed. Rolling on my back, I contemplated the stars overhead for a moment and I recognized Cassiopeia. After that, I don't remember anything at all.

Chapter Twenty-five _____

De Quincey, in his *Confessions of an English Opium-Eater*, complained of the debilitating aspects of laudanum. The Chinese call it "eating clouds." The mind floats free, full of delusions of wonder and grandeur, and yet one is tethered to the earth by the ignominy of one's digestive tract, which is ruined by the drug. The only way I've found to get over it is to take it as long as the doctor tells you and then to smash the bottle. Never keep laudanum or laudanum-based elixirs in the cupboard; it is a siren singing mischief. *One sip,* it sings. *Just a tiny sip. I'll ease your pain.* Laudanum helps one up over the scraping edge of agony, but sometimes I wonder if it would be better to simply endure the pain.

All my teeth felt loose and the bones in my face ached. My ribs, which had sustained hit after hit from Nightwine, were bandaged so tightly I could barely breathe. My wrists, which had been bloody and numb from being tied behind my back, were swathed in gauze and a sharp pain pulsed up and down my arm.

"Where am I?" I asked to someone hovering nearby. I regretted speaking, for it broke the crust of scabs around my mouth and the gauze stretched painfully across my face.

"The Priory of St. John," a voice said. "It is a private hospital."

I thought for a moment I knew that voice. I turned my head slowly and saw a form standing in the doorway whom I did not recognize. The pain, which came from more parts of my body than I could count at that moment, seized control of me and I cried out.

"It's all right," the man said. "Try to rest."

It was easier to do as he said than to think for myself. I closed my eyes and slept again. Sometime later, who knows how long, Sofia Ilyanova's features came into focus from far off, like a view through the wrong end of a telescope.

"How long have I been here?" I asked.

"Two days," she answered.

"God," I said. I wasn't certain whether I was calling for help or simply uttering an interjection. Probably both. I was staring at a cross on the opposite wall, with Christ's body writhing on it. My laudanum-addled mind wanted to pull the pins and let him down. "What are you doing here?"

"Seeing what my brute of a father has done to you."

"Any word from Mr. Barker?" I asked hopefully.

"None. Perhaps he doesn't know you're here."

"He knows," I answered, though it still hurt to speak. My lungs contracted painfully with each breath. "Wherever he is, he knows."

A pair of cool hands lifted mine and held them. I didn't mind that at all. We sat in companionable silence, and I savored her icy fingers.

"Is he awake?" a man's voice eventually interrupted. A heavily mustached fellow in a dark suit stood by the bed. Was it the same man who had been there before? I wasn't certain. He took my hand away from Sofia, and pressed his thumb against the veins of my wrist. His hands were as dry and callused as he was. The steady throb of blood pumping through my veins told me Thomas Llewelyn had survived yet another scrape. I was awfully short in the tooth to be an old warhorse.

"You've taken a serious beating," he said. "Who did this to you?"

"I did it to myself," I told him, which, as far as I was concerned, was accurate under the circumstances. Delivering myself to Nightwine's gang had been entirely my own fault.

"Oh, I can see we'll have some fun with you. I may have to deputize this young woman to keep you in line." He turned to look at her. "Keep his spirits up, if you can, but don't coddle him. Patients grow insufferable if you coddle them."

"He's insufferable now."

He moved to the door and then turned back again. "He'll live," he pronounced, and departed.

"You do insist on getting yourself in trouble, don't you?" asked Sofia. "You didn't have to march into my father's garden like that, you know."

"I was hunting for the Elephant and Castle gang."

"Well, you certainly found them. I almost feel responsible for what happened to you. He's my father, after all."

"How did you find me?" I asked, wishing I

could remove the bandages that constricted the movement of my face. My hands, however, weren't quite up to doing anything useful yet.

"One of the Elephant Girls saw you being put into a priory vehicle at Charing Cross Hospital."

We sat quietly for a minute or two. I was having trouble concentrating. As I lay there, her face swam in and out before me.

"I'm tiring you. I shall give you your medicine and leave you to rest. Open your mouth like a good boy."

I obeyed. She inserted a spoon of laudanum and I swallowed, grimacing at the taste.

Then she stood and collected her reticule. "I shall be back in the morning."

She leaned over and kissed the top of my head. After she was gone, I could still feel the moist print of her lips.

"Quite a nice young lady," the doctor remarked, coming back into the room. "Ah, and reliable, as well. She got you to take your medicine."

My memories of that afternoon are disjointed. I recall a monk with a long beard and spectacles coming in to change my bandages. The gauze he took away was bloody and stained with discharge. It turned out I was something of a mess. He told me I had three broken ribs, a broken nose, the muscles and ligaments in my jaw were torn, my lip was split, two cut and rope-burned wrists, and most of my face and chest deeply bruised. I blamed it on the spectacles I gave to Soho Vic. If I hadn't been so proud of myself over them, I would not have been foolhardy enough to think I could investigate on my own. Perhaps I had underestimated Sebastian Nightwine. His hatred of my employer was greater than I realized. There was no possibility of my being any use to Cyrus Barker at all in my current condition.

"How did I get here?" I asked the monk through clenched teeth.

"You were brought here from Charing Cross Hospital."

"Why?" I asked. "Who sent for me?"

"That's priory business, I'm afraid. You'd have to ask the Order of St. John."

As I lay in bed and the laudanum wore off, I began to think. If my grasp of history was correct, the Order of St. John was also known as the Knights Hospitaller. They had been formed during the Crusades to recapture the Holy Land. It was beginning to come back to me. The Crusades themselves had been planned in this very building. The Knights Hospitaller were a brother order of the Knights Templar, but later the pope ordered the Templars destroyed because they had grown too powerful and rich. In spite of it, the remnant of the Templars had fused with the Hospitallers later to form one single order. The Masonic order. I had worked it out. It was Pollock Forbes. He was the one who had seen that I was brought here.

I passed a long and fitful night, alternately staring at the ceiling and having strange dreams. Normally, one's day is broken down into minutes and quarter hours, but in hospital, time has no relevance. There were sounds that night that I couldn't identify, probably not unusual for a building as old as this one. A draft came in from the corridor every time someone opened the door. Through the darkness, I could see nothing clearly. Someone seemed to look in now and again, but did not approach the bed so as not to disturb. I slept again, having no idea how much time had passed until I woke. One minute, I was alone, and the next Sofia was there again.

"Good morning," she said quietly.

"What o'clock is it?"

"A little after ten," she responded, resting her elbow on the bed close to my face in an intimate gesture. She wore a three-quarter-sleeve dress and I saw my breath move the short white hairs on her forearm.

"You came again."

"I have. Here, take your medicine."

After I swallowed the bitter dose, she dared lift the bandage on one eye to inspect my face, which had been painted in iodine.

"To tell the truth, I think you are in more danger here than you were in my father's basement. I'm afraid they'll neglect you dreadfully when I'm not here."

"I don't care for hospitals," I admitted. My head still felt fuzzy, but I liked the sound of her voice. I could have listened to it all day.

"Talk to me. Say anything," I asked her.

"What shall I talk about?"

"Tibet. Tell me about Tibet."

"Every couple of years, my father goes to Simla, and then up into the Himalayas with bearers and a Sherpa guide. He took me there last year. There is a village along the Tibet-Nepalese border called Karnali, where my father has marshaled a group of men to form an army. He is treated there almost like a king. He has trained them using all the skills he's acquired as an officer. It is a beautiful place, Thomas. The mountains must be seen to be believed. I should like to take you there someday. Far away from civilization and its artificial laws—"

Gradually, the opium took effect and I began to fall asleep, carried by her quicksilver voice. I dreamed I was in a monastery on the side of a hill. There were dozens of open rooms there and bridges spanning impossible chasms. Was this Shambhala? There were rows of bald monks in saffron-colored robes chanting in meditation, and a tall screen made of gold, studded with jewels as big as a man's fist. I wandered into a library filled to the ceiling with books and scrolls. The architecture seemed ancient and yet more advanced than our own, supporting platforms and structures that appeared insupportable.

And all about us were snowcapped mountains that were purple in the distance. The books on the shelves in front of me were classics which had long been lost to time. There was Shakespeare's *Love's Labour's Won*, the collected works of Pythagorus, the lost manuscripts of the Incan empire. A monk murmured in my ear that Sofia was waiting for me and that I should follow him. She stood in a long robe of white silk that pooled at her feet, at the edge of a precipice. As I reached her side, she pulled her gaze away from the scene before her and regarded me with cool golden eyes and impossibly black lashes.

"Thomas, wake up. Can you hear me?"

I tried to open my eyes, but it was no use. I had no defense against the effects of either laudanum or the tantalizing vision of Shambhala.

Chapter Twenty-six _____

I awoke sometime later to find myself in a strange bed. I was no longer at the St. John's Priory, and by the look of the ornate but impersonal furniture in the room, it appeared that I was in a hotel room. Mystified, I looked about, trying to place where I was and to figure out how

I had been transported there. Had someone told me I was being moved and I'd simply forgotten it in my haze?

"Hello?" I called out weakly, hoping to rouse someone.

Sofia came in then, wearing an elegant white day dress with an apron tied about her waist and holding a large bowl containing a clear, gelatinous substance.

"You're awake," she said.

"Where am I?" I asked.

"You're at the Albemarle Hotel. I was concerned that they were not taking proper care of you, so I had you moved to a residential hotel. I told them I was your sister."

"You're holding me hostage."

"Don't be like that. I'm trying to help you."

"I need a doctor," I protested.

"I'm well trained in tending wounds," she said, trying to assure me. "Far better than the priory with its iodine washes. I would not have moved you unless I was sure I could restore you to health."

She began painting my face with the pungent concoction.

"What are you doing?" I asked.

"I'm using a mixture I've made up. Your bandages are off so the wounds can air for a couple of days. I know what I am about. I've used this before several times. It will minimize the scarring considerably. Your face won't be the worse for my father beating on it, I promise you."

I suppose I am a very private person. Before being ushered in front of someone the caliber of Miss Ilyanova, at least in regard to her beauty, I like to be freshly shaven, my hair trimmed, and wearing one of my better suits. Instead, I lay in a strange bed, my face about to be coated in something that resembled aspic, while a woman I barely knew tended to my wounds.

"I should let someone know where I am."

"Later," she said, raising a glass to my lips. Unfortunately, I knew that odor. It was Thompson's Licorice Elixir. I tried to cough it up, but most of it went down my throat anyway. She dabbed at my mouth with a serviette.

"Get some rest, Thomas. It's really the best medicine for you."

The next day, she told me later, we repeated almost the entire conversation word for word. Mostly I slept around draughts of laudanum. I was concerned that Sofia was dosing me too readily, but I could do nothing. I was as weak as a kitten. There I was, being tenderly looked after and all my needs met, yet at the same time I knew I was a prisoner. My ribs began to ache exceedingly and in my drug-laced delusions I believed I was being eaten by worms. No amount of assurance from Sofia that the medicine was actually working gave me any peace and I was agitated or sedated all day.

On the third day, I finally felt better and she assured me the worst was over. I was able to sit up and we played cards for a time. She had laid out a strip of oilcloth under my limbs to keep the sheets from being soiled from her concoctions. As bad as the cuts looked, they had stopped bleeding and in no way looked as if they were becoming infected. I began to believe I was actually going to recover from this ordeal. Had Cyrus Barker tried to get in contact with me? Had others noticed my absence? Who knew what sort of mischief Nightwine had gotten into during my convalescence?

"I must go," I told Sofia when she brought in breakfast.

"Out of the question," she said. "You still have one more day of treatment with my ointment before you will be properly healed. Anyway, what do you propose to do, hobble about London with broken ribs? I doubt you can even stand."

To prove she was wrong, I insisted upon standing there and then, but in doing so I proved her point better than my own. While I could stand, it would be a day or two before I could walk properly again, and then upon a stout cane. I sat back on the bed, considering my predicament.

"I'd like a mirror, please," I said.

She opened her mouth to protest, but saw the determined look in my eye. Opening a drawer in a chest, she pulled out a hand mirror and gave it to me and I surveyed the damage. There was now a bump on the bridge of my nose and the skin under my eyes was yellow and purple. Thankfully, my teeth survived intact. There were various abrasions and a scratch along the left jaw. It was an unpleasant sight after several days of healing. I gave her back the mirror.

"I fear for your reputation, having a man in your rooms for so long. What must the people in this hotel think of us, closeted here?"

She covered her mouth with a hand, hiding her smile. I was still quite callow then, in spite of all I had encountered in life and as Cyrus Barker's assistant.

"Oh, Thomas," she responded. "This is a residential hotel. I have paid well for whatever opinion they have of us."

"But are you not concerned about your reputation? This is London, after all."

"I am a woman of no reputation. I have not so much as spoken to a woman since I arrived. I shall meet nobody of good society while I am here and would not care to impress them if I did. The rules of the English bourgeoisie are of no concern to me. I can do whatever I like and generally do. You need not leave early on that score."

"Very well," I said, admitting to the truth of what she said. "But I still must go. I need to get back to the office. Who knows what has happened since I was brought here? Barker might be in trouble."

"If he were, pray tell me what you could do in the state you are in? You came very close to death a few days ago. I am stronger than you at the moment and will have my way. One more day and you may go."

"Why am I here?" I countered. "You have not answered that question."

She looked vexed and for a moment did not speak.

"If I had not brought you here, my father would have had you killed. Your death is not something he would leave unfinished. He despises you."

"Yes, I never quite got that. Why does he hate me so?"

"You work for Mr. Barker. You're the one who is the closest to him. I think he may even be jealous of the relationship between you."

"He should have thought of that before he killed the Guv's brother."

"What?" Sofia asked. For once, I had shocked her. "What are you talking about?"

"You hadn't heard, then?" I told her of the events Barker had relayed to me about himself, his brother, and her father during the Taiping Rebellion. She took it all in and thought it over.

"That's just like him," she finally said. "My grandfather had taught him to set aside all feelings of familial bond. He never had brothers or sisters with whom he could experience a relationship. I must admit I have wanted a brother or sister of my own; I covet a family's bonds."

"I have nine brothers and sisters."

"What's that like?" she asked, moving closer to me.

"Oh, no," I said. "I will not be sidetracked so easily. Thank you, Sofia, for saving me from your father while I was in a weakened state, but I really need to go."

"Leaving today would be foolhardy. Give me one more day and I will let you go without an argument. I realize you must be at your master's side, wherever he is, but I seriously doubt you will make it as far as the lobby."

"I still don't like it," I grumbled.

She patted me on the shoulder. "Tomorrow, I promise."

Lock two young people together in a room for a few days and they shall talk about everything under the sun. They'll discuss their hopes and dreams, their concerns, the battles they have faced in life. I had begun to get over my surly mood and relax in her pleasant company, and so, of course, I ruined it. That's the way humans are; we can never leave well enough alone.

"I'm going out for more bandages," she told me after lunch, putting on her hat. "We can wrap your wrists without the danger of the bandage sticking now. Is there anything else I can bring? Chocolates, perhaps?"

"Whatever appeals to you."

"I'll return in half an hour. Don't move about much. You're still unsteady on your feet." She picked up her reticule, and feeling some need of intimacy at our parting, patted me on the hand. Then she left me alone in the hotel room.

When she was gone, instinct took over. There were questions to which I wanted answers, answers which might be found in Sofia's luggage. Now that I was able to move about again, if slowly, I searched the rooms.

Rummaging through the dresser drawers, I marveled at the sheer variety of feminine articles of which I had little knowledge, items that buttoned and hooked and laced, some stiff and some hard, others so thin and silky as to be almost gossamer. Though I was alone in the room, I felt embarrassed searching through Sofia's intimate apparel, but thought it likely she might hide something of importance therein. It proved to be a waste of precious time.

I was in no condition for a strenuous search, but that was what was needed after the drawers revealed little of interest save that Miss Nightwine purchased her foundation garments from expensive places in Paris, as near as I could tell. Like her father, she had excellent taste, and must require a good deal of money to live.

The first thing that made me realize that all was not as it seemed was her parasol. A superficial glance at it revealed nothing out of the ordinary, but as soon as I lifted it I saw the shaft was made of metal and not ash or malacca. Raising it by the middle, I immediately realized that the tip end was heavier than the handle. A sharp tug upon the tip removed it, revealing a thin needle about four inches long. A tiny hole at the bottom showed it for what it was: the tip of a syringe. A bit of fumbling on the shaft opened a hollow compartment, and farther up near the handle was a small catch which, when pulled out, formed a kind of trigger. I put it down again as I had found it and continued my search of the room.

It was under the wardrobe, pushed far to the back, that I found what I was looking for, a thin case tightly squeezed into the small space. I put a pillow on the floor and lay on it in order to work the case from its location, and when I did, was rewarded with the realization that it was locked. True to form, the woman preferred to keep her secrets.

No matter. There were hairpins to hand and I was not unacquainted with picking locks. It took precious moments, and I shall never again believe stories in which the hero uses a hairpin to open a locked door with relative ease, but eventually I got the thing open. Immediately I wished I hadn't. Once it was unlocked, I could not stuff the demons and evils back in fast enough. I sat on the bed pillow and contemplated the array of weapons in front of me.

The case belonged in the Black Museum at Scotland Yard. Exhibit 43, Case of Professional Assassin, Female: one unassembled air rifle; vials and ampoules containing what must surely be poisons; a thin silk rope for climbing and garroting; various small spring-loaded devices for shooting projectiles; and a few weapons I had no clue about whatever.

No wonder Poole hadn't found any evidence of Nightwine killing anyone. His daughter had done it for him. It was she who had delivered the package to O'Muircheartaigh's offices, and met Lord Clayton in the folly on that dark night. Then I found a slip of paper squeezed in between the ampoules and the velvet-lined case. It was folded over, so I opened and read it. It was an address: 821 Mile End Road. Immediately my shoulders sagged and I leaned back. The possibility that she had ended the life, aye, and the ministry of that fine man, and the work he did against all odds in a section of London that needed him desperately, was unspeakable. It was a near fatal wound to my psyche, the only part of me that had not been injured so far, and was until that moment still intact.

She came in then, her arms full of packages. I did not bother to hide or to look like I wasn't searching through her things. I am an investigator, an enquiry agent. It is what I do, what I am, for good or ill. I am innately curious. I could not

283

stop myself, even if it meant finding out things I wish I had never known.

"Oh," she said, putting down her burdens on the bed. She'd brought back some treats for me, for us, but I never found out what they were. She had aplomb, I'll give her that.

She was not shocked or angry and made no pretense to be. Had she been emotional, it would have made her less the consummate professional. In fact, I would have preferred it had she shied something at my head.

"Did you kill Brother Andrew?" I blurted into the deafeningly quiet room. I lifted one of the glass ampoules, which held a green-colored liquid. "Did you jab him in the stomach with one of these?"

"No," she responded. "It's meant for the leg. It was designed to kill someone in a crowd, or someone highly dangerous, which, of course, the Reverend McClain was."

"It must be convenient to be able to turn off one's emotions as if with a gas cock. I'm not certain I could do it."

"You have not had the training I've been subjected to. Are we going to have a row?"

"I'd like to yell at you right now, but I don't think it would do much good. I don't think I could convince you of anything, and I honestly believe the circumstances of your life were not of your own choosing. You are what your father made you."

"But you do want to leave as soon as possible," she said.

"Oh, yes. Whatever this was, it is over."

"Nothing I can say will make you forgive me? I was not aware that the Reverend McClain meant so much to you."

"He was a friend," I said, putting the vial of green liquid back in place in the brown velvet of the case. "More than that, he was a good man."

"I wish," she began, and as she said it I wondered what it was she really wished, what regrets she had or whether she was merely saying what I wanted to hear. "I wish I could only kill men who desperately need killing, instead of disposing of obstacles to my father. I am leaving him, you know. But I'm afraid it's too late for Brother Andrew."

"What is it you really want, Sofia? Why did you bring me here?"

"I wanted to be with someone my own age who wasn't tainted by the world, a nice, normal young man who might help me attain some sort of ordinary life."

"I don't think I am untainted by the world," I stated. "I have my own demons to fight."

"Yes, but you are succeeding. You're resilient. You heal quickly."

"You helped heal me."

"Yes. Now I was hoping you would heal me."

"I'm not sure I can. You need more than I'm

able to give. You might even require an alienist," I pointed out.

"If I find one he would lock me away. I've killed several people. And the worst thing is that I like it. I derive satisfaction in a duty well done, and in besting someone larger and stronger than I. That's what I was thinking when I killed the Reverend McClain. He was heavyweight champion of the world. It was only afterward that I realized he was also a good man. Do you know how many good men I have met in my life? Just the two of you. And you see, I had to kill him, because I was not able to kill you."

I instantly recalled the raised parasol at our first meeting. "You were sent to kill me, but you didn't."

"I had to make up for it by killing the Reverend McClain." She sat on the edge of the bed, folding her hands in her lap. "Isn't it ironic that the very principles that attracted me to you are the very ones that are making you leave?"

I wanted to say something then, but I couldn't think of what, and the moment passed.

"I'm not all bad. Tell me you don't hate me," she said. "That you don't thoroughly despise me for what I've done. I won't ask you to forgive me."

I closed the lid of the case and slid it back under the wardrobe. Then I stood. She looked as fragile as the blown glass in the ampoules I'd been handling, though every bit as deadly. She desperately wanted something from me I was not able to give.

"Thomas?" she choked out, extending a hand.

In spite of everything she had done, I couldn't help but respond to her pain. I ignored the outstretched hand and hugged her to me instead. She did not move at first. In fact, she went rigid for a moment. But then she relaxed and held me in return, resting her head against my chest.

"You're not thinking of turning me in to Scotland Yard, are you?" she asked.

Actually, I was, but unless she came with me willingly I doubted I could do it. At the moment, she was by far the stronger of the two of us.

My mind was still forming a response to the question when the door opened and her father walked in.

_____Chapter Twenty-seven

We jumped apart as he strode toward us. When Sebastian Nightwine reached us he shoved us apart still further, and before I could stop him, slapped his daughter across the face. I was instantly furious and struggled against the hand he pressed against my chest. I may know two dozen ways to attack a man, but with three broken ribs, I could do little to defend her.

Sofia drew a pistol from beneath the mattress and pointed it at her father.

Nightwine looked at her, undaunted by the weapon in her hand. "Don't be stupid, girl," he said. "I don't know what you see in this chap, I really don't. You should have killed him when you had a chance."

"Stop it," she said, her aim never wavering.

"This is quite a love nest you've made between the two of you. It's nice to know in the midst of this crisis you can play house together."

"Get out!" she ordered.

"What are you going to do without me? We both know you'd never make it on your own. There's only one suitable occupation in London for a girl like you."

"You forget I've learned a few skills. I might find my services in need."

"What do you expect to do?" he retorted. "Advertise in *The Times*? 'Situation wanted for professional poisoner and assassin'?"

"Something like that, perhaps. Whatever I do, it is my decision to make."

"It is now. You are sacked. I have no need for your inconsistent services any longer. I have found a more suitable replacement."

"He's welcome to it. No more slaving as your bondservant, seeing to your slightest whim, traveling ahead to make sure that everything is perfect for your arrival. No more killing for you, because someone stands in your way, or must be made an example of, or because they simply irritate you. Thank you, Father. This is the only kindness you have ever shown me."

Taking her parasol from the sofa, she walked cautiously to the door before slipping the pistol into her bag. Without another word, she quitted the room, closing the door behind her. She had left me to handle her father on my own when I could barely even stand. Nightwine pulled a small silver case from his jacket pocket, lit a cigarette, and seated himself on the sofa.

"Mr. Llewelyn, I must congratulate you on giving the Elephant Boys the slip. I gave them a most thorough dressing-down. I do not brook failure, either in my subordinates or in my own children. Now that you're back on your feet again, perhaps you would be willing to take a message to your employer."

"What sort of message?"

"Tell him that I now hold all the cards. I've got Commissioner Warren in my pocket. We've become great friends. Do you know what I did last night? I played baccarat with the Prince of Wales. The Foreign Office is very pleased with my plan and has taken possession of my maps. I'm keeping the more vital ones myself, such as the map of the city of Lhasa. For most of the week, I've been working with Her Majesty's

Army. The Sirmoor Rifles will see us as far as the Tibetan border. I'm to be made brigadier general. One cannot have a common colonel lead an important expedition."

"You're not a common colonel, Nightwine. You're a common criminal. I don't know how you have successfully pulled the wool over so many eyes."

"Careful, Mr. Llewelyn. There are slander laws. As you can see, I did not commit the murders your employer has attempted to lay at my feet. I have an alibi for each one. You have no proof that I've done anything wrong and your own credibility is as lost to you as your employer. Neither Scotland Yard nor any official office of government will believe any of your accusations against me. Meanwhile, Cyrus Barker hides like a rat in a hole. He is of such little account to me, in fact, that I have rescinded my request for protection from Scotland Yard. Barker is defeated. He can no longer touch me."

I eased myself into a chair opposite him and tried to appear as unconcerned as he was. "I should tell you I had a fine chat the other day with a friend of mine at the Foreign Office, detailing your plan to sell Tibet to the highest bidder. He was interested to hear it and promised to pass it on to his associates. Don't be surprised if your reception at the Foreign Office is decidedly frosty the next time you go."

"When I was at the Foreign Office this morning, they handed me a banknote for nine thousand pounds sterling. I wondered why they had decided at the eleventh hour to send along a major to accompany me on the expedition. Now I see I have you to thank for that. It's of little concern, however; I'll have him shot the minute we reach the Tibetan border. A frontier accident, you understand. I'm disappointed in your Foreign Office, I must say. They haven't near the guile the Chinese or Russians have. They are almost as naïve as you."

"What is to keep me from going to Scotland Yard and swearing out a complaint against you?"

"Stupid boy. Don't you know Commissioner Warren would stop your complaint in a heartbeat? More likely you'd be the one to end up in jail. I believe you've already been there once this week. I've seen your record and it is the only proper place for someone like you."

I stopped, thought for a moment, and then chuckled.

"You win, Mr. Nightwine. My hat is off to you. Congratulations on your successful scheme to bilk the British Empire of thousands of pounds. I'm no match for you, I confess it, but Barker will get to you. Neither of us knows where or when he's going to turn up. I only hope I'm there to see you brought low. That is something I'd really like to see. You know, someday, when your bones are rotting in the ground, I'm going to write about these last few weeks. It should make an interesting book."

"You do that. Write your little book. Then step out of your office and look down Whitehall Street where my bones are interred in Westminster Abbey as the Liberator of Tibet."

"Liberator?" I repeated, rising to my feet. "I'm sure that's a word that shall be on every Tibetan's lips."

Summoning as much dignity as I could, I walked from the room where I had been held prisoner. I went down a corridor and a staircase to a lobby, trading curious glances with the desk clerk. Opening the door, I stepped out into a cool April afternoon. I walked, or rather shuffled, to a corner and looked at a street sign attached to a building. Praed Street in Paddington. My ribs ached when I raised an arm to hail a cab in Edgware Road, and crawling into the vehicle was a painful process, but I was finally on my way home.

Leaning back in the cab, I rested my head on the cushion, trying not to think. There had been enough torturing myself over the past several days. No more Sofia hovering over me, no more Thompson's Elixir. I would sleep well in my own bed that night. The last of the laudanum worked its way out of my system and I was lulled to sleep, waking only when we came to a stop in the

New Kent Road. I eased out and strained my ribs again paying the cabman. It was gratifying to shock Jacob Maccabee from his usual decorum. When I walked in the door, his jaw hung open and I thought his eyes would pop out.

"My word, you're a fright!"

"Thank you, Mac. That's reassuring."

"Where have you been?"

"Beaten nearly to death by Sebastian Nightwine and then restored back to health by his daughter in a hotel in Praed Street."

"You're having me on," Mac insisted, arms akimbo.

"I'm not, and don't argue. It hurts to talk."

"Sorry. It just doesn't make sense. Unless you and she "

"Yes?"

"Unless there was an understanding."

"There is no understanding. I've merely been trying to stay alive."

I sat down on the staircase in the hall. I still did not have much stamina. My epidermis might heal over the next month but Nightwine had bruised both muscle and bone. Mac's look of horror didn't assure me that when I healed I would look like my former self. Was this another price to be paid?

"Have you heard that the Metropolitan Police dropped the charges against us?"

"It was in *The Chronicle* this morning. Mr.

Zangwill wrote an article claiming that the reward money on the Guv comes from no recognized source, and if it is true, must have come from the criminal Underworld. I'd like to think that would give some citizens pause."

"Good old Israel. He is a better reporter than he was a teacher. Is everything back to normal here?"

"For the most part. The safe manufacturer has scheduled an appointment to replace the front panel. And I should tell you that Etienne has returned."

"Has he? That's a relief."

"Of a sort, perhaps. He appeared one morning, I think it was Thursday, and went into the kitchen for twenty minutes or so, then came out again and made a telephone call on the set in the alcove. He spoke for about five minutes in French; then hung up and propped open the back door. Suddenly he began throwing everything from the kitchen into the garden: pots, pans, plates, glasses, silverware, crockery, utensils; in short, anything he could lift. Thank heavens the best china and silver is kept in the dining room."

"He left it all for you to clean up?"

"No, an hour later, a wagon arrived with several employees from his restaurant. They brought packing cases full of all new equipment for the kitchen and took away all that had been thrown out. It took two hours, at least, before everything was unpacked to his specifications and the garden in order again. During the entire time, and even after, he didn't say a word about it to me."

"He's a funny old bird, Etienne, isn't he?" I noted.

"If by funny you mean peculiar, then most certainly," Mac replied. "Do you think the Guv will come home soon, then?"

"I hope so." By this time, I was holding on to the banister for support. "I'm exhausted. I need to go to bed. Pretend I'm a badger that has gone into hibernation and don't disturb me. I'll call if I need you."

"But you need a doctor's care," he pointed out, with at least some degree of concern for my welfare.

"No hovering, please. I don't want a face swathed in sticking plasters. I just want to rest. I think I could sleep for a week."

He helped me upstairs to my room. Oh, how I loved those homely four walls. At a turtle's pace I changed into my nightshirt and closed the curtains so that not a beam of sunlight could be seen. Then I crawled into my bed. My own bed: the best phrase in the English language.

Very well, so a week was an exaggeration. I slept until the following day just before noon.

Mac brought a light lunch and I slept again until after dinner. I woke around six o'clock, unable to get the conversation with Nightwine out of my

295

mind. His preening over what a success he had become was too much to bear. He could not possibly triumph after all we had done to stop him. Perhaps he was lying to discourage us. Saying something enough times and to enough people can sometimes cause it to occur. That was Sebastian Nightwine's way. Take away the rank, the suave manner and pleasing looks and what have you got? Merely a confidence man with an unchecked opinion of his own worth.

I climbed out of bed and began to run a brush through my hair. Opening my wardrobe, I chose a suit reserved for when I was not in the office, brown with velvet lapels. I wore a white shirt with a soft collar, and a waistcoat of tan gabardine. I tied my favorite Liberty tie, an Indian paisley of red and gold. Lastly, I donned a pair of Barker-style spectacles that reduced the view of my eyes to a smoky brown haze. It was not mere affectation, but covered the purple bruises under my eyes.

Studying myself in the mirror, I couldn't call myself handsome, but certainly stylish. I should fit in very well among the evening crowd at the Café Royal. It was time to ask Pollock Forbes what the government meant by fraternizing with the likes of Sebastian Nightwine.

Chapter Twenty-eight

I suppose one cannot have everything, although I wouldn't mind trying it sometime. I had long intended to visit the Café Royal during the dinner hour, but not with a face that looked like a summer peach left in the sun for two weeks too long. My cheeks and chin were tinted pink as if growing a new layer of skin. Had I bumped into Mr. Whistler I'm sure he would have asked to paint a rendering of my bruised eyes, *Nocturne in Purple and Puce*. I kept my spectacles on, though they made the dark, elegant room look even darker. People noticed and pointed me out to their neighbors as I passed, but then, that was the point of going there in the evening, to be seen and noticed and especially discussed. Who is that fashionably dressed young man with the roughened face and the dark spectacles? Isn't he that detective fellow mentioned in the *Gazette*?

I finally spotted Forbes in a corner, talking with a tall woman with an ostrich-feather band that quivered as she spoke. He was dressed in the height of nouvelle fashion, with a navy-colored shirt and a white tie tucked into a charcoal-colored waistcoat. I regarded him for a moment, almost afraid to interrupt his evening with important matters. He was a contradiction, Forbes was. On the one hand, he dealt in vital political matters and concerns from the Continent, and on the other, he had to know the latest gossip, what people wore, and who was seen with whom. To him, perhaps, it was all one larger picture and I was too close to the canvas to make it all out.

Finally, unbidden, he caught my eye during one of those casual glances he made across the room every five minutes or so. He raised a brow, but whether it was my presence there, the sight of my injured face, or he was dazzled by my tie, I couldn't be certain. Rather than approach him, I confiscated a table for two when the last patrons left and ordered some café mocha, which is even better than the mocha at the Barbados coffee-house in St. Michael's Alley, and that is saying something. I sat and sipped and waited. Five minutes later, give or take a minute, Forbes deposited his lean frame in the seat across from me.

"Well," he said, at a loss for words for once. "You're here."

"Yes, and before you ask, I don't know where Barker is. Thank you, by the way, for my stay in St. John's Priory. Had I remained in a casual ward in Charing Cross, I'd probably be dead by now."

"You certainly didn't stay long," he said, as a

demitasse full of mocha was set in front of him, unbidden. I'd heard that on a good day he had as many as thirty of them. "I stopped in to see you and discovered you had gone. Really, Thomas, the doctors were only trying to help you get better."

"I was removed from the ward without my knowledge by a woman who tended my wounds."

Pollock Forbes opened his mouth to make some comment, probably at my expense, but closed it again. He was known for his diplomacy, after all.

"Glad that you survived it," he finally said.

"I spoke to Nightwine yesterday," I told him, stirring the cocoa at the bottom of my cup. "He was insufferable. Surely he can be stopped somehow."

"I don't see how. His plan, audacious as it is, is simply too good to pass up. I mean, my God, man, we could practically own the whole of Asia by 1900! That's earth-changing."

"He says they're going to make him a brigadier general."

"It gets worse than that, Thomas. I have it on authority that he's getting a knighthood. That's only the start. Remember, Disraeli became Earl of Beaconsfield when he made Victoria an empress."

"Meanwhile, Barker has a price on his head."

"I've done what I could," Forbes said. "You have no idea the prejudice against your employer at the moment. Military deserter, possible murderer. You know, he's never given a reasonable explanation of how he acquired his wealth in China. There's even a popular concern over his beliefs as a Baptist. It's out of fashion, whereas Nightwine's are more . . . worldly, shall we say?"

"Old-fashioned," I repeated, thinking of Mrs. Ashleigh.

"I beg pardon?"

"Nothing. So, would you say that the conflict between the Guv and Nightwine has become common knowledge?"

Pollock Forbes shook his head like he was a schoolmaster and I a wayward pupil. "No. I'm saying you can walk into any betting establishment in London and find out that not only are there bets that one will destroy the other, either figuratively or literally, but the odds are three to one in Nightwine's favor."

"Is that even possible?" I asked, more to myself than him.

"Of course it is. You can be sure Nightwine has placed a wager on himself to win as well and told his friends to do the same. He's in this to win. Every pound he makes is used to influence someone. The more irons you place in the fire the less chance the flame will go out. Do you know what Barker should be doing? Instead of disappearing, he should be showing his face any and everywhere."

"But he's got a price on his head," I pointed out. "Five hundred pounds."

"Who is stupid enough to go after Cyrus Barker? Would someone pull a gun on him, knowing how good a shot he is? Would someone dare take hold of his sleeve, knowing he'd wake up in hospital, if not the morgue?"

"So, some are betting on Barker, then."

"Aye," he said, reminding me that like the Guv, Forbes was a Scot. "And you can tell his supporters everywhere. Like yourself, they're all wearing colored spectacles."

In spite of my cut lip, I couldn't help but smile and think of a box of spectacles I'd seen in a shop window. I had Soho Vic to thank for that.

"It's become common knowledge, then."

"I wouldn't go that far," he admitted. "It isn't in the newspapers per se, though any news on Barker is quickly exploited. The odds rose significantly in his favor when he was cleared of the charges against Clayton."

"Have you placed any bets yourself? I notice you're not wearing the dark lenses."

"I cannot be seen to take one side over another, if I wish to continue to do my work. If I decided to have a flutter on the side, that's my business."

I looked at him hard. Every Scotsman enjoys a good gamble, or so my father always said. Did Pollock bet where his pocketbook told him to, or did he go for the sentimental favorite?

Another cup arrived. Who knows what number Forbes was on? I could feel my body thrumming with the stimulant.

"Pollock," I heard myself say. "Do you know where the Guv is?"

"You're asking me?" he said, tapping his chest.

"Yes, I am. I need him to know something. Something very important about the case."

"Sorry, old man. I honestly would tell you if I knew. He hasn't confided in me or anyone else that I know about. He could have sailed to the Continent, for all I know, though I doubt it. He doesn't like to leave London for very long."

I drank my cup and looked at him speculatively.

"What?" he finally asked.

"I hold an awfully large piece of this puzzle, one that even Barker doesn't have. If I die, the information would die with me."

"Why not tell me, then? Is it because I wouldn't tell you which way I would bet?"

"Something like that. When we were last here, he told me that while you generally helped him, your interests are mainly for the good of London itself. Or the government, or the empire. I forget precisely how he put it. In other words, he trusts you, but your main concern is not necessarily the welfare of Cyrus Barker and his agency."

Forbes discreetly coughed into his pocket handkerchief and replaced it in his pocket again. "Quite right. Take this Tibet matter. It is so very much in the best interest of the government, I'd be a fool to say we shouldn't do it. It doesn't matter in the larger interests of the country who suggested it or supplied the maps."

I nodded and sipped my coffee again.

"I'll give you some advice," he said. "Free of charge."

"What's that?"

"If Barker is destroyed, killed, I mean, you must run away as fast as you can. Go back to Wales. Farther, if possible. There's the chance that you know too much, you see, that Barker may have confided in you. You might know, for example, where he has some money hidden. It's not just you, either. There's your clerk, your butler, anybody intimately connected to him. Even shopkeepers who trade with him. Nightwine won't stop with his death. He won't rest until the name Barker is used as an example of everything that is wrong with society. He will lie and cast aspersions until you would cut out your own tongue rather than admit that you even knew the man."

"Would you?" I asked. "Would you deny you knew him?"

"You're damned right I would. Believe it or not, I'm trying to do something here that's larger and more important than the reputation of just one man. If you intend to jump on his funeral pyre, there are plenty willing to add more faggots to the flames. London loves a good spectacle."

"That's harsh, but honest, I suppose. And since you've been honest with me, I will tell you.

"If you can get this to Barker, I'd appreciate it. If not, I hope you'll keep it to yourself. Nightwine has a daughter in town, named Sofia Ilyanova. She is responsible for the deaths of the men and women in O'Muircheartaigh's office, Lord Clayton, probably Gerald Clayton, and even Andy McClain, too. By using her, Nightwine was able to establish an alibi for himself each time. However, she despises her father and wants to get away from him."

"Is she the one who kidnapped you from the priory?"

"Yes, she was."

Forbes sat for a moment, blinking. Finally, he stood and motioned me to follow. He led me to the lodge room at the back and ushered me inside. I recalled when he had censured Barker for taking me there, but I supposed a quiet place to talk was more important than standing on ceremony.

"A daughter, eh?" he said, beginning to pace. "Is she married?"

"No. She's the result of a union in his youth with a Russian countess. The mother killed herself. He's taken the girl all over the world. She's an expert at poisons."

"Do you have any idea where she is staying?"

"I know where she was last night."

"You're not involved with her, are you?"

"How could I be?" I countered. "She killed a close friend of mine. Mr. Barker and I are targets number one and two. However, she's had several opportunities to kill me and didn't take them."

"Is she loyal to her father?"

"She held a gun to his head for about five minutes, but didn't pull the trigger. They've parted company, but knowing how duplicitous he is, it could have all been staged for my benefit. Her visit to the office a week earlier to hire Barker may well have been a ruse to kill him."

"I see your difficulty," he said.

I thought that was a bit of an understatement myself. I paid my bill before stepping out into the cool of the evening. The moon was scudding between clouds and a few stars peered out, twinkling remote and unconcerned. In Charing Cross Road, I saw a betting establishment, and though I'd never even thought to enter one before, I walked in. It was nearly deserted at that time of night. On the wall was a chalkboard, giving odds on various games. I crossed to a small window where the bookie sat.

"What are the current odds against Cyrus Barker?" I asked.

"Five to one," he responded.

I reached into my pocket. "Ten pounds in his favor."

"It's your funeral, mate," he said, trading the bill for a slip of paper.

Outside again, I hailed a cab and sat back, feeling discouraged. The advice Forbes had given me kept rattling around in my head. *Get out of town. You're not safe.*

At home again, Mac opened the door and let me in. We barely exchanged words. If anything, he looked more dispirited than I. As I walked down the hall, the telephone set in the alcove jangled. Mac and I shared a look of dread as I picked up the receiver and put it to my ear.

"Barker residence," I said.

There was a crackle at the other end of the line, and then a low voice spoke.

"Good evening, lad."

Suddenly, Mac glued himself to my shoulder and listened in behind me.

"Sir!" I cried. "Sir, how are you? *Where* are you?"

"I'm safe and in good health. Let us leave it at that. I understand you were attacked by Nightwine and have been in hospital yourself."

"He held me hostage briefly, but I managed to escape. I have so much to tell you! Nightwine's being aided by a daughter, Sofia, about my age. She's the one who has been committing all the murders with a parasol containing a hypodermic needle. She came to the offices last week asking for our help, claiming he forced her to kill for him."

"Is she Russian?"

"Yes! Her family name is Ilyanova. How did you know?"

"Nightwine told me once years ago he'd been sent down from Sandhurst for seducing the daughter of a Russian count. When I first heard O'Muircheartaigh's package had been delivered by a young woman, I speculated he had brought along an accomplice."

"She kidnapped me from the hospital while I was drugged, sir, and nursed me back to health. Perhaps she thought you might rescue me."

"You're fortunate to be alive," he said.

"Did you ever get hold of some money? Tell me you haven't been starving yourself."

"I've eaten today, thank you," he said, which wasn't what I had asked. "How is the agency and the house?"

"Mac is here with me, sir. A gang broke into the house and locked him in his room. They stole the cash reserve."

"Hello, sir!" Mac shouted right by my ear.

"Good evening, Jacob. Is Harm well? The intruders have not put him off his food, have they?"

"He's fine, sir," Mac said, unable to resist a curl of his lip. He took no pleasure in being caretaker of his master's dog. Mac had been held hostage, but the Guv seemed more concerned about his prized Pekingese. I felt his weight shift as he crawled off my shoulders and went back to work with a despondent air.

"Where is Nightwine's daughter staying?" Barker asked.

"In Praed Street, sir, at a private hotel called the Albemarle."

"How are you recovering from your injuries?"

"Healing up well enough, sir. Is there anything in particular I should be doing until your return?"

"I'm not going to risk sending you out to be injured further."

"I look worse than I feel," I assured him. "I'll be right as rain in no time."

"I was going to send you looking for Nightwine's maps of Tibet, but you should stay home and convalesce. I won't risk injuring you further."

"I'm fine, sir. When shall you be coming home? Soon?"

"Soon enough, Thomas. The trap is almost prepared and set. Cheerio."

"Trap, sir?" I asked. "What trap?" But he had rung off. In frustration, I pounded the wall in the alcove with my fist before putting the receiver back on the hook.

" 'Stay home and convalesce,' he says. 'I'm nae gang tae risk injurin' ye further, laddie,' he says."

I eased myself down on the first step and rested my injured chin on the palm of my hand. When this case began, I'd have done anything to get out of work. Now he was giving me carte blanche to sit about reading all day, but all I wanted to do was to help bring down Nightwine.

"Blast!" I cried. If our employer had called to reassure us, he had in fact done anything but.

Outside it had begun to rain again, and thunder rumbled overhead. Harm came in from the garden, pushing open the door with his short muzzle. He regarded me with the same remote detachment his master often did.

"What are you looking at?" I demanded.

The dog snorted and waddled off, oblivious to the anxiety in the house.

_____Chapter Twenty-nine

I found Mac in the front hallway with the door open, polishing the knocker and doorknob with another of his homemade solutions. It was good to see him quite his old self again, hale, hearty, and full of his usual energy, particularly since I wanted to talk him into doing something he would be reluctant to do.

"I say, Mac, could I see you for a moment?"

"What do you mean?" he asked suspiciously. "You're looking at me now. You want to talk; then talk."

"Yes, but I want us both seated."

"Seated? Have you ever once seen me seated in this house? This is where I work."

"Just come inside and sit for a few minutes. That blasted doorknob can wait."

"So now you're an expert on doorknobs? All right, I'm coming."

We went into the parlor and sat on the sofa. It was the least-used room in the house and had been decorated by a professional in the latest style. We almost never came in here, and didn't stay for more than a minute or two when we did. Mac sat down warily, as if perching on a satchel full of dynamite.

"Yes?" he asked.

"Do you recall Mr. Barker saying he wanted those maps of Tibet?"

"Of course I do. He said it over the telephone not fifteen minutes ago."

"Nightwine told me yesterday that he had given most of them to the Foreign Office already, but not the important ones, the ones hardest to get."

"What of it?" he asked. He was as skittish as a colt. I'd have to say this just right if I were to convince him.

"I know where they are. They are either in a room where I saw him studying them earlier, or in the club chamber where he sleeps. If I could go in disguised as a servant, I might be able to search for them. Chances are, we're talking about small scrolls, not large ordinance maps. They might even fit up my sleeve."

"You're not in a condition to do much more

than sit right now, Thomas. Remember, you were in hospital all last week. Besides, your arrival was witnessed by several people. I doubt you could go in without being spotted."

"You're probably right. If only someone could go in for me who knew what to do, someone who could make a more convincing waiter than I."

"Oh, that's subtle. Whoever could you mean?"

"The security in that building is very lax," I assured him. "Barker and I strode right through the front door."

"And because of that, it is not going to be so easy now."

"Barker would suggest going through a back door, I suppose," I went on. "He always favors the back-door approach."

"They're not stupid, Thomas. They'll be watching for fellows like me."

"As I recall, you wanted my position before I was hired. This is your opportunity to impress the Guv with your competence if you accomplished this mission."

Mac held up two fingers. "First of all, I do impress him with my competence every day, unlike some people, and secondly, it is not a mission at all. This is one of your harebrained schemes. It won't work, I tell you."

"Are you telling me you can't do this?" I asked. "Look, we'll go over the plan together, I'll listen to every suggestion you have, and if it seems

311

feasible to you, we'll do it. I won't force you into anything, and I'll even go with you."

"You know you can't go into the club, not with a face like that. You'd be recognized in a heartbeat and we'd both be thrown out or arrested."

"Then I'll wait nearby and lurk until you return."

"Couldn't I just go back to polishing doorknobs?" he asked, but it was a halfhearted attempt. Like the trout on the end of a leader, he was hooked.

"There are plenty of doorknobs there, which definitely require your expert touch."

Close to an hour later, we climbed out of a cab near Pall Mall. Mac had changed suits, even gone so far as to remove his yarmulke, and looked every bit a servant of the Army Navy Club. Trying to convince him of that was another matter.

"Suppose he comes in."

"Act like a servant. He won't know you from Adam."

"I don't even know what to look for."

"Maps or anything else that looks relevant. Anything with writing on it. If you can't find anything or seriously believe you're about to get in trouble, just walk out."

"I really can't go to jail again," he said. "It would break my mother's heart."

"Barker and I had a conversation recently, the

312

day we broke into Clayton's house. He said our current situation warranted our not being able to call ourselves enquiry agents anymore, at least not until we can rehabilitate our reputation. I say if Nightwine is the one responsible for making us mere detectives, then we should use every advantage we have at hand against him. There's no reason he should get complacent. I want the blackguard to feel we are breathing down his collar, quite literally, because we will be."

"I will be, you mean," he corrected. "You'll be outside walking about."

"Now you know the sort of work I'm forced to do day in and day out."

"How will I know what room he's in, and if he's there?"

"He's in room six. I called the hotel and asked. It's a marvelous invention for detective work, the telephone set. When you get there, knock. If he answers, say you've got the wrong room. If not, use the skeleton key."

"What if it doesn't work?" he asked, taking it out of his pocket, as if it were a fuse ready to go off at any moment.

"Look, Mac, it's a blank key. It goes in the hole and you jiggle it about. You're an intelligent chap. I'm sure you can figure it out, and if you can't, just leave."

"Just leave?"

"Yes. This is only an attempt. I'm not trying to

get you arrested. Do your best, do what you can, look for the maps, and then get out of there as quickly as possible. I have enough to answer for when the Guv comes home without bailing out his butler."

"I prefer 'factotum,' " he corrected.

"Yes, well, I prefer a clay pipe and a black Apollo at the Barbados, but we'll have to do without at the moment."

"There is no Jewish prayer to beseech heaven for a successful burglary," he said, and crossed the street.

As soon as he was gone, all his arguments fell on my shoulders. What was I thinking, sending a butler to do a detective's work? He was untrained and barely knew a betty from a bulldog pistol and I'd just sent him after the most dangerous criminal in all England. Cyrus Barker would have my guts for garters when he found out, and rightly so. It would have been reckless to do it myself, but sending Mac was irresponsible. Suppose he got hurt or captured or arrested. Suppose Nightwine shot him dead, poor Mac, who, while he might be a bit of a prig, had never actually done anyone any harm.

All right, I told myself, *nothing is going to happen. He'll be fine. At the slightest hint of danger, he can simply walk out. You're giving him the chance to be the enquiry agent he's always wanted to be. If he's successful, you'll give a glowing account to Barker when we see him again. Oh, how I hope he's successful.*

Five nerve-racking minutes later, he appeared at an upper window and gave the thumbs-up signal. The problem was, we hadn't discussed signals. Was he saying he was going into the room now or had already come and gone? Before I had the chance to wave back at him to come back and forget the whole thing, he stepped away from the window and was gone.

I began to pace up and down Pall Mall. The area was originally a grass court for Charles II a few hundred years ago when *paillemaille*, a game similar to golf and croquet, was played here. Back then, the area was nothing but parkland and the only danger was being barked in the shins with a wooden ball.

Ten minutes had passed when Nightwine's cab suddenly pulled up at the door. I stepped back into a shop, out of sight. Surely Mac must be done, I reasoned. Then it occurred to me how thorough he tended to be in all his work. If Nightwine caught him, I couldn't imagine the trouble we'd be in. I stared at the open front door, a black rectangle of space, waiting. Five more minutes creaked slowly by. Then a hand suddenly jostled me and I crouched in defense. It was Mac.

"What did—"

"Get out of here!" he muttered as he flew past.

I looked back the way he had come and saw two

porters from the club chasing after him. I was far too weak to follow. As they passed, I reasoned if he could make the open square of Trafalgar, he'd be lost among the people and pigeons there. It occurred to me that there was a second word to come out of that old game, "pell-mell," to run quickly and with great confusion.

Much more slowly, I made my way to Trafalgar Square. Eventually I passed the two porters returning unsuccessfully from their search. Stepping up to Nelson's Column, I scanned the view and eventually spotted Mac standing in front of the National Gallery. I crossed over to him.

"I thought you were done for sure," I said.

"Stupid idea! What were you thinking?"

"I thought maybe I could make up, you know, for getting captured by Nightwine."

"But you escaped."

"And got beaten and injured, and of no use to anyone. Face it, Mac, I made a hash of it," I admitted. I looked him up and down. "No maps, I take it?"

"No maps. I hunted down below and up in his room. He's got them locked up somewhere, I think."

"Did he walk in on you?"

"I jumped behind a sofa when I heard the door open and waited five minutes while he smoked a cigarette practically in front of me. I was so close I thought he'd hear me breathing. Then he crossed into his bedroom and I sneaked out as quietly as possible."

"It was a disaster from start to finish," I said. "I'm sorry I got you involved in it. It really was a stupid idea."

"Oh, I don't know about that," Jacob Maccabee said. Reaching into his jacket pocket, he handed me a folded slip of paper. I unfolded it. It was a bank draft.

Pay to Mr. Sebastian Nightwine the sum of nine thousand pounds.

They could have heard our cries of joy back at the Army Navy Club.

_____Chapter Thirty

The following morning, I placed this advertisement in the Agony Column of *The Times*:

Found in Pall Mall yesterday evening:
A substantial bank draft.
Name amount and bearer in order
to collect lost item.
Whitehall 042

Looking back on it now, I should have added a line such as "one call per person." The telephone set began to jangle at seven-thirty and didn't stop for hours. Half of the calls were people trying to guess the amount and the bearer. Some thought a pound substantial, while others went as high as ten thousand. The bearers that were proposed included the Prince of Wales, music hall comedian Little Tich, and the Archbishop of Canterbury. The rest of the calls were from reporters wondering what we were about and whether the offer was legitimate or a stunt in order to garner publicity. The agency's name, which Jenkins announced each time he lifted the receiver, was enough to cause every reporter to request an interview. Those intelligent enough to connect the number and the agency beforehand, with the aid of the telephone directory, were thwarted by a locked door. The Barker Enquiry Agency was not open for business.

Finally, about ten that morning, Jenkins called my name and held out the telephone set to me. I'd like to have thought that Sebastian Nightwine was reading *The Times* and saw the advertisement, and then ran about the room searching for his cheque in a blind panic before calling. Some things we will never know.

"Mr. Llewelyn," the voice said. One loses a good deal of nuance when speaking through the device, but I could sense the anger and even danger in it. "I believe you have something that belongs to me."

"Who may I ask is calling?" I said. Were Barker there, I'm certain he would have reminded me not to be jocose with men that have no sense of humor.

"You waste my time at your peril, sir," he warned.

"Very well, Mr. Nightwine," I said. "You have my full attention."

"I want that cheque returned, Mr. Llewelyn. I could have called a stop upon its payment, but it would not look professional asking the Foreign Office for a replacement. Presumably, you have a demand in return. What is it?"

"I'd like you to blanket London today with notices rescinding the five-hundred-pound reward on Barker's head. Oh, and keep the Elephant and Castle Boys busy all day visiting every public house in London to tell them the news. Do that, and you can have your precious note back."

"Done. Where shall we meet?"

"In front of the Albemarle. Bring your daughter, please. I want to be certain she can't sneak up behind me with her lethal parasol."

"Shall we say seven o'clock?"

"Seven it is, then," I said, and hung up the receiver.

To me, being in charge always means getting that feeling in the pit of one's stomach after every decision is made. Some take to it immediately. I never would. Oh, I'd roll the dice on my own life readily enough, I suppose, but with others it is different. One balances the dangers against the consequences, and then realizes one is considering the fate of a human being one actually knows.

There was a point to this. I was responsible for him, and Mac had expressed an interest in accompanying me to the appointment with Nightwine. He had suddenly become fearless. I would give him full credit for finding the cheque, while I could do little more than to take the blame for getting myself captured and escaping again.

Late in the afternoon, Poole entered with a yellow sheet of paper in his hand, its corner ragged from having been ripped from a telegraph pole. He set it down on Barker's desk without a word. Getting up from my own desk, I bent over and scrutinized it. The letters were large and filled the entire sheet:

The £500 reward for Mr. Cyrus Barker
has been rescinded.

"What's this about?" he asked, in his hangdog way, as if he were going to regret the news, but was obliged to ask for it anyway.

I stepped around to Barker's desk, and retrieving the bank draft, set it beside the sheet he had brought in. He immediately grinned.

"I take it Mr. Nightwine has lost this some-how?"

"Just happened to find it in the street," I answered. "Could have happened to anyone."

Poole nodded and the smile sloughed from his face again. He didn't have much to smile about.

"What are you going to do with it?" he asked.

"Give it to him. We have an agreement. He removes the bounty on the Guv's head, and I give him the banknote. He could always stop payment and request another."

"Are you giving this to him in person?"

"Seven o'clock at the Albemarle Hotel."

"I swear Nature must protect her idiots. Shall I accompany you?"

"Best not. You may not represent Scotland Yard's finest in Warren's eyes, but Nightwine won't know that."

"Do you mind if I hang about nearby, then?"

"You may if you like, but I requested Miss Ilyanova's presence."

"Nightwine's daughter?" he asked, as if her identity were common knowledge now.

"Yes. I want her in sight when I hand her father this cheque."

He rested his backside on the edge of Barker's desk, a liberty he never would have taken had the man himself been there, and crossed his arms.

"It won't do you any good, I'm afraid," he said. "I came across some news this morning. Ever heard of a bloke named Psmith, with a *P?*"

"Unfortunately, yes. O'Muircheartaigh's shootist, isn't he?"

"Not anymore. He's employed by Nightwine now. The girl's been out of sight. If I know Nightwine, he'd like to have your head mounted on his wall right now, and Psmith is just the hunter to give it to him."

"He can't have it," I told him. "I'm still very much using it."

"You're sure you don't need my help?"

"If you happened to be in a tall building nearby and saw Psmith setting up a rifle, I wouldn't mind if you stopped him from whatever he was about to do."

"I thought you might. It could get me reinstated, capturing a sharpshooter in the act, so to speak. Warren would appreciate anything that makes the CID look vigilant. So, you're just going to walk up to Nightwine alone and hope for the best, eh?"

"Not alone, precisely. Mac is coming with me."

"Mac?" Poole asked. "You mean your Jewish butler? The fellow that looks like Lord Byron?"

"It was he that found the bank draft, you see. I told him he could come."

His mouth flattened out as he reconsidered. "That's not a bad idea, actually. The more friends you have present, the less chance you'll be carried away in a hand litter."

"Is there a public house in that area you

recommend? As a place to meet with friends beforehand, I mean?"

"Try the Dickens, across from Paddington Station."

"Thanks."

He thought about that a while and then stood up again. "I think I suddenly have a desire to walk around Paddington. Cheerio."

After he was gone I considered what people I knew who were tall enough to stand safely behind. The last thing I wanted was to be shot in the head waiting to return a cheque to a criminal who didn't deserve one. I was minded to start a fire in the grate and watch his gift from the Foreign Office burn.

"I'm going with you, Mr. L, if you don't mind."

Our clerk Jenkins had the most intent expression I'd seen on his face in months.

"You're sure, Jeremy?" I asked. "You'll be missed at the Rising Sun."

"The Sun's loss will have to be the Dickens's gain. If Mac's goin', I can, too. He cares for the house and me the office. We have what you call a working relationship. When the bullets fly, I don't want anyone thinkin' to hisself, 'Where's Jeremy Jenkins, then?' "

"Is there anyone else we should bring along?"

"The runt."

"Runt? You mean Soho Vic? The Guv said he's out of it."

"No slight intended to Mr. B's judgment, sir, but ain't that a decision for Vic himself to decide? I mean, you can't treat him like an adult for years and then send him on his way with a sweet to suck on when things get dangerous. Not in my opinion, anyway."

"Your advice is well taken. Think you can get a message to Vic in time?"

"If he don't have a note in his hand in forty minutes, this ain't the town I grew up in."

As he put on a stovepipe hat and prepared to leave, I spoke up again.

"Could you do me another favor?"

"Sure, Mr. L. What is it?"

"Don't do anything I would do. If this Psmith fellow is out there somewhere, I don't want him thinking you are me."

"Right, then," he said, looking out the door as if deciding whether or not to take an umbrella. He disappeared into Whitehall. Say what you will about number 7 Craig's Court, we really have some of the most extraordinary conversations in all of London.

Jenkins returned without incident, and when Mac arrived, we locked up promptly at five-thirty. As we walked down Whitehall Street, we had to make way for two young men wearing black lenses. Barker still had his supporters, I was glad to see. The three of us stopped into the Rising Sun, where Jenkins spoke privately with his publican. There was no telling what sort of tales he spun there, but the assembly wouldn't hear of us leaving without a pint in our bellies. The way they looked at the three of us, we felt like young knights about to go out and vanquish a dragon. In a way, we were, I suppose. In fact, there was even a beautiful damsel, but I would hardly say she was in distress.

Afterward, we walked to Charing Cross and caught the Metropolitan Underground Railway to Paddington. Vic was waiting for us in front of the Dickens.

"Took yer time gettin' 'ere, din't yer? You tourists new in town?"

"Thanks for coming, Stashu," I said.

Vic took the cigar out of his mouth and spat a string of invectives. He was born Stanislau Sohovic, but anyone pointing out he had immigrant parents was in danger of losing some teeth.

"Let's go inside," I said.

The Dickens was more a very long hallway than a public house. The four of us could barely stand abreast and touch both walls, but the Dickens had a reputation as the longest public house in the city. We ordered standard pub fare: cutlets, roasted potatoes, and mushy peas, washed down with brown ale. Vic was forced to drink ginger beer, which I secretly found gratifying. He did manage, however, to get the first word in.

"Where do you suppose old Push is now, eh?"

he asked. "Reckon he's down in the sewers ready to jump out at any moment."

"No! I say he's brought the *Osprey* up from Sussex," Jenkins said, referring to Barker's steam lorcha. "He could be tied up somewhere along the Thames."

"I thought he might be in Limehouse, got up like a Chinaman," Mac replied. "You know how revered he is there."

I kept my mouth closed, which only made the three of them stop and look at me.

"All right," I admitted. "This morning I had a thought. What if the Guv were right underfoot this entire time? I went down into the basement and looked to see if he'd been there. I didn't find anything, but you know he owns the entire building and there are two empty floors above ours."

We each debated the merits of our case after the food arrived. Had I been alone, I later told myself, I'd have been too nervous to eat. As it was, we wiped our plates with homemade bread and had a second pint. We were well fortified when we left at ten minutes until seven.

"Jenkins," I said, sounding like a rugby team captain. "I want you to circle around north of the railway and come in from the far end. Vic, you come around from the south along Market Street and walk on the far side of the street as you come back."

"Wha' are we doin'?" he argued. "Wha' am I a-lookin' for?"

"You're making sure that I'm not murdered on the street by Nightwine or one of his cronies."

"Oh," he said, speaking around the cigar in his gapped teeth. "Thought we was 'ere to do somethin' important."

We split up and Mac and I continued down Praed Street. Like many streets in London, it is two solid rows of unbroken three-story buildings. Some very obviously formed residences, while others were a hodgepodge of shops, offices, and government buildings. As we walked I looked for open windows or someone standing on the roofs, hidden by chimneys. I probably wouldn't feel the bullet, I thought, not if Psmith was the shootist I thought he was. There was no way to prepare beyond common prayer. I looked over at Mac and found he was muttering under his breath, probably in Hebrew.

The Albemarle was there as I had left it, small, discreet, and elegant-looking, with the doorman in a long green coat and hat matching the trim on the building. As we came closer, he opened the door and Nightwine and Sofia exited, waiting for our arrival. I was nervous, conscious that anything could happen. Was this the way Barker worked, or did he prepare for every contingency? One would think after two years in his employ I would know.

"Mr. Llewelyn!" Nightwine called as we approached. "May we please get this business over with quickly? I have an appointment within the hour with someone far more important than you."

"Good evening, Miss Ilyanova," I said to his daughter, ignoring his remark.

"Look at you, Thomas," she responded in turn. "Your face is healing splendidly."

"Who is this fop?" Nightwine asked, pointing at Mac. "Or should I say, who is this *other* fop?"

"I thought you'd like to meet the man who found your bank draft in Pall Mall," I said.

"Are you associating with thieves these days?" he asked. "Of course you are. You criminals always work together."

I saw Mac's normally sallow cheeks turn red.

"Have you found proof that I withdrew the bounty on your employer's head?"

"I have," I answered.

"Then give me my bloody cheque!"

I pulled it from my pocket, folded in half. He took it, opened it, and visibly sighed.

He'd been actually worried. It was the first human emotion I had ever seen him show.

"Thank you, Mr. Llewelyn. Come, Sofia. We'll be late—"

"Barker!" a voice called out. I remember thinking it was Soho Vic. Immediately, the cry was taken up by another voice. My eye caught the face of a man who was crossing the street in our direction, the young man who had captured me behind Nightwine's house, the head of the Elephant and Castle gang. They had brought reinforcements of their own. Why did it seem so unfair that they should have done so, when we had, as well?

I looked down the street from where Mac and I had just come, and at first saw nothing, even though the call was repeated by others, as well. Then Mac or someone else moved and I saw him, walking down the middle of the street, stepping around vehicles and horses as they passed. He was wearing his familiar long coat and bowler hat. From where I stood, I saw he had grown his mustache again and dared wear his spectacles. I felt as if every person in the street had simultaneously taken a long intake of breath.

Nightwine was the first to let it out again, accompanying it with a curse. He reached into his pocket and retrieved a pistol, an Adams revolver by the look of it, with an octagonal barrel. Sofia laid both hands upon his forearm, not stopping him per se, but counseling him not to start shooting just yet. He looked about to shake her off, not being the kind to brook interference.

As Barker stepped under the light of the closest gas lamp, something caught my eye.

It didn't look right. I'd been worried that the Guv wasn't eating, but he looked well nourished, even immense. Upon closer inspection, it didn't look like the Guv at all, actually. I glanced back in time to see a hand seize Nightwine's shoulder and jerk him around. Not two feet from where I was standing, the doorman slapped a pair of gloves across Nightwine's face, with a dry leather snap. Sofia made a sound in the back of her throat as her father recoiled from the blow.

"Sebastian Nightwine," a deep, rumbling, and very familiar voice said almost in my ear. "In front of these witnesses, I challenge you to a duel."

Chapter Thirty-one _____

Almost immediately we were surrounded by people, some of Barker's allies, some in Nightwine's employ, and other citizens from the hotel or on the street, anxious, as we were, to see how this little contretemps played out. After all, it wasn't every day that one saw a doorman slap a visitor to his hotel.

Cyrus Barker removed his hat, revealing a small, closer-fitting pair of dark spectacles than the ones he was accustomed to wearing. His mustache had begun to grow in. There was too much happening to take in all at once: Barker's sudden appearance; Nightwine's reaction to being struck; the doppelgänger Barker, just about to reach us; Sofia, caught between two adversaries; and a mixed circle of men who, at a single word, might start a riot. That was not even considering the shot which at any minute might snuff out my life like a candle flame.

"You're challenging me?" Nightwine repeated, as if he weren't sure he'd heard correctly. "That means I have the choice of weapon."

"It does," Barker replied. "Tomorrow before dawn. Let us say six o'clock."

"I'll provide the weapons, then. I choose sabers."

"Sabers it is."

Just then I heard the creak of a boot behind me. I turned my head as the false Barker passed by, seemingly unconcerned. I recognized him immediately now, Bully Boy Briggs in an outsized version of Barker's clothes. Gone were his heavy side whiskers, replaced by a dark mustache and black lenses. As he walked, he twirled his metal truncheon in his hands, ready to use it if he were stopped, as unlikely as that was. So exact was the outsized gray-black leather coat to the original, it could only have been made by K and R Krause, Barker's tailors. The last time I had seen him, my employer had fished him out of the Thames after their fight, and had inexplicably given him twenty-five pounds. Was Barker so canny that he had conceived this event so far ahead of time?

I turned my gaze back upon Sofia, wanting to see her reaction, if any, to Barker's larger twin, but found I couldn't. In the confusion, she had vanished, leaving an empty space at her father's side. Nightwine still stared at Barker speculatively, as if trying to work out what trick he was trying to perform by giving away the choice of weapons. If it did prove to be some sort of trick, he could find no flaw in it.

Nightwine looked about, realizing his daughter was missing. Things had not gone as planned, yet he still believed he had the upper hand. He cleared his throat and addressed his old enemy again.

"Good, then," he responded. "I shall see you tomorrow. Where shall we meet?"

"The southwest corner of Hampstead Heath."

"I'll be there." He turned to one of his men standing at the curb. "Someone stop that vehicle."

One of the gang members ran out into Praed Street and stopped a passing cab, startling the horse. Nightwine strode out to the cab and climbed aboard. It bowled off, leaving his subordinates to beat a disorganized retreat.

"Good evening, Thomas," Barker said. He looked at Mac, Jenkins, and Soho Vic, who had gathered closer now that Nightwine's men were gone. "Gentlemen, it is good to see you all here together."

He shook each of our hands in turn, exchanging

a greeting with us all. Unbuttoning the long, green coat, he stepped inside an alcove just inside the entrance, and exchanged it and the doorman's hat for his own more familiar coat and bowler. I looked over and saw that Soho Vic was giving us all a gap-toothed grin. Mac had one as well, and even Jenkins looked pleased with himself.

"Is this a private party?" a voice called from across the street. Out of the shadows came the lean, laconic figure of Terence Poole. "Or can anyone join in?"

Barker went forward and grasped his hand. Then he turned and started walking fast, leaving us to follow him as a group.

"Did you find Mr. Psmith?" I asked, catching up with Poole.

"He found me, actually. He was quite put out to learn that the roof he had chosen to shoot you from already had someone occupying it."

"Seems a shame to spoil a chap's plans."

"My thoughts exactly."

Ahead, Barker was having a discussion with Soho Vic, while behind, Mac and Jenkins compared notes. It was time to have the Persian carpets cleaned and perhaps a new painting for the outer office. We followed as Barker turned onto Edgware Road, intent upon some unknown destination, but with a brief wave in our direction, Vic kept heading east. He had mouths to feed and a ragtag army of street urchins to bed down for the night.

I'd have preferred a cab, but Barker seemed determined to enjoy the night that was settling like a deep blue mantle over London. The North Star was the first to shine overhead, while a sluggish moon hung on the horizon, trying to decide whether it was worth the effort to rise that evening. Barker turned onto Oxford Street, in the direction of Charing Cross and our chambers.

"Did you see Barker slap Nightwine in the face?" I asked Poole.

"No! Did he? Blast, I missed that. Saw the big fellow dressed as Barker, though. Who was that?"

"Briggs."

"Jim Briggs? Last I heard, he couldn't decide whether he was a bodyguard or a strong-arm man. I'd rather have him working for Barker than the other side. His wife's sick, I heard, and he's got two little ones to feed."

"I only met him once," I said. I didn't explain the circumstances. I wasn't sure where to begin.

Barker had ducked into Dean Street. I had given up trying to decide where the man was going, but though I was still worn from my injuries, it was a good night for a walk in the finest city in all Christendom. All of us walked with our hands in our pockets save for the Guv, who had his folded behind him. Then I noticed him reach into his pocket and extract a key. Stepping into

Shaftesbury Avenue, he unlocked the door to the empty building Barker intended to eventually turn into a school of arms. The front room was empty, but in a back room I found a small bedstead, and a shelf containing potted meat, tinned peaches, and half a loaf of bread. I had finally solved the mystery of where he had been the last six days.

I had been present when he let the property, but now I saw he had made one improvement on it. He had added a telephone set. He now seized the instrument and gave the operator a number in Belgravia.

"Abraham," he said when the call had been put through. "This is Cyrus Barker. I regret the lateness of the hour, but I need a simple document drafted tonight. I shall compensate you for the conditions, of course. Are you able to come? Excellent. Meet me in Newington in an hour. I'll see you then."

He hung up. *Abraham,* I wondered, and then it hit me. He was talking to his solicitor, Bram Cusp, of course. It occurred to me that the only possible document the Guv required on such short notice would be a last will and testament.

Mac was incensed, but not because of the telephone call. He stood by the bed lifting the tins one by one.

"He's been sleeping in this hovel, eating food from tins?" he demanded.

"What have you been doing with yourself, sir?" I asked our employer.

"I have been training. I knew Sebastian would choose the saber, a weapon he excels at. Therefore, I hired the best instructor in London, Captain Alfred Hutton, to train me almost continuously in the art over the past week. I rely on the fact that Nightwine has probably not picked up a blade since he left his regiment, and may be out of practice. It is a slender advantage, I'm sure, but it is the best I could find. Right now, if I know him, he is raging about London looking for a good pair of dueling swords and someone with whom to practice."

"I would pay to see that," I said.

"Jeremy, do you need to see your father?" my employer asked suddenly, turning to our clerk.

"He'd understand, sir, if you require my services further."

"I think we are through for the night. Will you give him my regards?"

"I shall, Mr. B. He particularly likes to be remembered by you. I'll be on me way then. Good night, gentlemen!"

I thought to myself that he was winnowing us, one by one.

"I should be heading on, as well," Poole said, "unless you need something. Anything at all."

"Nothing, thank you, Terry. Give my best to Minerva."

336

"I shall."

They shook hands, but paused in the middle. The two were saying good-bye, in case Barker did not return from the duel. How does one compress six years of friendship into one brief handshake?

"Minerva?" I asked when he was gone.

"His wife."

"He's married?"

Barker shook his head. "Sometimes I despair of you, lad. You've spoken to him a hundred times and never learned a thing about him?"

"Sorry, sir," I said. He could crush so easily with a single word.

"Have you heard that Gerald Clayton is dead?"

"Aye, I have."

"I don't understand," I said. "He was on his way to propose. Now, suddenly, he has committed suicide? What happened? Did she turn him down? Did he turn to drink again and blow out his brains? I thought you had convinced him after your talk."

"I would not care to speculate without facts," Barker said.

"Oh, come now, just once! You're not in a court of law. I won't hold you responsible if your conclusions are not fully correct."

"It is a bad habit, nevertheless."

"It's not a habit if it happens one time."

"Look, we have not spoken to the girl, but I

think it highly unlikely he ever had the opportunity to see his cousin. We know for certain that he recanted his testimony that morning, so that I was freed. The next we know, he is dead. Knowing Nightwine, he could not allow such an act of mutiny on Clayton's part. It made him appear weak."

"So he killed Clayton and made it look like suicide?"

"Just think. He purchased that photograph. It proved of no use as a threat. The only way for it to be of any practical use to Nightwine was as seeming proof that Clayton had killed himself in remorse over some veiled but unspecified deed. To those who know no better it besmirches Clayton's name forever. To those who understand what Nightwine is capable of, it sends a message as to what will happen to anyone who thwarts him."

"I find it hard to believe anyone could be that ruthless."

"Ah, but you see, you were raised by parents who taught you right from wrong. Imagine having a father who taught you from the cradle that any thought for anyone's interests but your own was reprehensible and deserving of punishment. It isn't merely that he is a member of the aristocracy, although that is part of it. He was raised to be the new Adam of a post-Christian society.

"Let us lock up and go home to Newington,"

Barker went on. "I expect a full report before Mr. Cusp arrives."

I stepped out the door and flagged a hansom, and we went home in relative silence. Barker was remote, no doubt preoccupied with what was about to happen in the morning. Mac looked unsure whether to speak to him or not. As for me, I was whipping myself with the theory that something I had said or done had precipitated the duel. As usual, I saw through a glass darkly. I had done my best, and would learn presently whether anything I had attempted had made even the slightest difference. It was a long and silent ride back to the Surrey side of town.

Back at home, Mac hurried around turning up the gas lamps while I stood about the hall feeling useless. The only happy one among us was Harm, whom the Guv tucked under his arm like a large black book, narrowly avoiding being bathed by the dog's tongue. He stood there like a stone statue, while the dog's plumed tail made circles in the air behind him.

"Let's go into the kitchen," he said, and I followed him inside. Putting the dog down, he took up the kettle to get water while I prepared and lit the stove. When I had a flame going, he set the kettle on it, then turned around one of the chairs at the deal table and straddled it.

"Well?" he asked.

"You want to know everything that happened

since you sent me to the Foreign Office to get arrested, don't you?"

"Precisely. And I do mean precisely."

Soon, the kettle began to sing. Barker got up, opened a caddy of his green tea and measured the leaves into cups before pouring in the water. I preferred mine strained, but just then I'd choke on them rather than complain. He returned with the cups and took his seat again.

Over tea, I told him about my arrest and interrogation at Scotland Yard; my return to the office; the arrival of Sofia and, later, Mrs. Ashleigh; returning home to find Mac shattered; the visit to the British Museum; being captured and escaping; waking up in hospital; waking up in Sofia's rooms; discovering she was the murderer; walking out and going home; and coming up with the scheme which against all odds actually worked. That took about half an hour, at the end of which, Barker stood up and went through the dining room into the parlor to look at the safe. He removed the painting, set it on the floor, then turned the tumbler and reached in.

"It's empty, sir," I said.

"Is it?" he rumbled, moving his hand about inside. There was a sliding sound and he began pulling out packets of notes. "There is a hidden compartment. My valuables are behind a false wall. There was not more than fifty pounds for them to find."

"I'm glad, sir, but still. Fifty pounds! To think of that much money in the hands of the Elephant Boys makes my blood boil."

"No matter. I shall carve it out of their hides eventually. That was clever, by the way, to think of his former residence. I confess I discounted it."

"If only I hadn't been so stupid as to get caught." I felt keenly that I had done something to disappoint my employer, not to mention jeopardize the case.

"Could you tell the house was inhabited from the back gate?"

"No, sir. It did not appear to be."

"Then you've done nothing to flog yourself over."

"Was I wrong to meet Nightwine tonight and return the draft?"

"No. In fact, it gave me the opportunity to offer him the challenge I've been preparing."

"What about the entry into Nightwine's rooms?"

"That is something I want to talk to you about. Mac is not a professional, and could have been arrested. That note belonged to Nightwine. He actually earned it, much as it grieves me to say it, and you had no right to take it from him."

The tea had not been strained but I certainly was, as through a sieve. The Guv said it with his usual finality, but for once I wasn't going to take it meekly.

"I would offer a defense," I said, aware of the tightness in my own voice.

He gave a ghost of a smile, but squelched it. "Proceed."

"You weren't here—"

"Bad beginning," he interrupted.

"No, hear me out. You weren't here to see the condition Mac was in after they'd terrorized him for days. I promise you if something hadn't been done to help him achieve some sort of respect for himself he'd never be the same man again. The reason Mac is not a private enquiry agent is because you gave the position to me and I have felt his resentment ever since. You said you wished you had the maps, and I was in no condition to get them, and so I sent Mac."

"But you did not take the maps," he pointed out. "You took the bank draft."

"That was Mac's doing, but I would have done the same were I there. He couldn't find the maps, but refused to leave empty-handed. He was resourceful, and if I may say so, I've never seen a man so happy to be chased by porters."

Barker shook his head. "It was theft, lad, pure and simple."

"But taking the maps would not have been? This is the world of low detective work, sir. Perhaps someday when this case is over, we can see about deserving to call ourselves private enquiry agents again."

He finished his tea and scratched under his chin in thought. "Unfortunately, I can find no flaw in your logic."

I tried not to smile myself. Had I actually carried the day? He pointed a stubby finger at me and I stifled it immediately. Suddenly, I saw a gleam behind his spectacles that I only noted when he was surprised and his eyes opened wide. What now? I wondered.

"Tobacco!" he cried, and immediately he rushed up two flights of stairs to his aerie. It had been nearly two weeks since he had himself a smoke. I followed at a more subdued pace. Barker was seated in one of his armchairs, holding a large calabash pipe stuffed full of his own tobacco, blended for him in Mincing Lane: toasted Cavendish with perique for taste and a soupçon of latakia for bite. He struck a match and surrounded himself with a halo of smoke. Then his newly grown mustache spread out in a look of pure satisfaction. He smoked silently for about ten minutes, with Harm dozing in his lap, until there was a knock upon the thistle knocker of our front door.

"That will be Abraham," my employer said. "Go to bed, Thomas. Get some sleep. You'll need your wits about you in the morning."

Chapter Thirty-two _____

It was all too soon when Jacob Maccabee was poking about in my room and preparing to open the curtains. When he did, however, it was still as black as Barker's spectacles outside.

"What o'clock is it?" I moaned.

"Four-thirty. You know the two of you must be there at six."

"Mmmph," I said.

I got up, threw water in my face, and decided it was still too damaged to shave. Instead, I dressed and tried to batter the short curls that were already sprouting with a pair of handleless brushes the Guv had given me for Hogmanay. In the hallway, I was turning onto the stair when the aroma of fresh coffee assailed my nostrils. I took the stairs two at a time and burst into the kitchen.

"Etienne!" I cried.

"Toast," he muttered back at me.

"I beg your pardon?"

He took the short cigarette out of his mouth and spat on the flagstone. "The man goes to 'eez death and all he wants is toast and tea."

"Perhaps his stomach is unsettled."

"He has no stomach. Just a block of granite. I don't know why I bother. He would eat bangers and mash for a month entire."

"I could eat something," I said.

"But you do not go to your death."

"Actually, I thought about that in the middle of the night. If Barker dies, it would be two against one They have no reason to leave a living witness behind to identify them."

Dummolard snorted as if the thought of my death were rather droll, like something out of a Zola novel.

"Very well. What will you have?"

"Have you got truffles?"

"*Un petit peu.*"

"And bacon?"

"You would put truffles and the truffle-finder together in the same dish?"

"The pig is beyond caring. A condemned man's last wish?"

"Spare me the sentiment. Next you will be crying into my omelette." He turned and took down a copper pot from the wirework overhead.

Outside, Barker was in shirtsleeves conferring with the gardeners, who were repairing the damage that had been done during his absence. Some of his rare penjing trees had gone without water and were in danger of dying. The gardeners had paper lanterns on tall poles, but even then there was a line of silvery-pink on the eastern horizon. The sun would soon be coming up. What would the day bring?

First things first, I told myself, pouring coffee. Etienne understands coffee like no one else in England. His press is even better than the one at the Barbados, my favorite coffeehouse in St. Michael's Alley. It awakened one as fast as a bucket of cold water, without the ill effects.

After my omelette, which I ate slowly because Etienne considers eating quickly the grossest of insults, I went outside to see Barker. He actually went so far as to put a hand on my shoulder.

"The oldest penjing may live," he said. "We had to prune it back drastically, and we lost two others, but this one and five more shall live."

"I'm glad to hear it, sir. Perhaps you can start with a cutting from Kew Gardens or something."

"I thought that myself, lad. Are you nearly ready?"

"Just need to get my hat and coat, sir."

"Would you stop for a moment in my room?"

"Of course."

I followed him up two flights of stairs to his garret room. The dawn was just lighting up the red walls. Barker sat down at his desk, which was covered with various envelopes; ominous-looking envelopes.

"Oh, no, sir," I muttered.

"Better safe than sorry. My life is in God's hands now. Here is my will, the deeds of the

346

house and office, my bank statements. Everything that is necessary in the event of my demise."

"You're not going to die, sir. You're going to live. I insist upon it."

"I'm gambling, lad. He is still twice the swordsman I am. He can triumph yet. You do realize in the event that I die, they might—"

"Yes, I realize that, sir," I interrupted.

"Do you wish to write a will? Mac and I shall witness it."

"Sir, I own nothing. A shelf of books worth a few pounds that Jacob is welcome to."

"Don't you want to leave a message to someone? Anyone?"

"Who really cares, sir? My family is shed of me. I really am all alone in the world now. It's probably best."

"Let us try to keep you alive, anyway, lad, if only for Philippa's sake. She's awfully fond of you, you know."

"Glad to hear somebody is, sir."

"Let's go, then."

" 'Into the valley of Death rode the six hundred.' "

"Will I have to listen to you recite poetry all the way to Hampstead Heath?"

"No. Sorry."

"Who was that, Browning?"

"It was Tennyson."

"Still living?"

"Yes, sir."

"Mmmph."

Barker believes that all poets should have the decency to be dead at least a century or two. I feel the same way about politicians.

We walked to the stable a half mile away, past a milkman with his tall pails. I had the feeling I sometimes get from a fever that I was unconnected with reality. I could end up that day as dead as the Reverend McClain, yet somehow it didn't bother me. More correctly, it didn't interest me. It all seemed vaguely academic.

I thought of my late wife, Jenny, who had died while I was in prison. Would she be waiting for me when I got to heaven? Would I even go there if I died? I had certainly had it in for God after she passed away. It probably wasn't wise to get angry with the creator of heaven and earth. One would be certain to be in his hand sooner or later. I was still angry with him, but I realized now that everything wasn't his fault. I'd made choices and mistakes of my own. Not everything he had given me had been dross or else I wouldn't be so afraid of losing it. So far, I'd call it a draw, which is worlds better than I'd been two years before.

It is a long drive from Newington to Hampstead Heath, such a drive, in fact, that I scarce have been there five times in my entire life. It looks prosaic enough during the day with its hills

348

covered with East End families eating packed lunches and larking about.

In the early morning, however, it appears antediluvian; its furze-covered juttings grasping at tendrils of fog and land covered in scores of wet, glistening species of plants like the tops of a South American tepui. One would hardly believe that man had set foot there, which made it the perfect place for two implacable men to attempt to hack each other to death with good Sheffield steel at six o'clock in the morning.

They were awaiting us under a tree that cut the moving fog like the bow of a ship. From a distance I could see the carriage and Nightwine off to the side in a white shirt, hacking at the fog with his sword. It would not do to appear either too eager or too afraid, so I brought Juno up to him with a steady pace. Psmith suddenly detached himself from a tree he had been leaning against.

"You've arrived, then," Nightwine commented as we alighted from our vehicle. In his white shirt, tan trousers, and knee boots, he looked every bit the military man he was.

"Was there any doubt?" Barker asked as his booted feet landed on the wet grass.

"None, I suppose. You can be relied upon to do the predictable thing."

"It is my duty to stop you from plundering Tibet. They have enough troubles as it is. Not a single Dalai Lama has reached the age of twenty in the past fifty years."

"All the more reason to take them under our protection if they cannot run their own affairs. But we haven't come here to discuss politics. Psmith!"

Psmith stepped forward without a word, and I could see he was wearing a light gray suit almost the color of the mist. He opened an ancient sword case, lined in tattered jade velvet, containing French sabers of surpassing beauty. Barker must have noticed it, too, but he stood before the sword case, ignoring the weapons, and looking beyond them.

"Hello, Mr. Psmith," he said, extending his hand. Neither of them moved until it began to become ridiculous. Psmith finally glanced over at the top of the case and that seemed to settle matters. He closed the lid with ill grace and took the offered hand, which hadn't wavered once.

"Mr. Barker," he muttered, and then opened the case again. It had been a little thing, but then even little things added up in battle.

The Guv took out each of the swords and examined them thoroughly for straightness and quality.

"These are very good, Sebastian. How did you acquire them?"

"I bought them from an arms dealer in Bond Street at midnight last night. They belonged to a member of the king's musketeers. I could not resist them."

"I'll take this one," Barker said. "Shall we get on with it? I've got a man from Kew Gardens coming this afternoon to look at my penjing trees."

"I've got tickets aboard a steamer bound for Istanbul," Nightwine said, taking the remaining sword and beginning to slash at the air. "I do believe one of us will miss his appointment."

The sun was beginning to slash at the fog as if with a sword of its own. I could feel the dew slicking my hair and weighing down my suit and shirt. All creation seemed to be wrapped in wet cotton.

Barker slapped at a fly on his neck and looked absently at his fingers.

"*Êtes-vous prêt?*" Nightwine asked, after the time-honored custom.

"*Oui, je suis prêt.*"

"*En garde!*"

Both men charged at once and there was a clang of bell against bell as the swords came together and then sprang apart again. My employer retreated slowly, drawing Nightwine along with him, closing the gap, but at one point he stopped and would go no further. I noted then a small spot of blood on his collar, very red in the half sunlight, left by the insect that had bit him. I waved at one near my head and waited for the next clash, which was not long in coming.

I had fenced in school and knew a good match when I saw one. In this case, all the form went to Nightwine. Beside him, Barker, in his black waistcoat and striped trousers, looked ungainly. The saber did not seem as natural in his hand as, say, a claymore might have. It looked dainty, though deadly enough for the purpose. Had he been overconfident? I wondered. Barker had often told me to choose a weapon and stay with it. One will only get into trouble if tricked into using another man's weapon.

There was a third clash, a parry and riposte, and this time, blood was drawn. Nightwine was the first to spill claret, slipping his blade just past Barker's ear and cutting him near the back of the head. A second bloodstain appeared on the Guv's collar.

I stepped forward and Psmith's thin arm crowded me back, showing me how much power was contained in that wiry frame of his.

"A wound has been delivered, gentlemen," he announced in a public school voice, Eton, perhaps, or Rugby. "Is honor now satisfied?"

"No," Nightwine said shortly. "It is not."

"What would you know of honor?" Barker answered in return. "You who have none?"

"Oh, yes," Nightwine said, slashing at him and meeting resistance. "Cyrus Barker and his famous sense of honor. The natural, self-made gentleman of great renown."

Barker lunged forward, whether as a tactic or in anger over the slight I could not tell. They passed each other quickly, then turned and engaged each other in the other direction.

"I contend it is you who have no honor, sir!" Nightwine continued. "You're nothing but a lowborn Scot!"

Barker's blade finally found flesh, glancing past Nightwine's elbow and slicing a groove along the bicep. Nightwine, a little more sure of his skill over his opponent, had become momentarily arrogant. Each word Nightwine said seemed to sear into my memory, but at the same time, I thrust them away for now. Words didn't matter, not when lives are on the line.

"Forgive me for speaking plainly, Cyrus. I am your oldest and best friend, after all."

"Save your breath to cool your porridge, Nightwine," Barker answered. "Everything that needs to be said between us was said a long time ago. And if you're thinking you're leaving London any way other than in a pine box, you'd best think again."

Nightwine charged with a growl in his throat but Barker wouldn't be moved. The sun played on their flashing blades, too fast and bright for the eye to follow. I waited for a grunt of pain, a cry, hoping it would not be Barker from whom it issued. If there's anything I've learned by now, however, it is how rarely we get what we want.

"Aargh!"

The blade point pierced the Guv's shoulder and Barker added a third bloom of crimson to his white shirt. His blade slipped from nerveless fingers, bouncing off the hard ground with a dull ring. For a second he was unarmed and at Nightwine's mercy. The shoulder of his sword arm had been pierced. I felt the breath drawing in through my lungs, awaiting the fatal coup de grâce. Instead, Barker kicked the sword up into the air with his foot, and caught it with his left hand. When the inevitable blade came his way, he parried it and stepped back, holding the sword high over his head.

"None of your Chinese nonsense here, Cyrus," Nightwine taunted. "You're on English soil now. You're merely prolonging fate, you know."

"That's not water spilling down your arm," came the reply. "I'm sure we could do this all day."

The fight continued, becoming less civilized as it went on. They were no longer gentlemen duelists, I told myself, but gladiators. Both men were bleeding heavily and their shirts stuck to their frames. They were sweating in the moist heat, and their fencing form was long gone. *Will it never end?* I asked myself. How long had they fought already? Ten minutes? Twenty? Why hadn't I thought to bring a watch?

Both men showed signs of fatigue now and

were blowing like racehorses. I spared a moment to glance at Psmith, wondering if he was armed. There was no pistol visible on his skeletal frame, but another case of swords lay at his feet in the event that one was damaged. I looked back, just in time to see Barker stumble.

His boot heel struck a tree root in his way and he fell. His left heel slid across it and through the grass while his right lay straight behind him. His limbs scissored open and his sword hand came down in an attempt to correct his balance. His right shoulder passed just under Nightwine's guard and struck him heavily in the hip. Nightwine suddenly fell across Barker's splayed body, toppling forward. There they came to a standstill, with Nightwine curled over Barker's prone body.

I looked at Psmith and he back at me. Then as the sun pierced the fog, it illuminated the red-hued blade rising from Sebastian Nightwine's back. Psmith gave a low curse.

Slowly, the body atop him slid over onto its side and Cyrus Barker scrambled to his feet unsteadily. He looked down at his vanquished foe and the saber that pierced him through. His hand, his *right* hand, still held the hilt, I noticed. He looked at us as if aware for the first time that we were there.

Psmith stepped across and bent down to see if there was still life in his employer. He held two fingers to his throat for a few seconds, but could find no pulse and shook his head in my direction.

I turned to say something to Barker. I don't even recall what it was, now. Before I could say a word, the Guv gave a sudden moan and a spasm. Then he fell over onto his side and lay still. I froze, unable to move, unable to comprehend, my heart in my mouth. There was no new mark on him. Nightwine's sword had little blood on it. What in the world had happened? I flew to the body; not Barker's, but Nightwine's, ripped open his sleeve and found there a small engine strapped to his arm, a length of copper pipe containing a device able to shoot a small dart, tipped with poison, perhaps across a clearing into a man's neck, one which might be mistaken as the bite of an insect. Then I jumped to my feet, and began kicking at the ribs of the dead man in my rage.

Calm, matter-of-fact in that desiccated way of his, Psmith crossed to my employer and checked his throat, as well. Then he turned to me.

"Dead as the proverbial doornail. I suggest we call this a draw."

Then he turned and walked away into the early morning mist and was almost instantly swallowed up in it. I had never felt so lost and alone in my entire life.

_____Chapter Thirty-three

Dead. Cyrus Barker was dead. Everything was over. No more following after him in the teeming streets of London. No more putting up with his moods and tricks. No more nights in my little room with Harm snoring at the foot of my bed. With leaden feet I crossed to his body and looked down. He was a bloody mess. One arm was scarlet with it. He lay profoundly still, as if carved in stone. *It is ironic,* I thought, Stone Lion, *Shi Shi Ji,* his name in Cantonese.

I heard a branch move overhead, though that sort of thing didn't matter much anymore. Then Sofia Ilyanova landed beside me, trying to get her balance. I was so astonished at her appearance, I couldn't speak.

"Open his shirt," she ordered, fiddling with the tip of the parasol in her hand.

She sounded so sure of herself that I obeyed, opening his waistcoat, shirt, and singlet until his pale, cold flesh lay exposed. I saw the hypodermic apparatus with the strange green liquid that was attached to the tip of her parasol. Before I could stop her, she lifted the black folds of her gabardine skirt and straddled him with her dainty boots. She raised the parasol high, and then brought it down with all her weight, dead center, piercing the breastbone. I watched with horror as the green, viscous liquid pumped into the wound.

Immediately, she crossed to where her father lay crumpled in death.

"He finally did for you, Father," she said with something approaching disdain. "You never could let well enough alone."

I jumped when the corpse beside me started. Cyrus Barker's body suddenly drew a deep, agonizing breath.

"Dear God in heaven, what have you done?" I demanded.

Abruptly, the figure at my feet shot up to a seated position and exhaled in something approaching a roar, before falling over inert once more.

"It is the antidote to Father's poison, mixed with some adrenaline and a few other things," Sofia explained. "It's quite a potent little concoction. I offer no guarantee, you understand, but your master is rather tough. If anyone will pull through, it is he. You'd better get him to the priory immediately. This lying about in cold, wet grass cannot be good for him."

I sprinted to the cab and brought Juno through the grass to where Barker lay and then climbed down again. It was a hard scrabble dragging his dead weight up into it. I could hear him breathing now, a blessed sound. Then I climbed back onto my perch and looked down on the little angel of death, who had unexpectedly brought life instead.

"Are you going to be all right?" I called down to her.

"I always land on my feet, Thomas."

"Will I see you again?"

"Go!" she cried. "You look after Mr. Barker and I'll attend to my father."

"But he weighs almost fifteen stone. You couldn't possible move him."

"Thomas, you should have learned by now that I am not without my resources; however, I cannot guarantee that your master will survive such a shock to his system. I suggest you get him to a hospital as soon as possible."

There was no time to argue. I flicked the reins and turned the cab about. Then, with a final glance her way, I seized the whip and cracked it above Juno's head.

"Hee-yah!"

That morning I was being unaccountably aided by females, first Sofia, who had brought Cyrus Barker back from the grave, and now Juno, our cab horse, who stretched out her feet and ran like the wind. She instinctively avoided the snarls of slow morning traffic and at one point even hopped the curb and clattered down the pavement for a hundred yards. She knew my desire instinctively and has been the most reliable female of my life's acquaintance, all this for a chance of a gallop, a good brushing, and a bag of oats.

I opened the trap and looked down into the cab as we sped east toward Clerkenwell.

Barker lay sprawled in the corner, his head lolling with its motion. I had lost him, my teacher, my mentor, only to find him again, to lose him to death, only to see him brought back to life. Surely that was enough for even the two of us to go through in as many days. His life was now a burning ember, the merest spark, but surely it would not go out again.

"Come on, come on, come on, come on." I realized I was chanting under my breath, but whether I was speaking to Juno or to God I couldn't say. If the latter, it wasn't the most reverent prayer he'd ever heard, certainly nothing compared to one of Barker's declamatory speeches which lasted half an hour while the Sunday joint went cold.

Finally, I was turning into the cobblestone alley with the stone archway, and Juno clattered to a stop when I set the brake, skidding the last ten feet. Good old Clerkenwell, mundane as a Sunday afternoon. I hopped from my perch to the ground and ran into the building.

"I've got an injured man here!" I yelled to no one in particular. Two men in morning coats came running to the cab. One of them called for a hand

360

litter, and within two minutes, Barker was being carried inside. I followed him, but was stopped by one of the men.

"Name, sir?"

"Mine or his?"

"His."

"Cyrus Barker. Is this going to take long?"

"Not if you answer succinctly. Age?"

"I've never asked him. He's around forty, I think."

"Is he a member of the priory?"

"I believe so, yes. I was a patient here myself last week."

"What seems to be the trouble?"

"He was in a duel this morning and was cut by a saber in the back of the head as well as stabbed in the shoulder. Just after that, I think, he was struck by a poison dart, because he collapsed in a heap after the duel and registered no pulse. Then he was given an antidote to the poison by an injection directly into the heart. I understand the serum contained a dose of adrenaline. It brought him round in that his heart is beating but he's not conscious and is pretty much like you see him now. Do you think you can do something for him?"

The porter or what-have-you simply stood there with his pencil poised over his notebook, not writing or doing anything, but standing with his jaw half open.

"Do something, you idiot! The man may be dying!"

The porter wheeled about and went into the room where Barker had been taken. I had intruded into his ordered world with my reanimated corpse and my talk of deadly toxins. I followed him into the room. A second man came out and pushed me out of the way to use one of those metal tubes to listen to my employer's heart.

"It's Cyrus Barker," I said to him, a stocky sixty-year-old man with brown hair shot with gray and a beard white as snow, a much more confidence-inspiring sort than the one before him.

"Oh, we know Mr. Barker here," he said. "No idea what sort of poison he was given?"

"No, sir. I'm sure it was probably exotic."

"What physician administered the antidote?"

"No physician, sir. It was a bystander."

"I see," he said, as if he got this sort of emergency all the time. "And did he say most definitely that what he injected was an antidote to the poison?"

"Yes, she did," I told him. "I gathered she had created both."

The doctor opened Barker's shirt and inspected the wound on the breastbone, an angry pucker of red skin.

"Wait outside in the hall," he finally said. "We'll do what we can."

"I'll see to the horse and be right back."

I'd seen a few stables in the area before and found one that I thought would take good care of Juno. Then I walked back to that medieval alleyway which now contained a secret hospital where, right then, the Guv was strapped to a gurney, fighting for his life.

I sat in a wooden chair against a wall near the front entrance. One hour stretched into two, and two became three. I told myself this wasn't a simple case. He'd been stabbed twice and poisoned twice, for in a way, the antidote itself was a kind of poison. Administer it to a healthy man and I'm sure it would kill him stone dead. I couldn't expect to go in a few hours later to find the Guv sitting up and taking nourishment. The doctor, a man named Strickland, finally came out and took a seat in the chair beside me.

"We can't do a thing for him but wait," he explained. "Oh, we've sewn up his wounds, but with no idea what he's been exposed to, it would be negligent to start giving him useless medications. We'll administer digitalis if his heartbeat weakens. Other than that, we must let him rest."

"Has he awakened at all?"

"No, and I don't expect him to for a while. He's always had an iron constitution. We'll let him sort himself out for now and check his progress."

"Yes, sir. Whatever you think is best."

"Now, Mr. Llewelyn, let us talk about you. You left this hospital under rather unusual circumstances a week ago. Is that correct? Your sister had no business taking you from this facility in such a state."

"She wasn't my sister, actually," I admitted. "That was the girl I was talking about to your porter."

The physician raised his eyebrows. "Can you explain why she felt you were better cared for outside of this hospital?"

"You'd have to ask her."

"If she shows up again, I hope you will alert someone immediately."

"I shall. Thank you, Doctor."

An hour later, I thought to inform Terry Poole that our friend was in hospital and fighting for his life. Some people should know, I thought, such as Mrs. Ashleigh. I also sent word to Mac and Jenkins. Poole arrived within the hour and stood at the foot of Barker's bed listening to him breathe.

"Any idea when he'll wake up?" he asked.

"When he's good and ready, or so the doctor tells me. I say, are those dark spectacles you have there in your pocket?"

"Yes," he admitted. "Warren finally saw sense, but only after we threatened to form a labor union and strike. There were so many spectacles about the place by the end he said he'd fire the next man who wore a pair. I've been reinstated, but assigned to 'K' Division. It's a demotion. No more chances to nip home for lunch, it looks like, not for a while, anyway."

"I'm sorry to hear that," I said. "Mrs. Poole must be disappointed."

"She said she was just getting accustomed to my being underfoot."

"Have you heard anything about Sofia Ilyanova?"

"She has not been seen since leaving the Albemarle."

"What about Psmith?"

"I hope he's long gone."

"Keep me informed. I'm sure the Guv will want to know."

Chapter Thirty-four

The next morning I was at the priory at eight o'clock but was still not the first to visit Cyrus Barker. When I entered his room, I found a stocky, strongly built man sitting next to the bed, with the chair drawn up so that his back was to me. Even though I couldn't see his face, I still had no trouble recognizing him. It was Charles Haddon Spurgeon, the pastor of the Metropolitan

Tabernacle, Barker's church. I was not about to interrupt his communion with the Guv, so I took a seat out in the corridor.

The pastor came out a quarter hour later, and upon noticing me, walked over to shake my hand. He had a thick head of silvery hair and impressive jowls beneath his beard.

"Thomas," he said to me. "I understand you have been through quite an ordeal."

"I have, sir," I admitted, surprised the great man knew my name. I suppose it was because of his close relationship to Cyrus Barker.

"You will let me know when he awakens, won't you?"

"Of course." I had to admit, I liked that word "when."

"And when he does, tell him I won't have him dawdling in bed. There is work to be done and he hasn't earned a holiday just yet."

"Yes, sir," I answered. It took a moment to work out that it was spoken in jest.

"Take care of yourself, son," he said, patting me on the shoulder. "And take good care of your employer."

He turned and headed toward the entrance. A clergyman of his import must know every corridor of every hospital in the city. As he left, I took Spurgeon's chair and sat looking at my unconscious employer. His color was better and he appeared to be in a deep sleep. I missed his stentorian voice. In fact, there were a lot of things I missed. Even being at the office, when we had time to talk about things not related to any case, or training together at night. I had taken this situation to keep from starving, not realizing that it would eventually become my whole life.

"Thomas," a voice said, interrupting my reverie. It was Mrs. Ashleigh, with a doctor in tow. I jumped from my seat.

"Dr. Hilliard has been giving me the latest on our patient," she said, walking to the edge of the bed. She began to remove her gloves. "Tell Thomas what you just told me."

Dr. Hilliard, a tall, elderly man with pince-nez spectacles, nodded gravely. "The tests have been inconclusive. However, he's suffered no setback and looks better today. There's full hope of recovery. I was telling Mrs. Ashleigh that all we can do now is wait for him to awaken."

"I'm pleased to hear it, sir."

The doctor nodded and left, and Mrs. Ashleigh turned and looked me square in the eye. I could see the mettle in her that morning. She was someone to reckon with, despite her fashionable dress and delicate features.

"Thomas, you look a fright. Sit down and tell me everything that happened."

I pulled up a stool next to her, and unburdened myself of most of what had happened since I had seen her last. It felt good to be able to say the words and know that someone actually cared. At one point, she put her hand on my arm and smiled as if she wished she could take away my pain.

"I prescribe a good long rest for you." Then, looking at Barker, she said more wistfully, "For both of you."

She stayed at his side for more than an hour, saying nothing, but holding his thick, meaty hand between her own. I thought it the best medicine he could possibly have.

After she left, a steady trickle of people came throughout the day to sit by Barker's bed: Etienne, Mac, and even Jenkins. Around five o'clock, Pollock Forbes came to the bedside and asked for another retelling of the story. It was the first time I'd ever seen him outside the confines of the Café Royal.

"He looks well," Forbes noted. "Any sign of movement?"

"None so far."

"Are we taking good care of him?"

"We?" I asked. "I always read the Knights Templar and the Knights Hospitaller were enemies after the Crusades." While nominally a Freemason, Forbes helmed a group comprised of the remnants of the Knights Templar.

"We were, for a century or two. But that was a very long time ago."

"I see."

"This year we shall inaugurate an ambulance service in London," Forbes said.

"And what, pray, is an ambulance?"

"It is a vehicle for transporting sick or injured people to hospitals. The service will be offered by subscription, something your employer should take advantage of."

"Excellent!" I said. "I'm glad to hear it. I shall agitate the Guv to subscribe. You wouldn't believe how difficult it is to transport a man his size in a hansom cab. I was thinking of trading it permanently for a dog cart."

"I've got some other news for you," Forbes said. "The murder charge against your employer has been dropped. Before he died, Gerald Clayton made a statement to Scotland Yard, exonerating Barker. The warrant for his arrest has been withdrawn, though don't expect it to be heralded in the newspapers."

"What about the assault charges?"

"I thought it best to not interfere on that score. It's no more than a slap on the wrist and a fine. It will soothe the ruffled feathers of Warren and the Police Commission, particularly since the charges against you were dropped."

"Did you do that?" I asked.

"I put in a good word for you. I thought you might not want another blot on your record."

"It's blotty enough as it is, thank you."

"I must say, your police record made for some interesting reading."

"You saw it? Is there any document in London you cannot lay hands on?"

"I don't know," he said, smiling. "I haven't tried. It's best not to press one's luck."

"Thank you for everything you have done for us, Pollock," I said. "I know you must have gone to a great deal of trouble."

"Only as far as Commissioner Warren was concerned. He was hoping the arrest of the dangerous criminal Cyrus Barker would secure his position for a year or two."

"Why should he have what the prime minister cannot even claim?"

"Mind you, the duel is still hush-hush. The fact that it took place in Hampstead Heath is known to less than a dozen people. I'd like to keep it that way."

"So you can trade on the information later?" I asked.

"You catch on. About now, the Foreign Office must be wondering what became of their Colonel Nightwine. His bank draft was not cashed and his room at the Army Navy Club is not occupied. I believe I'll let them wonder about it for a few days more."

"Poor chaps," I said. "They nearly had a new empire in their grasp. I feel sorry for them."

"Don't," he counseled. "They're rats to the core."

"Anderson's all right."

"He's not really one of them. He merely shares space in their building. Between you and me, he's too good for his situation. I'd like to see him moved up someday soon."

"Is that what you do, go from soirée to meeting to late-night supper, trading favors and making suggestions?"

"Your employer can save the world in his way. I'll do it in mine. How many people have you told about Miss Ilyanova and her murderous parasol?"

"Three, perhaps four. Only those in Barker's closest circle."

"No more, please," he said, as if he were speaking to a child or a simpleton. I'd like to think I was neither.

"Why not?" I challenged. "It's the truth."

"You're an adult now, Thomas. One cannot go about indiscriminately telling the truth. It must be doled out in bits and pieces or no one shall ever believe it. If what you say is true, this girl Sofia has killed more people than almost any soldier presently in England. Don't get me wrong; I believe you, but think about it for a moment. What does that bode for the future? A woman who can kill better than a man? You do realize she was here for over two weeks, strode about in broad daylight, killing close to a dozen people, and yet no one recalls her or so much as suspected her. Scotland Yard and the Foreign Office hadn't a clue."

"Of course they hadn't. Nightwine gave them a quarry to hunt, and there he is," I said, pointing to the bed where Barker slept.

"It's also not good to go about showing everyone the Yard is incompetent. For one thing, it isn't true, and for another, it is dangerous. We don't need the public afraid that their police force isn't up to scratch, you see."

"Don't worry, Pollock, I'm not going to start another Turf Scandal at Scotland Yard. If Inspector Abberline is any indication, they have become too competent, in my opinion. Besides, who would believe me? A beautiful young girl, not over seven stone, forced by her father to become a professional killer? It's preposterous."

"Was she? Beautiful, I mean?"

"Oh, you have no idea. Skin the color of a moonbeam, with eyes like a golden sunrise. But she had no conscience whatsoever. It's as though she was a clock put together in the factory with one of the cogs missing. Perhaps it is an anomaly peculiar to the Nightwines."

"You'll keep this quiet, then," Forbes said.

"So you may trade upon it?"

"No, not this, Thomas. Some things are best never spoken of."

"I'll keep it silent unless my employer tells me otherwise."

"Fair enough," he said, rising. I watched him change from the serious social manipulator to the idle dandy instantaneously.

"Do keep me informed," he said, shaking my hand.

"You'll know when I do."

About a half hour after he left, there was a sharp intake of breath from the bed, followed by a cough. Barker's head moved slowly from side to side, taking in his surroundings.

"Don't try to speak, sir," I said. "You're in St. John's Priory. Nightwine is dead, but you're alive, thank the Lord."

He nodded, and after a moment I heard his low, steady breathing again. He'd fallen asleep as fast as he'd awakened. I stood and went to inform the monk who acted as a nurse there.

An hour later the Guv lay propped up on several pillows, being fed gruel by Mrs. Ashleigh under the watchful eye of the monk. Barker spoke only one or two words, and there was no volume behind them. I wondered if he had any memory of dying. The widow, who had nearly become one twice over now, provided conversation enough for both of them. I had sent a small batch of telegrams, stating he was awake but not receiving visitors. Barker's face looked ashen and he was so weak he could barely raise a hand, but when I chanced to sit beside him once, he seized the coat button of one of my sleeves and gave me a brief, urgent look. It occurred to me he had no idea how he had got here or what had happened to him. The last he recalled, he had been dueling with Sebastian Nightwine. Perhaps he did not remember the duel at all. Memory can be a very tricky thing.

I hadn't spoken in a while myself. It was pleasant to have Mrs. Ashleigh's kind words wash over us like a balm. She balked a bit when the monk suggested he needed rest, but promised to return the following day. When she left, I sat at the head of the bed and spoon-fed him information, one morsel at a time. *Nightwine is dead. He shot you with a poisoned dart. His daughter gave you the antidote.*

Eventually, the monk returned and shooed me out as well. Apparently I was keeping the patient awake, too. I promised to return later, and before I knew it I stood in Clerkenwell Street again. Hospitals are cottony places, insulated against the outside. It's always a shock to step back into the bracing workaday world and hear dray vans passing or news vendors crying the latest disaster. The sun seemed unusually bright now and I noticed the air was gritty with soot.

I went south into the city and had a chop and a glass of wine at the Barbados. Afterward they brought the long clay pipe with my name on it that hangs over the bar and I smoked and pondered for a while. This death and resurrection of my

374

employer, was there a cost? Had the shock to his system shortened his life? All these demands I had seen him make on his body, were they all being subtracted from the end? Someday, I wanted to see him living on the Sussex coast with Mrs. Ashleigh, enjoying a long and well-deserved recompense for his many years of service.

Afterward, I went back to the office long after Jenkins had gone, more to be able to tell Barker I had been there than anything else. There wasn't much to learn, anyway. Abberline had been in, requesting information about a certain woman named Sofia Ilyanova. A few people had wished to engage the agency, but had been put off, and some reporters had arrived, wondering how Barker felt about the charge of murder being dropped and the reward being mysteriously lifted. I didn't respond to any of them.

Where is she now? I wondered. There was the matter of her father's body to dispose of. I doubted Sebastian Nightwine would ever lie in a cemetery somewhere with an ordinary tombstone over his head. He had held no belief in the afterlife, but I did not doubt he would have liked a monument built over his remains. Now he would never have a stone erected describing him as the Hero of Lhasa, and it was all due to Cyrus Barker. If there is such a thing as Eternity, and I believe there is, then the Guv had given Nightwine something to wail and gnash his teeth over for all of time.

Chapter Thirty-five _____

"Thomas, wake up," Barker said to me the following morning.

I opened my eyes instantly and realized I had nodded off while waiting for Barker to waken. Sitting up in my chair, I rubbed my eyes for a moment before they finally focused on the Guv. He was sitting on the side of the bed with his feet on the floor.

"Can I help you do anything, sir?" I asked. "I can call for a nurse."

"That won't be necessary, but I need you to get me a new set of clothes and my long coat."

"Were you thinking of leaving today, sir? I'm positive the doctors here would be against it. You're still weak."

"That does not change the fact that this case is not finished. There's a killer loose in London and we must stop her before she kills again or escapes to the Continent."

"Are you serious? The woman just saved your life!"

"Aye, she did, and I am grateful, but she has still taken eleven lives, and that's just here in London. There is no telling how many she killed elsewhere before coming here."

"But she was forced to work for Nightwine, sir," I argued. "He made her do it. I'm sure she has no intention of doing so again now that he is dead."

"That does not change the fact that she is a murderess. She must be held to account for the lives she has taken. Besides, if pushed against the wall by person or circumstance, she is bound to use those skills again. She is a menace to the public welfare and must be incarcerated for the rest of her life, if not—"

"If not hanged?" I interrupted.

Sometimes I despise my own imagination. Suddenly, I could picture her with a noose about her slender neck, the pale blond hair pulled up behind her head. They've dressed her in a drab, blue-black prison dress. She has been moved about from cell to cell for weeks, never knowing when the final day may be. Finally, they slide a partition to one side, and the noose is there. She's trussed up quickly and a priest reads from the Psalms. Then the trap is sprung and she falls through.

"Oh, God!" I moaned.

"Tell me you haven't fallen in love with the girl, Thomas," Barker said.

"No, sir, I have not."

Barker clasped his hands and rested them on his knees. "One can train a docile dog to attack, but afterward, it can never go back to its old life. It has become too dangerous."

"She's not a dog, sir," I argued. "She's a person."

"That doesn't prove your point, lad. A human is infinitely more dangerous than a dog."

"She killed eight people at once. Suppose she sent one of her packages to the royal family, or left it on a train, or exposed it at a station. The carnage could be in the hundreds."

I said nothing, but put my face in my hands, feeling miserable.

"I've nothing against the girl, personally," he went on. "I do not believe her heart is naturally black because her father was a Nightwine."

"Do we have to do this?" I pleaded. "Couldn't Scotland Yard handle it for once? Abberline is a keen fellow."

"He is, but I'd have to convince him that she was responsible for all the killings. By then, who knows where she would be. No, Thomas, it has to be us."

"You can barely stand, sir, and I'm injured, as well. How are we going to subdue her or convince her to come with us?"

"We'll cross that bridge when we come to it, but be certain to bring along a brace of pistols for each of us."

That was that. He had patiently answered every one of my questions, but would not be dissuaded from his quest. I left Barker to haggle with the staff about whether he should or shouldn't be traveling that day. Taking a cab to King's Cross

Station, I boarded the Underground for Elephant and Castle. Coming up the stairs into the bright sunshine by the old public house and the Baptist Tabernacle, eternal enemies, I promised myself that Sofia would not be harmed when we found her.

"Thomas!" Mac called when I entered. "How is the Guv?"

"Belligerent," I said. "He's determined to track Miss Ilyanova to her lair today."

"What do the doctors say?" he asked, coming out of his room. He wore his cheater spectacles, which meant he'd been reading. The hall smelled of beeswax and not a mote of dust hung anywhere, so I supposed he deserved his rest. I knew Mac's deep, dark secret: he liked to read romances.

"It doesn't matter what the doctors say," I countered. "Unless they can successfully tie him to the bed, I've got to get him some clothes and his pistols."

Harm came out of the parlor where he'd been napping on a hassock and favored me with a reasonably enthusiastic wag of the tail. It was only me, the Fixture, nothing to get excited over. I reached down and scratched the back of his head.

"Can you recall precisely what time the Guv collapsed the morning of the duel?"

"They fought for about ten minutes and there

was a bit before and after. I'd say a quarter past six. Why?"

"This is going to sound odd. At six-fifteen, Harm suddenly began howling in the garden. I've never heard anything so loud and strange in my life."

"Pekingese were bred as guard dogs for the emperor, Barker told me. They do have an alarm cry, but are you having me on? It's miles between here and Hampstead Heath. How could he possibly know?"

"He couldn't," Mac insisted. "He's completely untrainable, and has a brain the size of a walnut."

"How long did he howl?"

"About a minute and a half. I came out the back door to see if something had happened, like a cat getting in the yard. Then he suddenly stopped, and got himself a drink from the pond. I doubt he even remembered doing it."

"Strange, indeed. Well, I'd better get on. I'm sure the Guv's waiting impatiently."

I gathered the items, loaded the pistols, and carried everything out to the Newington Causeway where I found a cabman willing to go as far as the priory. When we arrived, he waited while I entered with the clothes. Barker had prevailed over the doctors, or at least was being released on his own assurances. Having failed, the doctor turned on me, giving me a list of things to look out for: if he looks faint, looks tired, starts to wobble, turns pale, has trouble breathing, et cetera, I was to bring him back at once.

Cyrus Barker stood in the lobby of the priory, pacing like a Regent's Park lion at feeding time. I brought him his clothes and he changed in his former room. He came out looking pale and damp, as if the exertion of changing clothes had been taxing to him. I knew he wouldn't admit it, but he was barely holding himself together.

I saw no good outcome from this, but plenty of horrid scenarios: Barker's weakened heart giving out a final time from too much activity; Sofia captured and denounced as a gruesome murderess in the newspapers; Sofia jabbing the Guv with her poisonous parasol, and he shooting her dead on the spot. It is times like this that I long for a normal situation, like a patent clerk or a shop-keeper.

In the cab on the way to the Albemarle, Barker sat back and rested, marshaling his energy for the coming battle. The last one had killed him. What drove this self-appointed guardian of the city to perform the acts he did? He was rarely paid and never thanked. Generally, he made more enemies than friends. Perhaps I would never understand what drove this man to do the things he did.

When we arrived in Praed Street again, I had the strangest sensation. I had stood there so recently facing Sebastian Nightwine that I recalled him in vivid clarity, the color of his bronzed skin, his blond mustache and eyebrows almost white against it, the honey color of his remarkable eyes. Now he was gone: to a just punishment in Barker's opinion, to oblivion in his own. Is not infamy another form of fame?

Barker spoke to the doorman as if they were old friends. This was the man who had lent him the hat and coat and had traded places with him two nights before. I speculated he had met him earlier than that, keeping an eye on me when I was carried there against my knowledge a week earlier by Sofia. The doorman informed us that Miss Ilyanova had not vacated her rooms, although he had not seen her in a couple of days. Barker led me up the stairs to the door to her rooms and stopped. He pulled out his pistols and I mine. Another scenario presented itself: me shooting her dead, and having to carry that on my conscience for the rest of my life.

"What's wrong?" I asked, when he hesitated.

"The room could be awash in ricin. There could be an unknown poison on the door handle. She could have packed the place with explosives."

"Oh, lovely," I muttered.

"Or she could have left it as she found it. I'm trying to piece together her actions based upon what little I know of her. Have you any insight?"

"I would say she fears you, based upon her sudden departure the moment you appeared here the other night, but she bears you no malice for her father's death."

"Good, then," he said, and before I could stop him, he unlocked the door with the betty he kept in his waistcoat pocket and threw it open. He trusted me far more than I did myself.

There was no poison, unless it was a slow-acting one, no ricin, no explosives. The room looked deserted. There were no suitcases and her clothing was gone. I even looked for her weapons case under the armoire. She had decamped while Barker was convalescing. *Good girl,* I thought. *I hope you're far, far away from here.*

"Thomas," Barker said, directing my eye to the fireplace. There was a leather case there, a tube-shaped affair leaning against the side. She'd pinned a note to it that read "Mr. Barker."

"The maps!" I cried.

The Guv crossed the room and squatted beside it.

"Ricin" he repeated. "If it is anywhere, it would be here."

"No," I assured him.

"Very well," he said, and opening the lid, poured the contents out upon the floor. I held my breath, expecting to see powder pour from the tube. I had assured him, but there was no one to assure me.

Barker reached inside and pulled out a half-dozen parchment maps. They were yellowed with age and lettered in what I supposed to be Tibetan script. These were Nightwine's private maps, the ones too precious or valuable to simply hand over to the Foreign Office. Nightwine was dead, but with them Britain could still launch an offensive action against Tibet of its own.

Still resting on his boots, he spread out the maps on the floor. Some were larger scale, showing mountain ranges and entire countries. Others were plans of buildings.

"Shambhala," he said, pointing to the smallest of them all, no more than two feet by three. "Here is Lhasa. This one appears to be a detailed map of all the monasteries in the Himalayas, and this looks like a map of the Dalai Lama's chambers. There's even a hidden chamber marked to get in and out without detection."

"Some of them look new and some look very old," I remarked.

"They know how to preserve manuscripts in Tibet. Some of them could be as much as five hundred years old."

Right after saying that, he lifted the corner of one and began to rip it in two.

"Sir!" I cried. "Stop!"

"It's too dangerous, lad," he said. "Far too dangerous. If these were in the hands of the Foreign Office, they would get into all sorts of mischief."

"But is that your decision to make? I mean, we

could bring them missionaries and medicine and education—"

"And smallpox and instability and slavery," he continued, still ripping and destroying the maps. Some were on fresh onionskin and made a sharp, crisp sound as they ripped, while others crumbled into powdery pieces. It hurt my eyes to see such beautiful ancient works of cartography destroyed.

Barker stopped at the final map, the one of Shambhala. His hand hovered over it.

"I believe I'll keep this one," he said. "I've destroyed the one showing its location."

He set it aside and then began shoving the torn maps into the room's grate. A single match and they all ignited like tinder. I watched the fire consume them in the reflection of Barker's lenses.

We lowered ourselves cross-legged on the floor and watched the fire. The blaze crackled with whatever resins or varnishes had been painted on the old parchments.

"She's gone, then," I said eventually.

"Aye," he rumbled. "She's gone."

"I suppose we could alert Scotland Yard and have the ports blocked."

"She would anticipate that," he responded, watching a perfect little jewel of a monastery begin to char and curl. "She is no fool. Anyway, I don't feel like aiding Scotland Yard at the moment. They must work their way into my good graces again."

"You don't regret letting the killer of Brother Andrew get away?"

"That's just like you, Thomas, to argue one side on Monday and another on Tuesday."

"Actually, it's Sunday, sir," I pointed out.

"Leave it to you to keep track of your day off."

"Somebody must, until there is a private enquiry agents union."

"You'll be founding president, no doubt."

"They'd need someone bright as a new penny."

Carefully, Barker rolled the Shambhala map and put it in the leather cylinder.

"Come, lad," he said. "Let us go back to the office and see what deviltry London's got herself into now."

"Yes, sir."

In the lobby, Barker turned to the doorman he'd spoken to earlier, and tipped his hat.

"Give him half a crown, lad."

I paid him and we went out to our waiting cabman.

"Half a crown?" I remarked when we were inside. "A shilling would have done. This was a very expensive case, I must say. I intend to add it all up when we get back to the office."

"You do that," Barker said. Crossing his arms and tipping his bowler hat over his spectacles, he rested in the corner of the cab.

Chapter Thirty-six

There was an assault upon the knocker that night, shortly after half past ten. Barker and I were disturbed in our separate rooms, both reading with our dressing gowns thrown over our clothes. I was reading one of Mr. Verne's fantasies, certain if I tried to sleep without finishing it, I should dream of projectiles shooting me to the moon. When the knocker sounded, I wondered, What now? I put a marker in my book and stepped into the hallway, listening to the murmurs at the door. Actually, they were only murmurs on Mac's part.

"I don't care what time it is," a voice brayed in the corridor. "Wake him. Wake both of them, or they can rot in jail this very night."

"He does not receive visitors in his private home, gentlemen. If you wish, you may speak to him at his offices in the morning."

I've got to say this about Mac: as far as his duties are concerned, he's got all the brass a man could want. The entire Black Watch could be standing outside and he'd have denied them admittance.

Barker came up beside me and leaned over

the rail to hear what was happening, as I was.

"Who is downstairs?" he asked.

"I'm not sure. Someone official, I think. We've been threatened with a night in jail already."

The Guv proceeded down the steps, with me behind him. Two men stood in the hall. The first was Commissioner Warren. I knew him from images I had seen published in the *Gazette*. He was of medium build, with a brown mustache and an aggressive manner. He looked every bit the retired military man. Beside him was a man a little taller, with a lantern jaw almost gray with stubble. I speculated he must have to shave twice a day.

"Gentlemen, may I help you?" my employer asked with more politeness than the occasion deserved.

"Barker," Warren said. "Where is Sebastian Nightwine?"

"I'm sorry, he's not in this house. When we saw him last, he was in the company of a young woman. What was her name, Mr. Llewelyn?"

"Sofia Ilyanova, sir," I supplied.

"Were you responsible for the burning of some maps this afternoon in a grate in the Albemarle Hotel?" the other man demanded.

"I'm sorry, but I do not feel the need to answer questions from guests in my home who haven't had the manners to offer their names."

"I am Hoskins of the Foreign Office."

"Well, Mr. Hoskins, what sort of maps are you talking about?"

"They were maps of Lhasa, which you no doubt already know. They were of national importance to the British Empire."

"Did I miss something?" I asked. "Are we about to be invaded by Tibet?"

"My sources tell me, Barker, that you were just released from the Priory of St. John. What was the nature of your injury?" Warren demanded.

"An injury to my shoulder."

"How did you acquire this injury?"

"In a duel in Hampstead Heath with Sebastian Nightwine," Barker responded.

"Who won the duel?" asked Hoskins.

"Obviously he did. I am the injured party. I should have known better than to challenge a superior swordsman."

"When did you last see Mr. Nightwine?" Hoskins continued.

"I passed out at the scene and did not see him leave."

"Where could he have gone, then?"

"I believe he said he and his daughter had a ship leaving at noon."

"A ship?" Hoskins snapped.

"Aye. I hope you gentlemen have not lent him any money. He never was responsible with money."

"That's a lie," Warren thundered, as if by

389

slandering one military man, he'd slandered them all.

"I'm making no accusations against him," said my employer. "Just offering personal advice."

"Perhaps you've got him tied up or locked away somewhere. We will have this house searched from cellar to attic."

"As you wish," Barker said, as if the matter of his own house being searched didn't concern him in the least. "You may start there if you wish."

"There" was actually Mac's room, the closest to the entranceway. Hoskins turned the handle and pushed the door open. Immediately, Harm burst forward and froze upon his ankle. The Foreign Office man gave a cry of pain and surprise and began to hop about. I could have told him no amount of leg-shaking was going to dislodge the dog's little arsenal of teeth. Once locked in, I knew from personal experience, he was like a nutcracker with a fresh walnut.

Warren pulled a small pistol from his pocket and dared to aim it at Barker's prized possession, given him personally by the Dowager Empress of China herself. The Guv twisted his wrist and took the gun away from him, as one takes a slingshot from an incorrigible six-year-old. Warren turned red and began to sputter, choking on his own anger.

"Mac!" Cyrus Barker called, almost leisurely, as if for tea.

Jacob Maccabee appeared and separated the dog's jaws from Hoskins's limb.

"My apologies, gentlemen," the Guv said, returning the pistol. "I forgot our guard dog was in that room. Why don't you begin with the library?"

Hoskins had seated himself on the hall floor and was examining the bite marks on his ankle. "What's behind that door? A tiger?"

I tried to control myself, but his aggrieved look was too funny. I laughed, which under the circumstances was not the right thing to do.

"Oh, you think this is funny, do you, Mr. Llewelyn?" Warren snarled. "Do you know what I think is funny? Six months in Holloway Prison, for a start."

"For what?" I asked. I'd already been released for assaulting an officer.

"I'm sure we can come up with all sorts of new charges. Resisting arrest, causing an affray, aiding a known fugitive. In fact, I can keep you for months simply on suspicion. Your file says you are trained in the use of explosives. How do we know you are not an Irish sympathizer?"

"Give him to me," Hoskins put in. "I'll see that he disappears permanently."

"Gentlemen!" Barker growled, silencing everyone. "I do not believe Mr. Llewelyn or I are going anywhere tonight."

"What makes you so sure?" Hoskins demanded.

Cyrus Barker turned to me and put out a hand. "Mr. Llewelyn, the watch."

I stood for a moment, confused. Was he going to perform some sort of magic trick? I pulled the ticking engine from my pocket, removed it from its gold and platinum chain, and handed it to him. Immediately, he thrust it into Hoskins's hand. The man looked at it, as perplexed as I, then his brows rose and he handed it to Warren without a word. I had forgotten the inscription.

To Cyrus Barker,
from HRH the Prince of Wales
for services rendered to the Crown

Barker knew that the prince bestowed these upon his guests like party favors, and I knew it, but these gentlemen did not. If they did, they still couldn't tell what the service had been. It could have been anything from being a good baccarat partner to saving his life. In this case, it just happened to be the latter.

Without a word, Warren gave me back my watch, which I reclasped and put in my waistcoat pocket with all due reverence.

"You're sure Nightwine said he was leaving on a ship, and not a train?" Hoskins asked.

"Definitely a ship. Did you catch the name, lad?"

"I don't think he threw it, sir," I answered.

"There you are, then."

"You were still seen going into the Albemarle this afternoon," Hoskins said.

"We haven't denied being there," Barker answered. "We were as curious as you as to whether they had gone. One might assume Nightwine burned the maps himself, before he left."

Hoskins looked at Warren and Warren looked back. It wasn't that they wanted to believe the Guv. They didn't, but he had pulled a trump card from my pocket and they didn't know him well enough to know if he was bluffing.

Warren raised a finger. "If we learn you've been lying to us, you won't be able to tell the difference between my wrath and a ton of brickbats falling about your head."

"I shall certainly remember that, Commissioner," Cyrus Barker assured him. "I wish you luck with your hunt. You know there is no love wasted between Mr. Nightwine and myself."

"Mr. Barker," Hoskins said, now cordial enough to add the word "mister" to his name. "Can you offer an explanation as to why Nightwine would bring maps all the way to England merely to burn them?"

"I believe I can," he said. "He has had the maps for a while, the only maps that show the entrance and fortifications of Lhasa. By memorizing and then destroying them, he is assured that he alone has the knowledge of how to get in and out of Tibet. He may still intend to take the country, only for himself, with your money to finance it. You may recall I sent the lad to your office with just that suggestion over a week ago. Were I you, I would stop payment on that bank draft immediately."

If I ever felt at any time that my employer lacked imagination, it was disproven that day. While Nightwine lay in the grave somewhere, or in a coffin crated up and bound for the East on some steamer, Barker spun a tale of a mythical Nightwine attempting to bilk the government of its money and making it sound plausible enough to be true. There was enough truth to it that Warren and Hoskins were unable to punch holes in his logic.

"Sebastian would not do such a thing," Warren maintained, but I could sense a hesitancy in his voice.

"Believe what you will, sir. That is only my theory of what he plans to do, but I have known him more than twenty years and you not even twenty days."

"We'd need to stop the cheque, anyway," Hoskins pointed out.

"We should get to the Bank of England the moment it opens in the morning," Warren agreed. "I pray it's not too late. Come, Hoskins."

"Good luck," the Guv offered them again, and

even shook their hands. I wondered whether I would ever be canny enough to start a conversation with imminent arrest and end with a handshake.

Hats were adjusted, gloves pulled on, and eventually our guests left. Barker stood with his hand on the knob, listening for sounds of the two men walking away. Then his knees began to sag, and he toppled over like a pile of books stacked too high. I jumped forward and caught him by the elbows and cried out for Mac.

I'd hoped to prop him up, but instead he pulled me down to the floor with him. When Mac opened his door, I was pinned under our employer with the odd limb sticking out, waving feebly. He helped pull Barker up and each of us, holding an elbow, dragged him to the parlor sofa. There we opened his collar and I put my ear to his chest. His heart was beating, at least, but his face was ashen gray. The conversation and his appearing to be hale and hearty had taken every last ounce of his energy.

"Water, Mac. Bring some water," I said, waving a cushion to cool the Guv's face. I chided myself for allowing him to go downstairs in the first place. A good assistant would have said he was resting and "You'll have to go through me to see him." Of course, that discounted the Guv's iron will.

Mac brought a tumbler of water and I poured a

little down his throat. Barker raised his head and took the glass, drinking it down, some spilling over his open collar.

"He's not going upstairs tonight," Mac ordered. "Let's bed him down here on the sofa. I'll get a pillow and a blanket. You get his boots off."

I unlaced his boots and pulled them off, then unbuttoned his waistcoat and braces. It would do for the present. Mac returned with the pillow and a sheet and blanket. Together, we bedded him down for the night.

Harm came in from Mac's room and sniffed at Barker on the sofa. We had gone and changed things, and he didn't like change. As far as he was concerned, the house was his and we were all his servants, the prerogative of a royal dog, and all this changing things about was irksome. Didn't we know he had a schedule? Mac's bed from eleven to one, mine from one to three, and Barker's from three until he rose shortly after five. This was going to upset the apple cart dreadfully, I thought, as the little black Peke regarded us dourly.

"It's only for one night," I told him.

"If I had my way," Mac said, "he'd be chained to a stake outside, no matter what the weather."

The animal continued to glower at us dis-approvingly.

"He probably thinks the same thing about us," I said.

_____Chapter Thirty-seven

A month later we were seated in our chambers. It was a warm Monday afternoon in late May and Whitchall Street was baking like a kiln. The windows and doors were open as wide as they would go, hoping for the slightest movement of wind. We sat in our shirtsleeves, with the cuff links out and our sleeves rolled to our elbows.

I cannot say that Barker looked exactly the same as he always had, but he was getting closer. His mustache had grown in, but he was at least a stone lighter than before, though Mac and Dummolard took turns inducing him to stuff himself at every meal. He was getting about, though he tired easily. I tried to get him to take afternoon naps on the camp bed but he would have none of it. The Guv's idea of a compromise involves his giving twenty-five percent to your seventy-five, and you're feeling glad to get it.

We were puzzling over a case we'd just begun, making plans to go to various businesses that evening when travel was more bearable. However, the old case kept intruding upon the new. Events continued to transpire, set in motion when

Nightwine was still alive; for example, the booking agents and the various bets on Barker or Nightwine, mostly among the Underworld. The fact that the Guv was recovering and Nightwine nowhere to be found was proof enough who had emerged victorious. The losers attempted to kick up a storm, but the agents were intractable. It is far easier to change the mind of an MP than a member of the betting establishment and probably more healthy, too. It is their game and they play by their own rules. A few bettors were still inclined to grumble, but there were always bets to be made and opportunities to make money, and eventually the matter was forgotten.

Then there was the fact that by law, Barker had committed murder. It was while Barker was recovering that it finally dawned on me. What a predicament he was in. Dueling was illegal, and had been for fifty years. All that was necessary was for Sofia Ilyanova to present her father's body to the police with the assertion that she had seen the Guv kill her father with her own eyes, and all would be lost. All the claims that Nightwine had made against him would be brought up in court. Barker would go to prison, the agency would close its doors, and I would be tossed into the street. Nightwine would have his revenge, after all. Had Sofia saved his life in order to see him punished?

If this was a plot hatched by Barker's old

nemesis, it was a very good one. Sofia had seemed sincere. In fact, I wanted to believe her, and so I did. However, that does not mean I did not worry about it and think every footfall in the hall was an inspector come to arrest us.

Then there were the constant interruptions. Not long after Barker returned to work, a full week before any of us believed he should, we received an unwelcome visitor at our chambers. Seamus O'Muircheartaigh came into our waiting room, still looking ill and fragile, but without his breathing tank. I would not have called him a good-looking man before the ricin incident, but what looks he ever had were now ruined. He looked fifteen years older than his true age. There were heavy parentheses on either side of his mouth and his eyes had sunken into their sockets permanently. He looked like the father of the man I had first met. He entered, speaking not a word either to Jenkins or Barker or me until he was seated in our visitor's chair.

"Water," he said when he was seated. I poured him a glass from the pitcher on the table behind my employer and he drank it down. He had a spasm of coughing then, but mastered himself, an act of iron will.

"So, he is dead, then. You gentlemen saw it with your own eyes."

"A saber blade thrust through the heart," Barker said.

"The point came out near his shoulder blade," I added.

"No!" the Irishman exclaimed. "I thought that was impossible with a saber blade."

"I saw it with my own eyes, sir."

"I am gratified to hear it. Did he suffer much?"

"No. It was over quickly."

"A pity. If you had accepted my commission when I offered it, you would be several thousand pounds richer now."

"That may be true," Barker said, "but as you know, I didn't need the money."

"You are a poor capitalist. Fortunately, I am not. You won me a packet of money last month and I thank you."

"Congratulations."

"I am back in business as of this morning."

Barker looked at him levelly. "Still funding the financial side of the Irish Republican Brotherhood?"

"To my last sou and my last drop of blood. I will not stop until Ireland is free and this accursed city is a smoldering wasteland, as you would be if you had any pride in your heritage. That goes for you as well, Mr. Llewelyn. Cardiff and Edinburgh are no more free than Dublin, and won't be until London is covered in ash."

"And here I was thinking you a common criminal," Barker said.

O'Muircheartaigh's wizened face broke into a

nasty grin that was almost skeletal. "I'm sorry to disappoint you, Cyrus. Well, perhaps not that sorry. I've come here to say that our temporary truce is at an end. I cannot speculate and attend to my business concerned about anyone or anything save my own interests. I suggest you do not attempt to hamper me in my work or it will not go well with you. Let us go to neutral corners and lick our wounds."

"That is not bad advice, provided you understand that at some point our interests will conflict."

The Irishman lifted a wide-brimmed hat that he had been holding to his head. "I'm looking forward to it."

Slowly, he pushed himself painfully to his feet and began to shuffle out with no more of a goodbye than the greeting when he first arrived. He slowed, however, when he reached my desk.

"Survived another one, have you?" he asked.

"As you see," I answered with a shrug.

"Remarkable."

He continued on and a few seconds later I heard the door close. I let out my breath.

"He really thinks himself a patriot, then?"

"Aye. He uses the money produced by his own criminal enterprises to fund the government's enemies. It is ingenious when you think about it."

"Doesn't he keep a few pennies for himself?"

"Oh, he has a wealthy lifestyle, but I don't

begrudge him that. It's one less rifle or bomb that won't go off in London."

"I suppose I could live with that."

Then Jenkins came in with the second post on a silver tray, just as he always does. I noted a large envelope among the letters, but wasn't especially curious about it. Barker stopped leafing through the stack and stared at it. Then he gently put it on the tray again and pushed his green leather chair away on its casters.

"What is it?" I asked.

"It's for you, from Ceylon."

"Ceylon? I don't know anyone in Ceylon. I don't even know anyone who's ever been to Ceylon."

"I assume the package is from Miss Ilyanova."

"Oh," I said, reaching for it. The Guv caught my wrist in his big hand.

"Do you remember the ricin that nearly killed O'Muircheartaigh, lad? I think it's best if we take this outside."

It suddenly seemed to me that there were an inordinate amount of dust motes swirling about our chamber in the sunlight. Holding my breath, I followed my employer out into the small courtyard behind our office. I even followed his example and held a handkerchief against my mouth as a precaution. He cut the string with his dagger and sliced the top of the envelope open. Then slowly he tented it and peered inside.

"There doesn't appear to be any granular material. I'm going to let gravity pull the contents out. Be prepared to jump back if anything looks untoward."

He lifted one end of the envelope and decanted a letter, nothing more dangerous than that. Barker used the blade of his dagger, poking it about the envelope, looking for anything dangerous. The breeze I'd been waiting for all afternoon arrived unceremoniously and picked up the letter, and I was obliged to catch it before it went over the wall.

"Stuff and nonsense," I stated.

"Better that than gasping out your last breath," Barker said. He looked faintly disappointed that the envelope contained something as mundane as a letter.

I examined the letter at my desk. It was written in Sofia's hand. I laid it on the desk and unfolded it slowly.

14 May 1886

Dear Thomas,

I am sitting here on the veranda of a quaint little bungalow overlooking the Mahaweli and thinking of you. I hope Mr. Barker has recovered from his ordeal and your lives are no longer turned upside down as they were. I should be sorry, I suppose, for the events I helped to facilitate, but then if it had not happened I should never have met you, and I am glad I did. Kidnapping you from the priory was a whim, but our time together during your recovery may have been the best moments of my life. I have given over my father's body to a Buddhist monastery for burial and am now free to live as I choose. I have money enough to last until I decide what that life shall entail. Your chastisement of me for the murder of Andrew McClain was the first regret I have ever had for a death at my own hand. I would like to think it was my last, and that I may in time forget the training that was forced upon me. And yet, I understand I am my father's daughter. I have always liked shiny baubles, and I'm not very good at penurious living. If I return to my old habits, you must share in the blame for not coming to rescue me from it. I should not need to make the only sacrifice. And yet, dear Thomas, you have given me a seed of hope. Perhaps I may live a normal life yet. Certainly, it was what my mother wished and prayed for. Ceylon is so peaceful, and it would be wonderful to live here forever, working with my hands by day and sitting on the veranda at evening's end, watching the sun go down. I wish you could be here to enjoy it. But don't worry. I do not expect you.

Sofia

• • •

I read it once, twice, thrice over, while Barker sat in his chair regarding me and practicing his much espoused patience. It was a private letter, but I knew he would need to see it. I got up from my seat and put the letter on his desk. He leaned back in the corner of his swivel wing chair, resting his chin on his left hand while reading the letter as many times as I. It was that kind of letter.

While he read, I thought about Sofia in far-off Ceylon. It was certain to be an exotic place, with elephants and palm trees, and I could picture sitting on that veranda beside her at sunset. The vision evaporated when the Guv cleared his throat.

Barker put the letter facedown in the center of his desk, crossed to his smoking cabinet and selected a pipe. He chose one of his favorites, a lion's head in mid-roar, stuffing its skull with tobacco from his jar. Seating himself again, he swung his heels up onto the edge of his desk and crossed them neatly at the ankle. Then he struck a match against the little French porcelain striker and puffed until it lit. It was one of the few liberties he allowed himself, resting his heels on his desk, and he only did so while cogitating. His mind was like a vast difference engine, working out equations, and I knew it was only a matter of time before he started asking me questions.

"Are you contemplating a trip to Ceylon, Thomas?"

"No, sir. I am not," I lied.

"Then the two of you did not share a *grand passion*."

I shifted uncomfortably in my chair. "No. I wouldn't call it that."

"Are you under the impression that she may have been in love with you?"

"She was the practical sort, I'd say. She wouldn't lose her head over a fellow, although she might make him feel that she did."

"It's getting close to lunch. Go over to the Grapes public house and bring us some meat from the joint, and bread, and a pitcher of beer. I'm suspending work on the new case for the day, until I've studied the letter thoroughly. My thumbs are pricking. Pricking fiercely, in fact."

I returned with the food and drink, having liberated also a nice wedge of cheddar and a jar of pickled onions. We ate at our desks, making rude sandwiches of the beef and the thick bread. I believe it was his favorite meal, a businessman's lunch for busy men in the middle of Whitehall. In the Grapes, I rubbed shoulders with men from the Admiralty, the Foreign Office, Downing Street, and the Houses of Parliament. If Etienne Dummolard suspected that, he would have torn his hair out.

He was munching onions with the aid of a small fork Jenkins had brought from somewhere, and taking swallows of beer as he read the letter once more. Something about it truly excited him. At one point he even drew the lamp closer and perused it flat upon the desk with his face but a few inches away.

For my part, I was back as I had begun, with little to do, waiting for him to say something and unable to interrupt him. It was my letter, after all. Therefore, I studied my notes from the new case while he studied the old one. Finally, he tossed it across the glass top of his desk, where it fell off on my side and landed on the Persian rug.

"We've been fooled, lad," he said. "She tricked us. She tricked everyone to get what she wanted. I did not take this girl seriously enough. I thought it mere coincidence that I never encountered her the entire time she was in London, but she planned it that way before she even arrived. I was too preoccupied with her father."

"I noticed she disappeared the minute you arrived at the Albemarle," I said.

"In many ways, she's worse than Nightwine."

"Wait," I said, waving my hands. "You're the one who said a girl her age could not attempt such a complicated venture."

"I know," my employer said. "I was wrong."

That was a remark I never expected to hear from Cyrus Barker's lips.

"Go on," I said, looking at him skeptically.

"I didn't understand her motivation, or rather,

her desperation. She came here with the express intent to kill her father."

"But she couldn't kill her father," I pointed out.

"That's correct. But I could. She saw a chance for her own freedom, if she played her cards right."

I crossed my arms, thinking furiously.

"Don't forget, lad, Sebastian Nightwine was here two years ago, before he even met her."

"And caused her mother's death," I added.

"Precisely. When he was here last he already had the plan to attack Tibet, and had possessed it for over twenty years. Why should he choose now to go ahead with it, after all this time?"

"He said it was his pension," I said. "He was keen as mustard after it."

"Perhaps she put the thought in his head. She had to make her father think it was his idea in order for him to go through with it."

"It's too fantastic," I argued. "To come halfway round the world to rid oneself of one's father."

"Believe what you want, but think about this: why the British backing? They could have eventually gotten funding elsewhere and taken Tibet on their own, but Nightwine became convinced he must make his money here."

"Where you would be in his way."

"Exactly. And Miss Ilyanova knew we would inevitably clash. I was the blunt instrument she would use against her father. She would not kill her father on her own, but she could manipulate matters so someone else could do it for her."

"What about me?" I summoned the courage to ask. "She manipulated you and Nightwine. Was she manipulating me, as well?"

"Just because she couldn't kill you doesn't mean she couldn't manipulate you. Miss Ilyanova has been damaged by the events of her life, possibly beyond her ability to return to a normal existence. Despite her claims in the letter, which you must understand was written for a purpose, I cannot picture her living a life of quiet domesticity, even to please you." Barker got up and went through the entire ritual of lighting his pipe again. I suspected he was summoning his thoughts, or thinking how best to express them.

"Thomas," he said when his pipe was going again. "You're an intelligent young fellow, educated, bright—"

"Get on with it," I remarked.

"But you're not on her level. She is the daughter of a Russian countess and a famous explorer. She is beautiful, clever, and perhaps the most dangerous woman in Europe. She is an adventuress, as much as I deplore the term. She could have her pick of any man in London or Paris. Wealthy men, powerful men, aristocrats, even kings. Instead, she chose the son of a collier, a disgraced scholar, assistant to a man on the run from the law, with seemingly little going for him."

I saw it coming, but it stung anyway. Barker is a very good man but he can be uncommonly blunt. I felt I should say something in my defense.

"She said we were in unique positions, because of the battle between you and her father."

"Do not take everything she said at face value, lad."

"She was just using me, then?"

"I'm not saying she had no feelings for you. She has not invited you to Ceylon in order to punish this agency. However, you had one attribute no one else possessed. Her father despised you."

"Oh, he did," I answered. "But what does that have to do with anything?"

"Nothing, or quite a lot, actually. I suspect she used you to make her father irate. You wouldn't be the first unsuitable young man thrust under the nose of her father, I'm sure."

"Balderdash," I said, crossing my arms and leaning back in my chair.

Barker removed the pipe from his mouth and shook his head. "What happened between you and Miss Ilyanova does not concern the agency. I'll only say this. You have told me recently that you are content with your employment here and that you intend to continue with the agency indefinitely. What means could she employ to get you to abandon your career and follow after her? She tried to make you fall in love with her, but that did not succeed. You chose instead your responsibilities here. Her only way to bring you to Ceylon is by impressing upon you the belief that she has something more to offer."

Barker put his pipe in an ashtray on top of his smoking cabinet to cool. I started to go through the post, but suddenly stopped and looked up at my employer. "There's another letter here, sir."

"From whom?"

"From Sofia. And it's addressed to you."

The Guv stood and leaned over the desk, snatching it out of my outstretched hand.

Dear Mr. Barker,
I was going through my late father's effects and found this photograph. I thought it might be of interest to you.

Sincerely,
Sofia Ilyanova

Barker separated the letter from the photograph and studied it as if it might produce information beyond the few simple words it contained. Then he regarded the sepia-toned image with such intensity, I wondered what it could possibly be. His wrist dropped and he held it loosely between his fingers, looking stunned. It dropped onto the desk and I retrieved it, wondering what had astonished him so. The image was octavo-sized and someone had inked the date 1885 in the lower

411

right-hand corner. A group of men in large hats of the sort worn in western America stood formally in a group in front of a bunting emblazoned with stars and stripes. The men were all armed and one of their heads had been carefully circled in the same ink as the date.

"It's him," Barker said at last.

Who on earth is he talking about? I wondered.

After a moment, he finally found his voice. "It's Caleb," he said, breathing hard. "My brother is alive. And Nightwine knew it the entire time!"

_____Historical Note

W hen I write the Barker and Llewelyn books, I'm in the habit of using both historical and imagined people, places, and events without informing the reader which are real. My criteria for choosing a historical figure has to do with whether he or she was involved in whatever kind of situation or political movement the novel is about. They help bind the story to a particular time and place, while at the same time, they allow us to see that many of the issues from a hundred years ago are more than relevant in the world today. I'd like to draw back the curtain and discuss some of the historical figures who appear in *Fatal Enquiry*.

Charles Haddon Spurgeon (1834–1892) was the most popular evangelist of his day. His sermons were published in the weekly newspapers and read by such authors as Robert Louis Stevenson. He built the Metropolitan Tabernacle in Southwark, where it still stands today, and left behind dozens of books on various subjects which are still being published today. He was respected by leaders of other denominations and religions, as well as people from all fields of interest.

General Charles "China" Gordon (1833–1885) first made himself known to the British public by leading an army of troops to save Shanghai during the Taiping Rebellion. His success made him a household name, but he was also discussed for his controversial mystical interests in Christianity. The army did its best to keep him out of the limelight until he was sent to Khartoum in 1884 to help defend the city from the Mahdi's troops. His death there was an embarrassment to the British government. Gordon was considered a martyr, the English public cried for his body to be recovered, and eventually Lord Kitchener was sent to suppress the Mahdi's forces in the Sudan.

Frederick Townsend Ward (1831–1862) was an American soldier and adventurer who led a group of American soldiers against the Taiping rebels in support of the Imperial Government. He was trained at West Point in the same class as George Armstrong Custer. His devil-may-care attitude made him popular among his troops, but his risk-taking earned him an early grave.

Israel Zangwill (1864–1926), an Anglo-Jewish reporter, author, playwright, and Zionist leader, is best remembered for the phrase he coined: "melting pot." He wrote several books, the most famous being *The Big Bow Mystery*, which appeared in serial form. Each time someone wrote in to suggest the killer, he scratched that name off his list of suspects. At one point during his tenure as Jewish leader, he considered moving the Jewish diaspora to Galveston, Texas.

Frederick Abberline (1843–1929), Chief inspector for the London Metropolitan Police, is best known for spearheading the investigation of Jack the Ripper in 1888. He was also in charge of the Cleveland Street scandal of 1889, before retiring in 1892 with many awards and commendations. He was a quiet, methodical investigator, whose first occupation was as a clockmaker.

And finally, **Robert Anderson**, (1841–1918), later Sir Robert, was an Irish-born civil servant and barrister who eventually became assistant head of the Metropolitan Police. In particular, he was head of the Criminal Investigation Department during the Jack the Ripper investigation. He retired in 1901 and was made Knight Commander of the Order of the Bath. He was an evangelical, who wrote several books on Christian numerology and eschatology, as well as a memoir of his career, *The Lighter Side of My Official Life*, in 1910.

These men, who lived inspiring and often courageous lives, add a richness and depth to the Victorian world of Barker and Llewelyn. I am ever in their debt.

Center Point Large Print
600 Brooks Road / PO Box 1
Thorndike ME 04986-0001 USA

(207) 568-3717

US & Canada:
1 800 929-9108
www.centerpointlargeprint.com